3/94

ML

GODSPEED

Tor books by Charles Sheffield

Cold as Ice
Godspeed
One Man's Universe

GODSPEED

CHARLES SHEFFIELD

A TOM DOHERTY ASSOCIATES BOOK ■ NEW YORK

This is a work of fiction. All the characters and events portrayed in this book are fictitious, and any resemblance to real people or events is purely coincidental.

GODSPEED

This book is printed on acid-free paper.

A Tor Book
Published by Tom Doherty Associates, Inc.
175 Fifth Avenue
New York, N.Y. 10010

Tor® is a registered trademark of Tom Doherty Associates, Inc.

Design by Lynn Newmark

Library of Congress Cataloging-in-Publication Data

Sheffield, Charles
    Godspeed / Charles Sheffield.
        p.   cm.
    "A Tom Doherty Associates book."
    ISBN 0-312-85317-3
    I. Title.
PS3569.H39253G6   1994
813'.54—dc20   93-26547
                                    CIP

First edition: November 1993

Printed in the United States of America

0 9 8 7 6 5 4 3 2 1

To
Robert Louis Stevenson
and
Robert Anson Heinlein

Tell it all," Doctor Eileen said. "Just as it happened, before you have time to forget anything."

"Why?" I didn't want to. For one thing, I didn't know how.

"Because people will want to read about this, a hundred years from now."

"But it's . . ." I paused. Boring? It wasn't boring to *me*, but maybe to other people. . . . *"Who* will want to read it?"

"Everyone. It's danger and deception, and daring and death. There isn't a man or woman born who *wouldn't* want to read it."

"But why me? I don't know how to describe things. You would do a lot better job."

Doctor Eileen put her hand on the top of my head and ruffled my hair. I hated it when she did that. If I hadn't been sitting down she couldn't have. "If you mean I could do a smoother, more experienced job, you're right. I could do it better in that way. But you're a lot younger than me, and your memory ought to be ten times as good. Most important, a lot of what I said would be what they call *hearsay*. That means I *heard* about it, but I wasn't in the thick of it from start to finish, the way that you were—and *only* you were. You are the right one, Jay. You have to tell it.''

She left, abandoning me to the recording unit.

A quarter of an hour later she was back. I had got as far as, ''My name is Jay Hara.'' And there I had stuck. My head spun with thoughts of Paddy's Fortune, and Dan and Stan the two-half-man, and Muldoon Spaceport, and the Maze, and Mel Fury, and the Godspeed Drive and Slowdrive. But I couldn't talk about them.

Doctor Eileen sat down next to me. ''Problems?''

''I don't know *how* to tell it.''

''Sure you do. Just start anyplace. You see, Jay, you're not building a house, where the foundation needs to go in before the walls, and the walls before the roof. You can start anywhere you want, and go back and fill in where you like, or change whatever sounds wrong. And if there's any place that needs smoothing, I can help with that. But the main thing is to get going. No more excuses. Do it.''

She made it sound easy. To Doctor Eileen, it probably was easy. But I hated the idea that she might come in after I was done, and change what I said, and leave my name on it. So I made her promise that she wouldn't do that, only add here and there if I left out some fact needed to make things clear. And then I began, at the only place that I could imagine beginning.

My name is Jay Hara. I am sixteen years old. My earliest memories are of my mother and Lake Sheelin. Mother would lead me onto the porch of the house, facing out across the lake, and we would watch the winter sun glint off the windblown water, or laugh at the clumsy flying fish skimming across the surface. Some of them finished on the shore, and then in the frying pan. But there were always plenty more.

The lake was wide and, when I was little, I thought it reached to the edge of the world, but now and then, when the air was calm and unusually clear, there would be a hint of domes and steeples across on a distant shore. And most magical of all, when the sky was darkening towards night and the winds had died to nothing, Mother would sometimes take me outside and say, "Look, Jay. Look there."

She would point, to where there was nothing to see. After a few minutes a bar of glowing purple would start to rise across the lake and grow taller until it split the sky.

"You can't see it," Mother would say, as I stared at the topless column. "But there's a ship sitting on top of that." And then she would laugh, and add, "Up, up, and away, to the Forty Worlds. When you grow up, Jay, that's the place for you. You'll be an explorer, the best there ever was."

By the time that I was nine I had learned a good deal more about exploration, and it seemed to me that it was not nearly as wonderful as Mother painted it. For one thing, I had met some of the explorers. Every month or two, strangers would visit us, wandering in along the dusty road that led from the town of Toltoona, half an hour's walk away along the lake shore. They were always men, all different, and yet in some ways all very similar. I came to recognize the trembling, muscle-weak limbs, or the red, veined faces, or the horrible throat-tearing coughs.

And these were the famous explorers of the Forty Worlds! I could see how sick they looked, but it seemed that Mother could not. When they arrived, she became a different person. There was nothing like the appearance of one of those wheezing strangers to change her from a strong, self-sufficient woman to someone apparently too delicate to breathe.

"If you could just help me with this basket," she would say, her hand laid gently on a man's arm. "If you would carry it for me into the house . . ." And she would laugh, mocking her own weakness.

The man always carried it, although the chore was often far harder work for him than it was for her (or even for me). And once he was in our little living room, Mother blossomed. Her pale face took on a blush of color, her red hair floated free like a glowing crown, and her walk became an easy rolling of hips. In the evening she would go down to the cellar and reappear with a selection of wines, to accompany foods far more elaborate than usual, and Duncan West, Uncle Duncan, who was normally at the house almost every evening, mysteriously vanished.

Look, I don't want to sound like an idiot, even if no one is ever going to read this. I know *now*, very well, what that was all about. But I didn't know it *then*. To me, Uncle Duncan had been a fixture in our house since my earliest days. He was a big, easygoing man, always smiling, and known to me as "Unkadunka," because when I was only a couple of years old I could not pronounce his name. And if, when a stranger appeared, Duncan West disappeared, and came back a few days later when the man was gone . . . well, those were separate facts. I never related them inside my head.

Stupid? Maybe. But I think most nine-year-olds would have done no better.

As for me, I just loved it when the strange men came to stay at the house. It was not just the different and exciting food. Part of it was also the change in Mother. She became a laughing girl, full of fun and charm, all flashing eyes and tossing curls. And part of it was the excitement caused by the men, too, for no matter who they were they came to our house filled with tales from beyond the edge of the universe.

In fact, it was a tall, gaunt man with fiery-red burns all the way from his lower neck, where his shirt ended, to the top of his thinly haired head, who first told me about the Maze.

"They *call* the planets the Forty Worlds," he said. We were at the end of a long, leisurely dinner, and between them he and Mother were finishing a second bottle of wine. The newcomer's name was Jimmy Grogan, and although he talked mostly to Mother I suspect that I was his real audience, for I'm sure she had heard it all before. "But that's true only if you count the Maze as one world," he went on. "If you count the Maze at its true numbers, then our system is more like the Four Thousand Worlds, or maybe the Four Million."

The Maze. Mother's hand was on Grogan's bare upper arm, stroking it where new baby skin was still growing to replace the old scar tissue, but his face stayed worlds away. "There's untold treasure out there," he said, "if only we knew how to find it. I think that's what keeps a man going out, time and again." He sighed, and took a final big swallow of red wine. Suddenly he stared directly at me. "Imagine it, Jay. A great jumble of little worlds, more worldlets than you can count, all with nearly the same orbit, so that a ship has to skim and hop and scamper in the cloud of them, never sure from one hour to the next if there's a collision on the way. But if you dare to stay there in the Maze, and if you are lucky enough to hit the *right* worldlet, you come home to Erin the richest man in the Forty Worlds system. And you never have to work again."

At that time I was still sorting out in my head the difference between sun and stars and planets and worldlets, so I did not really follow his discussion of the Maze. But one word of his spoke to me loud and clear.

"Treasure," I said. "You mean—gold?"

He hardly gave me a glance, before he was turning to mother and laughing that creaking, wheezy laugh. "Gold!" he said. "Now, Molly Hara, you've been filling the boy's head with the old fairy tales. Next it will be leprechauns, and the Pot of Gold at the end of the rainbow."

He turned back to me. "Rarer than gold, Jay, and a damn sight more precious. There's gold aplenty to be had right here on Erin, but out in the Maze there's every light element in creation, including the ones that we never find here. I know men who've struck lucky on lithium and magnesium and aluminum. And that's only the start of it. There's the treasure of old times, too—some say it's out in the Maze we'll find the Godspeed Drive, the—"

"Godspeed Drive!" Mother broke in. "Now, Jimmy, and you accuse *me* of filling his head with fairy tales. Enough of that." She stood up, supporting herself by one hand on Grogan's shoulder and stroking his cheek with the other. "All right, Jay, it's getting late, and you ought to be in bed. Off upstairs with you. Mr. Grogan and I have things to talk about."

I did not argue. The table was a dreadful jumble of dishes and glasses and bottles, and it was a rare day when I was not made to clear and wash and put away. I would ask about the Godspeed Drive in the morning, when mother was unlikely to be around. After we'd had visitors, she always stayed late abed.

But as it turned out I couldn't ask Jimmy Grogan anything, for the next morning he was away very early, back around the lake to the spaceport on the other side.

Soon after midday, Duncan West stuck his broad, smiling face in through the front door. I had learned long ago that it was pointless to ask Unkadunka for information, about Godspeed Drives or anything else to do with the distant past. My questions had to wait.

CHAPTER 2

So far as I know, Jimmy Grogan never came back to our house. He had stayed only that one night, but from my point of view he was an important visitor. He awoke my sense of curiosity. It was after his arrival that I noticed how Uncle Duncan always disappeared when other men came to see Mother, and how he popped up again at the house as soon as they left.

And of course, it was from Grogan that I first heard the word that started this whole thing: *Godspeed.*

Mother's spacer visitors kept on coming, never more than one man at a time, sometimes a guest every couple of weeks, sometimes no one for half a year. They stayed as little as a night, and as long as a week. As I grew older I became more and more keen to talk to them and ask them about things "out there." But I was thwarted. For when I reached my tenth birthday, Mother, as though deliberately preventing me from asking questions of her guests, sent me off to old Uncle Toby's house in Toltoona whenever a visitor arrived. I was not allowed to return home until the man had gone. "You're growing up, Jay," was all the explanation that mother or Uncle Toby would ever give me.

Well, over the years I picked up information about space and the Forty Worlds anyway, but it was in such little bits and pieces that I'm often not sure just what I learned when. That doesn't matter, because Doctor Eileen told me I could set things down any way that I wanted to. I'm going to take her at her word, and tell what I knew—or thought I knew—by the time that I was sixteen years old, and Paddy Enderton rolled onto the scene.

Mother and the house and Lake Sheelin, and the town of Toltoona farther along the shore, had been my childhood world. Then I learned that it was one tiny piece of a great universe. We lived on the western shore of Lake Sheelin, which is long and narrow and extends much farther to the north of us than to the south. A person on foot could start from our home, walk around the southern end of the lake, and in three days reach the spaceport. The same journey by the northern route would take twelve days or more. And a journey around the whole great globe of Erin, if a man or woman could find a way of crossing great seas that would swallow up Lake Sheelin and not even notice it, might take a thousand days.

It was a shock to me to learn that there were aircraft able to make that round-the-world trip, moving so fast that the sun was always overhead, in a single day.

And Erin was just the beginning. Our world was one of many that circled our sun, Maveen. Moving outward, we were the sixth of twelve worlds before a great planet, Antrim, swept the space around it clear, to form the Gap. Well beyond Antrim lay the narrow band known as the Maze, where floated worldlets so numerous and chaotic in orbit that they had never been tagged and named. Then came another gasgiant, Tyrone, and finally the twenty-four frozen and lifeless bodies of the Outer System completed the Forty Worlds.

For the spacers out beyond Tyrone seeking the particular light elements that were so rare on Erin, that was all. But once, ten generations ago, there had been the Godspeed Drive. Travel to the far-off stars, and commerce between them, had been an everyday event. Until one day, quite suddenly, no more ships from the stars had arrived in the Maveen system.

It may sound odd, but having learned so much, my interest was less in the Godspeed Drive than it was in the space travelers who risked their lives on and around the Forty Worlds. The Drive, if it had ever existed, was long-dead history—Mother, when I asked her, denied that there had ever been any such thing; Uncle Duncan and many other people said the same. But the spacers were here, real, undeniable. They were *today,* they were excitement. I could not have Godspeed. But I could have space.

When I reached my fifteenth birthday, I was at last allowed to use our little sailboat that sat on the jetty downhill from the house. The rules were simple: I must stay close to shore, I must never venture out in anything but light breezes, and I must never sail after dark.

If I am going to be as honest as I know how in telling everything that happened, here is a good place to begin. I broke those rules, all three of them. But I did not do it when I was at the house, with Mother there to keep an eye on me.

When she had a visitor on the way, and I was ready to be packed off to stay with Uncle Toby, I always asked if I could go to Toltoona by water, sailing along close to the shore of Lake Sheelin. Provided that the weather was good, Mother would agree. Then I would be out of her sight for anything from a day to a week, and old Uncle Toby, blurred of vision, hard of hearing, and unsteady on his legs, was happy enough to see me away early in the morning, and back as late as I pleased.

I gradually learned by trial and error what I could and could not do on the lake. The ideal situation was a strong and steady breeze from the north. That would allow me to sail right across Lake Sheelin without tacking, and come back the same way. I thought that I could be at the eastern shore in two hours and home again, when I chose to come home, in two more. That would give me most of the day to be where I wanted to be: at the Muldoon Spaceport.

On my first trip across I was too nervous about what I was doing, and too worried about my return, to enter the port itself. I hove to just offshore, ate my lunch, and stared at a baffling complex of buildings. There were scores of them, and I could not guess what they were for. What I most wanted to see, of course, was a launch or a landing, close up, but there was never a sign of one. After an hour and a half of goggling at everything, and pretending to be fishing or busy with my boat whenever anyone came down one of the jetties where the cargo boats were moored, I reluctantly headed back to Toltoona. I arrived at Uncle Toby's house, to his annoyance and mine, with most of the day to kill.

On my next visit I was much bolder. With no signs telling me to keep out, I moored my boat at the end of a jetty and went ashore. One of the first things I came to was a board showing a layout of the whole Muldoon Port. It had been placed there for the convenience of people from the lake cargo vessels, but it served me just as well. I stood there until I had a general feeling of where everything was. Then I started walking. The rest of the day was like a dream.

The great launch circles were my first target. Even from a distance I had seen the sky towers and the communication systems surrounding them. Invisible to me were the open grids beneath their bases, awaiting the surge of energy that would power landings and take-offs. After a few uncertain minutes I moved close to the guarding fence. I watched and waited for a long time, and finally realized what I ought to have deduced from my own experience: The launch activity happened close to sunset. All I would see now were preparations.

I moved on, to the monster domes of the maintenance shops. I did not dare to go in—there were too many people whose job seemed to be only to watch what others were doing—but I hovered at the hangar doors and thrilled to the sight of the repair men swarming over the bowl-shaped ferry ships, each as big as our house. I stared in fascination at the glittering cushion plates being fixed underneath them. They could be removed after launch and left in high orbit, whenever a ferry ship was needed for use farther off in space. To most people those cushions might seem no more than big round concave dishes, but because I knew their purpose I thought I had never seen anything so beautiful.

On that visit I hardly noticed the dents and scars and patches and the mended metal seams. It certainly never occurred to me that ships so battered on the outside might be no better within.

But one of the men near the door finally had his eye on me, and was starting to edge in my direction. I had done nothing wrong, but I felt guilty, and walked away toward one of the huge, metal-roofed rooms that served as combination marketplace and restaurant.

I went in, and saw more spacers in the next thirty seconds than I had dreamed existed.

They lounged at tables covered with food and drink, or stood leaning on bare walls. And they were talking, talking, talking. The whole room buzzed with spaceman chatter. I wanted to hear every word.

Except that the heads turning casually to glance at me did not move away. I was conspicuous, not because of my age—there were dozens of boys no older than me, serving food and drink—but because of my dress. Everyone else was either twice my age, or wearing the service uniform of white coat and blue tight pants.

More people were staring at me. It was time to leave. I walked quickly out of the restaurant and retreated to the shore, determined to talk Mother into making me a white coat and blue pants when I got back.

When I got back. There was the hitch. I had lost track of

time, and I had also not allowed for the fact that the wind usually dropped in the late afternoon to a light air. I set sail for the west shore, but the boat crept along, hardly creating a ripple in the still lake water.

That is how I came to see my first close-up space launch.

Darkness had fallen across the lake almost before I left the jetty. I had no problem with my destination, because Toltoona was a sizable patch of lights on the other side. But when I was no more than a tenth of the way across the lake, there was suddenly light behind me. A strange violet glow lit my white sail, and everything in the boat changed to peculiar and unnatural colors.

I turned. A ship was going up, balancing on top of a violet column of light. The ascent was slow, almost stately. I was close enough to see the return beam, a thin stream of matter that I knew was moving at close to the speed of light. It was a paler blue, and its line followed exactly back into the center of the power laser. A faint crackle of ionization carried to me across the water.

And suddenly the boat was picking up speed. I could not tell how much was natural wind, and how much I was feeling a byproduct of the huge energies being generated and dissipated back at Muldoon Port. But by the time the launch was complete and the violet beam had vanished, we were finally moving at a decent speed. Two long hours later I was tying the boat up alongside one of the Toltoona wharves. I sneaked up the hill, on into Uncle Toby's house the back way—and learned that he was not nearly as blurred in vision or hard of hearing as I hoped.

"And where in the name of Kevin do you think you've been?" he asked, when I was hardly in the door.

And then, before I could say a word, "And don't you be giving me any of your made-up stories, either, Jay Hara. You've been away across the lake, you have, and that in the dark. And poor Molly worrying herself sick about you."

"Mother knows I've been away?"

"And why else would she be worrying? She was here earlier. She wants you home as soon as you can get. And how do you think I look, with never a word to offer her as to where you were, or when you might be back?"

"How did you know I'd been across the lake?"

"Where else would a boy be, who eats and drinks and sleeps space, and has a boat? Did you have dinner, then?"

"No. I've had nothing since before lunch."

I was expecting food, or at least sympathy. But Uncle Toby sniffed and said, "Well, that's your own fool fault, isn't it? Dinner has been and gone. Get on home now—and not in the boat. Along the road."

"But Mother has a visitor. I thought he was going to be at the house for three more days."

"He is. This is different. Home you go, Jay. If you're lucky, Molly might give you something to eat when you get there."

Uncle Toby had my little backpack all ready to go. I started out for home. It was cloudy and pitch-dark, but there was no chance of getting lost. The lake was on my right hand, the embankment on my left. The road ran from Toltoona to our house, and ended just beyond it. There was hardly ever any traffic. I walked briskly, because it was late autumn, and the nights were already turning cold.

My head was filled with visions of Muldoon Port and that nighttime space launch, and the memory of the sail back to Toltoona through ghostly darkness. I doubt that I gave one thought to Mother's odd change of mind, suddenly wanting me home even though she had a guest staying with her.

And once I arrived home, and had a chance to talk with Paddy Enderton, it seemed the most natural thing in the world that Mother should want me there with her.

CHAPTER 3

It was more than five years since I had stayed at the house while Mother entertained one of her visitors. In that time I must have changed a lot in how I saw things, for it seemed to me, as soon as I stepped inside, that the man sitting in our best chair was quite different from all the others that I had met.

As I opened the door he gave a great nervous jerk upwards in his seat, then abruptly swiveled in the chair to find out who had come in. I saw a huge head, thick-bearded and dark-haired. It surmounted massive shoulders, and a bigger chest than that of any spaceman I had ever seen. His face was very pale, and free of the usual spacer broken veins and burns. Instead it wore an odd expression of surprise and caution.

But the biggest difference was in Mother.

"About time," she said. "Mr. Enderton, this is my son, Jay. He'll give you a hand to carry your things upstairs. He's big and strong."

Not one word about where I had been, or what I had been doing until so late. Which was just fine by me. But odder than this was Mother's attitude towards the visitor. There was none of the *glow* about her that I had always seen with other men guests, no sideways cocking of the head, no little touches or quick glances. Instead she sounded very practical and businesslike as she pointed behind me to the doorway.

"Get to it, Jay," she said. "It's too much for me."

I had noticed the great box when I came in—I could hardly miss it, the way that it filled half the entrance. If I was supposed to carry that upstairs, I would need lots of help. But Paddy Enderton was already standing up and coming toward me. Seated, his size had been deceptive. He possessed the head and torso of a giant, but his legs proved to be so short that he was no taller than me.

"You're Jay, then," he said gruffly. He stared hard, measuring my build, but made no move to shake my hand. "Aye, you seem strong enough. Let's do it."

I could see the remains of dinner still on the table, and that would have been my first preference. But Enderton had gone past me, and was already reaching down to a handle on the side of the box. He lifted it easily, one-handed. I took the other handle without much hope that I would be able to move it at all. To my amazement, the chest came easily off the ground.

I wondered, had Enderton really needed my help?

Yes, he had. We headed up the stairs without my feeling much strain, but Enderton gasped and gulped at every step. At the top, to my surprise, he took a turn to the left along the landing.

To explain that surprise, I have to say that our house had three bedrooms. The one at the front, looking out over the lake, was my room. The two at the back were Mother's bedroom and a small guest bedroom right next to it, where visitors always slept.

The left turn off the landing led to my room, and only to my room. And when we went into it, I found that all my belongings had disappeared.

"It's all right." Mother had followed us up the stairs.

"Mr. Enderton said he absolutely had to have the front room. You're in the guest bedroom, Jay. I moved your things. It won't be for long."

"How long?" It was ridiculous, moving me out of my own room for just a couple of days.

Now mother did look at Enderton, but it was nothing more than simple inquiry.

He had put down his side of the box and straightened up, the breath rattling in his throat. "I told you," he wheezed at last. "I'm not sure." He had one hand pressed to his massive rib cage, and his face was even paler than before.

"I'm not sure," he repeated after another long pause. "Maybe three or four weeks."

He said nothing more, but stood there scowling and panting, and glancing every second or two at the sealed box. He was clearly waiting, and after a few more seconds Mother nodded at me. "Come on, then," she said, and led the way back downstairs.

"He's *horrible,*" I burst out, as soon as we were in the living-room and out of earshot. "Why are you letting him stay with us for even a night, let alone a month?"

Mother hesitated. She had been loading a plate with cold meat and bread. "Now then, Jay," she said mildly. She handed me the plate. "Paddy Enderton is not what I expected, that I'll admit. But he's going to pay more than anyone ever paid. And for nothing, too."

"It's not for nothing! You're feeding him, aren't you? And you let him have my room."

"That's . . . different."

"It sure is. Why didn't you leave me with Uncle Toby until he was gone?"

"So you could go sailing off across the lake again, and worry your old uncle sick?" But Mother sounded more thoughtful than angry. "I just feel better with you here, and Uncle Duncan, too. Eat your dinner, now, and clear up afterwards. I'm going off to bed."

So there was another surprise, something for me to ponder as I ate a rapid and solitary meal, and then washed up. Not only was I going to be around while Mother had a visitor, but Uncle Duncan would be dropping in, too. That had never happened before.

None of this was enough consolation, though, for my being deprived of my own bedroom. My dislike of Paddy Enderton grew when I went up to the guest room and found all my things scattered around haphazardly on shelves and floor.

That was not enough to keep me awake, once I lay down on the bed. The day had been too long, and too full. I relived the visit to Muldoon Port, the grandeur of the space launch, and the night journey back, with the boat whispering its way across the dark lake. My final thought was again of the sailboat. It was still moored at Toltoona. Tomorrow I would have to walk over there, and sail it home.

That thought came into my head again as soon as I awoke. It was barely light. The house was quiet. If I hurried I could be to Toltoona and back before Mother even knew that I had gone.

I dressed quickly, stole downstairs, and headed for the door—and jumped a foot in the air when a silent form came at me from the kitchen.

It was Paddy Enderton, a big sharp-pointed carving knife in his right hand. "Hah!" he said. "It's you." He lowered the knife. "I'm just getting myself a bite of breakfast. What are you doing up so early?"

"I left my sailboat over at Toltoona last night. I have to go and get it back."

"You sail, do you?" he said, after an awkward silence. "Going to be a sailor, are you, or a fisherman?"

"I hope not." I wanted to be away, but I had to be civil. This morning he was at least talking to me as though I was a human being. "I'd rather be a spacer," I added. "Like you."

"What's that?" The knife jerked upward again, its point toward me. "Who said I was a spacer?"

"Nobody."

"Do you think I look like a spacer?"

"No, you don't." I was scared by his eyes even more than the knife. "But you sound like one, the way you have trouble breathing. And all Mother's other guests, they've been spacers."

"Other guests?" His pale face reddened, and the breath wheezed in his throat. "You have spacer guests here?"

I wished that Mother was around to explain, but it was long before her usual rising time. So it was up to me. I told him the simple truth, that we had guests now and again, ever since I remembered, and that they had all been spacers. But it had been four months since one was here.

That last fact seemed to calm him, and he slowly nodded his massive head. "I should have checked," he said, "before I came. Too late now."

"*Are* you a spacer?" I asked.

Instead of answering he walked through into the kitchen and came back carrying a sandwich of bread and hot bacon.

"Here." He handed it to me. "Eat that. I don't have the appetite now." He studied me as I took a first bite. "So you're often in Toltoona, eh? And you're a sailor, too, who wants to be a spacer. Did you ever think to sail right across Lake Sheelin, to Muldoon Port?"

"I did it just yesterday," I said proudly. "I saw a space launch, close up."

"Did you now." He smiled for the first time, an awkward grimace of stained teeth. "Well, Jay Hara, you're quite the adventurer. Would there be any problem if you sailed across again, for me?"

Problem? It would please me more than anything in the world, but still there was a problem, a big one.

"Mother doesn't like me to sail far away from the shore."

"That's for pleasure. If it was well-paid, though, that would be another matter."

My reluctance to discuss the idea with Mother must have showed, because he went on, "Of course, I'd be the one asking her. And if you did a little something extra for me now and then, there'd be other stuff coming your way that's more than wages. Things you'll like, you wanting to be a spacer. See here. I'm giving you this right now."

He pulled from his pocket a coin-sized flat circle, like a tiny plate of stiff paper, and handed it across to me. I examined it on both sides, and saw nothing.

"Well?" said Enderton.

"It's just a flat piece of cardboard."

"You think so?" He seemed pleased. "Grab your jacket and come with me."

He led the way outside the house. It was a fine morning of late fall, the temperature hardly risen above freezing. In another week or two winter would arrive dramatically, with biting north winds and soon after that a thin coat of ice along the shallows of the lake. But today we could still stand outside without discomfort.

Enderton stared along the road to Toltoona, and then across the deserted surface of Lake Sheelin. He examined them closely, before he moved next to me and pointed his thick finger at the disk.

"Now, you want to be a spacer and not a fisherman, I know that, but I'll bet you still like to fish?" He saw my nod. "So let's say you're out on the lake, fishing. And suppose you're still out when it gets dark, and you come across a place where there's something good on your line every time you stick it down in the water. You'd love to be able to find the same spot again, but there's not a landmark visible to fix your place. Then you press this."

His index finger stabbed at a little red patch on one side of the card. So far as I could see, nothing at all happened.

"So now you go away, anywhere you like. Come on."

Enderton started walking along the road. I followed him, swallowing down the last of my sandwich, until we were a couple of hundred paces from the house. There he stopped.

"Now, say that tomorrow night you want to find your way back to that same place. Then all you do is press this." He touched a blue patch on the opposite side of the card. "And see what you get."

The front of the card had suddenly changed. Before it had been blank, now it was divided in two by a bright yellow arrow. In the middle sat a number.

"That points the direction you have to go, to get right back where you want to be." Enderton rotated the card, to show that the arrow turned to point always in the same direction. "And the figures in the middle, they tell you how far you have to go to reach your starting point. You just follow the arrow. Go ahead. Do it."

I did as he suggested, and found myself led right back to the place were we had started. When I arrived at the right point outside the house, the arrow vanished and the little disk buzzed softly.

I turned the card over. It was thin as a fingernail, and the underside was no more than a repeat of the top. Paddy Enderton laughed, then doubled over with a horrible coughing fit.

"You'll see nothing there," he said, when he had recovered. "And don't try to break it open to look, or it will never work again."

"I've never seen anything like this."

"Of course you haven't." He gave me a leer and a wink. "And no more has anyone else around here. That's spacer work—and not the sort you'll find around Muldoon Port, either. But you see how useful it would be, to fix a position in space. And it's yours. You help me when I need it, and there'll be more things like this for you. Are we on, Jay?"

He held out his hand. After a few moments I took it. His

big black-haired paw swallowed up my whole hand, and I pulled away as soon as I could.

"If Mother says it's all right to cross the lake, I'll do it." Attractive as it had sounded at first, I was having second thoughts. I hadn't liked Paddy Enderton when I first met him, and gifts or no gifts I decided that I didn't like him now. "Mother will have to agree."

"Sure. I'll square that with her, no problem. But there's other things, too, that your mother doesn't need to know about." He leaned close to me. "You're going off to Toltoona, right?"

"I should be on the way already." I glanced at the sun. "I wanted to be back before Mother was up."

"Don't worry about that. I'll tell her that you ran a little errand for me." He reached into his pocket, and handed me more money than I saw in a good month. "This is for today's work. Before you collect your boat, take a walk right through Toltoona. Every street of it. How many inns are there?"

"Three."

"Take a look in each one. You've seen plenty of spacers, right?"

I nodded.

"Keep your eyes open for anyone who looks or sounds like a spacer. If you see one, take a good note of him—how he's dressed, what he's doing, if he has any scars or strangeness. Don't tell anyone what you're doing, and don't make it obvious. And when you come back, you tell me all about what you've seen and heard."

He gave me a hard push, as though urging me along the road to Toltoona, then just as sharply grabbed my shoulder and pulled me back again. He leaned very close and turned me to him, so that I could see every whisker around his full mouth, and every vein in his bloodshot eyes.

"And there's one more thing, Jay." His voice was a hoarse whisper, and his stale breath filled my nostrils. "One more thing to look out for real special. And if you see it, or you hear talk of it, you come right back here *at once*, without waiting one second for anything. Look for a man with no arms, carrying on his back another man with no legs. The *two-half-man*, they call him. Anyone says those words, or talks about Dan and Stan, you let me know real quick. And then there'll be more money for you than you've ever seen in your life."

Just what Paddy Enderton told Mother, I don't know. But a careful walk through the middle of Toltoona, and a slow sail back against the wind, kept me away from the house until lunchtime. When I hurried in Mother was standing at the stove; she said not a word about my lateness.

Duncan West was sitting with his long legs under the kitchen table. He nodded to me. "Food. A healthy young lad can smell it a mile off."

Not quite true, but I could certainly smell it now. And I could see it, too, smoking hot and ready to serve. It was my favorite, peppered lake shellfish.

I went across to join Uncle Duncan.

"So, Jay," he went on. "How's life for my bold sailor lad?"

As usual he treated me like a six-year-old, and a none-too-bright one at that. Typical, although before I was ten I'd become sure that Mother was a good deal smarter than Duncan West. She didn't seem to notice, or at least to mind, because he did a lot of repairs around the house and when he was dealing with mechanical things even I admitted that he was unbeatable.

Fortunately I didn't have to answer, because before I could even sit down Mother was in front of me with a loaded tray.

"Second sitting for you, Jay. Ten more minutes. If you're going to be an assistant to Mr. Enderton, you can start assisting now. He want to eat in his room. Take this up to him.''

It was another difference from Mother's usual visitors. Everyone in the past had eaten with her, and usually there had been a good deal of talk and laughter and fancy ceremony.

"Eat in *my* room, you mean," I said, not quite under my breath. But she did not respond, and I took the tray from her and hurried upstairs. If it was going to be another ten minutes before I could get anything to eat, I could brief Enderton on what I had been doing.

The door was closed, and with no hand free I banged on it with my elbow.

"Who's that?" Enderton's voice was gruff and unfriendly.

"Me. Jay. I'm back."

"Ah."

The door opened, a hand grabbed my elbow and dragged me sharply in, and the door slammed behind me.

All he was wearing above the waist was a sort of leather vest, unbuttoned all the way down the front. It made the power of his arms and shoulders and chest even more obvious. It also showed, running from above his left nipple all the way down to the bottom of his right ribs, a deep, rough-edged scar. The ribs that it crossed were broken and twisted and gnarled in among the thick layers of muscle. The wound, whenever and wherever it had happened, must have healed without medical treatment. It was a wonder that Paddy Enderton had survived.

But he had, and there was still power in those great hands. He grabbed the tray from me, and at the same time pushed me easily back into a chair.

"What did you see?" He leaned over me. "Tell it quick."

I did, but there was not much to tell. I had walked along every street, and into each of the three inns, and nowhere had I seen anything remotely suspicious. There was the occasional sprained ankle, and even a merchant with his arm in a sling, but that was a long way from armless and legless men.

While I talked, Enderton picked up the tray, ate, and grunted. He ignored all utensils and worked with his hands and teeth, cracking the hard pink shellfish cases casually between thumb and finger, then noisily sucking out the tender white meat.

"Good enough," he grunted when I was finished. "You sure you covered every street?"

"Every one in the town."

"Here, then." He fumbled clumsily in his pocket, and seemed surprised when he came up empty-handed. "I'll pay you later. Tomorrow, I want you to sail across and take the same sort of look at Muldoon Port."

"If the weather's good," I said, "And if Mother says it's allowed."

"Mmph."

That hardly sounded like agreement, but I stood up. I was keen to go back downstairs, and not only because I was hungry. This didn't feel like my room any more, filled as it was with the smell of stale sweat and liquor.

"She'll say yes." But he stood between me and the door, and he showed no sign of moving. He was breathing heavily, and snorting through his nose. "You may not always see them together, you know. Sometimes they do things separate, quite ordinary things. You have to watch out for each of them. Understand? *Each* of them."

I finally realized who he was talking about. "What do they look like?"

"Why, like each other. Understand? They're brothers, and they were a whole lot alike. More in looks, though, than in behavior. But then there's the accident, see, and one loses his arms, and the other his legs. Understand? Not alike any more. Two years ago, that was, out on Connaught, same place where I got mine." Enderton rubbed at his twisted rib cage, then turned to pick up a half-empty glass of dark liquid from the dresser. He took a big gulp. "We all three got mangled—and we were the lucky ones. We lived. Understand?"

I said nothing, and he went on with never a pause, "So if you see a man with no legs, that's Stan. Not too bad, he is, compared with the other. But you come and tell me about it anyway. Understand?"

I understood at least one thing. Paddy Enderton was drunk, dead drunk, more drunk than I had ever seen anyone.

"But if you see the man with no arms," he went on, snuffling and snorting and rubbing at his tangled beard. "The man with no arms, that's Dan. And then it's God help me."

He put his hands up to cover his face, and I took the chance to edge around him and to the door. I opened it as quietly as I could, but he heard me, and turned around to grab my arm.

He pulled me close, and glared into my eyes. "If it's Dan, see, then it's God help me. And it's God help you, Jay Hara. And it's God help everybody. Because nothing else can."

He released my arm. I stumbled backward through the door and almost fell downstairs.

His final words followed me. They were just what I needed to put me off my dinner.

Except that they didn't, not the way they might now, because at that time I didn't know what Dan and Stan were. They were just *names*.

And anyway, the food was peppered lake shellfish. I hadn't found anything that could put me off that.

Not then. I wonder if I would still eat it, knowing what I do now.

CHAPTER 4

If there's any place where what I'm saying is likely to get interfered with, I guess that this is it. Because I'm going to be talking about Doctor Eileen Xavier—the same Doctor Eileen who made me start working on telling what happened.

But before I get to that, let me say that before I knew it, Paddy Enderton had been staying with us for over five weeks.

I hated having him in the house, and so I think did Mother, although he demanded little enough as a guest. He did not have his meals with us, or go outside for walks, or even bother to clean his room or wash himself. He wouldn't let me or Mother in to clean, either. He seemed to do nothing but sit upstairs, cough and wheeze, make strange drawings that were scattered all over when I took him his meals, and stare out across the lake.

But he paid, and he paid well. So every few days I went along the shore to Toltoona, mostly in the sailboat unless the weather was rough, and when I got back I reported to Enderton that there was nothing out of the ordinary that I could see. He never thanked me, just nodded in a satisfied sort of way. I felt I was taking his money for nothing, but nothing was apparently what he wanted to hear.

About once a week, when the wind was right, I sailed all the way across to Muldoon Spaceport and docked there. With funding from Paddy Enderton, Mother had made for me the blue trousers and white jacket of junior service staff. Wearing those I wandered nervously into the restaurants, and soon learned that provided I didn't go into the kitchens, no one paid me the slightest attention.

After my second visit I became bolder. I broadened my travels to include the repair shops and warehouses and, finally, greatly daring, I went into the launch lounge, where never a launch was to be seen during the day, but where the old retired spacers seemed to spend all their time. There, sitting on the outskirts of those groups and saying not a word, I learned more about space and the Forty Worlds than anyone at Toltoona ever dreamed.

For Mother and Uncle Duncan, the idea that we had once been part of a great commerce between the stars seemed hardly more than a legend. Even if it's true, Duncan once said to me, what does it *matter?* There's nothing like that *now,* is there?

He was right, of course. Our real world was Erin, and, to a lesser extent, the rest of the Forty Worlds.

But the spacers could not discard the past so easily. They talked, while I listened open-mouthed, about the great deserted structures that floated free in space out beyond the Gap, beyond the gasgiant worlds of Antrim and Tyrone, beyond the Maze. Some of the speakers had visited those empty shells themselves. All of them agreed that no technology on Erin, today or in the past, could have been enough to build those monster habitats. The structures had employed, and now were cannibalized for, elements and alloys hardly known in the Maveen system.

No doubt about it, said the old spacers. Those structures were built using the Godspeed Drive. And somewhere out there, who knew where, there might be a structure that was *not* deserted and empty. Somewhere maybe was El Dorado, the Pot of Gold at the end of the rainbow, the supply base used by the Godspeeders themselves before, for whatever reason, they ceased to visit the system of the Forty Worlds.

Which was a great pity, agreed the spacers, because with the Godspeed Drive the stars, even the faint and distant ones, must have been no more than a few days away. The Drive had served ten thousand suns. And the ships at Muldoon Spaceport today, even our best ones, were no more than a faint shadow of the ships that must have wandered the Forty Worlds, a few hundred years ago.

I had never in my life heard anything half so interesting. After my second visit I spent almost all my time sitting in the launch lounge. It's a good thing that Paddy Enderton had no way to check on me, because there could have been armless and legless men by the dozen wandering around the rest of Muldoon Spaceport, and I would never have known it.

My sail home became later and later, as the season moved steadily on toward winter. On my fifth trip across, Muldoon Port was more packed with newly arrived spacers than it had ever been. The place had the atmosphere of one giant reunion party. I could hardly bear to leave, and I stayed there until after dark. But I paid for it on the journey home, when I shuddered and shivered all the way back. It was not just the cold. The squalls that ripped the lake's surface twice came close to capsizing me. By the time that I tied up the sailboat at our home pier, I had decided that this must be my last trip across Lake Sheelin.

That was a great shame, because for the first time in my life I had money. It was hidden away in a bag beneath my bed. Paddy Enderton was often late now in paying Mother, but never in paying me. Usually it was cash, but sometimes other things—a little timepiece, that showed the passage of hours and days for a place that was clearly not Erin, or a tube that I could place on my skin and see the pattern of veins and sinews and even individual cells, deep inside.

It would sadden me to give up more of these wonders, but

it had to be done. I headed up the path, where a thin film of ice was already forming on the puddles. I intended to tell Paddy Enderton that I could not cross the lake again until the spring.

But although he was in his room, he was already asleep when I sneaked upstairs. Through the locked door I could hear him snoring and wheezing, with a rattle in his chest that was sounding worse and worse as the weather grew colder.

No matter, I thought. I would tell him first thing in the morning.

But next morning, before Paddy Enderton and Mother were up and about, Doctor Eileen paid a visit.

The day dawned late, under heavy grey skies. With it came the first real snow of winter, drifting down in big, soft flakes. It made perfect snowballs. I went outside, throwing the icy spheres at trees and birds and bushes, and laughing at our tame miniver, Chum. He was a bit witless, and he didn't understand the game. He tried to catch everything in his mouth, and he was scooting around looking a bit like an oversized snowball himself when Doctor Eileen's car came floating in along the northern path.

I pretended that I was going to chuck one at her when she turned off the engine and got out of the little runabout. She stood her ground and faced me down, grinning out from the fur hood that muffled her so only eyes to mouth were visible.

"I don't know about you," she said, "but I've been up all night. I decided to cadge something hot from Molly on my way home. Your mother up yet?"

It was her first visit for a few months. Doctor Eileen's patients were scattered over a big area west of Lake Sheelin, the "poor side," as she called it, and when she had been working to the north of us she had the habit of dropping in unannounced. The official reason was to perform a routine check on my health and Mother's, but I thought that was a waste of time, because it seemed to me that both of us were healthy as ticks. The real reason, I decided, was that Mother and Doctor Eileen got on well, and liked to sit and talk. And talk and talk.

But now I have to take a break, and point out that when I sat down to describe the quest for the Godspeed Drive, it was Doctor Eileen herself who told me that I must not take anything for granted. I had to describe everything, she said, people and places and things, even ones so familiar to me that I had never really looked at them before. In fact, *especially* ones that I had never really looked at before.

So she can hardly object when I apply that rule to her.

I don't remember a time when I did not know Doctor Eileen Xavier. She had been prodding and poking and making me say "Ah" since I was an infant, and probably before that. I thought of her as big, but she wasn't. By the time I was twelve, we were eye to eye. She was little and old, with a brown, wrinkled face that somehow stayed tanned summer and winter, and she was sort of roly-poly, a little bent forward and kind of thick through the middle. She was not strong, not in the way that people usually mean, like lifting things, but I had never seen her tired, even when she rolled up at our house after a day and a half on the road.

What she was, she was *there,* at all hours and in all weathers, whenever people needed a doctor. Mother said there wasn't a man or woman within thirty miles of Toltoona who wouldn't give Doctor Eileen anything they owned if she asked for it.

So there was never a question, on that brisk, snowy morning, that I would take Doctor Eileen into the kitchen without consulting anyone, set her cold outer clothes to warm and dry, and give her hot cakes and a mug of sugary tea, the way she liked it. And only after that did I start upstairs to tell Mother that she was here.

"What is *that?*" said Doctor Eileen, before I could set my foot on the first step.

I had to listen for a moment before I knew what she was talking about. I had become so used to it, that awful lung-collapsing cough.

"It's Mr. Enderton," I said. "He always sounds like that when he first gets up. I think it's the cold air. It gets to him."

The front bedroom, looking out over the lake, did not benefit much from the house's heating. It was always freezing in winter. I hadn't said anything to Mother, but as the weather became colder and colder, my objections to sleeping in the guest room were less and less.

"I'll tell Mother you're here," I went on. But before I could stop her, Doctor Eileen was stumping up the stairs behind me, her mug of tea still in her hand.

"I'm going to take a look at him," she said. She reached the top of the stairs, set her mug on the landing rail, and started toward the guest bedroom.

"Not that way." I grabbed her sleeve. "He's in my room."

That earned a quick, questioning look, then she had turned and was moving to bang on Paddy Enderton's door.

"Who is it?" The coughing had stopped for the moment, but his voice was a husky croak.

"This is Doctor Xavier. I'd like to take a look at you."

"I don't want no doctor." But the lock was being turned, and after a couple of seconds the door opened. Paddy Enderton peered out. He looked even worse than usual, face pale as chalk but eyes bloodshot and lips purple-red.

He glared at Doctor Eileen. "I don't want no doctor," he repeated, but then he started to cough again, in a fit that doubled him over and left him groping at the wall to support himself.

Doctor Eileen took the opportunity to advance into the room. "You may not want a doctor, but you need one. Sit down, and I'll examine you."

"No, damn it, you won't." Enderton was recovering from his attack and straightening up. He knotted his fists. "I'm doing fine, and I don't want any old woman in here, doctor or not. Get the hell out.''

His eyes flicked across the room, and I followed his glance. The big box that usually sat closed and locked had been opened, and a lattice of dark-blue tubes and bars stood next to the window. Enderton took a step to the right, so that his body was between Doctor Eileen and the blue structure, then he slowly moved closer to her. "Out of my room.''

She stood her ground. "I can't examine a man who refuses to be looked at. But I'll tell you this. The weather here is going to get colder and colder for the next four months, and if you don't seek medical treatment you're going to be flat on your back before spring arrives. And that's not the worst that might happen to you.''

He grunted, deep in his chest, and shook his tangled bird's-nest of dirty hair. "I won't be here for any four months. And you don't know the worst that could happen to me. How I feel is my business. Get out of here.''

"Molly Hara knows how to get in touch with me if you need me," said Doctor Eileen, as she turned and urged me back through the doorway. "Only make that *when* you need me. If you've not spent a winter by Lake Sheelin, you have an experience coming to you.''

The door slammed behind us. The lock went into position, violently. And before either Doctor Eileen or I could say a word to each other, Mother came hurrying along the landing.

"You've hit a new low, Molly," Doctor Eileen said, by way of a greeting. It was as though the two of them were continuing a conversation from an hour before, but Mother just laughed and said, "With that one? Never in this world—or any other. Come on in, and bring your tea with you.''

They went straight into Mother's room and closed the door, leaving me alone on the landing.

I could have gone downstairs, and back out into the snow.

If it hadn't been for Paddy Enderton, I probably would have done. But his face had been full of anger, and I was afraid that he would follow me outside and blame me for telling Doctor Eileen that he was there. I didn't want to be alone with him.

I sneaked into my bedroom, the one that used to be the guest room, and closed the door as quietly as possible. Just a few seconds later I heard Enderton's door open, and his heavy tread on the landing and the stairs.

There was only the one way down. I was stuck. I settled on my bed, ready to stay there until I heard him come back up. It might not take long. Maybe all he wanted was a hot drink, to which he could add from his own supply of liquor. That was his usual breakfast these days.

In the next room, Mother and Doctor Eileen were talking together. That was nothing new, it was all they seemed to do when they met. What was a surprise was the ease with which someone in the guest bedroom could hear every word that they said.

"Fine. Now let's do the back." That was Doctor Eileen. "Breathe deep, and slow."

"You'll find nothing, you know."

"I should hope not. You're healthy enough, Molly. Not that you do much to make sure you stay that way."

"I eat right." There was the sighing sound of a long, forced breath. "I get plenty of sleep. And those stairs are more than enough exercise."

"I'm not talking about that sort of thing, and you know it. I'm talking about *that* sort of thing."

I couldn't see what she had done, but Mother laughed and said, "With that one? I told you, not in a million years. Not for a Pot of Gold."

"I'm glad to hear it. But it's a first." There were a few seconds of relative silence, with only the sound of Mother's deep breathing, then Doctor Eileen went on, "It's terribly dangerous, you know, taking on all comers the way you've been doing.''

"Don't be horrible. I've never done that. I'm very careful." *Breath.* "I've only ever had the one accident, and looking back I'm not sure how much of an accident it was. You'd have loved him, Eileen." *Breath.* "Anyway, it worked out all right, didn't it?''

"Better than all right. Unless you're the odd sort that thinks everybody needs a father. But Molly, I'm not talking that sort of danger, and you know it. What about *diseases?*''

"That's why you're here, Eileen.''

"For the local ailments, yes. But I'm not thinking of them. There's a thousand viruses to be picked up around the Forty Worlds, and brought back here by the spacers.''

"You think that maybe Paddy Enderton—the man in the front room—''

"Oh, I wasn't referring to him. What he has sounds like ordinary spacer lungs, aggravated by a bad injury. He's in awful shape, but I'm worrying about something a lot worse. The viruses I'm talking about, we'll never have met them before. And you can bet that the nanos available here won't touch them. If you don't worry about yourself, you ought to worry about Jay.''

I goosebumped all over, the way you do when you hear your own name and were least expecting it.

"He's not been sick for years," said Mother.

"Not in a way that you'd recognize. But Molly, how old is he?''

"Just sixteen. His birthday was last month.''

"Sixteen. Do you see any signs of the change in him?''

"Puberty, you mean? Not yet. But is that unusual?''

"It isn't." And now it was Doctor Eileen's turn to sigh. "I see it all the time in my rounds. Boys who reach sixteen, or seventeen, or eighteen, and don't mature sexually. But it shouldn't be like that. And it *wasn't,* fifty years ago.''

"I've never known it different.''

"Well, I have. I remember it. And I've seen the old medical records, too, from a hundred and two hundred years ago. They're still kept, you know, over in Middletown on the eastern shore. It used to be that most boys reached puberty by the time they were twelve. And did you know there were as many girls born as boys?"

Mother's reaction to that was of course invisible, but I know the effect it had on me. *As many girls as boys.* I knew scores and scores of boys, and just three girls. And I hardly knew those three, because instead of going to the local school with us boys they were kept coddled indoors all the time. They were never allowed out, to play or fish or wander along the shore of the lake.

"But why is that?" Mother was saying.

"I wish I knew. It's something to do with this damned planet, I'm sure of that."

"I thought you loved Erin."

"I do. But not enough to make me blind."

"Why would it start to happen *now,* and not hundreds of years ago?"

"Because we're isolated. When there was the Godspeed Drive—"

"Not that again, Eileen."

"Hiding from the truth won't make the problem go away, Molly, even if everybody does it. There used to be a steady flow of materials into Erin, from a hundred different worlds. There were plants and animals and food and supplies, arriving here every day. With that, humans and Erin fitted just fine. But we're isolated now, and have been for centuries, except for bits and pieces coming in from the Forty Worlds. And that's bad news. Human biochemistry and native Erin biology, I don't think they fit. Close, but not quite. And it makes me worry for our future, a century or two from now. People used to live a lot longer than they do, did you know that? Thirty or forty years longer. I don't know if it's missing trace elements in the food, or diet deficiencies, or toxins, or something in the air of Erin—''

It was an unusually long and serious statement for Doctor Eileen, but I missed the end of it, for the clatter of Paddy Enderton's footsteps was again on the stairs. I listened carefully. He walked slowly along the landing, then halted. After a long and mysterious pause there came at last the sound of his door opening and closing.

I stood up. Back in Mother's bedroom, the conversation had turned to the idea that I ought to be made to eat more green vegetables. I made a face at the closed door. I already ate more of them than seemed decent.

It was the time, snow or no snow, to make a run for Toltoona. When I got back Paddy Enderton ought to have calmed down, especially when I brought to him the "no news" that he regarded as good news.

I still think it was a reasonable idea. Except that when I opened the door and sneaked out onto the landing, Paddy Enderton was there waiting, standing in his stockinged feet.

One great hand closed around my upper arm, and the other went over my mouth. He leaned to me, so that his mouth was only an inch from my ear.

"Not a sound, now, Jay Hara," he said in a growling whisper. "You and I are going to have a bit of a talk. And don't try to fight, or I'll have to hurt you."

He was hurting me already. But I kept that to myself, as we shuffled along to his room.

His door opened, and closed again. This time, I was on the wrong side of it.

CHAPTER 5

Enderton sat me down on his unmade bed and dragged a chair over so that we sat staring at each other, a couple of feet apart.

"The woman." He had no knife or other weapon, but I knew that with those hands he did not need one. "Who is she, and why did you bring her to my room?"

I quailed, and told him. I explained that Doctor Eileen Xavier was an old friend of the family, who never mentioned in advance that she was coming to see Mother. There had been no chance to warn him.

After I had said that I just kept going, blurting out anything and everything I knew about Doctor Eileen. All the time that I was babbling he sat fidgety in his seat, never still. I saw his eyes flickering from me, to the window where the silent snow was still falling, to the locked door, to the odd skeleton of blue struts that faced out across the lake. He was drinking, too, replenishing a dirty glass with colorless liquid from an unlabeled bottle.

"She saw too much," he said, when I was finished. He wiped his mouth with his grubby hand. "If I thought that she might . . . The question is, will she talk? Where does she live?"

"South of here, along the lake shore just past Toltoona. Doctor Eileen's not one for talking." Except to Mother, I felt like adding, but instead I said, "What do you mean, she saw too much?"

He stared at me for a long time, while I hardly dared to breathe. "Well," he said at last. "It's like this, Jay."

There was a quietness to his voice that I had never heard before, as he went on, "You're a smart lad, and conscientious, and I've come to rely on you a lot in these past weeks. And I've been good to you, or tried to, and I hope you know it. But I'd like to be better yet. Because I can see the day coming, not too many years from now, when Jay Hara will be known as the finest spacer that ever lifted off Erin. And when that day comes, I'd like Jay Hara to be able to say that him and Paddy Enderton were friends, and partners."

I didn't know how to answer, what with the insincerity oozing out of every pore of his big, sweaty face. But I didn't have to speak, because he had another spasm of coughing, then went on, "Partners, is it then? You and me. I'll treat you like a partner, too. There isn't a boy on Erin, and few men off it, who've seen and heard what I'm going to show and tell you now. Come look at this, Jay."

He got to his feet and walked across to the blue tubes by the window. They seemed too few and too simple to do anything at all, but while I watched Enderton fiddled with the array for a moment, lining up a pair of struts. Then he flipped a switch on one side and said, "Look into the eyepieces." He handed me a pair of ice-cold tubes not attached to anything else.

I did, and it was magic. I was seeing Muldoon Spaceport, its domes and launch towers and boost grids like fairy castles, the thin metal trellises covered with a sparkling layer of white snow.

Except that it couldn't be. The port was ten miles or more away, on the other side of the lake.

I lifted my head and stepped to the window. The wind was

rising now and snow was falling harder than ever, traveling almost horizontally past the house. I couldn't even see as far as the lake shore before everything was swallowed up in a haze of white.

"That isn't really Muldoon Port, is it?"

"It is." Enderton flipped another switch. "Try again."

It was the same thing, much closer. Now a single dome stood in the field of view, elevators rising up its side.

"But how does it see *through* the snow, when we can't?"

"I don't know, but it isn't a problem. Not for this little beauty." He threw another switch. "Try it now."

This time I was close enough to watch people on the roof of a dome, hurrying about with their heads hooded against the snow. And with that view, I had an awful thought. I had been sailing across to Muldoon Port, but once there I hadn't done much searching for Enderton's two-half-man. Instead I had warmed a chair in the launch lounge, listening to spacer tales.

And all the time, he had been able to sit back here and watch me! Except that I suddenly realized that maybe he hadn't. The scene was cropped at the bottom, and I could not see anything less than fifteen feet above the ground. It was the curve of Erin's surface, putting anything at ground level below the horizon and out of sight; it meant that although Enderton could see much of the activity at Muldoon Port, people would be invisible unless they happened to be high in the buildings.

Enderton must have mistaken my relief for amazement. He nodded, and said, "Now you know how to watch launches in comfort. That's what I've been doing, these past few days. And I think we're coming close to Winterfall."

Thanks to my trips to Muldoon Port I knew what he was talking about. Before Winterfall, the spacer crews that planned to come home at year-end from scavenging the Forty Worlds sent word ahead to Muldoon Spaceport. And as soon as all those returning crews had been safely ferried down from their deep space ships, Winterfall would be complete. The port would enter its quiet period of deep winter, as the crews left Muldoon and dispersed. Most would head away from the lake toward Skibbereen and the bigger towns to the east, but each year, a few spacers came our way, around the lake to its western shore.

"Can you see Toltoona as well?" I asked. The town was much closer, so no curve of Erin's surface would save me.

But even before he swiveled the setting, I knew the answer. Miraculous as the instrument was at seeing through falling snow, it did not look through walls. And Toltoona was mostly buildings, blocking off the view of streets and squares and the insides of inns and stores.

"How would you like to *own* something like this?" Enderton asked me, as I peered into the cold eyepieces and confirmed my thought about Toltoona.

"Own it? It must cost a fortune."

"It would—if there was any place to buy it. There isn't." He took the eyepieces from my hand, and led me back to my seat. "This telecon is pure space technology. It will be yours, if you'll help me a bit more. See, I must know who's at Muldoon come Winterfall. I'm nearly ready, but I must have a few more clear days."

"Ready for what?"

"Ready to head out." His eyes flickered to the window. "I mean, ready to head out *west* of here. Does that doctor of yours ever go over to Muldoon Port?"

"Never. Her patients are all west and north of us."

"That's good. But tomorrow and the day after, you have to sail over to Muldoon and keep an eye on things. Until Winterfall it's more important to do that than worrying about Toltoona."

It was the worst possible time to have to tell him, but I had no choice.

"Mr. Enderton, I can't sail across in weather like this. It's winter, and the lake winds are too strong. The boat nearly turned over twice yesterday."

"Can't sail, eh?" he growled, and his face was turning red. *"Won't* is more like it." His fingers began to twitch, and the look in his eyes petrified me. I had to keep talking.

"Do I really need to go over there? I mean, if I sat all day with the telecon"—I pointed to the super-telescope over by the window—"I could watch everything that goes on at Muldoon Port."

"You can't see ground level. I've tried often enough. The curve of the planet cuts off the view. It won't do, Jay Hara."

He was standing up, stepping toward me. Driven by desperation, I had the idea that I think killed Paddy Enderton.

"From here you can't see it," I said. "But the water tower that serves Toltoona is only a few minutes walk away. It's high. There's a ladder leading up it, and a balcony all the way round. If I was to go up there with your telecon, I bet I'd see Muldoon all the way to ground level."

Even as I spoke, I knew it was an awful suggestion. I was volunteering to climb the giddy height of the tower—I'd done it once before, in summer, for a bet—and then sit in the freezing cold, for who knew how long, peering across Lake Sheelin at the goings-on in Muldoon Port. It was hardly better than its alternative—the blind rage and murderous hands of Paddy Enderton.

He stared at me. "Maybe. Maybe." But I think he was talking more to himself than to me. He went across to his storage chest, opened it, and pulled out a flat black oblong, small enough to fit in his palm. "Three days," he muttered, after he had prodded and poked at a few places on its upper surface. "Aye, that would do it."

He sat down again. "I have to take a look at Muldoon *myself*, from the top of that tower. Then we'll see."

I thought for one ghastly moment that he was proposing we climb the tower then and there, heaving our way up the bare metal ladder in driving snow. But he had sunk in on himself, hands tight around the mug of liquor, and was ignoring me.

Or almost so. When I began to ease my way across toward the door, he was suddenly up and blocking my path more quickly than I would have thought possible.

"What are you going to tell the doctor and your mother about what we've been saying to each other?" His face was inches from mine.

"Nothing." It didn't need a genius to know the right answer. "Not a word."

He reached out, and I thought he was going to grab me again. But all he did was pat my shoulder, and mutter, "Good lad. Off you go, then. And when it stops snowing, you'll show me that water tower."

I was allowed to escape. As I left, I realized that I had found something much more dangerous than sailing across any winter lake. Soon I would be perched on the top of a high tower with Paddy Enderton. An angry Paddy Enderton. A drunk Paddy Enderton. A Paddy Enderton who, if he didn't like what he saw when we got up there . . .

I hurried downstairs. And not before time, because I was shivering. Enderton's room had been freezing, cold enough to make me tremble all over. Except that I noticed, half an hour after I had parked myself next to the warm kitchen stove, that my shaking still had not stopped.

Looked at from the bottom, the tower rose forever into the afternoon sky. From the top, as I knew from experience, it would seem even taller.

And I was supposed to scale this monster carrying a quarter of my own weight in equipment on my back. The telecon was marvelous, but it was not light. The only thing I could say was that Paddy Enderton was bowed under a load at least as heavy as mine.

One hundred and forty-eight rungs in the ladder. I knew that from my previous time up. After seventy rungs a little ledge would allow us to stop and take a breather. Then came the longer haul to the top, in one continuous effort.

I placed my gloved hands on the first rung, and began to climb. It had been Enderton's threat that had prevented me mentioning to Mother what we would be doing, but suddenly I was glad that I hadn't. She would have been terrified—almost as terrified as I felt now.

We had agreed that I would go first, and remain on the ledge until Enderton was within ten rungs of me. Then I would start up the rest of the way, while he took a breather.

I reached the ledge all right, but once there I found that I dared not look down to see how far he had climbed. Instead I stared far out across the slate-grey surface of Lake Sheelin, to the distant domes and towers of Muldoon Port. Yesterday's snow had ended in late afternoon, and now there was bright sun and just a breath of wind. I wished I were down there, sailing across the lake.

It was *cold*. We had waited until afternoon, when the sun would be in the best position for seeing Muldoon, and the temperature at its highest. Still my breath was icy vapor, freezing in the air as I exhaled. I was well swaddled in warm clothes, and as long as I kept moving only my cheeks and the tip of my nose felt chilled. But what about the hours I proposed to spend perched on top of the tower, peering into the telecon?

If I didn't fall to death, I was going to freeze to death.

At the moment of that thought I felt a tap on my ankle, and heard Enderton's impatient, creaking voice, "Get on with it. What are you waiting for?"

I glanced down at him, which was a big mistake. He was right underneath me, waiting for his turn on the ledge. Below him, spread out like toys, were buildings and roads and hedges and fields. It seemed impossible that our house could appear so small, from just halfway up the water tower.

To fight my panic, I started to climb as fast as I could. Too fast. It was only when I slipped a rung with my left foot, and hung for a moment by just my hands, that I slowed to a more sensible pace. I could hear my own breath, loud in my throat. But soon the round bulk of the water tank loomed above me.

And finally I was there, sprawled on the balcony and recovering my wind. Only then did I realize that I could hear Enderton's gasping breath, too, far below me.

It was obvious. Take a man whose lungs had already been damaged by space and by an accident. Place him in air so cold that even healthy Jay Hara felt the killing chill in the depths of his chest. And then make that man climb a hundred-foot tower with a load of equipment lashed to his back.

Enderton would never reach the top. He would weaken and fall. For a moment I hoped he would, but then I nerved myself to start back down and help him. At least I had to *look* down and see where he was. Before I could do it, the ladder below me was creaking, and a faint, hoarse voice said, "Grab it. Lift the pack. Or I'm done for."

I leaned out over the edge. There was one dizzying glimpse of the far-off ground, and a random thought—*Ridiculous. I want to be a spacer, and I'm scared of heights!*—and then I focused all my attention on Paddy Enderton. He was a few rungs below me, clinging to the ladder. His usually pale face wore a tinge of unnatural purplish-blue. His backpack of equipment, hooked around his great shoulders, was just close enough for me to grab the top straps, and hoist. Twenty seconds later we were lying head to head, panting and shuddering on the narrow balcony at the top of the water tower.

Paddy Enderton had his faults—more of them than I knew at the time—but lack of willpower was not on the list. While I still thought that he was dying he was heaving himself upright, gazing across the lake towards Muldoon Port.

"Ah," he said. "Ah." His breath was a series of short,

rattling gasps, enough for only brief, jerky speech fragments. "Right enough. Muldoon. Maybe. Maybe."

He gestured to me to help him, and began taking parts of the telecon from our packs. In his shaking hands the tubes seemed to join themselves. The skeleton was assembled in a couple of minutes, while I did nothing but sit and watch.

Last of all, Enderton lifted the twin eyepieces. He peered into them, out across the lake. And then he gave a whistling groan, as though all the air had gone from his lungs at once.

"It happened," he said. "Happened already. I'm a dead man."

He leaned back against the bulk of the water tank and laid the eyepieces on the balcony. I grabbed them and lifted them to my own eyes, their metal rims freezing cold against my unprotected face.

Muldoon Port was clearly visible, all the way to the ground as I had suggested. From the despairing tone in Enderton's voice I had almost expected the two-half-man to spring into view, a man without arms carrying a legless one on his back. But there was nothing unusual about Muldoon Port. It was quiet and peaceful, with only a handful of people walking between the buildings. Then I realized that *was* unusual. When I had last been there the port had hummed with life; now it was almost empty.

Winterfall. It had been and gone.

I was still staring when Enderton grabbed the viewing tubes from me again and rotated the assembly. From the direction that he pointed I knew what he must be doing. He was following the shore line, tracking the road leading out of Muldoon Port around the southern end of the lake toward Toltoona.

"Nothing to see," he muttered after a few seconds. "But nothing means nothing. They'll know how to follow. They'll be on the way. It could be any time."

Again the eyepieces were laid on the balcony, while Enderton stood up and leaned dangerously over the rail. He stared, first south to Toltoona, then away in the opposite direction along the line of the lake.

"The shore road," he said abruptly. "How does it run north of here? Does it carry on right around?"

"Not close to the lake. It goes off west, then curves round to the Tullamore bridge. I've never been there, but it's on Doctor Eileen's rounds. She says it gets just about impossible in deep snow."

Enderton said not another word, but he grabbed the telecon, took it apart, and stuffed all the pieces that we had both struggled to carry up into one backpack. I didn't see any way that a single person could manage the whole thing. It was only when he set his foot on the first step of the ladder that I realized we weren't going to.

"The telecon!" I said.

"Safe enough up here." He was already three rungs down. "It's yours. You can get it any time you fancy. Come on."

I had no idea what he was doing, but I didn't want to stay on top of that water tower a second longer than necessary. The sun was low in the sky, a north wind was rising, and the air was becoming colder and colder. I took a last look at the precious telecon, sitting wedged on the balcony, then hefted my empty backpack and followed him. I didn't look at anything, and especially I didn't look down. But I could hear Enderton below me, wheezing and muttering.

"Can't be north, and can't be Toltoona. They'll have the roads covered. Water, then. It has to be water."

I was counting the rungs as we went down. After seventy-eight we were again at the ledge. Enderton did not stop this time to rest on it, and nor did I. At the hundred and thirtieth rung I paused and finally risked a glance down. He was almost at the bottom, his face purple-red and his every breath a groan.

I kept going, and soon my boots were crunching into deep snow. I felt a giddy sense of relief and safety. Within a moment it was gone, because Paddy Enderton had me by the arm. He was leaning against me for support, but at the same time he was dragging me down the hill—away from the house.

"You're going the wrong way," I protested, and tried to pull free.

"No. The only way." His fingers tightened around my biceps, hard enough to hurt. "We're sailing across the lake, Jay."

"We can't. In another half hour it will be dark." And then, when he ignored that, "What about your things back at the house?"

"I have all I need." He patted his pocket. "No more talk. You take me. Tonight."

"Mother doesn't know where I am. I can't do it."

"If you want to live, you can. Or do you think Molly Hara would prefer a dead son? It's your choice." He reached with his free hand into his jacket pocket, and pulled out a thin-bladed knife. "You sail me to Muldoon Port, Jay Hara. Tonight. Or I cut your throat here and now, and take my chances sailing across by myself."

CHAPTER 6

I thought I would describe what it felt like to be out on Lake Sheelin at night, in winter, with a blustery wind rolling and pitching the little sailboat, and a murderous man holding a naked knife blade just a couple of feet away from me.

I can't do it. I think that terror must be like an earache or a stomachache. After it's over you know that you had it and you know that it hurt bad, but you can't feel it or even *imagine* it, once it has gone away.

I know it must have been freezing cold in the boat; but I have no memory of being cold. I must have set the sail, too, and used the distant lights of Muldoon Port to guide our course, but I don't remember that, either. What I do remember is the insane sense of relief, when we were a quarter of a mile offshore and Paddy Enderton put away his knife and pulled out of his pocket the same little wafer of black plastic that he had fiddled with back in the house, what seemed like weeks ago but was really only the previous day.

This time he must have done something different with it, because suddenly the plastic card disappeared. The volume around it became a three-dimensional pattern of colored points of light, moving in complicated spirals past each other. Enderton stared at them for a long time, then his hand reached out into the center of the display. The lights vanished. Once again he was gripping a plain black oblong.

It was the fascination of watching those lights that made me miss the other change, the one in Enderton himself. When we had first descended the water tower and floundered through deep snow down to the pier and the sailboat, my captor's breath had groaned and wheezed in his throat. Once seated in the boat, however, I had been too busy to take notice of it.

Now I heard his breathing change again, to a loud, painful grunt. Enderton's hand suddenly jerked up to paw at his throat. I could see his face only as a pale oval in the darkness, and I leaned forward to peer at it more closely. As I did so he gasped, shuddered, and flopped forward. His head met my knee, then slipped sideways to hit the wooden seat with a solid thud.

At first I thought he was doing it on purpose, and for a few seconds I was too scared to react. Then I reached out and shook his shoulder.

"Mr. Enderton!"

He lay face down, his legs caught under the seat. If it had not been for that, I think he would have toppled sideways and gone right overboard. As it was, the boat was too narrow for me to turn him over and I was not strong enough to lift him.

I crouched forward myself, my head down close to his. He was breathing, but in shallow, rasping breaths like troubled snoring.

I peered ahead of us, across the lake. We were less than a quarter of the way to Muldoon Port. The wind was with us, the lights of the port were plainly visible, and we could certainly keep going as we were. But what would I do when we arrived? I felt sure that Paddy Enderton had made his plans, but I had no idea what they were. With Muldoon Port almost deserted, it was not even certain that there would be anyone around to lift him out of the boat.

On the other hand, what would he do if I turned back, and then he recovered consciousness and learned that I had disobeyed his orders?

The weather made my mind up for me. As I sat hesitating, it began to snow again. Within a few minutes the lights of Muldoon Port blurred, then disappeared behind a veil of white.

I reached forward and groped around in Enderton's jacket pockets until I found the knife. I threw it overboard. Only then did I turn the boat around, reset the sail, and head back for the western shore of the lake.

The lights of Toltoona had also vanished into the falling snow, so I could not tell just where I was heading. It was luck, not skill, that brought me to shore no more than a couple of hundred yards south of the pier that led up to our house.

I eased us along to the jetty and tied up the boat, but even in the best of weather I could not have carried the weight of Paddy Enderton up the path. He had to stay there face down, the snow falling to cover his broad back and exposed head, while I ran all the way up to the house, praying that Mother had not gone off looking for me and that somebody would be there to give me a hand.

She was in the kitchen. So was Uncle Duncan.

"There, Molly," he said, as I blundered in. "I told you he'd be safe enough."

"Jay!" began Mother. "I've told you a thousand times—" Then she saw my face.

"Mr. Enderton," I gasped. "He's really sick. Down by the shore. I can't lift him."

When spacer visitors were around, Mother liked to act weak and helpless. She was neither, of course, and now she proved it.

"Unconscious?" she snapped.

"He was, when I left."

"Right," she said. And then, without another word to me, "Duncan, we'll need a blanket, and maybe something to carry him on. I'll find those. You get the flashlight and our coats. Hurry."

Mother had taken over. And with that, I became empty and deflated. All I wanted to do was sink down on the floor of the warm kitchen and go to sleep. But I couldn't, because Mother was hustling me out of the door so I could lead them to the pier.

Paddy Enderton had not moved since I left, and I thought for a horrible moment that he was dead. He groaned, though, when Uncle Duncan straightened him, and he was muttering something under his breath as they heaved him up onto the pier and wrapped him in a blanket. I stood by ready to help, but all I was allowed to do was hold the flashlight. Mother and Uncle Duncan between them carried him up to the house, where they laid him on a couch dragged close to the stove.

His color was awful, a uniform grey pallor except for isolated spots of purple-red flaming on his cheekbones. Mother lowered her head to his chest and remained stooped over him for a long time. Finally she straightened and came to where I was sitting slumped in a chair at the kitchen table.

"I'm sorry, Jay," she said quietly, "But you have to go out again. We'll do what we can, but without a physician's help he's probably going to die. Whatever persuaded him to go out on the lake in weather like this, with his chest and lungs?"

She was not looking for an answer from me, although I could have given one, and she went right on, "You know where Doctor Eileen lives. I want you to go to her house. Tell her what happened here. Tell her that your mother says it's urgent, and bring her back with you. Go now, as fast as you can."

Before I knew it I was pushed out again into the freezing dark, big flakes falling silently on me as I started along the southern road. No one had been this way since the snow began, and in places I sank to my knees in undisturbed drifts. I put my head down and struggled on. One good thing was that the wind was steady and at my back. My eyes and face could at least remain sheltered. But there was little else to comfort me. The day had been exhausting, mentally as well as physically, and I felt ready to drop. After less than a hundred yards I halted and stood panting in the road.

At this rate I would never make it to Doctor Eileen's house. Sheer fatigue would stop me. If I tried to keep going, the first person along the road in the morning would discover my frozen corpse.

It was the wind, pushing persistently at my back, that gave me the idea that saved my life—and not for the reason that I thought at the time.

It occurred to me that if I left the road and went down the hill to my left, I would arrive at the place where the sailboat was tied up. With the wind at its present heading, it would then be child's play for me to hoist the sail and allow myself to be blown all the way to Doctor Eileen's lakeshore house. Even at night, the darkness of the lake and the reflection of light from the snow on shore would be enough to leave me in no doubt as to the land/water boundary.

Before I knew it I had made up my mind. My legs seemed like weighted pendulums as they carried me down the hill towards the pier. Two minutes later I was in the sailboat, scraping snow off the seat and struggling to shake it off the sail. One minute after that the boat was away, gliding smoothly before the following wind.

It had sounded so easy, but real life never seems to work out quite as simple and pleasant as imagination paints it. My hands froze almost at once, so I had to keep one tucked into my jacket and hold the rudder lines with the other. My bottom was the next victim. Sitting for three-quarters of an hour on the bare plank seat of a sailboat, cramped and freezing, was no joke. I felt thawed snow, cold enough to be painful, seeping into the seat of my pants. To add terror to discomfort I had an awful few minutes when I lost sight of the snowy shore. But easing the boat steadily to the right solved that, and once I was past the lights of Toltoona I knew the worst was over. Doctor Eileen's house came next, and the lights were on there all the time. The only question was whether she was home, or had been dragged out into the blizzard for some other nighttime emergency.

Either way, I knew one thing for sure: Doctor Eileen's house would be my last port of call for the night.

I was wrong about that too, of course. For the past couple of days, it seemed that every time I thought I knew what would happen next, events took a hundred-and-eighty-degree turn.

Doctor Eileen was home, and despite the lateness of the hour she was up and fully dressed. She let me get only as far as "Mother says it's urgent," before she swept me into her cruiser and headed north towards our house.

The good news was that the vehicle floated as quickly and easily over snow as over anything else. The better news was that Doctor Eileen often lived in it for days, so hot food and drink could be produced on the little stove in the rear of the cabin. We were hardly through Toltoona before I was feeling, if not restored, at least human. I answered her questions as best I could, about my aborted trip across to Muldoon Port, about Paddy Enderton's collapse on the way, about his symptoms, and about my own desperate decision to reach her by water rather than by road.

It was the last answer that produced the most reaction. She had been sitting quietly in the driver's seat, taking us rapidly but carefully along the north road. I was behind her, paying no attention to anything outside, which from the moment we started had been little more than a whirlwind of white.

"Did I hear you right?" she said. "Did you say that you had trouble walking because the snow was unbroken?"

"Yes. From our house toward Toltoona, no one had been along it."

"Well, they certainly have now. A number of people. See for yourself."

The footprints were already filling, but they were unmistakable. Four or five separate tracks led in the direction we were traveling. There was no sign of them returning. I stayed up at the front of the cruiser and watched, convinced that at some point the trails in the snow would leave the road and head away, up the hill or down toward the shore.

They didn't. They continued, all the way to the path that served the front porch of my own house.

Even then I was not alarmed. Puzzled, yes. Who would visit us at this hour, and in this weather? But I had no sense of danger.

It was Doctor Eileen who halted the ground car twenty yards from the house, and stepped cautiously out into deep snow.

"You wait here, Jay," she said.

It was too late. I had climbed out of the cruiser behind her. I could see an odd patch of white and red on the porch, just beyond the farthest point that the blown snow had reached.

I ran to it and knelt down. It was Chum, lying in a pool of blood. My miniver had been skewered through from back to belly, pinned to the rough planks of the porch by one of our own long-bladed kitchen knives.

"Jay!" said Doctor Eileen again. But I was blundering in through the front door, dreading what I might find.

At first the scene inside seemed to match my worst fears. The living room was empty, a chaos of broken and overturned furniture. Beyond it, in the kitchen, Paddy Enderton lay stretched out on the floor. His face was purple, and he was not breathing. All the kitchen drawers and cabinets had been pulled open and their contents swept onto the floor. There was no sign of Mother, or of Uncle Duncan.

As Doctor Eileen bent over Paddy Enderton, I ran upstairs. The landing was deserted. The door of the guest room, my new bedroom, was open, and it was a shambles. Everything I owned was strewn randomly around the floor. Sick to my stomach, I pushed open the closed door of Mother's room.

She was there, lying face upward on her own bed. Her coat was off, and her dress had been ripped up the front from hem to waist. Her hands were bound in front of her, a broad cloth had been tied around her mouth, and the left side of her face was swollen and turning a dull red. But when I ran to her she opened her eyes and lifted her head.

"Doctor Eileen!" I cried. It emerged as a high-pitched scream. I turned Mother's head to get at the place the gag was tied. "Mother's here. She's alive. She's hurt."

Eileen Xavier came up the stairs two at a time, and was into the bedroom while I was still struggling with the knots.

"Look out, Jay." She pushed me out of the way and cut the gag through with one quick flick of a scalpel. Until that moment I had not realized that she was carrying it.

Mother was coughing, and pushing a ball of cloth out of her mouth with her tongue. Doctor Eileen stepped back, and did a quick survey of her from head to foot. "Duncan West?" she asked.

Mother shook her head. She tried to speak, but it came out only as another cough. Doctor Eileen turned to me. "Jay. Check the front bedroom."

Thinking back, I believe that she wanted me out of the way while she examined Mother. But I didn't know it at the time, and I stepped along the landing to my old room half-convinced that I would find Uncle Duncan stretched out on the floor there.

I didn't. The room was empty, at least of people. But the

mess inside was even worse than anywhere else. Everything had been taken apart—the contents of Enderton's big square box removed and smashed to fragments, dressers and desk overturned, drawers emptied out onto the floor. The curtains had been pulled down and slit along their seams. The mattress of the bed had been ripped open, and its stuffing lay scattered everywhere. Even the window had been thrown open, and someone had probed with a knife into the layer of snow sitting on the outside sill.

I rummaged helplessly in the debris for a minute or two, then went across and closed the window. I headed back to the main bedroom, where mother was now sitting up.

"Uncle Duncan—" I began.

"He's all right," Doctor Eileen said. "He went soon after you, to try to get other help. He left long before they got here."

Mother nodded, and gave me a lopsided smile.

"Mr. Enderton?" I said. "Is he—" I found I could not finish the question.

"Dead, I'm afraid." Doctor Eileen was helping mother to her feet. "Of natural causes, just a few minutes after you left. Whatever he'd been doing today, the strain was too much for his heart." She must have seen my guilty expression. "Don't feel bad, Jay. I couldn't have saved him, you know, even if I'd been here. He wouldn't look after himself, even after he was warned. Come on now, take your mother's arm and let's get out of here. The two of you are going to spend the night at my house."

"Do you think they'll come back?" I didn't know who "they" might be, but I was mortally afraid of them. They had spitted Chum for no reason at all. He had been the most harmless pet in the world, a goofy ball of fur who would never attack anybody.

"Since we don't know who they were," replied Doctor Eileen, "we can't say they won't be back. But they were certainly looking for something, and they searched hard, and they didn't find it. There were four of them, and I don't know if one or more may want to try again."

"I don't think they will." Mother's voice was a whisper as we helped her into her coat and out of the door. I noticed a big red blotch I hadn't seen before on her throat. "They were arguing among themselves when they left. They had—changed the subject."

She glanced down at her own ripped dress, and then at Eileen Xavier.

"You were damn lucky, Molly," said Doctor Eileen. "Lucky they had a lot on their minds and were pressed for time."

"Give me some credit, Eileen." Mother was sounding more like herself. "I made a few unkind comparisons, just to make them mad at each other."

"But where could they have gone?" I turned to the doctor, as she opened the door of the cruiser for us to climb in. "We saw their tracks coming, but nothing went back."

She said nothing, but pointed down the hill. Multiple footprints, half-covered with snow, led toward the dark lake water.

Apparently I was not the only one with the idea that travel by boat was easier than struggling along through soft, clinging snow.

But as I settled into the cruiser's comfortable seat, and felt my eyes closing almost before my weary head touched the cushioned headrest, it occurred to me that the mystery attackers perhaps had a different motive. One thing was sure: Deep water, unlike deep snow, left no trail to follow.

CHAPTER 7

I slept through all the next morning and the early part of the afternoon. So in spite of Doctor Eileen turning up her nose at the idea of anybody passing on "hearsay" to posterity, that's all I can offer for the day, at least until I was sitting in the Xavier kitchen working my way through a stack of sorghum cakes and scrambled phalarope eggs.

Uncle Duncan lolled opposite me, yawning and stretching and complaining of lack of sleep. It seemed he had finally gone back to our house in the middle of the night, bringing with him a vet—the nearest thing he could find to a physician without going all the way to Toltoona. What they encountered at the house had left them baffled: the whole place ransacked, Paddy Enderton dead on the floor, Mother vanished, and the building deserted.

Rather than heading out again into the snow, they built up the fire and stayed there for the rest of the night. The intruders had not returned, and finally Duncan had decided to make for Doctor Eileen's.

Mother was not much more helpful. Four men had burst into the house without warning, while she sat alone with Enderton's body. The sight of him lying dead on the floor had sent them into a rage.

"They could hardly believe it," she said. "The biggest one went across and kicked the body and swore at it, as though Enderton had died just to annoy him. Damned Black Paddy, he called him. He searched Enderton's clothing, then he set the other three to ransacking the house while he questioned me. I did my best to act innocent. Said Enderton was just a lodger who had the upstairs room, and hardly ever came down. I was vague about everything, and I acted dumb as I knew how."

"I'll bet you did," Doctor Eileen said. She had already been out all morning on a call, and was getting ready to go out again. "We'll need a full description."

"I'll give you one, but it won't help unless I see them again. I'm sure they were spacers, every one, but there was nothing out of the ordinary about any of them."

"Nobody with no arms, or no legs," I said, and felt myself blush when Duncan West stared at me as though I had lost my mind.

"I tried to get them to say what they were after," went on mother. "But that didn't work."

I started to open my mouth again, ready to mention the telecon still sitting high on the water tower, but Mother quickly disposed of that possibility.

"Whatever it was they were after," she said, "it must have been no bigger than your hand, because of the places that they were looking. And when they couldn't find anything they got more and more annoyed. They started to smash things at random. That's when they knocked me about a bit, too, just to take it out on somebody. Then they moved upstairs and tied me down. I think they were getting interested in other options for me when the big one said forget it, the boss was waiting and he'd told them go easy on the redhead woman."

"Lucky for you," said Uncle Duncan.

"Oh, I don't know." Mother smiled at him, but she had

her eye on Doctor Eileen. "I think in another five minutes I could have had a couple of them at each other's throats."

"Or slitting yours," Doctor Eileen said. "Molly, you're plain incorrigible. Come on. I'll give you and Jay a ride back to the house. We'll pick up a few strong men in Toltoona, to stay with you and make sure there's no more trouble."

I glanced out of the window. There was a clear blue sky, and outside the snow was melting fast. "I've got to take the sailboat back home," I said. "I might as well do it now, and get it over with."

"All right," Mother said mildly. "But no heading off across the lake again. 'Clean your room,' has a whole new meaning today. I wouldn't like to think you were trying to skip housework."

As the other three left the kitchen I realized that she was right. I *was* avoiding going home. But it was nothing to do with housework. It was the thought of Chum, casually slaughtered and skewered to the front porch. No matter what Paddy Enderton had done, and no matter what the others wanted from him, they didn't have to do that.

I had lost my appetite. I washed the dishes, put on my coat, and headed for the place where I had tied up the boat. My whole water journey and final arrival last night seemed like an awful dream. It was surprising to find everything just as I had left it, the sail still not properly furled, the seats and the bottom of the boat covered in snow.

Before I could sail home, the boat had to be cleared. I took a square of wood and began to use it as a makeshift shovel, scraping snow into heaps and dumping it overboard into the black lake water.

I had been at work no more than two minutes when I came across the rectangular wafer of black plastic. It was sitting in the bottom of the boat, just where it had dropped from Paddy Enderton's hands.

* * *

Mother's orders had been explicit: Go home, and at once. But no command in the universe could have stopped me from sitting down in the bow of the boat and staring at Enderton's little sealed device.

It was thin, hardly more than a plastic card, and at first sight the front was plain. Upon a closer look I could see dozens of faint depressions, each one the size of a fingertip. I pressed them tentatively, one after another and then in pairs.

No result. But just last night there had been that strange display of moving points of light.

What had Enderton done? I struggled to recall, and quickly realized that I had no idea. It was not that I failed to remember, it was that he had operated in the dark, and until the lights actually appeared all my attention had been on the knife that he had just put away.

I fiddled with the thin rectangle of plastic for another minute or two, pretty much at random, and at last gave up. I jumped out of the boat and stood on the pier. There I paused.

Doctor Eileen Xavier was no longer at the house. She had taken Mother home. The question was, would she stay there for a while, long enough for me to catch her if I started now? Or if not, was she likely to come back to the Xavier house before she headed off again on her rounds, and so make it worth my while to hang around here a bit longer?

All too often in the past couple of days my fate seemed to have been determined by the wind. Now it was blowing steadily, pushing the boat's little pink pennant like a pointing finger to the north.

Towards home.

I tucked the plastic rectangle in my jacket pocket so I would not be tempted to fiddle with it any more, unfurled the boat's sail, and was on my way.

It was perfect sailing weather, clear and crisp and with a following wind that was just right. The only sound was clean lake water, lapping at the bow. On another afternoon I would have revelled in every moment. Today I could not enjoy it at all. I felt dreadfully dejected, for what I'm sure anybody else would have said was quite the wrong reason. Mother had been gagged and beaten. Paddy Enderton was dead. Our house had been invaded and almost demolished.

But the only thing on my mind was Chum. When I got home I would have to pull out the knife that pinned him to the planks of the porch, carry his body away from the house, and bury him.

The picture in my head was very vivid: four men, frustrated and furious as they rushed out of the house into the snow. Chum, convinced that the whole world was friendly and anyone running must be playing a game, gambolling across to greet them. The men's jerk of surprise, the curse, the vicious thrust of a knife.

At least it would have been quick. With luck he had died before he understood what was happening. But that was little consolation.

I patted my pocket as the boat came close to the dock leading up to the house. If this had been what they were after, one thing I knew for certain: They would not get it from me—

—if I could help it. That qualification came into my head as I started up the path. My footsteps slowed.

In a few more steps I would be in full view of the house. There was no sign of Doctor Eileen's cruiser out by the road. In all likelihood she had been and gone and Mother would be safely inside with her tough-guy guards, beginning the long job of cleaning up the mess.

But suppose that they weren't? Suppose that Mother and Doctor Eileen had not arrived yet, and last night's attackers had returned and were lurking inside waiting for me?

And what I was carrying.

I back-stepped a little way along the path, then dropped to one knee. I was at Chum's favorite burrow, a hole that he had carefully dug out and furnished with dried leaves.

I pushed the rectangular plastic card into the round hole. Then I recoiled as my fingertips met cold, wet fur.

Chum's body. And no one outside the family knew about his burrow.

I stood up, still holding the rectangle of plastic, and ran for the house. When I was twenty yards away a window went up with a sound like a gunshot. Mother's head poked out.

"Jay! I thought I told you to come straight back here. Get inside."

I halted. "Chum—"

"I took care of him. I put him in his burrow. If you want him somewhere else . . ."

"No." I couldn't bear to look at her, though she had only been trying to help. "He's home now. He can stay there." I stuffed Enderton's black wafer into my pocket and hurried into the house. The kitchen drawers and cupboards were closed again, and the mess of the previous night had been cleared up. Three men from Toltoona were sitting at the table playing cards. I knew them. They were all big and broad and self-confident, and they nodded at me casually.

"I didn't touch your room yet," mother said. "I thought you'd prefer to do that yourself. Come on."

I followed her, waiting until we were at the top of the stairs before I spoke.

"Mother." I kept my voice down to a whisper. "I've got it—the thing that the men were looking for last night."

She halted at the door of the guest room and glanced back to the stairs. For the first time in my life, I had the feeling that Mother was frightened.

"Go on into my room," she said. She followed me and closed the door after us. "Now, what do you say you've got?"

I pulled out the innocent-looking piece of molded black plastic, and told her where it came from. She took it from me, turning it over and examining each side.

"He made it work last night," I said. "He made it show a

lot of lights in the air. But I don't know how to do it. What is it?"

"I'm not sure." Mother sat down on the bed. Her room, like the kitchen, was back to normal. She began to press the surface of the black oblong, placing her fingertips into its shallow depressions. "If I had to guess, I'd say it was never made on Erin—or anywhere in the Forty Worlds. That means it must be very old, from the days before the Isolation."

It was strange to hear her talk that way. "I thought you said there never was a Godspeed Drive."

She glanced up, all the while pressing the concave areas on the wafer. "Oh, that's just me agreeing with Duncan. He says there never was one. But if you ever went over to the big museum in Roscommon, you'd not doubt that we came here from another star, a long time ago, and that goods and people were coming to and from Erin for hundreds of years. Until one day, suddenly, it all stopped."

"Why don't you take Uncle Duncan over to Roscommon with you, and show him?"

"Because he won't take the time to go. He says, and I half agree with him, what's the difference? There's no Drive *now*, and we have to get on with our lives without it. I don't dwell on the past much myself, but there never was a man like Duncan West for living in the here and now. That's why I like him. He's all in the present."

"Where is he?" It had suddenly occurred to me that he was not in the house.

"He left, as soon as he was sure that I was safe home and protected. He said it had been chaos yesterday, but he still had to earn a living."

All the time we were talking, Mother had been studying what she was holding, and pressing in different places with various combinations of fingers. "There!" she said with satisfaction. "That's got it."

I leaned over. There was no sign of the beautiful three-dimensional display of lights that I had seen in the boat, but the dark surface showed a glowing set of numbers and open round spots. "What did you do?"

"Turned it on. It was just power-protected, against being turned on by accident. To activate it, you have to press here, and here, and here, all at the same time. See."

Three of her fingers moved down in unison. The display vanished, leaving dull black plastic. A second later the glowing numbers reappeared as she pressed down for a second time.

"But what *is* it?" I asked.

"I'm not sure, but I think it's probably a calculator. Anyway, it's hard to believe that this is what the men last night were searching for. Here." She handed it to me. "I'd say that with Paddy Enderton dead, you have more right to it than anyone."

She stood up. "Now, I want you to sort out your room and the front bedroom, and get them as far as you can back to normal. Anything that belonged to Mr. Enderton, you keep separate. Put it out on the landing. When you've done most of the job and feel that you need to take a break, see if you can get the calculator to work."

"It wasn't a calculator last night." But as I said that, I realized that all I had seen was a display. A strange display, sure, but what I was holding *could* be a calculator—or just about anything else. I had no idea what it was.

"Do you think that Uncle Duncan could make it work?" I asked, as mother opened the door to my room.

"You can ask him, but I doubt it. Whatever it is, it's surely micro-electronics. I think it needs more than the knack."

The knack.

It described Duncan West's gift very well without at all explaining it. He was known all around the southern end of Lake Sheelin, where he made a living, and a good one, fixing mechanical things that were not working right. I had seen cars towed over to our house by their cursing or despairing owners, and driven away an hour later in perfect running condition after Duncan had fiddled around inside their engines.

It was not always so quick, though. I have known him sit down with a broken clock after dinner at our house. The next morning, when I got up, the kitchen table would be covered with screws and cogs and bearings, and Duncan would still be sitting there. As Mother said, he lived in the present, so that made him hardly aware of time. Eventually, maybe by mid-afternoon, everything would go back together, to the last tiniest screw, and when Duncan left he was carrying a clock that worked perfectly.

I wished for a bit of the knack myself, as I sat by the window and pondered the mystery of Paddy Enderton's accidental legacy. Mother had said to clean up my room first, but I of course ignored her. The lure of the black plastic card was too great. Turning it on and off was trivial—when I had been shown how. Making it work as a calculator was not much harder, once I found the pressure points that corresponded to the arithmetic operators.

But that was surely not all it did. A whole triple row of blank circles were unaccounted for. So I went on working, if that's the right word for the unsystematic (and unproductive) poking and pressing and pondering that I did in the next few hours.

Mother looked in on me once, and saw me sitting there amidst unimproved chaos. Oddly enough, she went away again with not a word.

The breakthrough came at last, but I think I should be given no credit for it. There's an old story about monkeys writing all the world's books, if they stick at it long enough. That's more or less what I did. I finally pressed a sequence, no different to my mind from a hundred others that I had tried; suddenly the wafer vanished, and the air in front of me was filled with minute points of colored light.

I stared at them, while I desperately tried to recall exactly what I had done. At the same time, I realized two things.

First, this was not the same display that Paddy Enderton had conjured up in the boat last night, because these lights were not moving, and second, although the glowing surface of the little plastic rectangle was faint and dim compared with the bright points surrounding it, I could still see numbers.

It was a bad moment. On the one hand I had to be sure that I remembered the operating sequence, and could produce the same result again; on the other hand, I was afraid to turn off the display in case I could not get it back.

What I should probably have done is go and get Mother and show her that, even if I could not re-create the display, it was real enough.

What I actually did was turn off the power.

Then I spent an agonizing thirty seconds until I had repeated all the necessary steps and a volume of space around the black plastic filled again with points of light.

I did it all over again, three times, and wrote down the sequence. Only after that was I able to pay attention to the lights themselves.

They formed a ragged cluster in space, a thick doughnut shape rather than a sphere. I tried to count them. When I reached a hundred I gave up, but I decided that the total had to be more than four times that. I reached my hand in toward one of them, very gingerly, and felt nothing. When my finger came to the space occupied by a light, the bright point simply blinked out of existence. It came back when I pulled away.

Mother sometimes says I'm colorblind, but technically speaking I'm not. I'm just not very good at matching colors in clothes, because that's the most boring thing in the world. But examining the colors of Paddy Enderton's display was the most interesting thing in the world, and I distinguished twenty separate hues ranging from deep violet to blazing crimson. The most common color was orange. Maybe a third of the points ranged from a dull near-brown ember to the heart of a glowing wood fire. The only color that I did not see anywhere was green.

I found a piece of paper among the mess on the floor, and wrote down my estimate of the fraction of the total for each color. It was fascinating, but I could not help feeling that here came the busy monkeys, all over again. I was working hard, sure, but there was no *plan* to what I was doing.

It was time for more systematic experiments. I reached forward and pressed a number on the input pad. Suddenly the display was no longer static. The points began to move at different speeds, the middle ones a little faster than the outer ones. Like tiny glittering beads on invisible wires, they slid around a common center.

More pressing of numbers showed that I was controlling only the speed of movement of the display. Pushing "0" froze everything, pressing "1" moved the lights almost too slow to notice, and "9" revolved the whole pattern every few seconds. Two digits pressed one after the other increased the speed more, faster and faster, until ninety-nine produced a blurred torus of light. Any third digit was ignored.

So much for the numbers. What about the blank circular spots?

I reached forward, then gasped when I realized that Mother was in the room, standing just at my shoulder.

"Well done, Jay," she said. "You were quite right, and I should have had more faith in you. Come on downstairs now and get some food in you. You can do this again later." She said nothing about the fact that my room was in as big a mess as when I came into it, or that I had not even been into the front bedroom where Paddy Enderton had been living.

"It's not just a calculator," I said.

"No. Or at least, not like one I've ever heard of before. I want Eileen Xavier to see this. She promised to drop by later. Come on." Mother led the way to the kitchen.

I ate there. Something.

That's no reflection on Mother's cooking. My brain was still upstairs, and my fingers itched to be back pressing on the plastic wafer. Anyway, the three men that Doctor Eileen had recruited in Toltoona talked so much, and about such boring things—ways of preserving meat, mostly—that anyone's brain would have wanted to escape. They were nice to have around for protection, I suppose, but I gained a new appreciation of Mother's preference for spacers. Even Paddy Enderton, dead dirty Black Paddy, had found more to talk about than salting and smoking and drying and pickling.

The afternoon had flown away, and the sky was already darkening when I sneaked back upstairs. I felt a new pressure on me when I again turned on Enderton's calculator/display/what-have-you. If Doctor Eileen was coming to the house, I wanted to be able to say more than "I don't know" to all the questions that she would be sure to ask.

The hardest question was one that I had already asked myself and not been able to answer. If this was what the four men had been searching for, *why was it important?* I could see it as an interesting gadget, more like a toy than anything, but surely not something for which anyone would threaten and torture and kill.

I brought up the display, set it to run in one of its slower-moving forms, and began to explore the effects of the three rows of open blanks.

I found a way to use them at last, something it would have been very easy to miss. For with a static display, or one where the points of light were moving too rapidly, I doubt that I would ever have noticed it.

You had to be looking at the display at the same time as you pressed an area in the middle of the three blank rows. Then if you were watching carefully you would see an extra point of light appear, a clear, green spark that was different in color from everything else. It also sat stationary, within the other points of the doughnut-shaped cluster.

By tedious experiment I learned that pressure on other blank areas could move the green star around in any direction. Up, across, forward, back.

And so what? said the skeptical part of my mind. Big deal.

You've got a calculator, and a display. Now what about something that *interacts* with the display?

That didn't seem to exist. I froze everything by pressing zero, then brought the green glow to coincide with a point of bright orange. The spark of fire vanished, but nothing else at all happened.

I sighed, and muttered to myself, "I'll *never* get this."

And at that moment the green star changed, from a constant glow to a flashing point.

It was a triumph of sorts, but it sure didn't feel like one. For having come so far, I could go no farther. The green point flashed and flashed and flashed, taunting me to make it *do* something. And I could not.

I talked, I gestured, I pushed and squeezed and probed at the surface of the wafer. I did all of them together. The display obstinately refused to respond. It seemed to be challenging me to make it react.

And at that high point of frustration, Mother brought Doctor Eileen upstairs.

Like Mother, Doctor Eileen was much kinder to me than I felt to myself. I was nowhere near answering the basic questions of device function, but she listened to me as I described everything I had done, and watched as I worked the input and the output display.

Finally she said, "Voice activated, for a bet."

"You mean it should respond to what I say? I *tried* that."

"I believe you. But I think you don't know the right key words." Doctor Eileen turned to Mother. "Molly, what Jay has done so far is terrific. But we are going to need professional help, spacers and historians. I don't know what we have here, but I'm sure it's not of the Forty Worlds."

"You mean it's from before the Isolation? That's what I told Jay."

"I mean more than that. The technology came from somewhere else, sure it did. But look at the unit." We all stared together, as Doctor Eileen went on, "Look at the *con-*

dition of it. That's not two or three hundred years old. It's *new*. It came into operation within the past year or two.''

"But that means . . ." Mother paused, and for the second time in one day I saw in her an emotion that I had never seen before.

"If it *is* new," she went on, "and it's not our technology, then there must be more in the Maveen system than the Forty Worlds."

"That's right." And now there was something in Doctor Eileen's voice, too, an excitement that I had never heard before. "Molly, I think the thing Jay is holding, whatever it is, and however it came here, is enormously important. It was made in Godspeed Base."

And now it was Mother's turn again, her bewildered voice saying, ever so faintly, "Godspeed *Base?* But Eileen, there never *was* a Godspeed Base. Was there?"

CHAPTER 8

At midnight I stood on the front porch of our house and stared across the quiet lake.

"Go to bed, now," Mother had told me a few minutes before. "You've had a full day. You need your sleep."

She was probably right, but I knew it would be pointless to lie down. Not with the inside of my head still running wild. Instead I went outside. Mother and Doctor Eileen must have been almost as wound up as I was, because when I left they went on talking to each other as though I did not exist.

Godspeed Base.

"If you admit that the Godspeed *Drive* once existed," Doctor Eileen had said, "then logically Godspeed *Base* had to exist, too, somewhere in the Maveen system."

"Why?" I asked.

"Because every machine needs repairs sometime. The Godspeed ships must have had a place in each star system, somewhere they could go for refitting or maintenance work. And the Base wouldn't have disappeared when the ships stopped coming here."

"Why did they stop coming?"

"Nobody knows. I've heard scientists say that the whole

Godspeed Drive system contained the seeds of its own destruction, something to do with the nature of space and time, and it should never have been built. I've heard religious leaders say that the isolation of Maveen and the Forty Worlds is a punishment for our sins on Erin. And of course, I've heard a thousand times that there never was a Godspeed Drive, that it's only an old legend." She looked directly at Mother. "You can point out to those people that humans clearly didn't evolve on Erin, and ask how we got here. But you won't get anywhere. Because most of them don't believe in evolution, either. Any more than they'll believe that what Jay has sitting in front of him is important."

I had a suspicion that Doctor Eileen was taking a dig at Duncan West, without mentioning his name. In any case, it was obvious how she regarded all such people. I stared at the little plastic wafer, switched off now on the table. We still didn't know why anyone would kill for it. But if it had come from Godspeed Base, that seemed to make it important enough to Doctor Eileen, if not yet to me.

"Do you think that Paddy Enderton had been to the base?" I asked.

"I doubt it. There would have been other evidence."

"There is." I told them about the telecon, and the little direction finder that he had given me.

"I'd like to take a look at those tomorrow," Doctor Eileen said, casually condemning me to another blood-chilling climb up the water tower. "But I mean more direct evidence. If he'd actually been there, he'd have come home with proof. And he'd not have kept *that* a secret when he reached Erin. But from what you've told me, he was convinced that he knew where Godspeed Base was. And he was definitely planning a trip there. That's why he wanted you take him to Muldoon Port, before he collapsed. And those other men *knew* that he knew. That's why they came after him yesterday."

I still had a basic question. "If the Godspeed ships don't come here any more, *why* is Godspeed Base so important?"

"Jay, you can ask more questions than any sane woman can answer," Mother said sharply. "Go to bed."

But Doctor Eileen was answering: "Because there's a chance that a complete Godspeed ship, with a full Godspeed Drive, is sitting out there at the base. It would have been there as a backup. Otherwise a Godspeed crew would have risked being stranded if the ship they came in was destroyed, or if there were major problems with the Godspeed Drive."

If she had wanted to choose words to guarantee that I would be unable to sleep, she could hardly have done better. Two months ago, exploration of the Forty Worlds with the spacers had been my great dream. Now Doctor Eileen was telling me that somewhere out there, within reach of our ships, might be something to take us to the stars.

But mother was saying again, "Go to bed, Jay. Eileen and I have other things to talk about."

I picked up Paddy Enderton's device and left the room. A minute later I was outside, staring across at the distant lights of Muldoon Port. My thoughts about it had changed since yesterday. Enderton had wanted to go there. The men who had hurt Mother and killed Chum had left by water. They were spacers. Chances were, they had gone to Muldoon. The spaceport was the road out, the way to the Forty Worlds, and now to Godspeed Base.

But the men had left without the information that they came for. That was in my hand, locked away, waiting for someone to find the key.

Voice-activated, Doctor Eileen had said. Well, I had a voice, as good as anyone else's.

I went back indoors and up to my bedroom. But not to sleep.

It took a few minutes to get to the place where I had been stuck earlier, with a single flashing green spark that I could move around among the other lights of the display.

If I had to choose words that would make a display do more than just sit there, what would they be?

"Godspeed Base."

No response.

"Godspeed. Godspeed Drive. Godspeed crew. Forty Worlds. Paddy Enderton. Er, information. Data. Position. Location. Input. Output."

Nothing. Either the device was as stupid as it seemed, or I was missing the point.

I sat and frowned down at the innocent-looking little wafer. Stupid, *stupid*. Unless . . . Suppose, just suppose, that it was the other way round? Suppose that I was dealing with something very *smart*?

Then I ought to be asking questions or giving commands, instead of offering one word at a time that it would not know what to do with.

"I want access to data associated with the display that is now being shown."

The response was immediate. An open box appeared in the air below the main display. To its left-hand side glowed three words: *First Data Level*. The box itself was empty.

"That doesn't tell me anything!" I protested. "I want to know more. Tell me something else about the display."

Nothing new appeared.

I talked on and on, without being able to produce any change in what I was seeing. It was only when I ran out of things to say that I realized that the voice commands and the flashing point of green might be related. At the moment, the green spark sat in an empty area of space. If the problem was that I was asking for information about nothing . . .

I pressed zero, to freeze the moving set of colored lights. Then I used the controls to move the flashing green spark to coincide with one rustily glowing point.

At last!

The open box was no longer empty. It contained a word, *Liscarroll*. Beneath that were six nine-figure numbers. Five of them changed not at all, or slowly in their final digits, but the sixth one changed all the time, increasing steadily.

I found my piece of paper, and wrote *Liscarroll.* Then I said, "Give me the second data level."

If there is such a thing as too little information, there is also such a thing as too much. Words began to stream through the open box, line after line of them. I read, with little understanding: . . . *primary assay obtained as extrapolation of surface spectra, composition as mass fraction: hydrogen, 0.44; helium, 0.20; lithium, 0.00; beryllium, 0.01; boron, 0.00; carbon, 0.06; nitrogen, 0.05; oxygen, 0.08; fluorine, 0.01; neon, 0.00* . . .

The list went on and on. I did not attempt to write everything down, but instead moved the green pointer to a new light. This one was of pale amber. I said, "First data level."

The box emptied. And refilled.

Corofin was the first word. Below it, as before, were six new nine-digit numbers, five of them again close to unchanging and the sixth steadily increasing.

I had learned my lesson, and I did not ask for any second data level. Instead I began to move the green point systematically through the display, recording the names that popped into the open data box. *Kiltealy, Timahoe, Moynalty, Clareen, Oola, Drumkeerin* . . .

No two words were the same. Every one had its own string of six nine-digit numbers. I settled down, determined to record a complete list. I would begin with the topmost point of the display and move the green marker systematically down through the whole thing, light by light.

I was becoming very tired, and maybe what I was doing was my way of avoiding further real thinking. But I went on, through name after meaningless name. *Rockcorry, Ardscull, Timolin, Ballybay, Culdaff, Armoy, Tyrella, Moira* . . .

And then, almost without realizing it, I found that I was copying the words, *Paddy's Fortune.*

I stopped, tingling all over. It could be a name, no different from any other. The usual six nine-digit numbers that sat below it supported that idea.

Or *Paddy* might be Paddy Enderton. *Paddy's Fortune* might be his own words to describe what was shown in the data box.

It was the middle of the night, but that made no difference. I went through to Mother's room with the display still on, intending to wake her up. She was not there.

She was downstairs. The three guards were in the living-room, sound asleep—so much for their value as protectors. Mother and Doctor Eileen were sitting facing each other at the kitchen table, glasses and an open bottle between them.

It was the first time that I had seen Mother drinking wine when we did not have one of her spacer visitors. I suddenly realized that I might not be the only one having trouble sleeping. Although my own past couple of days had been hard, Mother's had been far more filled with stress. She had been questioned, and beaten, and threatened with worse. She had been the one who had to sit with Paddy Enderton's corpse, and dispose of poor Chum's body.

"What woke you up?" she said, when I approached the table.

"I never went to sleep. I couldn't." I put the wafer onto the table along with my written list, and pointed at the displayed data.

"That green point is on something called *Paddy's Fortune.* Do you think it means Paddy Enderton?"

Mother stared at the glowing nimbus of lighted points, but Eileen Xavier seemed more interested in the data box and the list that I had written.

"Where did you get this from?" she asked.

"It's the words that the calculator seems to give to the points. Each one has a different name."

"Just a name? Nothing else?"

"Lots and lots more. I just didn't know what it meant, so I didn't write it all down."

Doctor Eileen put down the paper. Her eyes were gleaming as she turned to the display. "Show me."

I moved the green pointer to a glowing red point that I had looked at before, and said, "First data level."

Ardscull, read the data box. Beneath that, as before, were the usual six mysterious numbers.

Mysterious to me, I should have said. Because Doctor Eileen exhaled her breath, as though she had been holding it for the past minute, and gasped, "Jay, you've done it! Molly, you ought to be proud of him."

"I *am* proud of him," Mother said. "Most of the time. But I don't know what he did."

"Those little sparks of light." Doctor Eileen pointed. "They represent *places*. Those names that Jay wrote down are the names of some of the bigger worldlets, out in the Maze. I think the whole display is of the Maze. And *Paddy's Fortune*, for a bet, is the place where Paddy Enderton believed you'd find Godspeed Base."

"But that doesn't tell you how to get anywhere," Mother protested. "It's just a picture."

"It would be—if it weren't for these." Doctor Eileen indicated the six nine-figure strings of digits below the word, *Ardscull*. "I'm no spacer, and I don't know that much about planets and moons. But six numbers are enough to fix the location and speed of any object in space. I'll bet that five of them, the ones that hardly change, describe the form of the orbit. And this sixth one, the one that keeps increasing, tells the object's *position* in its orbit. It's all you need to reach a place."

"There's other information, too." I returned the green marker to coincide with the point of *Paddy's Fortune*. After the name and the usual six numbers had been displayed again, I intoned clearly: *"Second data level."*

The display box became annoyingly empty. "That's funny," I said. "It worked for the others I tried. Why doesn't it work for this one?"

"Because *Paddy's Fortune* is different from all the natural worlds of the Maze." Doctor Eileen stood up and began to walk round and round the table. "My God, Molly, do you know what this means? No wonder the men last night were willing to beat you and smash your house to pieces to get this. We have to tell everybody what we've found. Then we have to hire a ship and go there."

"Just a minute." Mother held up her hand, stopping Doctor Eileen in midstride. "You're doing what you accuse me of—jumping to conclusions. First, you're assuming that *Paddy's Fortune* has to be the same thing as Godspeed Base."

"That thing Jay is holding was never made in the Forty Worlds."

"Maybe not. But you were the one who insisted that Paddy Enderton had *not* been to Godspeed Base. If that's true, where did he get the calculator and display?"

"I don't know. You're worrying over details. There's one good way to settle everything—go and see."

"All right. But the *last* thing you can afford to do is let a lot of other people know you're going." Mother glanced around and lowered her voice—though it would have taken a lot more than ordinary speech to wake up the snoring louts in the next room. "Let people learn where you've been and what you've found, *after you come back*. The more we keep this to ourselves, the less trouble we'll risk. The bruisers who were here last night would love to know your travel plans."

Doctor Eileen flopped down again on her chair. "Well, *somebody* has to know. You have to help me find a ship, and a few reliable spacers."

"All right. We'll find a ship. But I can't be directly involved, Eileen."

"Why not?"

"The men who were here last night. I would recognize them—and they'd recognize me. If they saw me, you might as well hang out a sign saying where you are going."

"Then I'll find a ship for myself."

"That's nearly as bad. You need a *man* to do it, Eileen, if you don't want to be conspicuous. Whoever heard of a woman going to space?"

"That's for quite different reasons, and you know it."

Mother might know it. I didn't, and at the moment I didn't care.

"They didn't see me!" I said. "They wouldn't recognize me. I'm a man. Let me help find a ship."

Mother shook her head. "You've done wonderfully well, Jay. But you're much too young."

Too young, after everything that I had done and been through! I grabbed Paddy Enderton's calculator and held it close to my chest.

"Too young to find a ship," said Doctor Eileen. "Yes, I agree. But is Jay too young to *go?* Look at his face, Molly. He's earned the right, if anyone has."

Mother did look at my face, and I at hers. It was the longest few seconds of my whole life, until finally she nodded.

"All right," she said slowly. "You have earned it, Jay. You truly have. You can go with Doctor Eileen—if she goes."

"I'm going," Doctor Eileen said firmly.

"All right," repeated Mother. "And now get to bed, Jay," she added automatically. "It's far too late for you to be awake."

CHAPTER 9

I know two ways to make time stretch forever.

One is to go somewhere you have never been before, and do a hundred new and interesting things. After two days you think you have been away for ages, and you just can't believe that so little time has passed since you left home.

The other way is to be waiting for something, waiting and waiting and waiting, and not able to speed up its arrival at all.

That's what happened to me in the two weeks after Doctor Eileen declared that we were going off to space to take a look at *Paddy's Fortune*. While others did the interesting work I had to stay home, helping Mother and keeping my eyes open for the possible return of the violent strangers.

That danger seemed to lessen toward the end of the first week. Since Paddy Enderton had left no one to inherit any of his possessions, Mother and Doctor Eileen arranged for them to be taken over to Skibbereen and sold at auction. The proceeds would go to pay for Enderton's burial and the repair of our damaged property.

As it turned out we didn't get a penny toward either one. Before the auction could take place, the storage place in Skibbereen was broken into and everything was stolen.

Mother seemed to think that this was a good thing, because it made us a less attractive target.

Another dull week followed. Duncan West, who knew far too much to be treated as an outsider, had been sent over to Muldoon. Sworn to secrecy, he was negotiating for a ship and crew. It wasn't likely to be easy, with crews scattered all over after Winterfall. Doctor Eileen was back on her rounds, quietly arranging for a physician from the north end of Lake Sheelin to serve as her substitute while she was away. She was also busy with something else that I didn't find out about until later.

She dropped in on us every couple of days, but the only visit of interest was when she gave me what she called a *Maze Ephemeris*. It contained names of worldlets and sets of numbers called *orbital elements*, six of them for each place.

Comparing her list and Paddy Enderton's calculator/recorder/display and who-knew-what-else unit, I was able to relate the two sets of numbers to each other. They did not quite match, but Doctor Eileen said that the difference was just that one set was centered on Maveen itself, and the other on what she called "the whole Maveen system center of mass."

I was also able to match most of the names on Doctor Eileen's place list to items on the calculator display, and vice versa. *Paddy's Fortune* was not on her list, but she said that was not surprising. There were far more worldlets in the Maze than anyone had ever surveyed, and small bodies in particular were liable to be left out. I didn't know at the time what she meant by "small," and I was astonished to learn that anything less than a mile or two across—the full distance from our house to Toltoona, and more—was unlikely to be on anyone's list. For the first time I began to develop a feel for the vast region covered by the Forty Worlds.

One fine, calm day, when there was no breath of wind and the temperature was above freezing, I ventured again to the top of the water tower. In four nerve-tingling trips I brought down the telecon, and demonstrated it to Doctor Eileen on her next visit. She said that it was more evidence of a technology no longer possessed anywhere in the Forty Worlds, but she could see no way to relate it directly to *Paddy's Fortune,* and she did not even take it away with her.

I put it up in the front bedroom, my bedroom again, and used it to stare every day across the lake at Muldoon Spaceport. The facility was very quiet. I saw only two launches in a week. Most of the rest of the time, when Mother did not have me running around helping her—I think she deliberately kept me busy—I sat upstairs playing with the calculator.

It was soon obvious that it was capable of many more things than I could understand. At the simplest level, I could point to one of the worlds of the Maze and obtain more and more detail simply by calling for "Second Data Level," "Third Data Level," and so on. The trouble was, most of what I was shown seemed useless. There were listings of object composition (that's what I had looked at and not understood the first time I used it); there were things called "delta-vee" lists, that told how easy or hard it was for a ship to get from any world to any other at a chosen time. And finally, at the most detailed level of all, the complete set of data acquired by *any* visit to or survey of the object was included. For a prospector, or anyone hoping to scavenge the Maze, the whole collection of data could be priceless.

For us, though, it was useless. We were going to *Paddy's Fortune* and only to *Paddy's Fortune.* But I did wonder if we had missed the point. Perhaps the men who had broken into our house were interested in data about the *known* worldlets of the Maze. Or perhaps they wanted something completely different, something we had not thought about.

I had spent a lot more time with Paddy Enderton than had either Mother or Doctor Eileen. He was rough and tough and dirty, but he was also *practical.* He had never mentioned the stars or the Godspeed Drive to me, not once.

No matter what Doctor Eileen might believe, try as I might I could not see him as a person who would care one jot about the existence of Godspeed Base, or the long-term future of human beings on Erin. If he called a place *Paddy's Fortune,* that's what he would expect to find there: something to make him rich.

Before I had time to worry about that, a thousand things happened at once. Time began to stretch in the other way, with so much going on that I have trouble remembering what came when.

It began when Doctor Eileen came to the house, late one evening. She had heard from Duncan West. He had located and hired a ship, the *Cuchulain,* complete with crew, and was now busy arranging for supplies to be ferried up to it from Muldoon. He needed help, and he told Doctor Eileen that I could join him as soon as I was ready.

I was ready that minute, and said as much. Mother stayed up half the night, making me a spacer's jacket and trousers of dark blue, and first thing the next morning she zipped me over to Toltoona in Doctor Eileen's cruiser. They loaded me and my little bag on board a ground transport to Muldoon. I thought for a horrible moment that Mother was going to hug me in front of the other passengers, but she didn't.

Muldoon Port was a steady four-hour run around the bottom end of Lake Sheelin. I spent the whole trip in a hot glow of anticipation. Every previous time at Muldoon Port, I had been an interloper. Now I was going in as an honest-to-goodness spacer.

At the dropoff point inside the port I slung my bag over my shoulder and strolled the long way round to the cargo staging area where I was supposed to find Uncle Duncan. I wanted to see everything, and I wanted everyone to see me. It seemed a pity that the port was in its winter quiet.

In fact, I don't think anyone noticed me at all. And my grand arrival at Duncan West's side in the staging area was an anticlimax.

He didn't even say hello. He just nodded at me and went on talking to a big-boned, lantern-jawed man with carroty-red hair and a scrubbed-clean red face, who glared at me, said nothing, and kept on shaking his head.

"That's where the money is coming from." Uncle Duncan never raised his voice, ever, but today he did seem more intense than usual. I had the feeling that an argument had been going on for some time. "I have no stake in this, so I have no authority to change the deal. But remember the golden rule: The one with the gold gets to make the rules."

"Not in space," the big man said. He had the gravel voice and breathy wheeze of a spacer, and with your eyes shut you might have taken him at first for Paddy Enderton.

"You ought to have told us what you had in mind when we started," he went on angrily, "so we could have stopped then and there. You say you can't change the deal. Well, neither can I. If you *want* to take a woman on board the *Cuchulain*, that's up to you. But I certainly can't *agree* to it. You know about women and space. You'll have to talk to the chief, see what he says. He'll be back down here tomorrow." He stared down his long, thin nose at me. "And what's this, then? Another winter surprise?"

"No. This is Jay Hara. I told you he was on the way." Duncan turned to me. "Jay, meet Tom Toole, purser of the *Cuchulain*. You're going to be working with me and him on the supplies."

Toole made no move to shake my hand, but he did give me a much longer, thoughtful stare. "Jay Hara," he said after a few moments. "You're a young 'un. But I started young myself. Can you organize a list of items by their masses?"

"Sure." If I couldn't, I was going to learn fast.

"Here, then." He handed me a long printed list. "You locate these items on the pallets over there, and you set them in order, most massive first. Then you wheel them to the ferry ship. They get loaded that way, see, heaviest near the ferry's center line." He turned back to Duncan accusingly. "If you can't change the deal at your end, who can?"

"Doctor Xavier. Doctor Eileen Xavier. I'll make sure she's here tomorrow to meet with your chief."

"Is she one of the women who wants to go up?"

"Yes. One of two."

"How old is she? The chief is sure to ask me."

"Pretty old. Maybe sixty-five."

Tom Toole grunted. "That's one bit of good news. How about the other one?"

"A lot younger. Thirty-five." Duncan seemed ready to say more, but he noticed that I was still listening. "Here, get to work, Jay. I didn't ask you to come over to Muldoon to stand there gaping."

I began to walk slowly across toward the pallets and the cargo loading area. As I did, I heard Tom Toole say, "In her thirties. And pretty, I suppose. Now that's damned *bad* news. Your doctor and the chief are going to have a good go-around on that one, I'll tell you."

Doctor Eileen and the *Cuchulain*'s chief did have a good go-around, just as Tom Toole had predicted.

I was there to hear it, but in a sense I missed the first minute or two, because of how it began.

Doctor Eileen had arrived at Muldoon sometime during the night. The next morning she was having breakfast with me and Uncle Duncan, at Muldoon Port's one open winter cafeteria, when Tom Toole came in. He had with him a slender man who wore his long brown hair carefully tied back behind his head. I wouldn't have taken him at all for a spacer, because he breathed normally and easily and neither his cheeks nor his bright grey eyes showed any sign of broken veins. But he did wear a blue spacer's jacket, plain of all decorations and molded to his shoulders and chest without a wrinkle.

They halted in front of us. "Doctor Eileen Xavier?" asked Toole. He sounded very quiet this morning. "This is the head man on the *Cuchulain,* Chief Daniel Shaker."

The slender man held out his hand to Doctor Eileen. "Better just Dan Shaker," he said. And, as I froze, "Pleased to meet you, doctor."

His voice was clear and musical, with no sign of spacer's lungs. But I hardly noticed that, because inside my head Paddy Enderton's voice was whispering, *"If it's Dan, see, then it's God help me. And it's God help you, Jay Hara. And it's God help everybody."*

After a few seconds my brain came back to my head. I stared at Daniel Shaker's outstretched hand as it shook Doctor Eileen's and saw that it was perfectly normal.

"Well, doctor," Shaker was saying. "I'm sure we'll be able to work together well, and have a successful voyage. But according to Tom here we have a few things to work out before we start. Let's talk."

He nodded at Tom Toole, with hardly more than a half-inch up-and-down motion of his head, and the other man at once turned and started to leave the restaurant.

Daniel Shaker nodded, just as casual, to Uncle Duncan. "In private, Mister West, if you don't mind." And as Duncan stood up, and I started to do the same, Shaker gave me the friendliest smile, one that lit up his sparkling grey eyes and his whole face, and said, "You must be Jay Hara. Looking forward to going to space, I'll bet. I know I was at your age."

"He can't wait," Doctor Eileen said. "But off you go, Jay."

"Oh, that's all right." Daniel Shaker pointed to my plate, where half my breakfast was still uneaten. "Let him stay and finish. I remember my own appetite at sixteen."

Doctor Eileen hesitated a moment, then she shrugged. "I've certainly got nothing secret to say. But Duncan West tells me you have certain concerns about this trip."

"I do indeed, Doctor Xavier." Shaker took a roll of bread

and broke it in two, but I noticed that he did not eat it. He just crumbled it in his fingers. "I have concerns," he went on, "but not on my behalf. On yours, and on behalf of my crew. Tom Toole says you want to take women to space."

"Just two women. Myself, and Molly Hara." Doctor Eileen nodded her head at me. "Molly Hara is Jay's mother."

"It doesn't matter who she is. You know that women in space are supposed to be bad luck."

"I do. And I know that is nonsense." Doctor Eileen smiled at Daniel Shaker. "You strike me as a very sensible man, Captain Shaker—"

"Not captain. The captain of the *Cuchulain* died in a space accident on the last voyage. I am serving as chief, but only until the owner brings in a new captain."

"So until then I'll call you captain. Anyway, I feel sure you know *why* women don't go to space. It's nothing to do with bad luck—that's only superstition. It's the same reason women don't have dangerous jobs, on Erin or off it. Do I have to say why?"

"Women are too precious. Too valuable to be risked." Daniel Shaker never looked away from Doctor Eileen, but I somehow felt that he was also keeping his eye on me. Except for his hands, absently crumbling bread, he sat perfectly still. "Women must be protected. Women must be guarded, kept away from all danger. And space is dangerous."

"You seem to have survived it very well." Doctor Eileen scanned him with a physician's eye. "If I didn't know it, I'd never suspect you were a spacer. You show no signs of vacuum exposure, in skin or voice or lungs."

"I take care. A man can be careful, in space or out of it. But I've had my share of accidents, even if they don't show." Shaker shook his head slowly, as though remembering, and finally went on, "I say it again, from personal experience: Space *is* dangerous."

"I'll accept that. But you agree with me, it's nonsense to say that women bring bad luck in space."

"I can say it's nonsense." Shaker put down the bread roll and crossed his arms, so both his hands were squeezing the opposite biceps through his jacket in a gesture that I was to see a thousand times. "And *you* can say it's nonsense. But what you and I think, doctor, that's not important. I've got a crew to manage, and there's no doubt how *they* think. And in practice, they are right. Women in space—especially young women, and attractive women—cause trouble for other reasons. My crew are young men, most of them. They're letting off steam now, after Winterfall, and they might be all right for a few days. But I suspect we could be away a good deal longer than that. And after a while a young woman on board would be a disaster. That's *not* superstition. It's hard fact."

"I see your point," Doctor Eileen said. "If there were as many women as men born on Erin, the way there used to be, we might see as many women in space as men. And then there would be no problem. But as it is . . ." She glanced at me, then back to Danny Shaker. "Young women, you said, and attractive women. That lets me out. I assume you have no objection to *my* going?"

Shaker gave a little jerk of his head, as though he was surprised. "That's not what I meant, Doctor Xavier. But I can't argue with your logic. With no disrespect, you're at an age where you ought to be safe enough on board. I can live with that. The crew will grumble some, but a crew always needs something to complain about. Better that than some other things." Still massaging his own biceps, he pointed one finger at me. "But not Jay's mother. We're agreed, aren't we, that taking Molly Hara would be asking for trouble?"

It's a funny thing, but the expression on Doctor Eileen's face seemed more like relief than anything else when she nodded, and said, "I suppose so. It's a pity, but I'll make it my job to tell Molly, and I'll explain your reasons."

I wondered if Doctor Eileen had already been worrying about Mother's effect on the crew. I had never thought of my own mother as "young and attractive," but she certainly seemed to be popular with spacers, judging from the number of them who had been to stay at our house. But I didn't have time for many of those thoughts, because Daniel Shaker was rising to his feet.

"It's a deal, then, Doctor Xavier," he said. "Now, if we're to lift tonight and have the *Cuchulain* ready to leave the day after tomorrow, there's a thousand things to be done." He patted me on the shoulder. "Come on, Jay Hara. You're a spacer now. Tom Toole says you're a useful extra pair of hands, and I need all the help I can get."

I had managed to listen and eat at the same time, and my breakfast was all gone. Even if it had not, I would have been more than happy to go with Danny Shaker. *You're a spacer now.* And the fact that Mother would not be going to space with us did not upset me at all. It pleased me. I wanted to be seen as a spacer, not as somebody's child.

It was a long time before I realized that Danny Shaker, even more than Doctor Eileen and me, had achieved just the result he wanted from that first meeting.

CHAPTER 10

I felt poised on the brink of space, but before I get there, I have to talk about the Muldoon Spaceport and the ferry launch system.

I had visited the port half a dozen times, and thought that I knew it well before ever I met Danny Shaker. Ten minutes with him taught me otherwise. I had seen things from the *outside*, so to speak, like a person who sees just the walls and windows and roof of a house, but doesn't realize there are people and furniture inside. Now I was going to be allowed in through the front door.

We went straight to the ferry site. It was a monster flat circle of concrete, with a ferry ship already sitting on the metal grid at its center. When the weather was bad the whole thing could be covered by a great sliding dome, and it would sit that way through most of the winter. But at the moment the sky was bright and clear, and everything lay open.

The place was almost deserted after Winterfall, but Shaker said that was no problem. "The only reason you need people here is to load cargo. Once that's done, the launch system is automatic. When we're ready we'll be carried to Upside rendezvous."

"What's that?"

"Upside. The rest of Muldoon Spaceport. It's up in stationary orbit. There's as much there as here—maybe more."

"But where's the crew?" I could see Tom Toole, pottering about with his back to us over on the other side of the circle, and that was all.

"Enjoying the last bit of their Winterfall holiday, most of them. They'll stay on Erin to the last minute, then join us on the *Cuchulain*. Come on."

He whistled through his teeth, an odd sound like a fluting birdcall. Tom Toole turned and nodded in greeting, but he did not move to join us as Shaker led the way across the concrete circle. I paused, suddenly nervous. Surely Daniel Shaker wasn't proposing to use the launch vehicle *now*, before Doctor Eileen or Duncan West were here?

I was reassured by the thought that it was morning, and all launches took place after sunset. I followed him. He had gone all the way across to the central metal grid. Now he was standing on it, staring downward. As I came up to him, stepping carefully, he pointed down.

"See that?"

I followed the line of his arm, and saw circles of dull red beneath the grid.

"If you're ever here when they start to flash on and off, run for it. It means the launch grid is going to operate in the next minute. If you were standing here when that happened, you'd die but no one would have to bury you. You'd go like a puff of smoke."

And we were going to space in a ship sitting on top of that lethal grid.

"Why doesn't it vaporize the ferry ship?" I didn't want information. I wanted reassurance.

"Because of this," Shaker said. He stepped forward, to the great pie-shaped cushion plate sitting beneath the ship.

"It can stand pressures and temperatures better than anything ever built on Erin."

"This wasn't built on Erin? Where was it built?" For the past few minutes I had been asking question after question, but Danny Shaker didn't seem to mind. He was so friendly and easygoing, it was hard to see him as a spacer captain. Captains ought to be gruff and tough and rigid, not smiling and softspoken.

"No one knows quite where—or when." He slapped his open palm hard on the cushion plate, and it rang with a high-pitched sound like a gigantic crystal glass. "But it's all ancient," he went on. "From before the Isolation."

His voice was quite matter-of-fact. There was clearly no doubt in *his* mind that the Isolation was real. There had once been travel to the stars, and a known universe far beyond the Forty Worlds, and that was that.

"But it works perfectly well," he continued. "Safer than anything we build today. In fact, there's no way we could build anything like this now. We don't have the tools, or the materials, or the knowledge. Erin is really lucky to have it. Without the ferry system I doubt we'd ever have been able to get off planet to scavenge the Forty Worlds. And without the light elements we get from them, Erin would be in real trouble.

"Ever see the inside of a ferry ship? Come on." He did not wait for an answer, but went right to the ramp that carried cargo and passengers up into the ship.

Seen from a distance on the great circle of the launch site, as I had always seen them, the ferry ships had appeared big, but not really enormous. Each one was a silvery half-sphere, without windows or any other features, sitting above its cushion plate. At the very top of each ship was an antenna like a black hoop. It was easy to imagine the ship as a great serving dish, to be lifted away from the cushion plate using the hoop above.

I knew that was wrong, because the ship and cushion

plate had to remain strongly bound together unless they were deliberately released in orbit. But what I did not realize, until I stepped *inside* a ferry ship, was just how huge it was. I followed Danny Shaker at least ten paces to a central control room, through a narrow corridor higher than his head. The internal partitions were transparent, and we were surrounded on all sides by great bales of stacked cargo.

And once I was inside, I could see that the dome was all beat-up and battered. The walls and the curved ceiling were full of nicks and dents and smudges, where cargo had collided hard against them.

"Not during take-off or landing," said Danny Shaker. He had followed my eyes and my thoughts. "Those are as smooth as you could ask. The dents happen during careless loading." He sat down before a whole bank of switches and dials. "All ready? If you are, sit down there."

"Ready for what?" I sat down, hurriedly.

"For a little trial run." His grin took a lot of my worry away. "I know that you're like most Downsiders, you've never been up before. So I thought we'd lift now, just a little way. Then when it's the real thing tomorrow, with Doctor Xavier and your friend Duncan, you'll be an old hand and know just what to expect."

He didn't actually give me a choice. Before I could say anything he had thrown four switches, and I heard a distant wailing.

"Sirens *outside* the ship," Shaker explained. "That's to warn Tom Toole and anyone else to stay clear. Not that he needs it. See, he's away already."

He pointed to screens set spaced around the circular control room. They showed the deserted flat plain of concrete outside the ferry ship. Somewhere, although I had never seen a sign of them, cameras must be fixed to the exterior of the ship, pointing outward and down.

"Now we'll have half a minute of the flashing warning

underneath the launch grid," went on Danny Shaker. "Then we'll be off."

My stomach gave a little warning quiver, like the time one summer when I drank too much cold lake water and it went right through me. But before anything horrible could happen I felt a faint discomfort in my ears, and Shaker said calmly, "And we're off. Take a look."

It was like a dream. We were not moving, we couldn't be. But the view on the screens was changing. The flat concrete had been replaced by domes and hangers and sky towers. We were looking *down* on them, and every second they were farther below us.

The strange thing is, I had none of the dizzy feelings that had so upset me when I was climbing to the top of the water tower. Even when the domes dwindled and dwindled below us until I could see across Lake Sheelin all the way to Toltoona, there was never the sensation of *height*. It was like sitting in a solid building and watching a moving picture.

"All right?" asked Shaker.

"I'm fine." I laughed. "This is wonderful. Will space be like this?"

"I'm afraid not. Much more boring—during launch or landfall there's always something to look at. In space there's nothing to see, sometimes for months. Well, I guess that will do."

Shaker flipped another set of switches. After a few more seconds the pictures on the screen stopped shrinking and began to grow. Soon I could again see the towers and domes of Muldoon, moving closer and closer.

"How high did we go?" The last thing I wanted to do was land.

"Half a kilometer. Not high enough?" Shaker smiled at me, reading my disappointment. "Don't worry. You'll get the rest of it tomorrow—all the way to space."

We landed, as smoothly as we had taken off.

*   *   *

That was it, the whole thing. My first ride: not *to* space, but *toward* space. It may not sound like much as I've described it, and the whole rest of the day was spent hauling supplies with Tom Toole, who I don't think spoke ten words to me more than he needed to.

But it was a lot to me, and something must have showed. Because late that night, when Doctor Eileen came back from her trip around Lake Sheelin, I was still up, sitting in the apartment at Muldoon that we were sharing between the three of us. She took one look at me and said, "What's so wonderful, Jay?"

"Daniel Shaker." Uncle Duncan replied for me. "Took him for a joy ride in a ferry ship. Made him into a Shaker fan."

"I believe it. I'm close to being one myself." Doctor Eileen took off her coat and helped herself to a hot drink. I didn't blame her. The night outside was the coldest of the year.

"Daniel Shaker is a thinker," she went on, "and that's a rarity—especially among spacers. I'll bet he's a reader, too. How did you find him, Duncan?"

"Find him?" Uncle Duncan looked vague as ever. "I don't know. Asked around Muldoon. Talked to people. There isn't really much choice at this time of year. Not many crews want to go out, and not many ships are available to take them."

It was a typical nondescript Unkadunka reply, but it seemed good enough for Doctor Eileen.

"So we were lucky." She settled with a sigh into a chair, and sipped her drink. "That's good. I talked to Molly, and she didn't mind much that she isn't going. She has more than enough to do back home. But she did say that she was worried about Jay. I told her not to worry, we were in good hands. It's nice for once to know that it's true."

CHAPTER 11

We were all ready to go, but then came one last hitch. The next morning, when Danny Shaker was away from Muldoon, Doctor Eileen asked me to take her over to meet Tom Toole. When we got there she told him that two more people would be coming with us into space.

"The devil they will!" Tom Toole, unlike Daniel Shaker, was the sort of spacer I was used to, raw-boned and tough and glowering as he put his hands on his hips and tried to stare her down.

He towered over Doctor Eileen by a head and more, but she did not budge. "The devil they will, indeed," she said. "They are necessary."

"Necessary for what? The *Cuchulain* has a full crew."

"Necessary as my assistants."

"That's the first I've heard of it. We can't add new passengers now."

"I don't see why not. I've certainly paid for ample supplies, Mr. Toole—enough to cruise the whole Forty Worlds."

"It's not supplies I'm talking about."

"So what is it, then?"

Tom Toole shook his head. "The chief knows nothing about this."

"So you can tell him."

He turned his head away from Doctor Eileen. I could see his face, and it had on it the oddest expression, an absolutely sick look. "I can't do that. We've had enough changes. Who are these people?"

"If you won't tell Captain Shaker about them, I don't see much point in my telling you. But they are scientists, from the university over in Belfast. Both of them men, if that's what's worrying you."

"Oh, *scientists.*" Tom Toole said the word as though he was spitting, but his face was back to normal. "Useless dead weight."

"That's your opinion. It's not mine."

They stared at each other. I could see that Doctor Eileen and Tom Toole were going to get on together like fire and water. At last he said, "I'll tell the chief you want to talk to him about it. If he agrees with you, all right. And that had better be the last of the surprises."

He turned and strode away without another word. But I couldn't forget that odd spasm of discomfort on his face. What was he afraid of? Giving Danny Shaker new information that might annoy him?

"Doctor Eileen," I said, "if a man were to lose his arm in an accident, is there any way that it could be regrown?"

She stared at me. "Jay, if there were a prize for asking the oddest question, you'd win it hands-down. What are you talking about?"

I felt like a moron, but there was no way I could take the question back. I told her about Paddy Enderton, and what he had said about Dan and Stan, and one having no arms and the other no legs. "And Tom Toole seemed really scared just now," I added. "As though he's afraid of Danny Shaker."

"Don't confuse fear and respect, Jay. You should be thankful we've got a captain whom the crew doesn't treat lightly. He's a strong boss. And there's an old rule, not just in space but everywhere: Nobody likes to be the one who gives the boss bad news. I gather that Shaker doesn't welcome extra passengers."

"But what's the answer? *Could* an arm or a leg be grown back, if it was lost?"

"Not with any technology available on Erin, or known through the Forty Worlds. It's a skill that we supposedly had before the Isolation, one of the lost medical arts. We still have nanos that can splice individual nerve fibers and muscle fibers, and we can usually reattach a digit or a limb that was cut off. But we don't know any way to *regrow* lost organs or limbs."

I had actually asked the wrong question, although I didn't know it yet. I tried again: "If someone had access to Godspeed Base, maybe they'd have the medical technology . . ."

"Use your brains, Jay. If they had *already* been to Godspeed Base, they would know where it is. So then they wouldn't need to *find out* where it was from Paddy Enderton. So then they'd not have been searching and smashing and threatening at your mother's house. By the way, the location of *Paddy's Fortune* is one thing I don't want you discussing with anyone. I'd hate to get there, then find someone else had beaten us to it."

If my suggestion that Dan, the armless half of the two-half-man, might have grown back his limbs made no sense, it seemed to me that Doctor Eileen's notion of a *race* to get to *Paddy's Fortune* was just as wild. From everything that I could see we were the only people in the whole of Muldoon Spaceport preparing for a winter trip out. But she had mostly quieted my worries about Shaker.

He completed that process himself when he came to see us late in the afternoon, with our launch to space scheduled for the same evening. Doctor Eileen's two scientists had arrived a few hours earlier, carrying even less in the way of luggage than the skimpy bag that I had brought.

("They're *theorists*, Jay," Doctor Eileen said to me, as though that explained everything. "Not experimenters.")

I had never seen a scientist before, so I stared at the two men with a good deal of interest. They apparently had little in common. Walter Hamilton was tall and blond and pudgy, with a long, long chin and a little wispy beard that looked ready to fall off the end of it. He had a pale, unhealthy face adorned with a lifetime supply of pimples, as though he'd never been out in the sun in his whole life. If I had a face like that I'd consider suicide. But Walter Hamilton seemed pretty pleased with himself.

James Swift, standing awkwardly next to him, had flaming-red hair, bright enough to make Tom Toole's look drab. He was thin and no taller than me. He was also clean shaven, with more freckles than I had ever seen. He somehow seemed younger than he looked, if that makes any sense.

At the time I found it impossible to imagine either one of them standing up for two seconds to somebody like Tom Toole. Later I learned that when James Swift got his temper up—which was rather often—he wasn't afraid of anything.

Maybe Danny Shaker shared my first opinion. Certainly, he gave them no more than a glance when he walked into the room. He came right up to Doctor Eileen in his direct way and stood calmly in front of her.

"Tom Toole says you want to bring more passengers."

"I do. Two of them." She turned, to draw the other men into the conversation. "Dr. Hamilton, Dr. Swift, this is Captain Daniel Shaker, master of the *Cuchulain*." And then to Shaker: "As you can see, Captain, neither one resembles an armed bandit or a destroyer of ships. I cannot understand Mr. Toole's reluctance to give his approval."

"It's natural enough." Danny Shaker pointed to the unoccupied chair at our table and sat down in it opposite Doctor Eileen when she nodded her agreement. "Tom

Toole is a solid, experienced spacer. He and I have been together on a score of trips out. But never one like this. Let me tell you what worries us." He tapped his index finger on the table. "First, we've got a woman on board. You."

"An old woman, Captain. Well past childbearing, and not with the age or appearance for men to fight over."

"True." Shaker made no attempt at polite disagreement. "Otherwise you can be sure I'd never have gone along with it. I did, but all the same it's a departure from custom that leaves Tom Toole uncomfortable. The other crew members won't like it any better than he does. But that's not the main thing that worries Tom—and me. Let me go on. Second"—another finger came tapping down on the table—"there's the fact that I don't know our destination, so I can't tell it to Tom or the rest of the crew."

"I explained that to you. If the crew knows it before we go to space, others may learn it, too. You'll be told our destination as soon as we're all aboard the *Cuchulain* and have left Erin orbit. You have my word on that."

"I appreciate it. But it doesn't tell me *why* you care if people know where you're going. And that leads me straight to my third point. The crew members aren't even on board yet, but already they're muttering that we are going out to the Forty Worlds to seek a great treasure."

I don't know how I looked, but my face felt as though it was burning up. A great treasure—*Paddy's Fortune.* But how could anyone else know that?

Doctor Eileen didn't blink an eye. "I don't know what your crew thinks a 'great treasure' might be, but I'll tell you this: I'll be amazed if we find anything on this trip that the average spacer would consider valuable."

"All that gives me is your opinion of an 'average spacer.' But I'm telling you what my crew is thinking. And anything that worries my crew worries me—and it ought to worry you. An unhappy crew is an inefficient one, maybe a dangerous one. Anyway, fourth and finally, you came along this morning and dropped another surprise on Tom Toole: You want to take along these gentlemen"—Shaker's smile to James Swift and Walter Hamilton somehow said that he at least had nothing personal against them—"without giving Tom or me one word of explanation as to who they are. That's a good way to start any crew muttering and grumbling."

"I didn't talk about this, because I didn't think you or the crew would care or understand. But I'll stop the muttering, right now." Doctor Eileen swung around in her chair. "Dr. Swift, will you please tell Captain Shaker exactly who you are, and what you do."

I have known Eileen Xavier's habits all my life, so what she had just done came as no surprise to me. But it certainly startled James Swift when he was suddenly called onstage. As he was facing Danny Shaker he had his profile to me, and I saw a pink flush creep all the way out to the tip of his ear.

"I'm—er—I'm James Swift." He glared accusingly at Doctor Eileen, and ducked his chin. "I am a professor—a *full* professor—in the Physics Department at Belfast University."

"And what do you do?" prompted Doctor Eileen. James Swift seemed reluctant to continue. "Do you teach?"

"Not usually. I do research. Into massive free fields. And the breaking of conformal invariance."

The prompting this time came from Danny Shaker, as a laugh and a rueful shake of his head. "Run that by me one more time, professor. In simpler words, if you can find them."

"I specialize in field theory. Some classical fields, but mostly quantum fields." James Swift raised his head, so he could look down his nose at Danny Shaker. "Actually, I'm particularly interested in certain formulations of quantum gravity. The theories lead to a group of bubble models, and some of those offer a number of different possible structures for space-time. All of them are fully covariant, even with third-order quantization. But none of them has ever actually been tested, because the energies are extremely high, while the distances involved are very short. That's why everything so far has been pure theory—but it is very promising theory."

He didn't sound as though he had finished, but he did pause for breath. That was space enough for Doctor Eileen to raise her hand and say, "Stop it right there for the moment. Captain?"

James Swift's words had all been gibberish to me, and I could very well see how Danny Shaker might think they had been designed to confuse him deliberately. But all he said was, "Quite right, Doctor Xavier. I won't be passing any of that on to the crew. If they want it, which I doubt, they can get it from Dr. Swift directly. But *two* scientists—"

Eileen Xavier nodded. "You'll see. Dr. Hamilton, if you would be so kind—"

The other man had had time to prepare himself. He nodded and began smoothly, in a loud, lecturing voice. "My name is Walter Hamilton. I also am on the faculty of Belfast University. My original degrees were in physics, biology, and communications, but for the past seven years I have specialized in the history of science. In particular, I have specialized in the period immediately after the Isolation."

He paused for effect, long enough for me to decide that he sounded pompous and probably was. "It may sound like a purely academic activity," he continued, "but it is actually highly practical. Following the Isolation, the near-collapse of Erin civilization was so severe that an enormous amount of scientific and technical knowledge was lost. It has never been regained. I seek to define that loss as completely as possible, with the final objective of re-creating what was once known."

In the past few days I had heard more talk of the Isolation and its effects than ever before. But little of what Walter Hamilton had to say seemed to be any surprise to Danny Shaker. He was nodding.

"Some spacers explore the Forty Worlds, professor, with

similar objectives. Though I must be honest, and admit that most of us are after things that bring a quicker profit. Technology is interesting, but light metals are *sure.*" Danny Shaker turned to Doctor Eileen. "I accept that these scientists are really scientists—something that Tom Toole was inclined to doubt. But I have not the slightest idea why you would want to bring them with you on board the *Cuchulain.*"

"I don't believe that, you know." Doctor Eileen stared right back at Danny Shaker. "Unless I misjudge you, Captain, you have a good idea what I'm about. But I'll say no more on the subject—until we're all in the *Cuchulain* and on our way."

Shaker's response was very strange. He didn't give a real reply at all. He simply shook his head, sighed, and said, "Thank God you're not one of my crew, doctor."

"Thank God I'm not," Doctor Eileen agreed. She and Danny Shaker were suddenly grinning at each other like lunatics.

"So that's it," said Shaker. Then he looked at me, winked, and added, "Three more hours, Jay. Just three more hours, and you'll be in the ferry ship, and off to space."

Baffling!

That was the first time I realized that you could hear every word of a conversation—and at the end of it have no idea what had happened.

CHAPTER 12

The ferry ship took off with six of us on board: Doctor Eileen, Danny Shaker, Duncan West, Walter Hamilton, James Swift, and me. Mother made a special trip all the way around the south end of Lake Sheelin, just to say good-bye. She upset me by giving me a big hug and kiss, in front of just about everybody. Danny Shaker, thank Heaven, had vanished away into the ferry vessel before her arrival, or my embarrassment would have been even worse.

Tom Toole stayed behind, to bring the rest of the crew as soon as they arrived at Muldoon. He said they would be up later in the day. They were squeezing out a last few hours of home leave. At the time I saw no reason to question that explanation.

It also never occurred to me that a launch at night might be quite different from a daytime liftoff. But it was. For one thing, I felt a powerful acceleration holding me down in my seat, in place of yesterday's gentle float upward. For another, during the day the bright sunlight had overwhelmed everything else. But at night, with only dark lake and countryside below us, the ionization produced by the lift system could be seen all around the lower part of the ship as a ghostly violet fire. It made me aware of the searing energy just beneath my feet.

That led to another thought: Suppose that the power applied by the launch grid *failed,* as we were rising toward orbit? The ferry ship was not built to glide. It would plummet back to the ground like a falling rock.

I don't think I was the only one with worries. In fact, the other passengers—even Doctor Eileen and Uncle Duncan, who usually never seemed bothered by anything—sat fidgeting in their seats and shooting nervous glances at the display screens. Walter Hamilton and James Swift appeared absolutely petrified. I wondered what Doctor Eileen had told them, to lure the learned professors into space. Only Danny Shaker sat calmly in front of the controls. He did not touch the switches once, and when he noticed my eyes on him he gave a little jerk of his head toward the others and winked.

Downsiders, his expression said. *Look at them!*

It was exactly what I needed. I stopped thinking of falling and dying, and began to take notice of what was happening around me.

The view below the ship was nothing more than a pale violet glow of ionized gases, but other screens set higher in the control room walls showed what lay above us or far off to the side. We were already a few miles up, beyond the deepest part of the atmosphere. I had a quick view of familiar stars, brighter than I had ever seen them. Then they vanished as the screen filled with dazzling light.

Danny Shaker glanced across at me again, but I realized what was happening and spoke before he did.

"Sunrise!"

He nodded approvingly. It was sunrise, or more accurately it was sunset in reverse. We had risen far enough that Maveen had become visible again in the western sky, no longer shielded by the dark curve of Erin's surface.

I realized for the first time that far out in space the sun would never be hidden; a spacer would enjoy perpetual day.

But we were not yet that far out. Under the urging of the launch grid, the ferry ship began to tilt and accelerate toward the east, picking up speed to move us to orbit. After a few minutes Maveen slid back below the horizon and we were flying again in darkness.

It was my second surprise. Danny Shaker had told me that we were going to Upside, which was in stationary orbit somewhere far above Muldoon. I had imagined that the ferry ship would simply fly straight up until we were there. Instead I now learned that we would spiral our way outward, passing through half a dozen brief days and nights before we finally came to rendezvous with the space docks.

As we rose higher I peered at the displays that pointed out and down to the surface of Erin. Where were the great towns, the cities that I had read about in my school lessons? I saw no sign of them. They were not even dark dots or points of light on the mottled surface. From this height the world below could have been a planet on which humans had never set foot.

On our way to Upside we had one more new experience, something that none of us Downsiders liked at all. The ferry ship moved along faster and faster, boosted by a series of launch grids spaced around Erin's equator. But in spite of that increasing speed, the forces on us became less and less. I felt myself easing away from my seat, and I stayed where I was only because we had been strapped down at liftoff.

My stomach wasn't strapped down, though. It was floating free, and ready to do terrible things.

It didn't, because with Doctor Eileen's approval Danny Shaker had given us a drug to quiet our nausea. But it was a close thing, at least for me. I was a full week in space before I got my "space stomach" completely and the occasional fits of dizziness and discomfort of free-fall sickness went away.

But that was a long way in the future. Still, I was better off than some of the others. I heard awful noises coming from Uncle Duncan and Walter Hamilton and Danny Shaker saying cheerfully, "Into the container. Right in front of you!" Apparently the drug was not working for them. I folded my arms across my middle, gripped the restraining straps, and told myself not to look at the others. Instead I stared at a screen showing the field of view ahead of the ferry ship, and resolved not to disgrace myself.

It seemed days before the bulk of Upside was visible ahead and we were closing in for rendezvous. But by that time the worst was over. When we floated into the big entry dock and the doors closed behind us, even Walter Hamilton and Uncle Duncan, as pale and empty-looking as two crumpled paper bags, were able to stagger and float off the ferry ship and through to the interior of Upside. Two station staff members took them at once to a section where gravity was maintained, less than that of Erin's surface but enough to dispel the feeling of free fall.

Doctor Eileen and Danny Shaker went with them, leaving me alone with James Swift. We sat holding our stomachs and staring at each other warily.

"Well?" he said at last. His face was pale beneath the freckles, an odd contrast to his flaming-red hair. For once he didn't look angry at everyone in the world.

"I wouldn't say *well,*" I said. "But I'm not as bad as I was a few minutes ago."

"Me too. Poor old Walter. He really didn't want to come, you know, he's happiest in a library. But Doctor Xavier talked him into it."

"I don't see why either of you came." That had been on my mind since I met the two of them. "You don't seem anything like spacers."

"*We* don't!" He glared at me, and his face took on a pinker tone. I realized that other things came along with that flaming mop. "What about you. How old are you?"

"Sixteen."

"That's what I thought. You're just a kid. What are you doing on this trip?"

That gave me a problem. I couldn't tell him, but also I couldn't tell him why I couldn't tell him.

"I'm a sort of trainee. I want to be a spacer when I'm old enough."

That last part was true enough, and James Swift nodded. He calmed down a little. "I used to think that way myself when I was your age. You'll change your mind, though, when you've met a few spacers."

I had met more than he suspected, but I didn't want to disagree with him or let the conversation go anywhere near Paddy Enderton. I switched subjects. "Dr. Swift, I still don't understand what you do."

"Call me Jim. We're not at the university now, and we're going to be spending a lot of time together." He held out his hand, something he hadn't done when we were first introduced, and I felt stable enough to be able to reach out and shake it.

"Be careful how you handle Walter, though," he went on. "Always call him *Doctor* Hamilton. He likes to sit on his title, though he's nowhere near as smart as I am. But why do you say you don't understand what I do? Weren't you listening this afternoon?"

And I'll be careful with you, too, I thought. But all I said was, "I listened. But I couldn't make sense of any of it. Nor could Captain Shaker."

We both looked to the door, wondering when Danny Shaker and the others were likely to be back. Until they returned we had nowhere to go and nothing to do.

"You said you don't teach," I added. "I never heard of a professor before who isn't a teacher."

"I had a few . . . disagreements. About the right way to deal with students who were idiots." He glanced away from me. "I think I may be too used to working with specialists. Let me try again on the explanations. You tell me the minute I don't seem to make sense. Do you know what atoms and electrons are?"

"Of course I do! I may be only sixteen, but I'm not a halfwit."

"Sorry. Well, the rules that tell how atoms and the things they're made of behave are quite different from the rules that apply for big objects. Movement from one condition to another, or the transfer of energy, takes place in individual steps."

"I know that, too. They're called quanta."

"Right. You're ahead of a lot of the people who come to study at the university. Some of them are allowed in when they don't know *anything.*" An irritated look, and the face reddening again. "Anyway, quanta just means *pieces,* and we say that energy and atomic states are *quantized.* But other things can be quantized. Energy is carried from place to place by things called *fields,* and those fields are quantized, too. That's usually called *second quantization.* And last of all, space itself is quantized. That's called *third quantization.*"

"You've lost me. You mean space, like *space.* Like there is out here?" I looked around me, but we were in an interior chamber of Upside and all I could see were walls.

"Yes. Space is quantized."

"But empty space is just—well, *empty.* It's nothing. That's what the word means."

"You'd think so, wouldn't you?" Jim Swift wrinkled up his forehead. "When I sit back and listen to myself, I have to agree with you. Empty space ought to be empty, by definition. We need a different word. Let's talk about *vacuum* instead. When you set up the theory correctly, you find that even when a vacuum has no matter in it, it's not really empty. It has *energy,* a thing called the vacuum energy. If you could get at the vacuum energy, and use it in the right way, then you might be able to do something else. You might be able to trade energy for movement. You could have very rapid movement, through point to point in quantized space."

"Can you really do that?"

"Well . . . no. But that's what I study, at the university. It's my specialty. And don't laugh, but I'll tell you what I think. And I believe that what I think on this subject is better than anyone ever thought before.'' When he was talking about anything but work—and wasn't busy losing his temper—his voice was easygoing and diffident. But when he was lecturing me, he took on the strangest mixture of arrogance and distant calm.

"I believe," he went on, "that there was a time, before the Isolation, when people knew how to tap the vacuum energy. And they could use that and third quantization to travel in space. Travel *fast*, much faster than light. Quantum transitions take no time at all.''

"The Godspeed Drive!" I wondered how much Doctor Eileen had talked, after swearing the rest of us to strict secrecy.

"Exactly. And if that's true, the big mystery is this: What went wrong? Why did the ships stop coming? Walter tends to be a bit stuffy and arrogant, but he actually knows his subject very well. And he insists that the old records—such as they are—show that everything went wrong *instantly*. One minute, ships and supplies arriving; the next, nothing. Erin was on its own, struggling to survive and only just making it. No messages, no warnings, no explanations. The spacers sometimes come back and tell us there are strange objects out in the Forty Worlds, things like the Luimneach Anomaly. But their information raises more questions than it answers. Maybe this trip will be different.''

I could see why Eileen Xavier wanted Jim Swift and Walter Hamilton along on the journey. But what had she *said* to them?

An answer to that question had to wait, though, because Danny Shaker was floating back into the room. "Your colleague is feeling much better," he said to Jim Swift. "How about you?"

"I'm fine. Where is Walter? I'd like to see him.''

"Come with me." Danny Shaker turned and floated out again.

Jim Swift followed, much more clumsily. Movement in little or no gravity was obviously going to take some getting used to. For lack of anything better to do I tagged along behind, bouncing now and again off walls, floor and ceiling and struggling to learn the right combination of muscles.

The corridor that we were moving in was long, straight, and featureless, but after thirty or forty meters I began to feel a definite sense of *down*. My feet didn't just touch the floor, they pressed on it a little bit.

The sensation of weight steadily increased, until at the end of the corridor we came to a big circular room. It reminded me of a ward in the Toltoona hospital, bare, overheated, and filled with uncomfortable-looking beds.

Walter Hamilton was sitting on one of them, his color much improved from the last time I had seen him. There was no sign of Doctor Eileen or Uncle Duncan.

"Food machines through there," Shaker said, nodding to a big sliding door. "Are you hungry?"

Walter Hamilton put his hands to his stomach and seemed appalled at the idea, and Jim Swift shook his head and sank onto a bed next to his colleague.

Danny Shaker turned to me. "Jay?"

It was hard to believe, but although my stomach still wanted to float up into my throat, I was suddenly starving. I nodded.

"I thought so. Come on." And then, as he led the way through the doors, which opened automatically at our approach, "You're a natural, Jay. You're going to make a fine spacer."

When he said that I couldn't help thinking of Paddy Enderton, with liquor on his breath and his big, sweaty, insincere face pushed close to mine, saying, "You'll be the finest spacer that ever lifted off Erin." But there was a world of difference between the two men: Enderton gruff and slovenly, Danny Shaker soft-spoken and precise in speech and movement. I resolved to study the easy, economical way he moved in low gravity, and learn to imitate it.

We reached the machines, and Danny Shaker showed me how to operate them, how to make the food selection and key in the way that I wanted it cooked and prepared.

The food itself was a curious disappointment. It was edible enough, but somehow I had expected that space food ought to be *different* from the food down on Erin. Of course, it was exactly the same. As Shaker pointed out to me, every morsel of food that I—or anyone else—consumed in space was grown down on the surface of Erin, and shipped up. The only exception was salt. There were huge deposits of that on Sligo, the fourth moon of Antrim, and ton after ton was shipped down to Erin before Winterfall.

"And lucky for us that we can go to Sligo and mine it," said Shaker. "Because there's precious little to be found on Erin. Salt is sodium chloride, and sodium's a rarity back down there."

"I don't like salt."

"Maybe not. But you need it. A human can't live without it. If we couldn't get into space from Erin, I doubt there'd be a person alive there now."

It was something else to ponder. Back home people gave the impression that the things coming to Erin from the Forty Worlds were nice to have, but not really essential. Now I was hearing that Erin couldn't exist without the spacers.

"Come on." Danny Shaker had watched me eat, without showing any interest in food himself. "We've got work to do."

"I thought we were ready to leave."

"We are. Tom Toole and the rest of the crew ought to be up from Erin by now. They'll be on board the *Cuchulain*, along with Doctor Xavier. But we are going to be away for a long time, and I always do the final check of supplies and ship condition. That way I can't blame anybody but myself, if we get into deep space and things aren't right.''

I had been longing to see the *Cuchulain* since I first heard the ship's name, but there was one more scary experience to go through before I could do that. Only a small part of Upside held an atmosphere. The rest of it, including the access paths to all the deep-space ships, sat in vacuum.

With Shaker's help I eased my way into a suit, making the thirty-six point checks that in a few weeks would become automatic: air, filters (dual), heat, insulation, temperature, communication, nutrition, elimination (dual), medication, attitude control (triple), position jets (dual), joints (thirteen), seals (four), and suit condition displays (three).

Then came the two minutes while the pumps returned the air of the chamber we were in to the pressurized part of Upside, and I watched my suit's external pressure gauge drop steadily to zero. Soon there was nothing between me and hard vacuum but the thin shell of my suit.

Danny Shaker saved me again, acting as though what we were doing was the most natural thing in the world. "If you're ever not quite happy with anything while the pressure's going down," he said casually, "all you have to do is press the *Restore* panel on the wall there. The chamber will repressurize within five seconds. Hold tight, now. We're off.''

He was actually the one doing the holding. Almost before I knew what was happening he had taken the arm of my suit in his gauntleted hand, and was steering us out of the lock. I had assumed that we would emerge into open space. Wrong again. We were in a corridor no different from the one that had led us to the chamber—except that the external pressure showed as negligible, and the external temperature was a hundred degrees below zero.

The final surprise was the *Cuchulain* itself. It floated in a gigantic open hangar, controlled in its position by gentle electromagnetic fields. Its shape was neither the bowl of the ferry ships, nor the slim needle of an atmospheric flier.

Instead I found myself staring at a long warty stick, with a flared cone at one end and a small sphere attached to the other.

"Drive, cargo area, and living quarters," said Danny Shaker's voice through my suit communications unit.

I could see that the ship was far bigger than a first sight suggested. The little sphere showed glassy pinpricks and dark flecks on its sides. They had to be viewing ports and locks.

"There's no place for cargo," I said. "Do you hang it outside?"

Shaker laughed, his voice no different in my ears than it had been back on Erin. "I sometimes wish we could. The midsection between the drive cone and the living sphere is a flexible membrane around a rigid column. When the *Cuchulain* is carrying its maximum cargo load, it looks like a big bloated ball with a little pimple on each end. Balancing it for flight can be a pain. But I don't think you'll be seeing it like that on this trip."

I ought to have asked myself why he thought that, since according to Doctor Eileen our mission was supposed to be a secret. But I didn't think of it. Instead I said, "How do you land? There's no place for a cushion plate."

"Very true. The *Cuchulain* doesn't land. Ever. This is a deep space ship."

"So how do you pick up your cargo?"

"With the cargo beetles. See them?"

And I did, when he pointed them out. Each of the little warts along the axis of the ship was a whole ship in itself, a rounded shell hugging the central column.

"But *they* don't have cushion plates, either."

"Because they don't need them. The Forty Worlds are a low gravity environment except for Antrim and Tyrone, and those two are gas giants where we never land. Nowhere else has a hundredth the pull of Erin. Lucky for us, or scavenging would be impossible."

While I was asking questions—I still had a hundred

more—we had been approaching the structure at one end
that Danny Shaker called the living sphere. It loomed ahead
of us now, twice as big as a whole ferry ship. I could see that its
exterior, a uniform cloudy grey from a distance, was a whole
patchwork mess of seams and scars and scratches.

"And not surprising," Danny Shaker said, in answer to
my question. "The *Cuchulain* is like the rest of our ships. It's
old. Old and beat up. Built long before the Isolation, and
been through a lot."

"But why don't we build new ones?"

"Ah, that's a fair question. We'll talk about that when we
have a bit more time. All right?"

He sounded casual enough, but something made me
think that he didn't want to talk to me about that at all until
he had first discussed it with Doctor Eileen. With every
kilometer that we moved away from the surface of Erin, I had
the feeling that the balance between life down on the planet
and life out in the Forty Worlds shifted. The Isolation
loomed more real and more significant, changing from
vague myth to a central fact of survival. Living with Mother
on the shore of Lake Sheelin, I had felt myself in a safe, stable
world. Now I was hearing that Erin survived only because
space systems in place before the Isolation were still
working—and those systems were becoming steadily older
and more worn as the years went on.

The interior of the *Cuchulain,* when we finally passed
through the entry lock and shed our suits, did nothing to
change that idea. The chambers where I first met the rest of
the crew were clean enough, and kept in good order. But
everything showed the signs of long, hard wear. It's tempting
to say that the crew themselves showed those signs most of all.

With only two samples to judge from, I don't know what I
had expected. Captain Shaker and Tom Toole were as
different as two men could be: Tom Toole big-boned and
gravel-voiced and argumentative; Danny Shaker slender and
soft-spoken and neat.

The rest of the crew seemed just as diverse when I was introduced to them by Danny Shaker.

"This is Patrick O'Rourke." Shaker led me to the first man in the line. "Patrick and Tom Toole are like my right and left hands. They keep things going when I'm not here. Anything you need, Jay, you ask one of them. Now, here's Sean Wilgus, Connor Bryan, William Synge, Donald Rudden, Alan Kiernan, Seamus Sterne, Dougal Linn, Joseph Munroe . . ."

There were nine general crew men, in addition to Pat O'Rourke and Tom Toole. I lost track of their names after the first two, although I did notice some peculiarities. Donald Rudden was so fat that I could not imagine how he carried his weight around—though that problem should be less in space than down on Erin. Sean Wilgus didn't even pretend to be pleased to meet me, he glared when I came to him.

Everyone wheezed as they growled their greetings, just about as bad as Paddy Enderton, but Robert Doonan certainly held the record for that. Every breath turned into a gasp. Apparently Danny Shaker was a real exception among spacers in having good working lungs. He was also an exception in size. Patrick O'Rourke was a black-haired giant, the biggest man I had ever seen, and the others were all huge. Tom Toole, whom I had thought of as big when I met him, an inch or two taller than Uncle Duncan, turned out to be one of the smallest.

There was one other thing that they had in common, but I didn't know what it meant. As each crewman bent to shake my hand, he stared at me with genuine interest and curiosity. I could even sense it in Sean Wilgus, behind the hostility.

By the time that I reached the last man in line, Rory O'Donovan, I began to feel that perhaps they all recognized something unusual in me. Maybe, as two people different as Paddy Enderton and Daniel Shaker had suggested, I was going to make an outstanding spacer. Maybe these men saw that potential, and instinctively reacted to it.

I decided to do my best to make the prophecy come true. When Dan Shaker asked me if I would like to go around the ship with him as he made his final inspection of supplies, drive, control systems, and cargo beetles, I leaped at the chance.

And when, eight hours later, everything was pronounced ready and the *Cuchulain* left the hangar on Upside and swooped off for deep space and the Forty Worlds, I didn't have a worry left in my head. I had no doubt that the next month or two would be the happiest of my whole life.

CHAPTER 13

Twenty-four hours after the *Cuchulain* started our outward journey, the inside of my head began to sort itself out. So much had happened to me, in so short a time, that it had produced what Doctor Eileen called an "experience overload." I didn't have a name for it. All I knew was that I had seen masses of stuff and I'd had it all explained to me—but often I only understood when I met the same thing for a second or third time.

Even then I had problems.

For instance, before we left the Upside hangar Danny Shaker had shown me over the interior of the ship. We had visited the engine room, and the drive unit at the far end—off limits during powered flight to everyone except suicides—and we had been all through the labyrinth of the expandable cargo hold, corkscrewed down now into its tightest form. Shaker had pointed out the electrical supply system, and the air duct system, and the various vacuum escape systems, and he even explained the waste disposal apparatus in the living area. But it was only late the next day, wandering around with Doctor Eileen, that I began to get any feeling for what was where.

And then it became really embarrassing. Doctor Eileen knew I had been through the ship before, and naturally she asked me questions. Half the time, I had no idea of the answer.

"Look at the mess there," she said, when we were in the living quarters and walking along a tight little corridor. "Why is that room different from everywhere else?"

The corridor was clean. But one room that led right off it was filthy, coated in what looked like years or decades of dust.

I shook my head. Shaker had shown me that same room, and said something about it. But as to *what* he had said . . .

I went inside, bent down, and pulled the air duct grille away from the wall. It was a mistake. Dust clouded around me, in my hair and up my nose. The duct tunnel itself was clear, and I could hear air sighing along it. I remembered Danny Shaker telling me that the air duct passages were usually a couple of feet wide. They formed an alternative programmed pathway for the cleaning machines, and they could also be used in an emergency by humans as an escape route from one part of the ship to another. But none of that explained why the cleaning robots had chosen to ignore this particular room completely, while diligently collecting the dust and trash everywhere else.

I came out of the room sneezing and feeling like a moron. I had been told, and I *knew* I had been told. But I had been told a thousand and one other things, too, at a time when I was sick and nauseated from a first exposure to free-fall, and giddy with the novelty of everything. I simply didn't remember.

We didn't get an explanation until that evening when Danny Shaker came by to report on his progress in producing a trajectory for us.

That's another thing that I ought to have mentioned earlier, right when it happened. But I didn't, so rather than fiddle with the record back there, I'm going to stick it in here.

It had happened on the previous day, before we had been heading out from Upside for an hour. Danny Shaker came to see Doctor Eileen as we were preparing for our first night of sleep in low gravity.

"I want to remind you of your promise, Doctor," he said. "You indicated that you would tell me our destination as soon as we were on the way."

"You certainly haven't wasted much time in asking." Doctor Eileen sounded more amused than annoyed.

"That's because I don't want to waste your money or your time. As soon as I know where we are going, I can calculate an optimal trajectory. At the moment, though, for all I know we have the *Cuchulain* heading in exactly the wrong direction."

I knew from what Doctor Eileen had told me that this was a crucial moment. Once she informed Danny Shaker where we were going, there was no way to keep the information secret. A message from our ship to another one, closer to the destination, might allow someone to reach *Paddy's Fortune* ahead of us. On the other hand, there was no way to hold the information to ourselves indefinitely.

The doctor knew all that. She merely nodded, and held out a folded slip to Shaker. "Here are the coordinates. The position in orbit is given for midnight today, Erin Standard Time."

Shaker unfolded the slip and stared at it in silence for a few moments. Then he placed the paper in his pocket and sat down, uninvited, opposite Doctor Eileen. "That is an orbit in the Maze." His face was as calm as ever. "Do you know what that means?"

"I thought I did. From the way you ask the question, I suspect that I do not. Do you have trouble taking us there?"

"No more trouble than to anywhere else in the Maze. And no less, either."

"So you can take us?"

"Certainly. What I can't do is take you there *quickly*. How much do you know about the Maze, Doctor?"

"That it's hundreds of different bodies, of all sizes. That their orbits aren't accurately known, for any but the biggest ones."

"Change *hundreds* to *millions*, Doctor Xavier, and you have a better picture. The Maze is a great jumble of rocks, everything from midsized planetoids to pebbles. Constantly perturbed by the gravitational fields of Antrim and Tyrone, and mostly uncharted. A ship can certainly go there. But unless you want to risk running into a thousand-ton boulder at a relative velocity of a few miles a second, and shattering your ship and yourself to bits, you don't *fly* through the Maze. You *creep* through it. That's why I say I can get you there—eventually."

"How long?"

"I don't know." Shaker stood up and patted his pocket. "I have to feed these coordinates into the navigation computer, and see what we come up with as the best approach trajectory. The Maze is complicated. It may take us a while. I am a coward, you see, by both experience and natural inclination."

Then he winked at me, as though he was joking and I knew it, and left without another word. And now, twenty-four hours after that first discussion of where we were going, he was back.

We were sitting around the table, me between Doctor Eileen and Walter Hamilton, with Jim Swift and Duncan West opposite us, and an empty seat between them.

"You won't like this any too well," Shaker began, direct as usual. "We've done the trajectory calculation, Pat O'Rourke and I, and the safest route to where you want to go has to skirt out wide of the Maze. It will take us nearly four weeks."

I don't know if he could read the doctor's wince, but I could. In making her plans she had hoped to be out and home again to Xavier House in less time than that. But all she did was nod, and say, "Keep it safe, Captain, that's the first priority." And then, in what seemed like an odd change of subject, "Tell me, is the *Cuchulain* a safe ship?"

Shaker must have been as puzzled as I was by the question, but he didn't let his feelings show any more than she had. "I certainly believe it is," he said, "or I would not fly in it. As I told you, in space cowardice is a virtue. But why do you ask?"

"Jay and I did a quick tour earlier today. I noticed that some areas of the ship are neglected and dirty. It made me wonder how well your central control computer is working."

Shaker sighed, and sat down between Uncle Duncan and Jim Swift. "Doctor Xavier, I believe that the *Cuchulain* is perfectly spaceworthy, at least for the moment. But I don't pretend that the ship is as good as new. It has been in use, more or less continuously, for hundreds of years. There is natural wear, in everything from main drive to maintenance, and when certain things go wrong we do not have enough knowledge of the original design to fix them. I'm well aware that some parts of the ship are being neglected by the cleaning robots, and I assume that the problem lies in the controlling software in the ship's main computer. But I have no one able to understand that software, and safely change it."

His answer, oddly enough, seemed to please Doctor Eileen. She was nodding.

"Captain Shaker," she said, "you have been very patient with me. You have never asked me the natural question: *Why* are we going to the Maze? But I think that now you deserve an answer."

Doctor Eileen really liked Danny Shaker, I could tell she did. There was a lighter tone in her voice when she talked to him, and a different little smile on her face. It did not surprise me. I felt the same way myself. He was different from any man I had met in and around Toltoona.

"Let me start by asking a question," she went on. "You and I both know that the Isolation is real, and that before it happened there was travel between the stars. Materials and people came to Erin from far away, from planets around other stars. Why do you and your crew think they stopped coming?"

"Me and my crew? To be honest, Doctor, I doubt if anyone else on this ship spends two minutes a year worrying that question. But I do. I think there must have been some great emergency, far from Maveen. All the Godspeed ships were called there to help. And every one was destroyed. Perhaps in a great battle, but much more likely in some natural disaster. Maybe the whole fleet was turned to vapor in one flash of a supernova. Maybe they were all trapped around a chasm singularity, and they are still there. But we don't know. And I have to agree with my crew: Without real *information*, guesswork like this is no better than a game."

"I totally concur. But what do you think happened to the *other* worlds, all the other destinations served by the Godspeed ships?"

That made Danny Shaker's smooth forehead wrinkle, and he crossed his arms to massage his biceps through the sleeves of his blue jacket. "I don't like to think too much about that. I've been to libraries in Skibbereen and Middletown. There's not much left in the general data banks, but you get the feeling that our survival on Erin after the Isolation was not easy."

"That's a prize understatement, if ever I heard one." Walter Hamilton had been sitting aloof, still not fully over his spacesickness but much improved in the tenth-gravity field of our living quarters. Now he was showing signs of life.

"The first generation after Isolation survived by an eyelash," he went on. "Without the space launch system, and the local space fleet, and the access to minerals and light metals from the Forty Worlds . . ."

He hiccuped, put his hands on his stomach, and lapsed back to silence.

"So we came through—just." Danny Shaker turned again

to Doctor Eileen. "But you know that we're not really in the clear. The records show that every human on Erin, and many of our most useful plants and animals, came here from somewhere else. We're not *native* to the planet. It's not right for us. We keep struggling along, but we do it by hauling in what we need from the Forty Worlds. And we do it with a fleet of ships that can't be replaced, and gets older and more worn every year. I know that from personal experience—every year, something else goes wrong with the *Cuchulain.*

"But the old records make another fact even clearer. Of all the planets settled and colonized by humans, Erin is *the most like Earth,* the most like the original home world. So I think—and as I said, I don't like to think about this too much—I think that we have been very lucky. We have survived. Maybe a handful of other planets have, too." He glanced my way, and this time there was no wink or smile. "But for most of them, and for the *future* generations on Erin—"

"I agree with every word you say." Doctor Eileen cut him off before he could finish the sentence, I think because I was present. "And now I'll tell you why I'm asking you to fly us into the middle of the Maze. I believe we will find evidence, on the body whose coordinates I gave you, of something new about the Godspeed Drive."

"Something new?" Shaker's face was impassive again. "What?"

"I can't tell you—because I don't know. It could be as little as an old base, empty and deserted. Or it could be as much as a whole ship, with a Drive intact. But as I'm sure you'll agree, *anything* about the Godspeed Drive has to be investigated. Erin's future may depend on it."

"Indeed it may." Danny Shaker stood up. "I appreciate your sharing this information with me."

"You've earned it. And of course, you are free to pass what I have said on to your crew."

Danny Shaker's mouth quirked, and there was again a

gleam of humor in his eyes and mouth. "I will certainly do that, Doctor. But I ought to be honest with you, and say that I do not expect them to show much interest—unless we find a ship that's designed for in-System use, and might replace the *Cuchulain* with something newer. They're a pretty practical bunch of people, my crewmen—and I'm glad of it. Give me a crew that keeps the waste disposal system working, and I'll take them any time over a group that spends their energy on future worries."

He was turning to go, but Duncan West, who had been sitting blank-faced through all the conversation, suddenly spoke. "I'll bet it's not that," he said.

Doctor Eileen stared at him as if he were a statue that had just come to life. "Not what?"

I understood her reaction. Uncle Duncan *never* contributed to such general discussions of the past and future.

"Not the computer software," he said. "I bet it's not that that's causing the problem with the cleaning robots. I'm no computer specialist, but I've never heard of a glitch that could just drop individual rooms off, here and there, and leave the rest serviced."

"What else could it be?" Danny Shaker was staring at Duncan, too, as though he had never seen him before.

"I don't know. But I'd be more than willing to take a look."

"A look? No touching the computer, you realize—hardware or software."

"Of course not. I told you, I don't know computers. Well?"

Danny Shaker shook his head at first in refusal, but then he gave a what-do-I-have-to-lose shrug of his shoulders. He turned to Doctor Eileen. "Can you show him the place you were talking about?"

"I think so. But Jay could do it better."

Danny Shaker raised an eyebrow at me. "Jay?"

"I'm sure I can."

"Then let's go."

I led the two men away, suddenly unsure of myself. I had been there twice, but I'd seen proof that spacesickness made me forget things. There was a lot of relief in me when I opened a door, and revealed the dusty and neglected room beyond it.

Uncle Duncan went in and stared around for half a minute, a vacant look on his face. "How would they enter and leave?—I mean the cleaning robots."

Danny Shaker did not speak. He just pointed to a little panel, low on the far wall. Uncle Duncan walked forward without another word, leaving tracks in the deep dust, and knelt in front of the panel. He slid it carefully to one side. "It doesn't stick."

"I'm sure we checked that. I feel sure it's the computer, hardware or software."

But Duncan was shaking his head, and lying flat to stick his head past the open panel. "The cleaners come right through here." His voice was muffled. "Everything up to the back of the panel is vacuumed and polished. Which means . . ."

He wriggled back a foot or two, and began to feel carefully around the rear side of the panel's perimeter. After a few moments he grunted, rolled over onto his back, and inched his way forward until his head had again vanished behind the panel. His hands went up.

"Here we are."

"Did you find something?" I couldn't see what he was doing in there.

"Inhibitor circuit." He had his forearms close together, and he seemed to be pushing hard on something. "Met this sort of thing—before." His voice was uneven, grunting with effort. "Seen it back home. Break—in strip. See, Jay,"—he finally brought his arms down, and wiggled his way back out—"you see, Jay, there's times when people don't want cleaning robots in a room. Maybe they're using it themselves for something that needs privacy, or maybe they have something in there that they're worried about because it's super-fragile or valuable. So some rooms have an inhibitor circuit strip that you can turn on. It sits just where a cleaning robot enters the room, and it inhibits the robot, tells it not to go in. The normal condition has the inhibitor turned off, so the room gets cleaned. But if a circuit cross-connect goes *bad,* like it did here, then you can get the inhibitor permanently *on* . . ."

He stood up and dusted himself off. The hair on the back of his head was thick with grime. "Well, that's it. We won't know for sure, of course, until the cleaners come through again."

The whole thing, from our entry into the room until I was helping Duncan to dust himself off, had taken no more than three minutes.

Danny Shaker's face was a picture. "Do you do this sort of thing often?"

"I make my living at it—I don't mean cleaning machines, I mean with all sorts of mechanical fixes."

"Then would you like to earn some money while we're on the way to the Maze? If you would, I'll have Tom Toole add you to the ship's pay roster. We have a hundred little things that need fixing, all over the *Cuchulain.* "

"Sounds good to me. No promises, though. And no computer work—I'm just a tinkerer."

Duncan was as laid back as ever. I don't really think he cared much about the money, but he sure did like to fiddle with things.

Anyway, from that moment on he began to work with the crew of the *Cuchulain,* just as though he had been one of them for years. And every day he had a meeting with Danny Shaker, to discuss problems and progress.

It was typical Uncle Duncan. No matter where he was, or what was going on, he always managed to make his easygoing way right to the center of things. I envied him, and I wondered how he did it.

CHAPTER 14

The next day the cleaning robots went into the room where we had been and scrubbed, vacuumed, and polished it spotless. I know, because I went there especially to check.

Duncan didn't bother to go with me. He *knew* his fix would work. It was the knack.

He did a couple of other small jobs for Danny Shaker, but the big one came four days later.

Shaker appeared early in the morning—the ship kept Erin time—in our living quarters.

"I know some of you are going to hate this," he said, "but we have to go to free-fall conditions for five or six hours. We have a slight drive imbalance, and it's costing us time and energy. We're going to do a partial strip-down and take a look." He glanced at Duncan. "You'd be welcome." And then to me, seeing my longing expression, "You, too, Jay, if you want. You said that you'd like to see the drive close up."

I had, and I did. But I couldn't go with them at once, because I had promised to help Jim Swift move things out of a spare cabin filled with junk. He had been sharing a place with Walter Hamilton, which was no new experience for either of them, except that now Jim complained that in low gravity his cabin companion snored like a handsaw.

The drive went off while we were in the middle of the move, and working in free-fall slowed us down a lot. Nothing would stay where we put it! It was forty minutes after the drive went off before I started along the column that led aft from the living section through the empty and collapsed cargo hold, and on toward the drive area. On the way I paused to take another look at a cargo beetle, clamped to the column. The controls inside looked so easy. I wondered if one day I might get to fly one.

No use asking Patrick O'Rourke, that was sure. I didn't know why, but he glared at me from his great height whenever he saw me, as though I was some sort of ship's vermin scuttling along at his feet. But maybe Danny Shaker or Tom Toole would let me fly.

The rear compartment when I came to it was dark and gloomy. It was frightening, even filled with good air and with the drive off. I knew what monstrous energies were generated here. The feel of those energies was somehow still present, lingering on like an odd taste in my mouth.

I thought for a moment that the others were right there, in the first aft compartment that I came to. Then there was a moment of horror, when the four shapes I had seen in the dim light turned into four headless, legless corpses. The working men had taken their jackets off, and the blue clothing hung suspended in the middle of the compartment. Something (I learned later that it was static electricity) had made the chest and sleeves billow out full, as though there were torsos and arms inside them.

I took a deep breath, told myself that I was an idiot, and moved on to the main drive compartment.

Of course, the work of dismantling and inspecting the suspect drive unit had not waited for me. The housing had been swung free, and Uncle Duncan and Danny Shaker, together with two general crewmen, Joseph Munroe and Robert Doonan, were inside it, peering along the huge conical channel. Their legs all stuck out in different directions. I shivered again, because if the drive went on their heads would be vaporized in a microsecond. But it didn't seem to worry them in the least.

"I'll bet it's that." Uncle Duncan's voice sounded strange, echoing off the hard vault of the drive chamber. "Is it easy to take apart?"

"No problem." That was Danny Shaker. "Once I can get my hands on the right tools."

An arm came groping in the air, toward a length of rough cloth in which wrenches were secured every few inches.

"I'm here," I said. "I can get it for you. Which one do you want?"

"Give me the whole thing. We may have to try a few." Danny Shaker's right hand was still groping about behind him. I reached out to give him the set of wrenches, and saw that his shirt sleeve had somehow been snagged on the edge of the drive opening.

The sleeve was pulled up, to reveal his bare upper arm. I saw, with a horror that made anything earlier seem like nothing, the vivid red line of a scar across his biceps, midway between elbow and shoulder. As I placed the tools in his hand I moved my head to get a view of the underside of his arm. How far did the scar extend?

All the way—all the way around his arm!

I was in the drive chamber for another two hours, while Duncan and the crew made their repairs to the drive. I have to take Duncan's word to Doctor Eileen that that's what they were doing, because I took no notice of their actions. My mind was far away, back in the front room of the house with Paddy Enderton, while he raved about Dan, the armless half of the two-half-man. The bad one, the one much worse than brother Stan.

When they were all done with their work on the drive and came back to put their jackets on, Danny Shaker laid a friendly arm around my shoulders. "Hats off to Duncan

West, Jay," he said. And then, to Duncan, "We couldn't have done it without you."

I'm sure I cringed at his touch, but Shaker didn't notice, because at that moment Joseph Munroe gave a snort of disapproval and disagreement.

Shaker turned to him. "Don't give me that, Joe. I've been asking about that drive segment for the past two trips, and you've never had the ghost of an idea how to fix it."

His voice was mild, but Munroe went completely still. "You're right, Chief," he said. "I'm sorry about that."

He added nothing more, but I suspected that at least one crew member didn't approve of Uncle Duncan's temporary addition to their number. As for me, I didn't want to listen to praise of Duncan, or discussion of the balancing problem and Duncan's fix-it solution, or anything else. All I wanted was to get back to Doctor Eileen.

"You remember what I asked you," I said, as soon as I had a chance to get her alone. "About growing back a man's arms if he lost them?"

"I told you. It's impossible. If we still had the limbs, we could re-attach them, but that's all."

"I know. But suppose you had *someone else's* arms. Could you attach *them*?"

"We could try. But it would be quite pointless. The muscles wouldn't match, the nerves wouldn't match, the bone sizes would be wrong. Worse than that, though, there would be tissue rejection."

"What's that?"

"Your body has a set of biological defenses built into it, what's called your *immune system*. If something comes in from outside, bacteria, or foreign tissue, your body's immune system develops a reaction to that. It does its level best to destroy it, to swallow it up and get rid of it. That includes rejection of tissue or organs from somebody else. We can control the rejection with drugs, but it's very tricky. It only works if the donor—the person the tissue comes from—is very similar to the person receiving it. Even then, you usually get problems."

"What do you mean, very similar? The same age, or the same size?"

"Jay, what *is* all this? Age and size don't have much to do with it. It's much more important to be *genetically* similar—a mother, or a father, as the tissue donor."

"Or a brother?"

"Sure, a brother would be good. Best of all, of course, would be an identical twin. Then there's absolutely no chance of tissue rejection, because genetically speaking the two are identical. Jay, what is the point of this?"

I told her then, the whole thing. "And I thought," I said at last, "that maybe Danny Shaker killed his twin brother, so that he could steal Stan's arms and have them attached to his own body, to replace the ones that he lost."

Even as I was saying it, it sounded ridiculous. Doctor Eileen just stared at me.

"Did you see scars on both arms?"

"No. Just one."

"Well, did Paddy Enderton tell you that Dan and Stan, the people he was afraid of, were identical twins?"

"No. He said brothers. But—"

I realized, at that precise moment, how final death is. I had been about to say, we can ask him and find out. But Paddy Enderton had gone where he could never answer another question from anyone, about anything.

"Look, Jay." Doctor Eileen was doing her best to take me seriously, but I didn't think she was succeeding. "If you're worried about this, there's one very simple way to get an answer. I'll ask Captain Shaker about the scar that you saw on his arm. Would you like me to do that?"

I didn't. Part of the reason was that I hated Doctor Eileen to think I was that much of a fool, but I suspect that as big a reason was that I didn't want *Danny Shaker* to think the same thing. In spite of the goosebumps that had run over my body in triple-deep layers when I first saw that red scar, I still could not relate the Danny Shaker that I knew, the man who treated me more like an equal and an adult than anyone I had ever known, to the faceless bogeyman who had haunted Paddy Enderton's last days.

"No, it's all right," I said. "Don't say anything to Captain Shaker. It was just that Paddy Enderton seemed so *scared.*"

I was cheating, passing off my own fears as belonging to somebody else. But it satisfied Doctor Eileen.

"Enderton was a dying man," she said, "probably with a lot on his conscience, and plenty to be scared about if he were at all religious. But I'm quite willing to forget all about this, if you are."

"I am."

"So we'll drop it. Tell me what Uncle Duncan did to repair the drive. You know, at this rate I ought to be charging Captain Shaker for Duncan's presence on board, instead of paying his fare."

I would have told her readily—if I had known. But all the time I had been in the drive chamber I had been far too jittery about Danny Shaker's arm to notice what was being done to the drive itself.

I suspect that I was a big disappointment to Doctor Eileen. I could read her thoughts. She had brought me so far, and had hoped that I might be useful. But ever since I boarded the *Cuchulain,* I seemed unable to remember the simplest things.

What would she tell my mother when we got back?

After the work on the drive, the flight of the *Cuchulain* felt smoother. Whether this was real or imagined, I don't know. But as the days and weeks wore on, and began to seem more and more the same, everyone on board settled into a mood that was both timeless and impatient.

The final stage was the most tantalizing of all. We reached

the edge of the Maze, and we knew that at normal rates of deep-space progress we could have been at our target world in a few hours. But at Captain Shaker's insistence, and with Doctor Eileen's concurrence, we went creeping along the outer edge of the Maze like a mud-eel along the bottom of Lake Sheelin.

As we moved I saw, through a telescope, a dozen little worlds of whose existence I had first learned through Paddy Enderton's little computer.

Clareen, Oola, Drumkeerin, Ardscull, Timolin, Culdaff, Tyrella, Moira . . . Now, instead of being rusty or flaming-red points in a hand-held display that could be extinguished by a poking finger, they were new and whiter points of light. But in a way they were hardly more real or tangible.

Somewhere, a day or two ahead, lay our true goal: *Paddy's Fortune*. Was I excited? I certainly was—but no more so, I suspect, than the doctor, or than Jim Swift and Walter Hamilton.

The oddest thing was the crew of the *Cuchulain*. Danny Shaker had as good as told us that his crew didn't give a hoot for the Godspeed Drive, or the possibility that we might be heading for Godspeed Base. But something was certainly winding them up. I came across Patrick O'Rourke and Tom Toole, heads together, talking confidentially in one of the corridors. They shut up at once when they saw me, but there was no hiding the gleam of excitement on their faces. And not just O'Rourke and Toole. Every hour, it seemed, I came across little knots of crewmen, taking time off their duties to talk together in low voices. Once I even thought I heard the whispered phrase, "Paddy's Fortune." But that seemed impossible. Doctor Eileen had never used those words on board the *Cuchulain* to describe where we were going. I knew that I never had, either.

The only exceptions to the excitement and expectation that filled the whole ship were Danny Shaker and Duncan West. Shaker was as calm, organized, and pleasant to me as ever. It was impossible not to respond to him, and I felt those strange suspicions of mine fading.

As for Duncan, he had been hidden behind his bland, pleasant face for as long as I had known him—which was all my life. He continued to work on ship repair and maintenance, where according to all the crew (except for sullen Joe Munroe) he had been performing miracles. Duncan didn't seem to care when, if ever, we reached *Paddy's Fortune.* He derived his pleasures from immediate results, knowing that another ingenious fix had worked.

Finally, there was no more time for speculation. The word came to Doctor Eileen—I don't know who told her—that a body had been sighted at the exact location that our coordinate set predicted. It was only a minor worldlet, according to the telescope data, no more than a couple of kilometers across. But it was there, right where it should be.

Of course, we knew no details of the surface or internal composition. But that didn't matter, because in just a couple more hours the *Cuchulain* would be parked in a neighboring orbit, close enough for a very good look, and after that a visit.

The plan that we would follow on arrival had been laid out long ago, by Doctor Eileen. Danny Shaker and all his crew would remain on board the *Cuchulain.* So, to my huge frustration and chagrin, would I. Doctor Eileen told me that she had promised my mother that I would be exposed as little as possible to any unknown dangers, and landing on a new worldlet could certainly provide those.

So Duncan West, Jim Swift, Walter Hamilton, and the doctor herself would take a little humpbacked cargo vessel and fly across to *Paddy's Fortune.* Based on that initial exploration, they would either return to the *Cuchulain,* or send the signal for others to join them. The third possibility, thought of I am sure but never discussed in my presence, was that they would neither return, nor send us a signal. If that happened, I believe that the next decision would have been left with Danny Shaker.

Rather than going along to the cargo area and watching the cargo beetle be launched, I chose to stay in an observation chamber in the living quarters and stare at *Paddy's Fortune* through the best image magnification device that I could find.

We were maybe fifty kilometers away from the surface of the little worldlet, a distance that Doctor Eileen, or more likely Danny Shaker, must have judged sufficient to keep us clear of danger. It was still close enough to let me see the details of the surface—such as they were. But what I stared at on the image screen was absolutely baffling, and here's why.

On the way out from Erin, three or four sessions with Danny Shaker had taught me a lot about the Forty Worlds, and also a good deal about the Maze. I knew that a little worldlet, like the one that I was staring at, could have many things—rocks, light metals, salts, and water. Even carbon dioxide, ammonia, and methane. But those gases would have to be frozen, or trapped in the interior. Because the one thing above all others that no world as small as *Paddy's Fortune* could have was an *atmosphere*. The gravity field was simply too tiny to hold on to gases.

However, the surface details of the world on the screen were, without a doubt, softened and blurred by *something* between them and the *Cuchulain*. And when I stared hard at the limb, where the surface of *Paddy's Fortune* showed a half-moon horizon, I could see a thin blurry ring where light from Maveen was scattered back toward the imager on the *Cuchulain*.

That was the way that the rim of Erin itself had looked from a distance, as sunlight scattered from the layer of air.

Except that *Paddy's Fortune* couldn't have air.

It was too much for me to stand. I left the observation chamber and hurried along to the main control room of the ship. Danny Shaker was there with Tom Toole. They were watching a different viewing screen, one that showed the cargo beetle drifting smoothly away from the column of the collapsed cargo hold, and out into free space.

"Now then, Jay," said Shaker, "I'm surprised that you aren't down there to see them off."

"I was watching—the little world." (I had almost said *Paddy's Fortune*.) "I knew that Doctor Eileen and the others would be flying down to it, so I thought I'd follow their approach. But I can't understand the way that it *looks.*"

"Join the club," Tom Toole said, and he laughed.

"We had the same problem," Shaker said, "when we made our first observations. You mean the blurred surface?"

"And the way the horizon looks. You told me that a little worldlet—"

"I did. And I still say it." Shaker turned to the control board, and an image of *Paddy's Fortune* sprang up there. "It can't hold an atmosphere, right? So how can it possibly look like that? I'll tell you how. There's a complete translucent shell, extending over the whole world and about a hundred meters above the surface. Artificial, of course, and suspended we don't know how. Somebody didn't want the bare surface exposed to space.

"But that's not the half of it. Come on, Jay, let's test how good you are at guessing. What's under that see-through cover?"

"An atmosphere." It was the obvious answer.

"Too easy, eh? All right, what else?"

What else? Here was a whole worldlet that somebody had gone to the enormous trouble of covering with a layer through which gas could not escape, just so *Paddy's Fortune* could have an atmosphere. Why would anyone want to give such a small world an atmosphere? Who or what *needs* an atmosphere?

"Life! There's living things, down there under the cover."

Shaker turned triumphantly to Toole. "Now didn't I tell you, Tom, that he'd figure it out?"

"But how can you possibly know that there *is* life?" I said. I had peered at the surface with the best imager on board, and seen no plants or animals.

"I could ask you for one more guess, but it wouldn't be fair, because there's instruments on the *Cuchulain* that you don't know about yet." Shaker touched another couple of keys on the control board, and a small inset appeared on the screen. It was a jagged line, rising and falling above a horizontal axis. "That's what we get when we look at the surface of the world out there with a thing called a *spectrometer*. It measures how much light comes back to us at a whole set of different wavelengths. Well, we know exactly what's going in—that's just the light from Maveen itself. So when we put those two pieces of information together, we can often tell what material we're looking at. What we find here, and over a lot of the worldlet's surface, is something called a *chlorophyll signature,* a curve that tells us for sure that there are plants down there. Chlorophyll means plants."

"And animals?" I asked.

Now it was Tom Toole who guffawed and turned to Danny Shaker. "He's got you, Chief."

"Indeed he does." Shaker turned off the display. "There could be animals, Jay, and there probably are, even if they're only single-celled ones. But we've seen nothing that's a unique signature for them, the way that chlorophyll is for growing plant life. We'll know in a few hours, though. Because Doctor Xavier promised to send us a message back. She knows we're as curious about it as she is."

It was all right for him to say that, and act as calm as could be. But I don't think any of them was as keen to know what was down there as I was.

It wasn't fair. I felt that it was *my* world. I was the one on the expedition who had found out that *Paddy's Fortune* even existed. Yet now I was the one sitting up here, left behind while the doctor went to look at it.

I told myself, for about the hundredth time, that Doctor

Eileen was carrying her feelings of duty toward my mother to ridiculous lengths.

It was going to be another few hours before I learned that the idea of leaving me behind on the *Cuchulain* had been strongly supported by Danny Shaker.

CHAPTER 15

One of Mother's favorite sayings, used whenever she was making me do something that she wanted me to do as opposed to something that I wanted to do myself, was, "The devil finds work for children's idle hands."

From what I had been told of history, the devil had even better success with adults; however, it was never any good arguing that point with Mother. And if she had known about what happened next on the *Cuchulain,* she would have said that it proved she was right.

With Doctor Eileen off to visit *Paddy's Fortune,* and the ship's crew busy at their own work, I was left with nothing to do. For the first few hours I didn't mind that at all. I took out the little calculator/display unit that had belonged to Paddy Enderton, and I tried to find out more about how it worked. It was something I had been wanting to do for weeks, but I hadn't dared, because Doctor Eileen believed that the unit was back home at our house by Lake Sheelin.

I hadn't exactly lied to anyone. When we left, Mother had packed my bag for me. She didn't include the calculator, though I knew that she and Doctor Eileen had talked about it. I didn't believe that she had left it out by accident, but at the last moment, when everyone was ready to leave, I nipped upstairs and slipped the little plastic wafer into my pocket.

I told myself that no one had actually told me *not* to take it with me; on the other hand, I felt uneasy enough about what I had done that I left the unit hidden away, all through our trip out to the Maze.

Now that Doctor Eileen and the others from Erin were finally out of the way, I sat down at the table in our living quarters and started work. What I was after was more information about *Paddy's Fortune*. When I had asked for information at the Second Data Level before, nothing had appeared on the display. The assumption we had made then was that it was blank because nothing more was stored about *Paddy's Fortune,* and the data bank contained only its coordinate set. But suppose that was wrong. Suppose Paddy Enderton had deliberately *hidden* additional information about the mysterious worldlet that was supposed to make his fortune? What a coup it would be if I, sitting back aboard the *Cuchulain,* could come up with more information about *Paddy's Fortune* than Doctor Eileen, Jim Swift, and the others, over exploring the planetoid itself.

Pure wishful thinking, I guess, because if Paddy Enderton had stored other data about his worldlet in the little unit he had done it too cleverly for me. After three or four hours that got me nowhere, I was frustrated and irritated. I turned the unit off, hid it away in my pocket, and left our living quarters. I went wandering away along the length of the *Cuchulain,* heading toward the cargo hold but with my mind still on the little calculator unit. Where had it come from?

Paddy Enderton, according to Doctor Eileen, had never visited *Paddy's Fortune.* Also, according to the doctor, the calculator could not have been made anywhere in the Forty Worlds. That left a real mystery: How had the gadget come into Paddy Enderton's hands?

It was while I was chewing on that problem, and getting

nowhere, that I noticed one of the bulkhead doors, halfway along the cargo column, standing a few inches ajar.

According to everything that I had been told about shipboard procedures, it was an unforgivable sin for anyone to leave those doors open. They divided the ship into a number of airtight compartments. This limited the damage that could be done by a seal failure, anywhere in the whole structure, to a loss of air in a single part.

I closed the bulkhead door, carefully dogged it to, and hurried along to check the rest of the cargo column. Everything was in order, all the way to the drive unit. The drive was switched off, because the *Cuchulain* had been placed in a free-fall orbit that matched the orbit of *Paddy's Fortune*. I took a few minutes for another inspection of the drive. In spite of all the maintenance work that had been done on it there was a used, battered look to the equipment. How long did Danny Shaker say it had been in continuous use?

A couple of centuries, at least. So how much longer would it last? Long enough, I hoped, for us to complete our journey.

And with that thought I became aware of a violent knocking, back along the cargo column. I hurried that way. Before I was halfway there I knew that the sound was coming from the bulkhead door that I had closed.

I slipped the latch and waited, afraid of what would happen next. Sure enough, the door banged wide and Patrick O'Rourke popped out. He was wearing a suit with its helmet open, and his face was an angry red.

He glared at me. "Did *you* do that?"

It was tempting to play innocent, but I knew it wouldn't work—there was no one else around.

"The bulkhead was open—I was told it always had to be kept closed. . . ."

"It never occurred to you that at the end of every long trip, a systematic check is made on *all* seals? To do that, you have to leave them open, one after another. It's a long job. We were halfway through, and now the whole thing has to be started over. Hours of work. You stupid—stupid—" He stared at me pop-eyed, searching for the worst insult he could think of. "You stupid *child*. Well, you'll not cause us any more trouble today."

He grabbed me by one arm and the back of my neck, hard enough to hurt, and pushed me along in front of him.

"Stop it," I complained. "You don't have to do that, I can walk for myself. Let go of me!"

But he didn't, not until we were at the living quarters that Doctor Eileen and I and the rest of us from Erin had been assigned. Then O'Rourke opened the door and threw me inside. "Get in and stay in," he shouted after me. "For your own sake. I'm going to have to explain to the chief why my whole maintenance crew is three hours behind in their work. And let me tell you, he's not going to like that one bit."

The door slammed shut, and was locked from the outside. I rubbed at my neck—O'Rourke had left bruises there. For maybe two minutes I worried about what I had done, and what would be said to Danny Shaker.

Then I started to feel angry. I couldn't be expected to know about ship's maintenance, or what was done at the end of each trip. So far as I could see, I had behaved perfectly responsibly. The bulkhead had been open, when it wasn't supposed to be. I had closed it, like a safety-conscious passenger—and been *blamed,* instead of praised.

I went to the door and hammered at it. A couple of minutes of that was enough to convince me that it was pointless. O'Rourke and his crew were far away along the cargo column, and no one else had any reason to come to our quarters, not when Doctor Eileen and the others were away on *Paddy's Fortune.*

I was stuck, until Patrick O'Rourke took it into his head to come along and let me out. From the look of him when he left, that could be many hours.

I went back to the table and took Paddy Enderton's calculator out of my pocket. But in my irritated and impatient mood working on it appealed even less to me now than when I had left. I put it away again and went wandering around the living quarters. After a few minutes I crouched down next to one of the air duct panels.

No one on board the *Cuchulain* could really be locked up. There had to be emergency routes, ready in case the usual ways were blocked. To escape from our living quarters, all I had to do was remove the grille, crawl along an air duct until I reached a point outside the locked region, and push my way out past another air grille.

Which was, I decided, exactly what I was going to do. I would find Danny Shaker and give him *my* version of events, to balance out whatever it might be that Patrick O'Rourke was going to tell him.

I pulled the air grille away from the wall, lay flat, and peered inside. The passageway was about two feet across: big enough for any but the fattest crew member, and high enough for me to crawl along comfortably on my hands and knees. I started out. The duct was cool and pleasant, with fresh air sighing past me as I crawled.

In less than a minute I had gone far enough to put our living quarters well behind me. Grilles, placed along the wall of the duct every ten yards or so, made sure that I could get out any time I chose. I peered through one. I saw a groundhog's view of a deserted companionway.

This is where there may be some truth to Mother's saying about the devil and idle hands. I still had nothing to do. It occurred to me that hidden away in the air duct system as I was I could see and not be seen, and hear but not be heard. If I wriggled my way along to Danny Shaker's cabin I might be able to hear whatever Patrick O'Rourke was going to accuse me of doing. When the time came for me to refute what he said I would be ready, point by point.

It was not easy to judge distances, crawling along as I was

in a darkness relieved only by light scattering in through the air grilles. On the other hand, I could hardly go in the wrong direction. All the crew quarters lay in the same part of the ship, aft of ours. I went that way, taking my time, and pausing every now and then to take a peek out through a grille.

After a while I knew I was getting close. I could hear voices just ahead. A little farther, sneaking along cautious on my hands and knees, and I could identify them: Connor Bryan and Rory O'Donovan. Two of the general crew and, in my humble opinion, far from the smartest people on the ship.

In another few seconds I could see them, or at least I could see their legs. They were sitting close together, and they were talking, but not about me or *Paddy's Fortune* or the Godspeed Drive.

"Big and fat and pale-skinned," Connor Bryan was saying. "Big chest, big belly, big hips. None of your stick figures for me. I want something blond and buxom and wide enough to wallow in."

O'Donovan laughed. "That's all right, then, we won't be competing. Give me red hair, nice and slim, with smooth hips and long legs. Sort of like the one we'd have had in that house by the lake—except we had to leave before we could even get started."

"She wasn't bad. But she was old. Older than me, for a bet. I want something young."

"She wasn't old. She was middling. Middling can be better—if it comes with *lots* of experience."

They were silent for a moment. "But they won't have experience, any of them," Connor Bryan said at last. "If it's nothing but women, with never a man to share out among them for a century, how can any of them have any experience at all?"

"Dunno," said O'Donovan. "I guess you and me will have to teach 'em." They both laughed, then O'Donovan added in a quieter voice. *"If* any of it is real."

"Paddy Enderton was sure of it."

"Aye, and look what pleasure it brought Black Paddy. Running for his life at the end, then stiff and staring. I wonder if he was lying about everything. It's hard to believe, thousands of women and no men. Sounds like a fairy tale."

"Doesn't it, though? But we'll find out soon enough. Come on."

I hadn't taken much notice of the last few sentences, because at the words "Paddy Enderton" I had jerked up and banged my head on the duct ceiling. Fortunately they didn't notice. Connor Bryan was standing up and saying, "Let's go see the chief. He's supposed to be getting reports back soon."

As they left the room I turned myself so that I could sit crosslegged. *Paddy Enderton!* They had said the name, when they were not supposed to have heard of him. And they knew that he was dead. Suddenly I realized who that "middling old" red-haired woman might be.

But all the other talk of women made absolutely no sense. We were billions of miles away from Erin and women. Also, there had been never a word said between Bryan and O'Donovan about Godspeed Base, although that was the whole point of our journey to *Paddy's Fortune.*

Maybe the wise thing would have been to head back to our living quarters at that point, and ponder what I had heard. But from their talk it was quite clear that they were going to a meeting with Danny Shaker, and something new about *Paddy's Fortune* was likely to come from it.

I examined my palms (grimy), rubbed my knees (a bit chafed, after all the crawling), and pressed on through the air duct system.

Finding a particular cabin or chamber was much harder than just crawling in one direction. The ducts divided from time to time, and I didn't know which branch to follow. I seemed to go on scrambling around forever, to and fro in the darkness, and after half an hour or so I was tired. I stopped and took a rest. I was ready to give up. That's when I heard faint voices somewhere ahead of me.

I crawled forward, reached one more branch point, and took the duct in the direction of the sound.

Even before I got there I could tell that an argument was going on. Voices were raised, and people were interrupting each other.

"—at the place. What more do we need? *We* should be down there, not them."

I recognized the voice. It was Sean Wilgus, a slim, sly-faced man who was unpopular because he acted as though he was superior to everyone. But now there was a murmur of agreement.

"I have to second that." It sounded like Patrick O'Rourke. "You said, be patient. But we *have* been patient. And now we're here. What more is there to be patient about?"

"You've got it backwards." It was Danny Shaker, calm and reasonable-sounding as ever. "You tell me what the rush is. We're not going anywhere. They *can't* go anywhere without us."

"So what?" Sean Wilgus again. "They've served their purpose. We don't need them, we haven't needed them since the second day out, when she told you the destination. I agree with Joe, we should have dumped them out the lock right then and there."

"Right," Danny Shaker said. "Very intelligent. We let them all breathe space, and then when we get to the coordinates she gave us, we find that she held back a little bit of information, and we're sitting in the middle of nowhere with no idea what to do next. It's not like you to be so trusting, Sean. She's old, but she's nobody's fool. Until we actually got here, there was no guarantee she wasn't playing her own game."

"But we *did* get here." That was Joe Munroe, surly as always. "After we arrived there was no reason to wait one minute more. But still you insisted we do nothing. You let *them* go down and explore the woman-world, instead of us. Why?''

"Use your brain, Joe," Shaker said. "You have it backwards. You should ask, why *not* let them explore? They're not *expecting* to find women down there, I told you that. So if they do, they'll surely call back here and tell us. And then we'll act.''

"Maybe we will. And maybe not. Maybe some people here are getting soft.''

There was a dead silence on the other side of the partition. I peered through the grille, but I could see little. The last speaker had been Joe Munroe. From the way that Danny Shaker's voice varied, I knew that he was on his feet and pacing about, as he often did in conversation.

"Are you by any chance referring to me, Joe?" he said at last. "You ought to know better. I don't shy away from *necessary* death. But if they don't find what we want—if there's nothing interesting or valuable down there—why, then, we'd be fools to kill anyone. We'll take them back to Erin, get triple pay for winter work like a good, dutiful crew, and go our way.''

"That may be all right for you," Sean Wilgus said. "You've got your own tastes and preferences. You and that bloody boy, you ought to form a mutual admiration society. But what about the rest of us? You drag us away from the women on Erin, with Paddy Enderton's promise of thousands. And now you keep us away from them. We could all be down there. We could maybe be having a woman apiece, this very minute.''

"Ah, Sean Wilgus," Shaker said softly. "I don't like to hear that sort of thing from you. 'Your own tastes and preferences,' indeed. That kind of remark doesn't do you justice. It's a good thing I'm so fond of you, or I might feel tempted to do something about it. But you know I love you—love you as much as if you were my own dear brother.''

There was a deadly silence. All movement in the room ceased.

"No, Chief." Wilgus's voice rose an octave. "I'm sorry. I misspoke. All I meant was, I wish I could be down there exploring the woman-world—we all feel that way. But I'm not questioning your judgment. None of us are. We never would. Right?"

There was a mutter of assent.

"Well, that's good to know." Danny Shaker laughed. He sounded very close. "Because, you see, I'm going to exercise my judgment again, right now, and it's nice to know you won't question it. If you hadn't given me that assurance, Sean, I think maybe you'd want to act differently when I show you—*this.*"

Before I knew what was happening the grille in front of me was whisked away. A hand reached in, grabbed me by the hair, and hauled me through into the control room.

"You see, men," Danny Shaker moved his grip to my arms, and pulled me forward to the middle of the group. "When you get right down to it, most things are a question of judgment. So here's a judgment test for you. Suppose that you find a little surprise like this in the air duct system."

He glanced at me and shook his head. "Jay, I told you that you'll make a first-rate spacer, and I stick with that evaluation. But you have to learn a few things first. For example, there's nothing on a ship more important than the air supply system. Anything that changes the air flow pattern, like a foreign body in the duct system, will flag an alarm on the control board, even if it's not dangerous." He gestured to the banks of displays on one wall of the room. "Maybe no one else noticed, but I've been tracking you for an hour."

He turned back to the watching circle of men. "So, as I say, you find this little surprise, and you ask, how much did he hear? We can't be sure. So what do we do with him?"

No one spoke. But I looked from face to face, and saw murder on every one.

So must have Danny Shaker, because he laughed again and said, "Out of the lock, eh, for a bracing whiff of vacuum? Let's think about that for a moment. Suppose we dump him, which is a natural temptation. Then it's no more Jay Hara. And good riddance, you might say.

"But wait a minute. Once Jay is dead, there's no bringing him back. Now, maybe you can think of cases where a man might be more useful dead than alive—I certainly can. . . ."

He stood up straight with his arms crossed, absent-mindedly kneading his biceps through his spacer's jacket. There was a kind of group flinch, as everyone around him winced and drew back.

"But we'll all admit that's a rare event," Shaker went on. "A dead Jay Hara is probably worth nothing to anyone. But a *live* Jay Hara is a valuable item in negotiation. Why do you think I wanted him here with us, when the others went exploring? What negotiation, you ask me? I don't know, I reply. But since there's no *risk* in keeping him alive, I'll take the possible value of a live something over the guaranteed zero value of a dead one." Shaker glanced around him. "Now, is there anyone who would like to debate my analysis? Or relate it in any way to my *tastes and preferences*?"

There was not a word, not even a murmur of assent.

"So I guess we keep him," Shaker said. "Tom?"

Tom Toole stepped forward. "Yes, Chief?"

"Number Four confinement cabin. Locked, of course." Shaker turned back to me. "This will be much more of a challenge, Jay. The brig has five-inch air ducts, solid door and walls, vacuum beyond. So far as I know, no one has ever managed to get out of a Number Four cabin and live. Don't let that discourage you from trying, though—ingenuity and persistence bring their own rewards. All right, Tom. Take him."

Tom Toole twisted my right arm painfully up behind my back and grabbed the nape of my neck, which was still sore from Patrick O'Rourke's earlier grip. He marched me out of the control room and off toward the front of the spherical living region. It was a part that I had visited only on my first general tour of the ship with Danny Shaker.

"You're hurting," I complained.

"You don't know how lucky you are to be around to be hurting," he said. "The chief's a deep one. With anyone on board but him in charge—me included—you'd be gone. Aye, and before that I thought that Sean Wilgus was going, too. What with him taking on the chief, and then that 'I love you like a brother' bit."

"Does Danny Shaker have a brother? A twin brother? Are they the two-half-man?"

I didn't expect answers, and certainly not the ones I received.

"Of course they are," Tom Toole said cheerfully. "Or were. Where else do you think the chief got his arms?"

"You mean Danny Shaker's arms used to belong to Stan Shaker?"

"You heard the chief say he didn't shy away from necessary death, and he could think of cases where a man might be more useful dead than alive. That was a good example. Stan Shaker was never the man that Dan is."

"You mean that his brother didn't just die—Shaker had him *killed*?"

"Well, you don't think Stan *volunteered* to give away his arms, do you? His own preference would have been to take his brother's legs." Tom Toole laughed, as we reached the door of the cabin and he opened it. "Ah, that was a fine piece of planning. Stan didn't just have to die, you see, he had to die at exactly the right time and place, when an operating team was in position and ready to go to work. That took real organization."

I was thrown into the room and staggered forward to hit a hard wall only a few feet away. The door was already closing when I turned back to Tom Toole.

"Danny Shaker killed his own twin brother! He stole his arms, and destroyed the rest of the body!"

"Now when did I say any such thing?" Tom Toole's tone was reproving. "The chief killed brother Stan, sure enough, and he did take his arms. But I'll wager good money that he didn't destroy the rest of the body, although I've never asked him about it. I'm sure he's got it tucked away in cold storage somewhere out in the Forty Worlds. He can't tell, you see, when he might be needing another few bits and pieces. I say it again, the chief is a deep one."

The door slammed shut, leaving me in darkness. I lay on the floor, just where I had been standing. Even had there been light, I would not have had the strength to explore my cell.

Paddy Enderton had told me, long ago, of his fears. Now, at last, I shared them.

CHAPTER 16

The confinement cabin showed me a new side of spacer life. I don't mean the rock-hard bunk, which in low gravity was no hardship at all. I don't mean the dim lighting, either, or the sanitary facilities. None of those worried me a bit, because they were little different from ordinary crew quarters.

The difference was simple, but enormous: The confinement cabin offered *no emergency exit*. If a failure of any kind occurred on the ship, and no one came to let a prisoner out, that was the end. He would die. And it was clear to me that no one on board worried about that for one second. To them it was just part of the rules that a spacer lived with, and sometimes died with.

I lay in near-darkness, half-asleep, wondering what was going to happen to me. The cabin had running water to drink, but no food. Doctor Eileen and the others might be away on *Paddy's Fortune* for days and days. Unless Danny Shaker gave explicit instructions to some crew member to feed me, I might starve. I could not see Joe Munroe or his buddies bringing me a meal from the goodness of their hearts. In fact, given a choice they would not only let me die of hunger—they would like to hurry it along.

So I had very mixed feelings when the door opened, and I found myself squinting in the bright light at a figure who stood on the threshold.

"Good news, Jay." It was Danny Shaker, as cheerful as ever. "Come on. I know you've been aching since we got here to take a trip across to *Paddy's Fortune*—we might as well all call it that now, though I can hardly think of a worse name for it. We're going there, as soon as you've had something to eat."

I had come to my feet at once when he entered, with some ridiculous idea of overpowering him. But I didn't move toward him, and not just because he was a lot bigger and stronger than me. I was afraid.

"You killed your brother," I said. "You killed Stan Shaker."

"What!" He stared at me, the smooth high forehead wrinkling. And then he laughed aloud, throwing his head back so that I could easily have reached forward and slashed his smooth throat. If I'd had a knife, which of course I did not. But he could not have been sure of that.

"Jay, Jay," he said. "What have you been dreaming, to keep you awake at nights?"

"You killed your brother. You stole his arms."

"Who told you that?"

"Tom Toole. And don't say he was just making it up to scare me. He believes it, himself."

Danny Shaker walked casually past me and sat down on the bunk. "That's good. I hope the whole crew feels the same way." And, as I gaped at him, "Jay, I still say you'll make a great spacer, but you have an awful lot to learn. You've seen the crew of the *Cuchulain*, every one of them. You know they're tough men, and they're rough men, and there isn't one of them who couldn't tackle me and destroy me, if he decided to try it. True?"

"True." I didn't know what he was getting at, but he sounded so relaxed it was difficult to stay scared.

"But they don't, Jay. *Why* don't they? I'll tell you why, it's because they don't *dare*. You see, all that nonsense about me and my poor dead brother—Stan was killed in the same accident where I was injured, the one where I came close to losing my arms—it's not just that I *permit* nonsense like that to be muttered all around the ship, and all around Muldoon Spaceport. I *encourage* it. I like Tom Toole to tell people I'm a monster. That way anyone, like maybe Sean Wilgus, who has a mind to take on Danny Shaker, will think twice before he actually starts anything. Here's a great truth for you, Jay: Authority doesn't come from a piece of paper, or the way that you behave; it's all defined by the way that *others behave toward you.*"

He stood up.

"We ought to be going. I talked to Doctor Xavier, not more than-half an hour ago, and promised that I would be down shortly."

I still hesitated.

"Look," he said, "I happen to think that Doctor Eileen Xavier is one very smart woman, and I believe that you do, too. When you and I get over there, why don't you talk to her about all this dead-men's-arms stuff, and see what she says?"

"I already did."

"You did? Well, what did she tell you?"

I was silent for a few moments, until Danny Shaker stared at my face and started to laugh. "Didn't buy it, did she?"

"No, she didn't." I took a wild shot. "Did you ever hear of a man called Paddy Enderton?"

It produced a reaction, but not one that I was expecting. Shaker looked thoughtful, and said, "Black Paddy? I certainly did. I know him well. He used to be navigation officer of the *Cuchulain*. How did *you* ever hear of him?"

"He stayed with us for a while—me and my mother."

"How's old Paddy doing?"

"He's dead."

"I'm sorry to hear that." Shaker frowned down at me.

"But you know, I'm starting to put things together. Paddy Enderton—*Paddy's Fortune.*"

"How did you know it was called that?—the world, I mean, the one we're near."

"Why, from Duncan West. He called it that name a couple of times."

So much for total secrecy. But Danny Shaker was continuing, "As I say, this all begins to make some sense. You're probably going to hear bits and pieces anyway, from other crew members, so you might as well hear the whole thing from me. I wasn't being totally honest with you a moment ago. Paddy wasn't just the navigation officer for the *Cuchulain;* he also deserted the ship. Under very odd circumstances."

Shaker sat down again, and patted the bunk beside him. "Sit down, Jay."

I did, and he went on, "We were out in open space, eight months ago, when suddenly our radar picked up an artificial signal. An odd one, too, not like the usual identification for a Forty Worlds vessel. We headed that way—anything unusual can be valuable. It didn't respond to our messages, so when we got close enough Paddy Enderton took off in one of our cargo beetles. Alone. He reported back that it was just a little ship, not the sort of thing that was designed for long interplanetary travel, and he would try to board it.

"He managed to dock, and he went inside. That's when things turned strange. He called on a standard communication frequency, to say that he was aboard a two-man scoutship, and the crew were both dead. But it wasn't a two-man crew at all, he said; it was a two-*woman* crew. If you know anything about the rules, written and unwritten, for women in space, you'll realize that what Paddy was telling us was just about impossible.

"After that there was a twelve-hour radio silence. Just about the time that I was ready to call Paddy and tell him to return with or without the scoutship, its drive went on at high acceleration. There was no chance at all that the *Cuchulain* could catch it, even if we'd been all powered up and ready to go. We never heard one more word from Paddy Enderton. I thought at first that he'd been carried off in some sort of accident that turned on the drive. But when we finally arrived back at Muldoon Port, months later, we learned that he had been through there. He had gone to ground somewhere, no one could tell us where. We decided that Paddy must have found something valuable on board the scoutship, and wanted to keep it all for himself. But there was no reason to think that the 'something valuable' might be *out in space*—until now."

"What do you think it is?" I was intrigued in spite of myself.

"Well, it's supposed to be something on *Paddy's Fortune*. That's clear enough. The crew think it must be women. That's partly because Paddy Enderton said he found two women on the ship he stole, and partly because that's what spacer crews think about half the time—make that three-quarters of the time—while they're out in space. But you ask me, what do I think? Well, I prefer not to speculate. Not when you and I can be over there to see for ourselves in an hour."

I was ready to go, and not just because his words were making me more and more curious to see *Paddy's Fortune* at first hand. It had also occurred to me that I couldn't be *more* under the control of Danny Shaker and the crew of the *Cuchulain,* no matter what happened. And if he indeed took me down to be with Doctor Eileen and Duncan West and our two scientists, I would be much safer there than I was here.

Maybe Danny Shaker knew that's how my thoughts would run. Certainly, he did not say one more word about women or Paddy Enderton while I was eating, or grabbing a little bag of necessities in case I had to stay down on the worldlet for a day or two. We boarded a cargo beetle. Then he looked at me and past me, and said, "In case we need extra muscle-power for any reason."

Behind me, four more men were crowding through the beetle's little port. Patrick O'Rourke, Robert Doonan, Joseph Munroe, and Sean Wilgus. I could understand that the first two made sense, but I wondered if Shaker wasn't inviting trouble by taking Wilgus and Munroe. They were the ones who had been openly critical of him only a few hours earlier. Was Shaker doing it *deliberately*, to point out to me and to them that he was completely confident of his authority?

Either way, not one of them said a word when they were inside the beetle, though Joe Munroe gave me a very hard stare, as though to say, what the devil are *you* doing here?

I did plenty of staring of my own. Not at the men, but at what they were carrying: guns, and deadly looking knives.

Danny Shaker saw me flinch. "Something wrong, Jay?"

"The weapons. Why are you taking those with you?"

"For exactly the same reason that Doctor Xavier and your friends took theirs, at my recommendation. When you are heading for a place that supports life, and you don't know what you might encounter, you don't take risks. *Paddy's Fortune* may be dangerous."

"But Doctor Eileen is already over there. She must know that's not true."

"Ah, I forgot that you'd been out of the loop, so to speak, for a few hours. When we talked with the doctor, she didn't say that at all. I'll tap us into the *Cuchulain* data banks while we're on our way across, and you can listen for yourself."

It was a strange experience, to hear Doctor Eileen's voice in my ear describing their approach to *Paddy's Fortune*, while the little world itself grew steadily before my eyes. The recording put her about ten minutes ahead of us, so that when we still had twenty kilometers to go she was already describing their flight low over the translucent shield, seeking an entry point. By the time we got there, she was describing the touchdown on the real surface. Her actual recording had included video, but I was getting only sound, so what I heard was not too satisfactory. But it was clear from Doctor Eileen's words that they had emerged to stand on a tiny world with very low gravity, a perfectly breathable atmosphere—and vegetation denser than anywhere on Erin except right at the equator.

"The best word to describe it is *jungle*," said Doctor Eileen's voice in my ear. A disappointed voice, I thought. What she was seeing did not match her ideas of Godspeed Base. "It's a consequence of the low gravity, which does almost nothing to constrain upward growth. As you will observe, moving around is not going to be easy. Exploring may take us far longer than we expected. We are going to stay together and concentrate our firepower until we know that nothing dangerous is here. We are not sure yet that there is animal life, but we think there must be. Dr. Swift heard something moving off through that patch of thorns you can see in front of us."

I, of course, could not see that. What I saw was the curve of the little world itself, as our cargo beetle floated around it. We had negotiated the upper shield through a lock that worked itself automatically at our approach. Whatever it was that kept *Paddy's Fortune* operating and with an atmosphere right for humans was still doing fine. Soon we were within a hundred feet of the actual surface.

But I couldn't see that surface at all. What I saw was growing plants, apparently covering every square inch. It was only when we came lower that I noticed little pools of water, washbasin-sized, with lines of flattened growth running between them like animal trails. But there was no sign of the animals themselves.

The worldlet was turning on its axis and, as I watched, parts of it slipped away into shade for a brief night. The whole daylight period could be no more than an hour or two. I had a sudden vision of an accelerated world, with animals catching brief half-hour naps between nightfall and a new dawn. Then I realized that part of the world, what I imagined as its "north pole," was going to remain in shadow for a long time. Maveen was to the south, and would not illuminate much of the north at this time of year. Did animals—if there were animals—migrate south, to enjoy a season of perpetual sun? Or head north, to hibernate? It would not be a difficult journey, because the whole distance from north pole to south pole was no more than an hour's walk.

Assuming that you *could* walk, through such unbroken vegetation. Even from a hundred feet or less, I could not estimate the height of the plants. I had to take Doctor Eileen's word that it was difficult going.

I was not the only one peering down with huge curiosity. The four crew members were just as interested. Sean Wilgus was actually licking his lips in sheer excitement and anticipation, something I had never seen anyone do before outside of a theater show. Only Danny Shaker stayed at the controls, bringing us in for a gentle landing that nonetheless crushed a broad circle of tall succulent plants with spiky purple flowers.

He had no choice. *Paddy's Fortune*, at least to my first inspection, was *all* vegetation. Doctor Eileen had been forced to flatten a patch, too, when they landed. No wonder she was disappointed. An industrial world, as she had pointed out to me on the journey to the Maze, should show signs of that industry even from a distance. The transparent shield around *Paddy's Fortune* supported that idea. But now—this.

We opened the port of the beetle, and squeezed through one by one to stand on soft black soil. I at once found myself at a disadvantage. The surface was level enough, but the plants were head-high—*my* head. Shaker and the other crew members could see over the tops of the plants. My view was limited to green leaves and purple flowers.

And something else. I reached out and picked a tiny

object from the underside of one of the leaves. I held it out to show it to Pat O'Rourke.

"Look. Some sort of bug. There *is* animal life."

He glanced at it without the slightest interest. "Yeah. We know that. The other party showed us bugs."

I had heard only a small fraction of the recordings sent back by Doctor Eileen. I put the little green multilegged creature on a leaf, and turned back to explain the reason for my ignorance to Patrick O'Rourke.

He had vanished.

I could see the way that he had gone, from a few broken plants among the whole mass of springy vegetation. I took three steps in that direction, and suddenly I was right behind him again. It proved how easy it was to get lost—at least for me.

The others probably did not have that problem. Patrick O'Rourke seemed to know where he was going, and other sounds were coming from each side of me. Sean Wilgus was cursing at something black and sticky that he had trodden in, while Robert Doonan, easily the most broken-winded of the crew, was wheezing and grunting in front of him.

"How much farther, dammit?" he complained. "I thought you said we—aha, about time."

Within a few more steps I understood that mysterious comment. I emerged abruptly from green and purple jungle, to a place where the plants grew less than knee high. Danny Shaker and Robert Doonan were already waiting. I hardly gave them one glance, because standing there also, to my huge relief, was Doctor Eileen.

I don't think I was ever so pleased to see anyone in my whole life. It must have shown, because as I ran to her side she shot me a funny look and said, "What's the good news?"

I don't think she cared whether I answered or not. I was sure pleased to be with her, but from the look of it she wasn't all that happy to see me. She turned to Danny Shaker without waiting for my reply.

"What's this, Captain? You never told me that you were bringing Jay with you. I'm not sure this place is safe."

"Safer for him than the *Cuchulain,* when I'm not there. I'll vouch for that." And, when she stared at him, "You know my crew, Doctor. They're hardworking and they're well-seasoned. But they're a rough lot, and one thing no spacer will stand is a spy. I'm sorry to tell you that the crewmen are convinced that Jay has been spying on them. Crawling through the air supply system, snooping around, listening in on private conversations."

"Nonsense! Wriggling along air pipes? I'm sure he did no such thing." Doctor Eileen turned back to me. "Did you, Jay?"

"Well . . . I did—but it wasn't like that at all. You see, I heard them talking about women—"

"And when did spacers ever talk about anything else?" Shaker glanced across at the four crew, who had slumped down on the soft earth half a dozen paces away. He stepped closer to Eileen Xavier and lowered his voice. "I'm going to be honest with you, Doctor, even though you'll maybe think the less of me for it. Privacy in space is hard to come by, and spying on your shipmates is one of the very worst things you can do."

"But I wasn't—"

"Shush, Jay." Doctor Eileen waved her hand, but she didn't look at me.

"They *thought* you were spying," Danny Shaker said, "and that's what matters. The way the men were talking after they found Jay in the air ducts, that was real ugly."

"But *you* were the one—"

"Jay!"

It was useless, she would believe him more than she would me.

"Some were even suggesting space-walking him." Shaker shook his head ruefully. "I had trouble controlling them—as Jay himself can tell you. And I certainly wasn't sure enough of myself to leave him *behind* when I came down here. I brought him along for his own safety."

It was ridiculous. But the odd thing is that I almost believed it myself, the way Danny Shaker said it. Doctor Eileen certainly did. She sighed, and shook her head.

"Jay, I'm sure you didn't mean any harm. But you should have known better. What now, Captain Shaker?"

"A little breathing space, I think, to let the crew back on board calm down. Jay ought to stay here for a day or two. And if you don't mind, I'd like to ask one favor of you."

"Anything within reason."

"It's the men. Part of the reason they're so angry has nothing to do with Jay's snooping. He was quite right, you see, the crew *have* been talking about women—because they've got the odd notion in their heads that was why you came here in the first place."

"That's more than *odd*. It's crazy."

"I know. But somehow the word's been going around the ship that this little worldlet has women on it. Living, human women. *Young* women."

"Then that rules me out. Your crew certainly entertains some bizarre ideas, Captain."

"They do. But that won't change just because you or I wish it. So this is the favor I'm asking: Will you let some of my crew roam around here for a day or so? Then they'll find nothing, and go back and tell their mates that they saw for themselves and there's nothing hidden. After that, you and your professors can go on exploring for as long as you like."

"Which won't be for more than another hour, the way things have been going. This is an artificial world, no doubt of it, but we've found *nothing*. Nothing to suggest that it was ever a Godspeed Base, I mean, and nothing to hint that it ever had anything to do with one." Doctor Eileen snorted. "You know, if you hadn't come down I was thinking of going back to the *Cuchulain* anyway, sitting down, and going over everything that's happened one more time to try to make sense of it.''

"Perfect. Do it. The crew would like that, too, knowing you weren't trying to steer them away from anything.''

"Wait a minute, though. Walter Hamilton says he wants to stay even if the rest of us go back. This place seems to have nothing to do with a Godspeed Base, but it does date back to before the Isolation, and it has its own unique biology. Hamilton wants to study it.''

"Tell him to study away, Doctor, and welcome to it. So long as he doesn't try to advise my men where to go and not to go. I'll tell the crew to let him wander where he likes.''

"And I'll tell Jim Swift and Duncan to get ready. They're back at the other cargo beetle.''

She pointed up across the thicket of plants. She was too short to see over them.

"What about me!'' I said.

"You can come with—'' But Doctor Eileen paused and raised her eyebrows at Danny Shaker.

"Not a good idea.'' He was shaking his head. "Without me on the *Cuchulain*—or even *with* me . . . why, that's the whole reason I brought him. Jay should stay here. But don't worry, Doctor. The men here are the pick of the bunch. He'll be safe with us. I pledge my life on it.''

I wanted to shout, but what about *my* life? I didn't, though. It would have been pointless. Doctor Eileen was convinced that I had been acting like a moron on the *Cuchulain*, and she thought that Dan Shaker was just worried about my safety.

As she started back along a trail of flattened plants, I hurried along after her. I just had to talk to her some more. But as we went I had another thought.

Suppose she believed every word that I said. Even though Danny Shaker carried no weapon himself, his men all had them. He had told me that Doctor Eileen's group had guns and knives, too, but I saw no sign of one on her. If Danny

Shaker wanted to, he could just order his men (the "pick of the bunch"!—who'd pick Sean Wilgus or Joe Munroe for anything but dirty work?) to kill me, and kill Doctor Eileen, and kill all the rest of our party.

That's the sort of gloomy thought you have when you're struggling along head-down through tall leafy plants that catch you as you go, and you know that just behind you there are men who have already said they'd be more than pleased to chuck you out of an airlock into naked space.

I'll take those thoughts though, anytime, over the ones that I had ten minutes later; I'm talking about the ones that came as I stood at Walter Hamilton's side with Danny Shaker and his men just behind me, and watched the cargo beetle rise up, ease its way toward the softly glowing shield that surrounded *Paddy's Fortune,* and quietly disappear. Doctor Eileen, Jim Swift, and Uncle Duncan were all on board. I had tried one more time to talk to her, and she wouldn't even listen.

As the ship vanished beyond the translucent shield, my thoughts lurched from uneasiness to cold terror. Even now, I don't like to recall them.

CHAPTER **17**

I never did like Walter Hamilton. I suppose it all goes back to what Danny Shaker told me: You are defined not so much by what you are, as by the way that you are treated by other people.

Doctor Eileen might occasionally pat me on the head or ruffle my hair, but she did it sort of absentmindedly, without thinking. And although I hated it, in a way she had the right to do it because she had been around me ever since I was born.

Walter Hamilton was different. He hardly knew me, but he acted as though I was a nothing. He didn't talk *to* me, he talked *through* me.

I would ask him a simple question (though not often after the first few days); something like, "Dr. Hamilton, you said that Erin's contact with other stars was cut off right at the time of Isolation. But Dr. Swift said you don't need a Godspeed Drive to transmit radio signals. Why didn't people send *those* from star to star?"

And he would suck in his pimply cheeks, and sniff, and stare at nothing. Then he'd come out with something like, "Let us not be quite so crushingly naive. An interstellar subluminal communications network may well have preceded the existence of the superluminal Godspeed Drive. However, once the latter had been fully established, the obsolescence of the former was guaranteed. And of course, following the cataclysm of Isolation the presumed problems of basic civilization survival totally inhibited subluminal communications redevelopment.''

And I would think (but not say), *Ugh!*

Yet both Jim Swift and Doctor Eileen had told me that Walter Hamilton was a serious and competent research worker, someone who really cared about his subject. I didn't argue. So far as I was concerned she could have my share of him. For most of the trip out to the Maze I had done my best to avoid the man.

But now, on *Paddy's Fortune,* he was the closest thing to a friend that I had. I must say, the competition was not great: Danny Shaker, who *said* he was my friend, and O'Rourke, Doonan, Munroe, and Wilgus, who made it perfectly clear that they were no such thing.

We all stood in silence, watching the cargo beetle lift off. Danny Shaker waited until it had eased its way beyond the atmospheric shield and was out of sight, then he turned to Patrick O'Rourke.

"Well, you asked for it, boyo, and now you've got it. You can go anywhere, poke into anything you find."

The four crewmen laughed, and O'Rourke said, "You can sure count on *that,* Chief—if I can find anything to poke into."

Shaker nodded. "Go ahead, then. I've got other things to do. I'll be at the cargo beetle if you need me. I expect your report in four or five hours."

Without another word he turned and headed into the tall plants, moving along a faint line of disturbance that showed the way to the cargo beetle that we had arrived in. The vegetation sprang into position as soon as he had pushed through. I was starting right after him when Sean Wilgus moved to block my path.

"Not you," he said softly. "You stay with us." He lifted a hand to his belt.

"Now then. First things first." Patrick O'Rourke stepped in front of Wilgus. "You're too hasty, Sean, as usual. Don't forget what we came for." He turned toward Walter Hamilton. "You there. You've been here for a while. Are there any breaks in all this mess of plants?"

Not "Dr. Hamilton," you see, but "You there." Danny Shaker wouldn't have allowed such rudeness, only he wasn't around to stop it.

Hamilton glared at O'Rourke, but he answered quickly enough, and in a tone not designed to please. "If you'd bothered to use the eyes in your head on the way down, you'd know there are no totally cleared areas. But there are certain regions, like the one where we are presently standing, at which the natural climax species attain a reduced height. They seem to be associated with deep, narrow fissures in the surface. We found a dozen or more of those, up to ten meters deep and with more vegetation at the bottom of them. And then there are the trails."

"Aha!" That was Sean Wilgus. He came around to face O'Rourke. "I *told* you they'd been holding out on us. Trails! For *people!*" He swung to face Hamilton. "Right?"

The scientist stared down his nose at him, if you can do that to somebody taller than you are. "Don't sound like a bigger fool than you are. There are no people on this world. The trails are made by the frequent passage of small animals."

"How do you know?"

"There couldn't be people here. This world isn't big enough to support them."

"Just like it couldn't possibly have an atmosphere, according to all you big experts. But it has one." Wilgus was stepping closer to Hamilton. Patrick O'Rourke pushed in between them.

"Either there are or there aren't," he growled. "People, I mean. I told you, Sean Wilgus, calm down. That's what we're here for, to stay cool and see for ourselves. Make one of your wild moves, and the chief will skin you when we get back to him—aye, and me, too, for letting you do it. This isn't a big planetoid. Let's get down to finding our own answers."

O'Rourke was so big and broad that Walter Hamilton and Sean Wilgus could hardly see each other around him. For the moment it put an end to their argument. The four crewmen from the *Cuchulain* ignored Hamilton and me and started to organize their own search effort.

What they decided was simple-minded, but it ought to work. They would line up thirty or so paces apart, close enough to be in easy earshot, and walk around *Paddy's Fortune* in the direction of the setting sun. A "day" on the planetoid was a couple of hours, but on the other hand its circumference was only five or six kilometers. The walkers would catch up with the sun. By the time they had walked until Maveen was twice overhead, they would have performed more than one full circuit of the world. At that point they would either have found something interesting, or they would have found nothing. They could perform another sweep, farther north or south, or they might try something completely different.

No one suggested a role for me or Walter Hamilton. We trailed along after them, the two of us walking one behind the other in the path of flattened vegetation left by Sean Wilgus. I was in front, and I gradually slowed our pace so that we lagged farther and farther behind the crewman. I wanted to tell Walter Hamilton what Doctor Eileen had refused to hear: the full details of everything that I had heard when I was hidden on the *Cuchulain*.

I ought to have known better. If Doctor Eileen, who knew

me so well, found it impossible to believe me, what chance did I have with a near-stranger?

I talked for maybe five minutes. Finally Hamilton caught up with me and pushed past, saying as he went, "Would you for God's sake shut up! It's hard enough to think without your blathering. And I've got plenty to think about."

He hadn't even been listening! But then *he* started, about the observed ecology of the planetoid, and how it all had to balance, and how anybody with half a brain and a first course in population dynamics would realize that the biggest animal you could find on *Paddy's Fortune* would mass no more than a mouse, or at absolute maximum a small miniver, and Sean Wilgus and anyone else who talked of *people* on this worldlet had to be morons.

Then all of a sudden he stopped dead, and said, "For the love of Kevin! A *natural* world's balance. But of course it can't possess any such thing." He went down to one knee on the muddy ground, and pulled a little calculator and an electronic book from his pocket.

"What is it?" I said. "What have you found?"

"I told you, shut up," he muttered. "I've got to think." He ignored me as he did a whole bunch of calculations, then started to key new entries into his book.

I wanted to tell him that nobody could tell *me* to shut up, and I had plenty to think about, too. But I didn't want to make him angrier than he already seemed to be. Although he wasn't my choice of company, whatever he did he wouldn't kill me. I couldn't say that of any of the others. And Hamilton had a gun at his belt, a white-handled pistol that he could use if anyone tried violence.

Meanwhile he was back on his feet again, and moving fast. We were closing on the line of four crewmen. I knew that was the case, because although we were again in the middle of tall, scrubby bushes and I couldn't see anything but leaves and twigs and soggy black earth—how did it stay so damp, without rain?—I heard voices ahead.

Angry voices. Everyone was cursing. The crew had arrived on *Paddy's Fortune* looking for women, but what they had found so far was mostly mud. They had stopped for a rest, calling to each other to compare loud and angry notes.

Walter Hamilton went up to Sean Wilgus and waved the electronic book in his face. "Listen to me," he said.

Wilgus had his right thumb in his mouth. He was squatting down, peering along a low archway that ran through the tight-leaved plants, and he took no notice of Hamilton.

With loud complaints coming in from all sides, that was not too surprising. The only person who wasn't shouting was Robert Doonan, and that was probably because he was in such bad physical shape that he needed all his energy just to walk and breathe. But Patrick O'Rourke, off to the left, had encountered a patch of thornbush, with spines hard and sharp enough to draw blood. Joseph Munroe, next in the line, had not been looking where he set his feet. He had stepped into one of the little pools. It turned out that it was not so much a pool as a deep pothole, only a few feet across but as deep as it was wide, and Munroe had plunged into cold water up to his crotch.

Sean Wilgus himself had just crossed a little trail and seen a brown thing like a small kangaroo rat jumping along it. He had tried to grab it as it passed, but it had bitten him on the thumb and got away.

If he had been in a bad mood before the search began, he was in a worse one now. He had taken his gun from his belt, and he was aiming it along the dark tunnel.

Walter Hamilton stopped waving his book and crouched down at Wilgus's side. "What the devil do you think you're doing?"

Wilgus did not even look up. "I'm waiting. Next time I see some damned jumping thing, I shoot. I'll teach that son of a bitch."

"You will not! This is an unexplored world, a whole new

balance of nature. You are doing too much damage already, smashing a way through the plants.''

I admired Walter Hamilton's courage in taking on Sean Wilgus, even if the balance of nature on *Paddy's Fortune* didn't seem like a big deal to me. But I don't know if Wilgus was even listening. He certainly took no notice. As we watched he crouched lower, sighted along his gun, and fired twice. There was a high-pitched sound, somewhere between a bark and a scream of pain, from farther along the tunnel.

"Got it!'' Wilgus shouted.

Walter Hamilton produced his own high-pitched sound, a cry of outrage and disbelief. He reached down with one hand, grabbed the shoulder of Sean Wilgus, and lifted. In the low gravity of *Paddy's Fortune,* Wilgus came easily up into the air, still in his crouched position.

"You will stop that!'' Hamilton was stammering in his fury. "There will be no more killing of native life. Do you hear me? None! Or I will—I will report you to Erin's central council.''

If Hamilton had left his threat at that, Sean Wilgus might have been too busy laughing to do anything else. Threatening a spacer with a pack of Erin bureaucrats was no way to command respect.

But Walter Hamilton did something much more provoking. He released his hold on Sean Wilgus's shoulder, and reached for the white-handled gun at his own belt.

He wanted to threaten, that was all. I feel sure he wouldn't have fired—I bet Walter Hamilton had never fired anything in the whole of his life. But I saw the look on the face of Sean Wilgus as Hamilton's hand closed around the pistol butt. It was a moment of surprise, followed by an expression of anger and pure, vicious hatred. And his own weapon began to lift.

"Dr. Hamilton!'' I cried. "Let go of it.''

I was too late. Wilgus aimed his own weapon and fired three times, so quickly it all sounded like one shot. Walter

Hamilton, his hand still on his gun, fell backward into the bushes.

For a moment Sean Wilgus and I both stared at Hamilton's body, as blood spouted from great wounds in its chest and neck. Then we turned to look at each other.

I could hear Wilgus's panting breath. I fancied that I could hear his mind working, too. He was in deep trouble. He could tell Danny Shaker that the murder was self-defense from Walter Hamilton's armed attack, and the pistol in the other man's hand would support his statement.

But not with Jay Hara as a witness to the whole thing.

Wilgus's gun started to lift again—toward me. I cried out in fear, and threw myself sideways into the bushes. The gun fired again before I had gone half a dozen steps. But already the dense vegetation hid me from view. I heard a strange hissing, as bullets swept through tough leaves, but I was left untouched. I ran blindly on—and almost went smack into the grasp of Joe Munroe.

Like all the crewmen, he must have been heading for Sean Wilgus to find out what was happening. I couldn't expect any help from him. He had been a big supporter of the idea of throwing me into space without a suit. I ducked, wriggled away from his grabbing hand, and plunged deeper into the jungle of plants.

The first two minutes were pure panic, when all I wanted was to put distance between me and the crewmen. After that came more rational worry. I could run, but I couldn't hide. Every step that I took left its mark, in the form of flattened or broken plants. The others were a lot slower than me, but all they had to do was follow. They had plenty of time, and they outnumbered me. They could work as a team, following me one after another until I was forced to stop for rest and sleep.

I moved as gently as possible, trying to repair damage by lifting twigs and blades back into position after I passed through. It didn't work. There were still signs, and it would surely be days before they faded. Even if the plants did not show where I had been, I was leaving footsteps in the soft earth.

I crouched down, head bowed and ready to cry. *Paddy's Fortune* had seemed like a big enough place when I was walking around it with Walter Hamilton. Now it had become tiny, offering no possible hiding place.

The shadow of my own head on the floor in front of me finally told me what I had to do. As I sat despairing, it had crept slowly across the ground. The world was rotating, and Maveen moved across the sky. In another half hour it would be dark. Tracking me through the plants would be impossible. But less than an hour after that, the sun would rise again. I would again be in danger.

Unless . . .

I stood up, took my bearings, and started north. That was a move with its own dangers, because it took me back toward Walter Hamilton and possibly to my pursuers.

I stared in all directions at every step and crept along as quietly as possible. The only time that I stopped was to lean down and drink from one of the deep little ponds. The water tasted fine, cool and clear as Lake Sheelin. I would have drunk anyway, even if it had been warm and muddy. I was parched.

I was also absolutely starving. How long since my last meal? Only eight hours or so, but it felt like days.

I crept on. There was a terrible moment when I heard a nearby shout that sounded like Joe Munroe, and an answering call from the other side. It sent chills through me, and I froze. But there was no safety in that. I started moving again, through growing twilight. I was following my own tracks but I could hardly see them. Then came another awful moment, when I almost tripped over the body of Walter Hamilton.

He was dead and lying face-up, eyes open and staring. I huddled down at his side. I could hardly bear to touch him, but I had to. I wanted his gun.

It was gone. Either he had dropped it, or one of the others had already taken it. I groped around on the floor in increasing gloom, until my fingers located something hard. Not the gun. The electronic notebook that he had been holding. I took that and put it in my own pocket, along with Paddy Enderton's tiny computer and display unit. I felt again for the gun, all around the body. Maybe it was there, somewhere among the flattened plants, but I could not find it.

At last I gave up the search. I moved on, always north. Half an hour later I was easing forward into noiseless twilight.

If I had my directions right, in front of me lay not the short-lived darkness of nighttime on *Paddy's Fortune;* I was approaching the months-long night of the region around the worldlet's north pole.

Ten minutes more, and I could barely see where I was going. I sank to the ground and stretched out on soft, damp earth. For the first time in hours, I was free to relax. If I could not see where I was, no one else would be able to track me here without hand-held lights. Even then it would be difficult.

I said I was free to relax, but of course I couldn't. I was too wired up. There's a big difference between seeing a dead man, like Paddy Enderton, and seeing a man die. The image of Walter Hamilton's throat and chest kept coming into my mind, the bright blood gouting out. I had never realized before that blood could run like water. I hadn't liked Hamilton much. Now I felt guilty about that.

The ground beneath me was unnaturally warm, but I was shivering. I told myself, over and over, that I was safe, except that a part of my mind kept asking if that word included a situation where a person was without food, drink, light, or shelter, and had absolutely no idea what was going to happen next.

* * *

What actually happened next was ridiculous. Although I would have sworn that it could never happen, I fell asleep.

When I opened my eyes, it was raining. That was impossible. How could a tiny world like *Paddy's Fortune* support a layer of cloud? But certainly those were cool raindrops falling on my face.

I realized then what ought to have been obvious from the time I first set eyes on that artificial shell around *Paddy's Fortune*. If the planetoid could have an atmosphere, it could have anything. It was not a natural world. Something *controlled* conditions on the surface, and a shower of rain was probably no more difficult to arrange than breathable air.

My next thought was that the rain itself had awakened me. Then a bright light shone in my eyes, only a few feet off to one side, and I heard the rustling of leaves in the darkness.

I did not wait to see who it was. In one movement I was on my feet, running doubled-over through the clutching plant life. It was a dangerous thing to do, because I couldn't see an inch in front of my face. If a wall of rock had been in my path I would have run headlong into it.

It wasn't quite that bad, but what happened next was even more unnerving. The ground vanished from beneath my feet and left me running in midair. I had encountered one of the deep fissures that Walter Hamilton had talked about. In the low gravity of *Paddy's Fortune*, the long fall down the crack in the surface should have been more frightening than dangerous. Actually it was both. While I was still falling and moving rapidly forward, my hands hit a hard surface in front of me, skinning my knuckles. My body turned and dropped. In three more seconds I landed, rolling over on one hip and elbow.

Every bit of breath was knocked out of me. I lay flat on my back, struggling to bring air into my lungs and staring straight up at a light that was steadily approaching.

Sean Wilgus? Patrick O'Rourke? Or even Danny Shaker himself?

It made no difference. I couldn't stand up and run to save my life.

The white light brightened, moved down to within a foot of my face, then lifted higher. It was being held in someone's hand. As the arm was raised I had a first look at the person himself.

It was not Sean Wilgus, or anyone else of the *Cuchulain*'s crew. Nor was it Doctor Eileen, or a member of our party. It was a stranger, a thin, short-haired boy maybe two years younger than me, with ragged pants and jacket of light grey and a face and limbs smudged all over with mud and earth. He was holding a little backpack made of brown leather in one hand, and a bizarre-looking pink ring that threw off a bright beam from its center in the other.

Sean Wilgus had been right. The learned Walter Hamilton, with all his degrees, had been wrong.

There were people on *Paddy's Fortune.*

CHAPTER 18

Who are you? What are you doing here?''

The kid had helped me to sit up, but he didn't wait for me to get my wind back.

"I'm—I'm—'' I started, but then I was too breathless to do more than parrot his question. "Who are you?" I croaked. "And what are *you* doing here?"

He sniffed and picked up the pink flashlight from where he had placed it on the ground.

"I *live* here, that's what I'm doing." His voice was high-pitched and a little bit foreign, like somebody from over on the other side of Erin. "And I know what *I'm* doing. That's more than you can say, dashing around in the dark. You could have killed yourself. But I'll answer you. My name is Mel Fury."

"I'm Jay Hara."

I thought, *You sound like a smart ass.*

We stared at each other.

"Why did you run away from me?" he said.

"I thought you were somebody else. I was being chased."

Then I had to explain everything, about coming from Erin and our arrival on *Paddy's Fortune* and Walter

Hamilton's murder, but before I was fairly begun on that I started to worry about the light that Mel Fury was holding. Sean Wilgus and the others could use it to home in on me.

"Turn that off!" I said.

"If you insist." He sounded cool and superior.

The light vanished. After a few seconds I realized that I could still see a little. Although we were close to the pole this was a tiny world, and some sunlight was being scattered in by the translucent shield of *Paddy's Fortune*. There would never be around-the-clock total darkness, even at the bottom of a narrow crevice. So much for my idea that I could be free from pursuit.

"They may still be after me," I said. "We have to find somewhere safer than this."

"No problem." He stood up and hitched his backpack into position. "Let's go. I'm getting hungry anyway."

The crack in the surface that I had fallen into was only the width of my outstretched arms. I followed Mel Fury along the uneven floor of it, testing a sore ankle and rubbing my skinned knuckles as we slanted upward. As we went I thought about his last comment. He might be hungry, but I was *starving*.

We emerged onto the surface, and I stared all around me.

"I haven't seen anything you can eat anywhere." I kept my voice to a whisper—there was no knowing where the crew members of the *Cuchulain* might be. "Do you catch the animals and eat them?"

Fury gave a condescending snigger. "What a disgusting idea! Of course I don't. I eat regular food. You'll see, if you'll just be patient. And walk *quietly,* for heaven's sake. No wonder you worry about being followed."

It was a mystery. He seemed to glide through the vegetation without disturbing it at all. I tried to imitate his way of walking, and at the same time explained to him in a tense whisper where we had come from, and what we were doing on *Paddy's Fortune.*

"Where?" he said. And, when I told him how we came to call the worldlet that, *"Paddy's Fortune?* That's ridiculous. This place doesn't need a name. It already has one."

"What is it called?"

"Home."

Home? Well, that struck me as one of the dumbest names I had heard in a long time. But I didn't have a chance to say so, because we were emerging into full daylight and Mel Fury had turned to face me. His thin, dirty face wore a superior, skeptical expression.

"If there are people chasing you," he said, "which I'm inclined to doubt, and *if* they are *really* as dangerous as you say—which I'm inclined to doubt even more—then we'd better be careful. We're going to be in sunlight for the next few minutes. So no more talking until we get there."

"Get *where?"*

"To the access point. And I said, *no more talking*—until we're inside."

It was obvious that Mel Fury didn't believe we were in danger. He was just using that as an excuse to boss me around. His attitude would change a few minutes later, though not in a way that could give me any pleasure.

We had been heading steadily toward the equator, with Maveen higher and higher in the sky. I was itching to talk, full of a thousand questions, but I managed to hold my tongue. Until suddenly Mel Fury stopped and inclined his head to the left. "Someone. Voices. Over that way."

I couldn't hear a thing. And if I had, the last thing I would have done is head *toward* trouble. But that's what he did, snaking silently through a dense ferny growth with spiky leaves and blue flowers at the top. I had no choice but to follow.

Soon I could hear voices, too. Or at least one voice. It was Sean Wilgus, loud and high-pitched. I wanted to back away, but Mel Fury went on moving forward on his hands and knees. I slowly crawled after him, until at last he halted.

We had come to a roughly oval area where the ferny plants diminished from head-high to knee-high. Fury and I, lying flat on our bellies and out of sight, had a worm's-eye view of the whole clearing. Sean Wilgus stood at one side, a gun in his hand—the same gun, I was sure, that had killed Walter Hamilton. On the other side, arms folded and massaging his biceps, stood Danny Shaker. His knees and elbows were crusted with mud and his hair hung damp over his forehead, but he had a half-smile on his face. And now I could hear his voice, too.

"I'm accused of many things, Sean," he was saying. "And some of them are even true. But not what you've been saying."

"You're the only one as thinks so." Sean Wilgus's voice was angry, but he also sounded nervous. "You can't deny it. Drag us to the ass-end of the universe, promise us wealth, promise us a new ship, promise us women—"

"Not me, Sean. I said no such things. It was others made up all those. I told you I *hoped* that we'd find something valuable on this trip, but I said there was a good chance we'd receive no more than our pay—and very good pay, as you well know."

Wilgus didn't seem to hear him. "All this way," he went on, "for nothing, in a ship that's on her last legs. You know the *Cuchulain*'s not what it was. A few more trips, the engines will be done for. And you drag us out here."

"True enough. The *Cuchulain* is creaking at the joints. But that's exactly why we gambled on a trip to the Maze. We need more money than we'd get from a dozen scrounging trips for light elements, if we're to get the *Cuchulain* in shape." Shaker had not raised his voice. He sounded relaxed, almost soothing. "But don't change the subject on me. You've never said one word to answer *my* accusation, Sean. Are you going to? You can't deny you killed Walter Hamilton, others vouched for it. Aye, and for all I know you killed young Jay Hara, too, and hid his body. You say it was all done in self-defense, but I don't accept that. You have a temper, Sean. I think you killed in anger. If you didn't, then let me hear you deny it."

"I did it to protect myself. Hamilton was going to shoot me. I never touched Jay Hara."

"So you say." Shaker finally moved, but only to shift his hands from his biceps to his trouser pockets. He took one step, to lean forward balanced on the balls of his feet. "But you're a good crewman, Sean, and one that we need. So I'm going to give you the benefit of the doubt. Hand over your gun now, and let me make sure you don't have another one hidden away somewhere. Then I'll let you go back to work as one of the crew. There'll be no more firearms for you, though, on this trip."

Wilgus hesitated. "And no punishment?"

"That's for all the crew to decide. I'll not make that decision alone."

"Bullshit! You control them, and you know it."

Danny Shaker sighed and took his left hand out of his trouser pocket. He held it palm up toward Wilgus. "The gun, Sean. Let me have it."

Sean Wilgus lifted the gun he was holding. But instead of offering it handle-first, he sighted it at Danny Shaker. I could not see his face, but his arm was trembling.

Shaker laughed. "A shoot-out?" he said. "Now, Sean, you know me better than that. You know I've never been one to carry firearms." He might have been saying that he didn't like artichokes, or wearing green shirts, for all the tension and worry in his voice. He took three more steps forward, so that he was no more than fifteen feet from Sean Wilgus. "The gun. Come on, man, be sensible. Hand it over."

"No."

Shaker took another couple of steps. "Don't do something you're going to regret, Sean. Give me that gun."

Wilgus nodded. But he wasn't going to obey Shaker's order. I could see his finger tightening on the trigger. I was tempted to leap up and shout a warning to Danny Shaker. No matter what I thought he had done, I couldn't see him shot down in cold blood.

It was too late. I heard two shots, and instinctively flinched. When I looked up again at Danny Shaker, he was still standing exactly where he had been.

I couldn't believe my eyes. Wilgus, incredibly, had missed.

And then I glanced over to Sean Wilgus, and saw him crumpling silently to the ground. His face turned my way, and I could see the two holes, one next to his nose and one in the middle of his forehead.

Danny Shaker removed his right hand from his trouser pocket and stared down at the white-handled pistol he was holding. He walked forward to stand by Sean Wilgus and shook his head.

"I told you I've never been one to carry firearms, Sean," he said quietly to the body at his feet. "And that's no more than simple truth. If I took Walter Hamilton's gun when I was trying to decide for myself how he died, well, some would say this was no more than justice."

I wondered if Wilgus was dead, or just pretending, because Danny Shaker was chatting to him as though the two of them were sitting down having a drink together. His next words ended that illusion.

"Rest in peace, Sean. You'll never know how sad it made me to press that trigger. A good worker, you were, maybe the best on the ship. But with one fatal flaw, the temper you never could control. What a waste of human talent." Shaker shook his head and glanced thoughtfully down at his own person. "Aye, and not only that. There's goes a perfectly good pair of trousers, too."

He ran his fingers over the bullet holes in the cloth, stuck the pistol back in his pocket, and bent to take Sean Wilgus's gun from the crewman's dead hand. As he straightened up he slowly turned, through a full circle. I had a moment of complete terror when I was sure he knew we were there and

was going to come across to us. Then he gave the odd, fluting
whistle that I had first heard from him on the Muldoon Port
ferry site. I heard a far-off answering whistle. Shaker gave the
call again, bowed his head toward Sean Wilgus, and pushed
his way into the ferns.

All during the confrontation in the clearing I had taken
no notice of Mel Fury, nor he I think of me. We had lain side
by side, silent and frozen as statues. As Danny Shaker
vanished I turned my head. Fury's face beneath its layer of
dirt was an awful pale-green color, and he seemed ready to
throw up. I doubt if I looked any better. In all my life I had
seen only three dead men, and two of those had been
murdered in my presence within the past twenty-four hours.

Mel Fury stood up, nodded vaguely at me, and stepped
carefully into the clearing. He circled its boundary, keeping
well away from the body of Sean Wilgus. So did I. If Wilgus
had another weapon on him, as Danny Shaker had suggested, I did not have the nerve to search him for it.

Fury headed south again through the ferns. I stayed close
behind. I had lost all desire to talk. There would be a time for
questions—when we were somewhere safe. My appetite had
vanished, too, although I felt totally hollow inside.

We were close to the equator of *Paddy's Fortune* when Fury
hopped across a little ditch, no more than two feet wide.
"Here we are," he said softly. "Stand still while we're sensed
and we'll go inside. Whatever you do, don't move once
you're on it."

I followed him, stared around, and saw that the ditch was
in the form of a complete circle with the two of us standing
within its boundary. The plants beneath my feet were a dwarf
version of the familiar blue-flowered fern, and the earth
beneath was soft and spongy.

Nothing new—except that while the thought was in my
head I realized that we were sinking. Not *into* the surface,
which was my immediate worry, but *with* the surface. A circle
of ground within the ditch was descending, and us with it.

I crouched, ready for an instinctive jump to get clear, but Fury grabbed my arm. We rode together, down and down, until the ground was level with my eyes, and then far above me. It was suddenly darker. I was peering into shadowy gloom as Fury pulled me forward, off the soft ground and onto some rigid surface. The circle we had been standing on changed its direction of travel, rising until it blocked the light from above and left me standing in frightening darkness. I thought of flesh-crawling horror stories of my childhood, with their trolls and goblins and trogs, the creatures that lived underground among the roots of trees and drank human blood.

And then lights came on all around us, and I found myself standing in a big room whose walls, floor and furnishings looked like nothing more than the internal partitions and fixtures of the *Cuchulain*.

We were "inside." Mel Fury, filthier than ever—I saw new streaks of mud on his backpack and clothes and skinny white arms and legs—was heading for the door of the chamber. I had no choice but to follow. But as the door slid open at our approach, I couldn't help wondering: Was I going to be any better off here than wandering the surface of *Paddy's Fortune*, pursued by Danny Shaker and his cutthroat helpers?

CHAPTER **19**

The first thing I saw beyond the door was as familiar in a way as anything could be; when Mel Fury and I went into the next room I found myself facing two filthy, straggle-haired stick figures.

One of them was me.

The whole opposite wall was metal, shiny and flat enough to be a good mirror. My reflection's face was a mask of mud interrupted by red scratches and welts, and my arms and legs showed through rents in my pants and jacket. I was in worse shape than Mel.

He did not stop to stare but gestured to the right, where the wall held a matched set of doors.

"It's a real pain," he said, "but we have to do it before we'll be fed dinner. Better get it over with. Take the one next to me."

He went through a door and closed it behind him. After a moment's hesitation I went through a neighboring one. I found myself in a little cubicle without windows or furnishings. There was an exit door at the opposite end, and a hatch by my right hand with two handles set above it.

What was I supposed to do next? The door in front of me

resisted my push, so after a few moments I turned one of the handles. Before I could move, jets of hot water were hitting me from all sides. I yelped in surprise and turned the handle the other way. The water jets cut off at once.

A shower; except for the controls it was not much different from the low-gravity units on the *Cuchulain*. The hatches below the controls ought to dispense clean clothes and take away dirty ones.

I emptied my pockets. Walter Hamilton's book was damp, but it was designed to work in all weathers. And if Paddy Enderton's computer had been able to survive a night of snow and slush in the bottom of the boat by Lake Sheelin, a brief wetting was unlikely to hurt it. I put them both on a shelf high above the level of the water jets, and stripped to the skin.

Three minutes later, laved in streams of hot water and then dried in the jets of warm air that followed, I felt ready to lie down on the floor of the cubicle and go to sleep. I also felt ready to cry, something I had not done since I was nine years old. It had been a terrible day. Only the conviction that cocky Mel Fury would mock me if I wept kept me dry-eyed.

I finally opened the hatch and placed my wet and filthy clothes inside it. They dropped out of sight, and I had a worrying minute until new ones rolled out of a slit in the hatch's rear. The clothes were clean, the same light-grey that Mel Fury had been wearing, and by some mystery they were exactly the same size and style as the ones that I had removed, even to being a little bit short in the legs. But there was no sign of shoes. My old, soaked ones had gone, and for the moment I would have to go barefoot.

I retrieved the book and computer from the shelf and looked unsuccessfully for some way to comb my wet hair. At last I gave up and pushed it back off my forehead with my fingers. While I was doing that, the door in front of me opened by itself.

When I went through and saw what was in the room

beyond, I had one of those strange moments in life when about eighteen thoughts at once hit you so fast and chaotic you don't know which came first.

I saw Mel Fury waiting for me, clean and dry and newly dressed—and barefoot—in the middle of a big low-ceilinged room with bright yellow walls and half a dozen doors. Without the coating of mud and grime, his face was pale, as though he had never been out in the sun. I realized that he really hadn't, compared with me, because *Paddy's Fortune* was so far away from Maveen. Around Mel stood a dozen other people. They were all about the same age, all dressed the same, and every one as skinny and pale as Mel. At first glance they looked identical, though I later realized they were all very different. Every one of them was staring expectantly in my direction.

I said *people*. But then I realized it was not just people. They were *females*. And not just females. *Girls*. More girls than I had ever seen in one place in my whole life.

And—at last—I caught on. Mel Fury, now that she was cleaned up, had to be a girl, too, though her hair was close-cropped where the others wore theirs long. I had been fooled by that, but even more by the fact that when I met Mel she was dirty and wild and energetic, running uncontrolled through the jungle growth of *Paddy's Fortune*. Girls didn't do that! Girls were delicate and protected and pampered. Girls were *never* exposed to any risk of being injured.

And then my other seventeen thoughts came roaring in. *Paddy's Fortune*. I never had been able to swallow Doctor Eileen's idea that Paddy Enderton would have a scrap of interest in Godspeed Base or a Godspeed Drive. But women—or girls who would soon be women—*that* would be interesting indeed, and worth a fortune, too, if Enderton could play it right. Up on the surface of the world at this very moment were crewmen who shared completely Paddy's point of view. I had heard them talking aboard the *Cuchulain*. Except maybe for Danny Shaker, whose thoughts remained a mystery to me, there was no doubt what each one of them was after: Women. And the crewmen above our heads were searching and scouring the planetoid for anything out of the ordinary. One of them, sooner or later, was sure to find himself standing on the access point. When that happened . . .

"That circle we stood on," I burst out. "Up on the the surface. Could anybody stand on it, and be carried down here?"

All the girls were staring at me. I had never received so much concentrated attention in my whole life. But Mel Fury answered quickly enough.

"Only humans," she replied. "Not animals. The sensors won't respond for them. And you have to stand still for at least half a minute before anything happens."

"Can it be locked in position? So it won't work."

Mel caught on to the reason for my question even if no one else did. She turned questioningly to the tallest girl in the group, who said "I can ask the controller." But she went on staring at me, and didn't move until Mel added, "It could be urgent, Sammy. There are other people outside *Home*. Dangerous people—I saw someone killed. We have to try to close the access points."

That started a general buzz of excitement. As the tall girl hurried out through one door I was surrounded by everyone else and swept away through another. They all started to talk at once, asking me questions as we went to another room with tables and chairs all around the walls. I had a thousand questions of my own. But everyone had to wait, because Mel Fury pushed me toward a chair, sat down next to me, and said fiercely, "Let him *breathe*, will you. And eat. He hasn't had any food for days."

And then, as hot food appeared from serving hatches in the wall, she sat down next to me—and promptly began to ask questions of her own. The others stayed to eat, listen, and make comments to each other. Apparently I was accepted for the moment as Mel's prize.

The food looked fine, but it tasted subtly different from anything on Erin or the *Cuchulain*. I was too starved to be choosy, and in any case the girls seemed to find nothing odd about it. So I ate and ate, and talked and talked. There was plenty to explain: about Erin and the Forty Worlds, about why we had come here, about Danny Shaker and the cutthroat crew of the *Cuchulain*, about the Godspeed Drive and the search for Godspeed Base.

That last bit stopped them cold. It was clear that they had never even *heard* of a Godspeed Drive. The chance that this worldlet was Godspeed Base, with a starship somewhere inside it, dropped suddenly to zero. They didn't even seem *interested* in the idea of a star drive.

But when I told of Paddy Enderton's discovery of the scoutship with two dead women on board, the room went completely silent.

"Our people," Mel Fury said at last. "They left *Home* to try to find another world with people on it. The controller didn't want them to go—there had been others, you see, and no one had ever come back. They were the last big ones. But they were determined. And they couldn't be stopped by us, because they were the oldest. Well, now we are."

That made no sense at all, but every minute less and less did. I wasn't just *tired* at this point, I was exhausted, and with lots of food inside me and the adrenalin level ebbing, no amount of excitement would keep my eyes open much longer.

"You are the *oldest?*" I made a final effort. "What about your parents?"

But I didn't get an answer, because at that moment Sammy came hurrying into the room.

"There's no way of closing the access points permanently," she said.

"So someone could get in any time?" Mel Fury asked.

"Normally they could." Sammy gave me a self-satisfied grin. "But the access points remain closed automatically when it's raining outside. So I asked for the longest surface rain the controller can give us. We'll have it for six full revolutions of *Home.*"

I closed my eyes and tried to translate that to a time I was familiar with. My brain would not cooperate—and when I tried to open my eyes, they too refused to obey. I was ready to collapse. And suddenly hands were lifting and carrying me out of the room. I was finally placed face-up on a soft surface, my new clothes were loosened, and my pockets emptied. A dozen hands touched all over my body, and I heard whispers and giggling.

I went on with my hopeless mental struggle to convert six revolutions of *Paddy's Fortune* to something I understood. The best I could manage was to decide that it sounded like a long time.

My last thought was an odd sort of satisfaction. I might not be safe, not really. But if the murderous crew of the *Cuchulain* were still searching for me, out on the surface, they were being soaked by steady rain. I knew how much they would like *that.*

Serve them right.

Doctor Eileen told me to describe anything I saw that was unfamiliar. Well, here is a fact I learned since I left Erin: When you are at home and things are quiet and something new comes along, you can describe it pretty well; but when *everything* around you is new, you won't take it all in no matter how much you want to.

So I'll just have to do the best I can.

I opened my eyes with only the vaguest idea of where I was, or how much time had gone by since I passed out. Then I lay for a few minutes idly rubbing and scratching myself.

Only after a satisfying scratch did two thoughts come drifting into my head.

First, the crew of the *Cuchulain,* no matter what, must never be allowed to suspect that I had vanished beneath the surface of the planetoid. I was beginning to realize exactly what they would do if they found Mel and the other girls.

Second, I had to meet the controller. The girls inside Home seemed to accept his—or more likely, *her*—word as law.

The room I was in contained its own bathroom. I used that and came out casually fixing my pants—then finished in a big hurry when I saw Mel Fury sitting on the bed I had just left.

"How did you know I was awake?"

"Monitors." She pointed up to the ceiling.

I recalled my very personal scratching, and wondered how much she had seen. And were there monitors in the bathroom, too? But that gave me an idea. "Is there any way to see what's happening *outside,* up on the surface?"

"Not directly. The controller must have sensors, but I don't know how to use them."

The controller again. That was where I had to start. I wanted all my questions about *Paddy's Fortune* answered, but it was not the most urgent thing in the world. Top priority was to make sure that the crewmen didn't find a way in. A close second was to send a message to Doctor Eileen, telling her all that had happened and warning her.

"Can you take me to meet the controller? Right now?"

"Well . . . if you really have to."

"I do."

She stared at me a little oddly, as though a meeting with the controller was to be more shunned than sought. But she led the way out of the room—and into mystery.

Paddy's Fortune was the worldlet that the *Cuchulain* had found its way to, and I continued to think of it that way. But *Home* was really the *inside* of that worldlet, a series of concentric habitation shells that honeycombed the interior. As Mel led me toward the middle of *Home,* I lost my grip on reality. I smelled peculiar odors like burning feathers and molten metal, heard horrible (to my ears) music coming out of nowhere, saw a thousand gadgets so unfamiliar I could not even guess their use, and at every turn I watched little blond heads poke around corners, stare at me, and then vanish. They were the other residents in *Home.* But on the plus side Mel had the time to answer enough questions to satisfy some of my personal curiosity.

For example, Mel and Sammy and the other big girls all turned out to be exactly the same age: fifteen years and two months. No one on *Home* now was older than that, not since the scoutship left with its pair of nineteen-year-olds. But there were plenty of younger children: ten-year-olds, and six years, and one year. Exactly fifteen of each. It seemed to me that I had seen every one in the past half hour.

"But *parents,"* I said. "And who looks after the babies?"

Mel Fury didn't answer in words. She changed her path down the long corridors and moving ramps that spiraled toward the center of *Home,* to take us past the wombs, creches, nurseries and schoolrooms.

I stared in through viewing windows, to where little mechanical figures like cleaning robots hustled back and forth, feeding and changing and teaching. Not a human in sight, except for the babies themselves. At Mel's insistence, I inspected an array of fertilized eggs, each with its etched label and in its low-temperature bath.

"They're all girls!" I said.

She nodded, but she seemed embarrassed. "Well, they are, but they don't have to be. There's frozen sperm, loads of it. It doesn't occupy more than a few cubic millimeters of storage, so you won't see it."

And who decided when an egg would be fertilized and a new child added to *Home*'s population?

Mel told me, but I should have guessed for myself. The

same agent who did everything else on *Home*. Fertilization
decisions, along with air content and surface rain and the
food supply and each child's individual education program,
were the job of the controller. Mel told me that her own
presence out on the surface of *Paddy's Fortune* had been an
education elective, something that few other girls wanted.
She enjoyed the privacy and the wild feeling of the jungle.

Wild, when the location of every crevice—maybe the size
of every plant, and the timing of every drop of rain—was
decided by the controller?

My growing bewilderment finally ended. "Here we are,"
Mel said. "This is the controller's main room." She sounded
uneasy as she led me to a circular chamber about a quarter of
the size of every other one. There was a tall vertical cylinder
in the middle, surrounded by a narrow round table and half
a dozen angular chairs. Other than that the place was empty.

I turned to Mel, but before I could speak I heard a
pleasant female voice. "Sit down," it said to me, "in the
white chair. Make yourself comfortable. As for you, Mel Fury,
you will be punished later. You have been warned, many
times, about unauthorized trips to the outside. Yet you
continue to make them."

So there was the reason for Mel's discomfort. And so
much for her "education elective." She had been running
wild when she found me, just the way I suspected. The
difference that I had sensed between her and the other girls
was apparently a real one.

But at the moment I had bigger worries. I sat down in the
white middle chair, and at once thin wires as fine as spider
silk crept out from its arms to swathe themselves around my
body. They tickled my arms and neck, and touched my ears
and scalp. "Relax," the voice said again, "you will not be
harmed. This is for inspection only."

I didn't relax, but I did kind of collapse and sag down in
my seat. Of course I should have realized, long before, that
the controller had to be a machine. No human could do the

thousand and one jobs that the controller performed. We had control computers on Erin, even if they were not this capable.

Well, why *didn't* I realize it? Because so much was different here, it was easy to make the mistake of assuming that *nothing* learned on Erin was likely to apply.

Anyway, the *Home* controlling computer really *was* different. It was kind of creepy, to sit and chat with a machine just as though it was a human being. For one thing, you didn't know where to *look*. I stared at the vertical cylinder, for lack of anything better, but I had no reason to believe the controller's computer "brain," if it had a brain, sat in there. More likely, the controller was spread all over the interior. For another thing, no computer on Erin was a hundredth as advanced as this. If it hadn't been for Mel, sitting there and talking to that machine as though it was the most natural thing in the world, I don't know if I could have handled it. But anything she could do, I decided I could match.

So I talked with the controller. I didn't think it was God, though, the way that Mel and the other girls seemed to. She had bossed me around since we met, any chance she got, but now even feisty Mel sat meek as a mouse. No wonder. I learned that the controller set their whole lives for them—or tried to: everything but the time they would die, and maybe that, too, eventually, although they had no experience of it, because no one had been developed in the wombs and born inside *Home* until twenty years ago, when the controller had initiated a female birth program.

"Why no boys?" I asked, when it told me that everyone was a girl. It seemed like an obvious question, but Mel stared at me in amazement. To her, I guess it seemed natural that people should be female.

"My analysis of *Home* and its resources suggested that male children might actually be physically preferred here," the controller said softly. "Examination of you confirms this. However, for psychological reasons the female choice was made, at least until such time as external contact had been reestablished; which has now occurred.''

That statement about male children being physically preferred turned out to be important, but I missed its significance at the time because I thought that the ''external contact'' the controller was talking about was Danny Shaker and his crew. I was struck dumb with horror, until I realized the controller was actually referring to *me*. But recalling yesterday, which today's weird events had made like some awful dream, started me worrying again about Doctor Eileen and the rest of our party. I had to warn them that Danny Shaker and his men were killers, and now the presence of two dead bodies on *Paddy's Fortune* provided evidence that could not be talked away.

I decided it would take days to explain everything to the controller—I had been explaining for Mel since we met, and I still hadn't finished. So this time I didn't even want to try.

Instead I said, ''I need to return to the outside, as soon as possible, and leave this world.''

It was a reasonable request, and I saw no reason why the controller would object. After all, *I* wasn't one of its precious charges, raised from some frozen fertilized egg.

But instead of answering at once, which it had done in every other case, the controller remained silent. To my relief, the web of wires that had enmeshed my body retreated back into the arms of the chair. I was free to wriggle nervously in my seat—and I did.

''Tell me why you came here,'' the controller said at last.

So much for my idea of a quick and easy escape to the surface. I had to start all over again, with the whole messy explanation that I had given Mel.

This time it went a lot faster, though, because unlike Mel the controller didn't interrupt me with a stupid question every two seconds. It knew all about the Forty Worlds, in far more detail than I did. It also apparently contained detailed data on every worldlet in the Maze. I decided it was a lot smarter than Mel and the other girls—particularly when I got to the Godspeed Drive and our journey to search for it.

The controller took that idea in its stride. "This world was established as a biological reserve against future need, which has now arrived, never as a reservoir of space hardware. There is no Godspeed Drive on *Home.*"

That news was going to devastate Doctor Eileen—if ever I had the chance to tell her. And if I had been Mel Fury, I would not have been pleased by my role as part of a sort of as-required supply house for humans. But the controller was continuing: "There may be no Godspeed Drive anywhere in the Maveen system. If there is, that information is not available here."

And then, just when I was ready to sink into the gloom of a wasted months-long journey, it added: "There is, however, a logical place to look. There are several related references in data storage that possess space hardware associations."

I could hardly breathe. "References—to places? In the Forty Worlds system?"

"It is not clear that all are places. They are names: the Net, the Needle, the Eye . . . The Net lies within the Forty Worlds system, and even within the Maze itself. It carries a designation as a 'hardware reservoir.' "

"Do you know how to get there?"

"Coordinates are available for the Net. However, the information is not easily conveyed orally. You must use a navigation aid. This one is appropriate."

A little machine no bigger than my hand came scuttling out of nowhere and extruded long, spindly legs that brought it up to the level of the table. Just when I was thinking that this was the most peculiar-looking navigation aid I could imagine, it reached out a thin arm and placed in front of me a flat black oblong and a little silver box.

I was speechless as I fumbled in my pocket and brought out an identical copy of the plastic object sitting before me: Paddy Enderton's mystery "calculator/display unit."

Naturally, I then had to explain how I came by *that*, and again reveal the news of the death of the two women on the scoutship. This time I was wide awake instead of totally exhausted, so I could observe the distress on Mel's face. The controller's voice showed no sign of emotion, and I assume it could feel none—or perhaps it just had no way to show it.

"Take the new one," it said, when I was done. "This navaid has been loaded with information about the Net itself, also with all that is known, conjectured, or rumored about the Godspeed Drive. Connect the aid to your navigator and it will define an optimum trajectory to the Net. Take the silver box also. The capsules that it contains are diet supplements. Swallow one each morning after you leave here, until none is left."

After you leave. I was going to be allowed to leave *Paddy's Fortune!* And the sooner the better. I absolutely had to get all this new information back to Doctor Eileen and Jim Swift.

But there were problems. I picked up the little plastic wafer and fingered the familiar indents on its surface. "We don't have a navigator on our ship. I mean, we do—but it's a *person,* not a machine. I don't have anywhere to connect this."

"Then you must employ it in manual mode. You know how to interact with it directly?"

"Not really. I tried for days and days."

"I know how!" Mel Fury exclaimed. "I've trained on those for years. I can do it."

Maybe she had, and maybe she could, but the last thing I wanted was Mel Fury up on the surface with me, or worse yet on the *Cuchulain.* She was a female. One sniff of a woman—or even a young girl—and the crew of the *Cuchulain* would be wild beasts. Mel had no idea of the risk she proposed to run.

Fortunately, the controller was on my side. "You appear to be suggesting that you might accompany Jay Hara away from *Home,*" it said to Mel. "That is forbidden. The biological reserve must not be further depleted." And then to me, "She cannot go, but you are expendable. Therefore you must learn to use the navaid yourself. It should not be difficult, even for someone of your limited capacities."

I realize it makes no sense to dislike a machine, but there are limits. After those last couple of cracks, I would never feel the same about the controller of *Paddy's Fortune.*

CHAPTER 20

Looking back, I see my time inside *Home* as a dream, a strange period where everything was touched with fantasy.

Strangest of all, I had the illusion of *safety*. Certainly, I knew that danger walked the surface above my head, and at any moment some crewman might find a way to the interior. But everything else around me was so different from what I knew, danger became unreal, too. Inside *Home* I could think about Danny Shaker rationally, even affectionately, and wonder if I was totally misjudging him. As Mel Fury pointed out, Shaker had killed Sean Wilgus only to defend himself, and it was no more than his good fortune that he happened to have acquired Walter Hamilton's gun to do it with. She did not see him as a cold-blooded killer. When she talked that way, I had trouble with the idea myself.

Well, all dreams ended six hours after my session with the controller. Reality came back like a plunge into cold lake water as I watched the circle of plant-covered earth descend toward me, stepped onto it, and was lifted through the access point to the drenched surface of *Paddy's Fortune*.

I was dressed again in my torn and ragged clothes. They were clean now, but that would not last long in the mud and undergrowth. In my pockets I had Walter Hamilton's electronic book and the new navigation aid. The hours of tutoring that Mel Fury had given me were not nearly enough, but at least I knew how to read out the coordinates and general information I needed. I would have liked instruction in the hundred other capabilities that the navaid possessed, but I dared not stay longer in the interior. The rain on the surface had ended. Danny Shaker, if no one else, would suspect the truth if the search for me continued unsuccessful for much longer.

Maveen was rising. In its pale dawn light I stared around me at the world of *Paddy's Fortune.*

The tall vegetation was water-logged and bowed down, and the ground underfoot was a swamp into which I sank ankle-deep. The controller had certainly done its job in providing rain.

Now I had to do *my* job. When I described the plan to Mel Fury she frowned and shook her head, although I made it sound simple and straightforward. I would return to the surface at the access point closest to the cargo beetle in which I had landed. From there, according to the controller, all I had to do was head slightly north of east, almost toward the rising sun. In a few minutes I would see the beetle itself. Then it was a matter of lying low, waiting until the beetle was unattended so that I could go aboard. I was sure that I knew enough to fly it away from the surface of *Paddy's Fortune* and up to the translucent shield. Even if I had trouble after that, I could send my warning to Doctor Eileen and the others aboard the *Cuchulain.*

Simple and straightforward—in principle. The trouble began with the first step I took on the surface. I had to assume that the crewmen were still hunting for me, so I dared not lift my head above the plants. But now the leaves were so heavy with water that the tops of the tallest plants came only to waist height. I had to squelch along doubled over, moving as silently as I could with one eye out for danger

and the other on the golden circle of Maveen. Twice I had to
detour sideways, to avoid a couple of the long, narrow
crevices that were scattered across the surface of *Paddy's
Fortune*. In such low gravity I could probably have cleared
them with a high, running jump, but I dared not take the risk
of exposure.

After a few minutes the vegetation around me began to
steam in the sunlight. Sweat trickled down my forehead and
into my eyes. My body must have been sweating, too, but I
couldn't be sure because my clothes had been soaked
through in the first steps.

Encouraging myself with the thought that at any moment
I would see the cargo beetle, I plodded on.

And on, and on. Finally I stood up to my full height and
stared ahead over the top of the plants. Nothing.

I stopped and squatted down on my haunches. It *couldn't*
be this far to the beetle. Somehow I had gone astray, too far
north of east or not far enough.

I stood up, turned, and looked back the way I had come.
As the rain water evaporated from the leaves of the plants
they were beginning to lift and straighten. I might be able to
follow my own track to the access point and start over—or I
might not.

But there was really no choice. I had to go back.
Otherwise I would be reduced to wandering randomly
around the surface. Chances were that the crewmen would
then find me long before I found the cargo beetle.

I stood upright, prepared to take a first disconsolate step.

And I saw the topmost leaves swaying, maybe twenty paces
away and directly in front of me.

I froze. If I ran, the noise would make my presence
obvious. If I did not, I would be caught without making any
effort to escape.

The only other option was to stay and fight. That didn't
hold much hope, either, because even if the crewman

following me was as weaponless as I was, any one of them was twice my size.

I took a couple of steps back along my own faint track, eased into a small gap between the plants that grew beside it, and as an afterthought bent down and scooped up a double handful of wet mud. It wasn't much of a weapon, but it was all I had.

I waited.

And heard nothing. It seemed incredible that any of the hulking crewmen, wheezing and broken-winded as they were, could be moving so silently toward me. Maybe what I had seen was no more than one of the little native animals, bustling along at the base of the plants and making their tops shake.

I stood with muscles locked, unable even to wipe the sweat from my eyes. Then, when I had to move or die of unrelieved tension, the curtain of leaves in front of me was swept aside.

"I knew it!" A familiar voice whispered, right in my ear. "You goofbrain. You're totally lost, aren't you?"

I dropped my handful of wet mud, though now I almost wish I had thrown it. Because peering in on me, grinning all over her bony and self-satisfied face, was Mel Fury.

She was mud-spattered and sweaty but she wasn't nervous and breathless, as I was. Mostly, she seemed terribly pleased with herself.

"What do you mean, why did I follow you," she said. "Don't forget I've seen you blundering around out here before. You may have fooled the controller, saying you knew what you were doing, but you sure didn't fool me."

"You'll be in trouble when you go back." We were both talking in whispers.

"Of course I will. Big trouble. *If* I go back."

"You can't come! You mustn't follow me any more."

"Follow you!" Her voice was fiercely indignant. "You dummy. If you're going anywhere on this world, I'll have to *lead* you."

I didn't argue, because she was right. *Paddy's Fortune* was her home ground, and in her rambles she had been over every square meter of it. She knew exactly where we were, exactly how to get to the cargo beetle with minimal exposure. I knew neither where I was, nor where I was going.

We set out, I following in her footsteps as silently as possible. In less than five minutes, she paused. With one finger she pointed up. I saw the top of a cargo beetle, and realized that we were moving through the tall purple-flowered succulent plants that I had seen on our first landing.

I moved to Mel's side and leaned to put my mouth near her close-cropped head. "Is there anyone aboard?"

"How would I know?" Her whisper had the rising tone of irritation. "You should be able to answer that question a lot better than I can."

She was right. But I couldn't. It was something else I had not thought through before I left the interior. I think it was embarrassment more than anything that gave me the resolve to take the next step. I would have to learn the answer to my own question the hard way.

"Wait here. And I mean *wait*. Don't move!"

I crept forward, until I could see the whole of the cargo beetle and the area in front of its entry port. There was no sign of anyone now, but plenty of evidence of earlier activity. The plants in the area around the port were trampled flat, and the ground beneath them was mashed into mud like a hog wallow.

I could guess what had happened. When the heavy rain began, the crewmen would have refused to remain unsheltered on the open surface. They would have rushed back here, and waited in the cargo beetle until the storm was over. Then they had gone off again to hunt me down.

The big question was, had anyone stayed behind, to sleep or eat or keep watch?

I couldn't answer that. All I could do was wait, knowing that Mel Fury was becoming more and more impatient behind me. At last I couldn't stand it any longer myself. I tiptoed forward through the disgusting squishy mud, until I could stand at the side window and see through to the interior. It was completely empty, and the rush of relief that gave me is indescribable.

I turned and nodded. It was not necessary to speak—Mel was sure to be watching my every move. Without waiting for her to appear I went to the hatch and climbed into the beetle.

As soon as I was inside I knew that I had been right. The crew *had* been here during the rain—there was mud and mess everywhere. But the area over by the control panel was relatively clear, and that was all I cared about. I went across to it and scanned it briefly, making sure that I knew what I had to do to take off. I didn't want another debacle, when I stood baffled and Mel Fury snootily watched my hopeless incompetence.

In less than half a minute I knew it was going to be all right. I could fly the beetle, no doubt about it.

I turned in triumph to Mel, who was climbing in through the hatch, wiping her shoes fastidiously at the entrance and slipping off her brown leather backpack. She stared around in disgust at the mess.

"Don't your robots take care of this for you?" she complained. "It's revolting."

"No robots here. But never mind that now." She was moving too slowly for my taste. "Come on, Mel, close that door and let's go. We can worry about cleaning up later."

"No need for hurry, Jay," a deeper voice said.

I went rigid with surprise and horror, and ran for the hatch.

It was too late. Danny Shaker, neat as the cabin was messy,

was already stepping into the beetle. As I watched, he turned and slammed the hatch shut.

"There," he said. "I'm sure that's what you were proposing to do anyway. But let's make it with me inside, shall we, and not out?"

It was absolutely typical of Danny Shaker. The other three crew members had been mad with impatience during the long rain storm, and at the end of it had insisted on dashing out to search for me. He had gone outside, too—about twenty steps. There he had made himself comfortable, and waited.

"It's the old principle, Jay," he said. "If you want to catch a bear, one way is to go and thrash through the woods looking. That's what the lads insisted on doing, they can't bear inaction. But an easier way is to set out a delicacy the bear wants more than anything else in the world, and then sit by it and wait. This cargo beetle was what you wanted most of all, to take you back to the *Cuchulain* and Doctor Xavier. How could you possibly have resisted it?"

He smiled at me, then nodded his head toward Mel. "But I must say, it was a real surprise for you to show up with a friend. You found a way to the interior, didn't you? And now I have to ask myself the important question: Is the inside of this worldlet Godspeed Base, and did you find a Godspeed Drive?"

Shaker was sitting in the pilot's chair, where I had been. Mel and I stood against the beetle wall, farthest from the port. He had told us to do that, and although I saw no sign of a weapon neither Mel nor I made any move to rush him. She didn't know him, and I knew him too well.

"It's not," I said desperately. "I mean, it's not Godspeed Base, and there's no Godspeed Drive here."

"Mm." Shaker sat rocking in the swivel seat, fondling his

biceps. "Nice to see you so cooperative, but you weren't listening closely. I said, I had to ask *myself* that question, not you." He pointed a finger at Mel. "What's your name?"

"Mel—Mel . . . Fury." No cockiness in her expression now.

"Well, Mel Fury, there's an old technique I've used often in the past to make sure people are telling the truth."

I gasped, and he glanced at me reprovingly.

"Now really, Jay, you should know better than to suspect me of barbarism. I'm talking of something quick, and painless, and just about foolproof. I want you, Jay, to go outside for a few minutes. And Mel, you stay here with me. Don't be afraid, all I want from you are answers to a few questions. And you, Jay, you can run away if you want to, but I wouldn't advise it. The others of the crew don't believe in the refined approach. Get outside now, and close the hatch. Be quick. For your sake, we want this all over and done with before anyone else gets back here."

I looked at Mel. With her backpack and her skinny, muddied legs and short hair, she didn't resemble any girl from Erin. I wanted to tell her, "Make him think you're a boy! Whatever you do, don't let him suspect that you or anyone else here is a female."

But there was no way to say anything to her at all without Danny Shaker catching every word. I went reluctantly through the hatch and stood outside leaning on the hull of the beetle. Even with my ear pressed against it, I could not hear what was said inside.

The wait seemed endless, though I know from the changing angle of Maveen in the sky that it was no more than a few minutes until the hatch slid open and Shaker was saying, "All right, Jay, back inside."

Mel was sitting down now. Shaker nodded his head toward her and said, "See. Good as ever. So it's your turn, Jay. What do you have to tell me about what you learned when you were inside *Paddy's Fortune?*"

It was obvious what he was doing. If Mel and I were telling the truth, we would have to be consistent with each other. But what had he asked her, and what had she told him?

I made the hardest decision of my life. To keep Danny Shaker and his crew away from the inside of this world, I had to offer something better. Doctor Eileen would have fits if she knew what I was going to do, but I had no choice.

I reached into my pocket and pulled out the navigation aid. "I learned that *Paddy's Fortune* isn't Godspeed Base. But a Godspeed Base and a Godspeed Drive may still exist, at a place called the Net, which seems to be some kind of hardware storage facility. The instructions to get there are inside this."

Danny Shaker took the aid from my hand and stared at it, with no trace of expression on his smooth face. "Did you get this from Paddy Enderton?"

"No." It was a good thing to be able to answer him honestly, because I was never a good liar. "It's like something that Enderton had, but I got this one here."

"You know how to use it?"

"I do. But Mel—he knows it better than I do." *There*. I had slipped in one lie after all.

"Does he now." Shaker turned his sparkling grey eyes to Mel and inspected her closely, while I wondered if I had made another mistake. What I had just said made Mel less likely to be killed, but more likely to be taken away with Shaker from *Paddy's Fortune*. But hadn't I made it *more* likely that I myself would be killed, since I had just stated that Mel was better qualified to use the aid than I was? Surely we would both be useful, even if only as backups to each other.

"Outside. Both of you, this time." Shaker spoke before I had time to consider further permutations. "I need five minutes solo thinking. Stay right by the hatch, now, or don't hold me responsible for the consequences."

He didn't bother to suggest what those might be, and I didn't choose to ask. As soon as we were outside again and the hatch was closed, I turned to Mel. We might not have much time to ourselves, and there were things that had to be said.

"Does he realize you're a girl?"

"Huh?"

At last I had managed to surprise her. "No matter what else Danny Shaker learns, he must never know that you are a female. None of the crew must even *suspect* it. Ever. Understand?"

"No."

"You will, but I've no time to explain now. You didn't tell him?"

"That I'm a girl? No. It never came up. But he asked me if there were females inside *Home.*"

"What did you tell him?"

"The truth, the same as you did—except when you called me a *he.* I said that there are. But I didn't say we're *all* females. Look, I don't see why you're so terrified of lying to him. I'm not."

"That's because you don't know him. He's smart."

"I can see that."

"Deadly smart."

"Then why are we standing talking, instead of running away?"

It was a question without a simple answer. Because I was convinced that Shaker would find a way to track us down? Certainly. Because I felt that Shaker was our only defense against the rest of the *Cuchulain*'s crew? That too. I knew it for a fact in my case, and Mel's sex put her even more at risk. The only place we could run to was the interior of *Paddy's Fortune,* and that would expose everyone in *Home* to the risk that we ran now.

Maybe that was the strongest reason of all, but I had no time to explain any of this to Mel, because the hatch of the beetle was sliding open again. Danny Shaker's head poked out.

"I have a problem," he said. "Come on in, and let me tell you about it. I think I need your help."

Mel stared at me. *He* has a problem? said her look. But she climbed back in through the hatch without a word, and sat down next to me where Danny Shaker indicated.

He sat down opposite us, and began rubbing the fingers of his right hand over the top of the navaid. "First, let me clear a few things out of the way. I don't know how to work this gadget—I don't even see how to turn it on. But I believe that the two of you understand it, and can make it work. Second, I accept that this world is not Godspeed Base. Actually, I decided that for myself a long time ago. *Paddy's Fortune*, inside or outside, does not contain a Godspeed Drive. What it *does* contain I'll come to in a moment, when I tell you my problem.

"Now, the two of you were told that if we follow the directions provided by this thing I'm holding, we'll be led to the *real* Godspeed Base. Fair enough. You may be right, and we *may* find a Godspeed Drive there. I'm not sure I believe it, though I believe *you* believe it. So we have the classic question: The value of the bird in the hand, this world, against the value of the bird in the bush, Godspeed Base."

I knew what Danny Shaker was saying, but apparently Mel didn't, because he looked at her and said, "Sorry, I'll try to make it clearer. What I *know* I will find inside this world has value. What I *may* find if we go somewhere else in the Maze could have enormously more value—almost infinite value, you might say, because I don't know how I would begin to put a price on it. That means there's a calculation to be done: the value of what we have here, compared with the value of what we may find elsewhere, multiplied by the chance that it's there when we arrive. All right?"

Mel nodded.

"Well, I've done that calculation, and the result isn't even close. If it were up to me alone, I'd go for the risk and the big prize. I'd take the coordinates you two feed us, and head for a

new destination and the Godspeed Base. But now let me tell
you my problem.''

Shaker looked right at me, and smiled as though I was his
best friend in the world. "I think Jay recognizes it already. It's
my crew. I told them at the start of all this that we were
heading out to find wealth. Somehow that got twisted, so all
they ever cared about was that we would find *women*. Wealth
to women, see, and nothing I've been able to say has changed
that. At the moment they're as mad as hell at me, because
after coming all this way there's been not a sign of a female.
They're close to mutiny. And now I want them to buckle
down to more hard work in space, heading for another
unknown destination. That will be uphill work. But I might
be able to do it anyway, mixing force and persuasion, so to
speak—so long as they never suspect there are women to be
found *right here.*" He pointed his index finger directly down.
"No more than a few steps, right, if you head in the correct
direction? The big job is to find an entry point, but once you
know one exists that's just a matter of time. If the lads knew
that, they'd go mad. And I'd never get them away from here,
except maybe back to Erin with their prizes. I'm quite sure
we'd not be making another trip to seek Godspeed Base.

"So now let me pull it all together, and tell you how you
can help. Number one: I need Mel Fury to work with the
gadget here, but as far as the crew are concerned Mel Fury
mustn't even exist. They have to think that this world is no
more than the way it looks from the surface, wild and
uninhabited. Certainly with no people.''

"But it's an artificial world," I objected. "Obviously
something inside must keep it going.''

"Obvious to you, Jay. But I've told you before, you're an
exception.''

I felt ridiculously pleased at the compliment, and
wondered why.

"But most don't think that way," Danny Shaker went on,
''so I don't see that as a problem. The existence of Mel Fury is

a problem, though, and that means we have a secret to keep. Mel must be hidden here on the cargo beetle before the crew return—no problem there, I can find a dozen hiding places—and stay out of sight until we get to the *Cuchulain* and are on our way again. All right?"

Mel nodded. I had the feeling that Danny Shaker had her practically hypnotized, but I didn't blame her for that. I had been there myself.

He smiled, as though Mel had just done him the biggest favor in the world, rather than having no choice but to do whatever he said. He turned to me. "As for you, Jay, you'll have to say you gave yourself up, voluntary-like, after nearly starving and dying out on the surface in the rain. And you'll say that after talking with me you want in with us, instead of sticking with Eileen Xavier. I'll tell the crew you gave me this"—he held up the navaid—"that Doctor Eileen had, and that used to belong to Paddy Enderton. But now here's the hardest part." His voice became soft, and he looked right into my eyes. "If we're to carry this off, Jay, Doctor Eileen has to think that way, too. She must believe you've betrayed her. Or it won't work. Can you do it?"

The honest answer was, I didn't know. But I really had no choice, any more than Mel had a choice. What would happen to us if we said no? I had a strong suspicion, but I didn't want to prove I was right.

"I can do it," I said firmly.

What he was asking of me would be unpleasant, especially when I had to face Doctor Eileen, but it didn't sound too difficult. And it seemed to me that Mel and I were coming out of this unbelievably better than I could have imagined just half an hour earlier.

For one thing—the main thing—we were *alive*. And now we would be operating with the protection of Danny Shaker himself. Not only that, we had kept the girls in the interior of *Paddy's Fortune* out of the hands of the crew of the *Cuchulain*.

I understood what that meant, even if Mel did not. It was a major achievement.

As Shaker discussed where to stow Mel safely out of the way in the cargo beetle, in a place where no one was likely to look for her, I felt nothing but relief. And the image of him that I had tried to paint for Mel, as a deadly, heartless killer, was one that I no longer found credible.

Why didn't I question more closely, at least to myself, Shaker's own motives in all of this?

I have no excuses, though I know I was ignoring Tom Toole's comment, that the Chief was a deep one. And I had forgotten, or at least managed to push to the back of my mind, Danny Shaker's own words to his crew, back on board the *Cuchulain, "I'll take the possible value of a live something over the guaranteed zero value of a dead one."*

Maybe that was it. Maybe I refused to reduce my own self-image to that of a mere live something.

CHAPTER **21**

The first job was to find a hiding place for Mel Fury. Shaker stowed her away behind a false bulkhead, tucked away among spare parts for the beetle's drive unit. It was crowded and not too comfortable, but he ordered her not to move or make a sound until he came to get her. By that time, he said, we would be on board the *Cuchulain*.

She nodded cheerfully enough, but I wasn't too happy. I was beginning to wonder about Mel. She had met her very first male—me—only a day or so earlier. A few hours after that she had seen Sean Wilgus killed. Then she had been explicitly forbidden by the controller that ran *Paddy's Fortune* to go back to the surface. She had followed me anyway. And now she acted as though everything was part of some big, exciting game. I decided that either young Mel had a few screws loose in her head, or she was at least ten times as tough as me. Maybe both. Would she sit still when she was asked to?

Then Danny Shaker came up with his own surprise. He wanted *me* out of the way, as well as Mel, when the crewmen returned.

"Just listen closely, and you'll find out why," he said, when I asked him. "Nine-tenths of running a ship, or anything else, is psychological advantage. I don't want you *hidden,* exactly, the way Mel Fury is, but I do want you in a place where you won't be noticed first thing. Aye, and you'd better be given a real job to do, preferably something that everybody hates. This should do fine."

He showed me a hatch in the floor of the cargo beetle. It led to a cramped lower level, a ring-shaped region with a ceiling only a couple of feet high. "That runs around the cargo beetle drive," Shaker said. "It's supposed to be checked for dirt and leaks and general condition every time the beetle flies. But you can imagine Pat O'Rourke or Tom Toole trying to squeeze in there."

Or Jay Hara. But Shaker forced me down through the hatch. "Shouldn't be more than a couple of hours," he said cheerfully. "I expect you to do a decent job of it while you're waiting to come up, too. Otherwise I'll be forced to put you back." He slammed the hatch shut.

I sat on a hard metal floor. At least there was light. Mel would be sitting in the dark. I didn't feel particularly sorry for her.

I did nothing for a few minutes, then began to crawl around the inner wall of the ring. I saw no sign of any breaks, but dirt and junk there was, plenty of it, and I collected it in the bag that Danny Shaker had given me.

I was almost back to where I started when the floor vibrated to footsteps above my head, and I heard voices. I stopped working and sat motionless. I could hear—but if only I had been able to see!

Because an argument was starting up, no more than a few feet away.

"Aye, and look at us." That voice belonged to Joseph Munroe, sulky as ever. "Starved and tired out, with nothing to show for it."

"The galley's on, Joe." Danny Shaker sounded conciliatory. "You'll have hot food in a few minutes."

"And soaked, every one of us. No more dry clothes, either."

"Not until you're back on the *Cuchulain*. I'm sorry, but I didn't expect rain here."

"Or much else that's happened, far as I can see." Munroe raised his voice, from sulky to angry. "I'm going to say this, Dan Shaker, if no one else will. This trip's been a disaster, botched from start to finish. And you can't say we didn't try to warn you. You ignored us."

"Never. I listen to everything any crewman wants to tell me. You know that, Joe, if you'll stop and think."

"What about the woman on board, then? Didn't we all tell you that was asking for bad luck, that nothing good could come of a woman on a ship?" There was a mutter of agreement from the other crewmen, Robert Doonan and Patrick O'Rourke. "And hasn't there been bad luck," Munroe went on, "and more than bad? That scientist fellow dead, and Sean as well."

"Sean Wilgus didn't have to die. It was from his own actions. He killed Dr. Hamilton, and he would have killed me, too."

"Maybe. But Sean was a good crewman, you've said so yourself."

"And I'll say it again, Joe. Sean was first-rate."

"So what do you call that, if not bad luck? A good man gone, with the *Cuchulain* ready to fall apart, and every able-bodied crewman needed to hold it together and fly."

"I know that better than anyone." Shaker didn't raise his voice, but his tone became more intense. *"Hold your distance, Joe Munroe, and listen to me."*

The floor above my head sounded with a sudden clatter of heavy boots. I was in agony. What was going on up there? If only I could *see.*

"Think, before you threaten me." It was Danny Shaker again. "Wasn't I the one who said we needed something more than the usual trip out, something profitable enough for us to afford a complete refit? Didn't we all agree on that, long before we left Erin?—back even when Paddy Enderton was aboard with us. Didn't *you* agree with it, and drink with me to fame and fortune?''

"You had the golden tongue, and you know it. Promising us fortune, more money and women than we knew what to do with—"

"Not women, Joe. I never said one word about women. That came from Paddy, and your own ideas about what he'd found. No, what I promised you was simple: triple wages, guaranteed, and a shot at something more valuable than anything on Erin. I said we'd have a shot at the Godspeed Drive.''

"Godspeed Drive!" There was contempt in Joe Munroe's voice, and again Doonan and O'Rourke were muttering in agreement, louder than before. Even without seeing them, I could sense the swing in mood.

"Aye, you heard me, the Godspeed Drive," Shaker said. He lowered his voice, so I could only just hear him. "You don't understand, even now, what that drive would mean to anyone who had it. All of you, I want you to think about it for a minute. Imagine this: Instead of the poor old *Cuchulain*, staggering along through space for months at a time, you'd have a ship that could whip across the whole Maveen system in *seconds*. From Erin to Antrim, like *that.* " I heard him snap his fingers. "And more than the span of the Forty Worlds. If you couldn't find what you wanted here, you'd be able to take a hop to another star, and find it there. With that sort of power, think about what it would bring to you and me and the rest of the crew. We wouldn't just *do well* on Erin. We'd control the supply of every rare material. We'd make every other ship in the system obsolete. We'd *own* the whole Forty Worlds, and everything in them. You talk about wanting women? People would find you women by the hundred—by the thousand—and push them at you, for a sniff at the sort of power we'd have. All of that, and more. It can be ours—it *will* be ours, once we get to the Godspeed Base. That's my goal now, as it has been all along: Find Godspeed Base, and lay our hands on a ship with the Godspeed Drive."

I thought it was a great speech, but it didn't work.

"Which we'll never do." It was a new voice, and so wheezy and throaty it could only be Robert Doonan. "I don't know where it is and what it is, this hellhole you dragged us to, but I know one thing. It's no more your damned 'Godspeed Base' than I'm the Skibbereen Whore. As for that rotten kid, the one who gave us the coordinates to come here and has had us running all over in the rain and mud for the past two days until we're ready to drop . . . if ever I set eyes on him again, I'll slit his skinny throat."

Doonan stopped, but only to start coughing.

"I hate to say this, but Joe and Robbie are right." It was Pat O'Rourke, his deep voice rumbling. "This can't be the Godspeed Base. Couldn't ever have been. We've been talking, the three of us, and we agree you've done us wrong. It's time for a change. A change of leader."

There was a long silence. I strained my ears, and heard no more than air pumps and the background hum of electrical equipment.

Something was going to happen, I just knew it. But what?

"So it's come to that, has it?" said Danny Shaker at last.

"It has," Pat O'Rourke replied, and the other two murmured assent.

"Well, I'll tell you something, Pat. I'm not a man to stay where he's not wanted. We'll go on back to the *Cuchulain,* and you and the rest can pick your own chief. But while we're doing that, I'm going to give all of you a few things to stew on. First, I never said this had to be Godspeed Base. Think back, and you'll recall what I did say. This was a place that we had to go to, because it could *lead us* to find the Godspeed Drive. It was, and if we just keep going, I say it will. Second, you'd better decide who's going to do the hard thinking for you when it's not my responsibility."

"We'll manage." But Munroe didn't sound too confident.

"You will? Then start with this one, Joe Munroe. You've been looking for a world full of women, a place to make you all rich. How? You'll have your fun with any women you find, that I believe. But women can't make you rich if you leave them out here in the Maze. Are you proposing to ship a load of them away on the *Cuchulain?*—you, who was the first to say that even *one* woman on board brought nothing but bad luck. No? What, then? Are you proposing to set up some sort of pleasure camp out here in the middle of nowhere, where other ships will come for a bit of bought fun? I could organize that sort of thing, yes, and make it work. But are you sure that *you* could? Just *how* are you going to become rich? I can answer that question, and see a dozen ways to turn women in the Maze into real wealth on Erin. But can you, Joe?"

There was a long silence, until finally Danny Shaker continued: "And even that's not the whole story. You see, thre's something else you don't know, something that happened when you were off on this last run around on the surface—a chase, you'll remember, that I told you before you left was going to be a big waste of time and effort. I walked a little way to see what conditions on the ground were like, but I stayed close to the ship. And guess who was waiting here for me when I got back."

I heard Shaker's footsteps approaching. The hatch above my head was suddenly lifted, and Danny Shaker's face appeared in the opening. "Come on out, Jay," he said. "There's a few people who'd like to talk to you."

The way the crewmen reacted to my appearance, I thought I was going to be murdered on the spot. Only surprise kept them fixed where they stood.

"Jay's been down there cleaning up the lower hold,"

Shaker said. "Everybody's favorite job." And then to me. "Here. Show the lads this, and tell them what you told me."

He was holding out the navigation aid. I took it with hands that trembled.

"This world," I said. *"Paddy's Fortune*—it isn't Godspeed Base, and there's no Godspeed Drive here. But you have to come here first, because this"—I held out the navaid—"gives directions as to how to get to the real Godspeed Base *from here*. If we hadn't come here first, we wouldn't know where to go next."

What I said was true, and I prayed they would not ask for too many details. Danny Shaker made sure of that.

"And now tell us all why you're here at the beetle, Jay," he said. "Explain why you came to see me."

I turned to face Joe Munroe, Robert Doonan, and Patrick O'Rourke. They towered over me, every one of them. What I was going to say sounded preposterous, but I had no choice. I had to assume that Danny Shaker knew what he was doing.

"I want to join Captain Shaker and the rest of you," I said. "I know I'm young, but every one of you started young. I'm tired of being told what to do every minute of the day by Eileen Xavier, and I'm tired of being treated like a kid. I'm not a kid. I'm sixteen years old. I know how to work this"—I turned on the navaid, set up to show as a sample a shimmering three-dimensional display of the Maze—"and no one else does, in Doctor Xavier's group or in yours. I can be useful, and I'm willing to work hard on anything that Captain Shaker tells me to do."

"Or he would have been," Shaker said softly. He was not talking to me at all. "Except that you lads will have a new chief, as soon as you get back to the *Cuchulain*. I don't know if Jay Hara will feel the same about working for him." He stared around vaguely, then headed for a seat by the control panel. "Well, that's going to be your problem," he said as he settled down. "That, and deciding how any women you do happen to find will give you more profit than an hour's fun. Me, I'll go back to being a simple crewman, and glad to do it. There's nothing takes the heart out of a man more than doing his level best for everybody, and then being spit on by the same people he was trying to help.''

I couldn't believe he could be so relaxed, because the anger on the faces of Pat O'Rourke and Robbie Doonan had to be obvious to anyone. Then I saw that they were glaring not at Shaker, but at Joseph Munroe.

"There, Joe Munroe," said Pat O'Rourke. "Now you've done it. Didn't I warn you we might be going off half-cocked? Do you think you're the man that can lead us all to fortune? Because if you do, I'll tell you something: It'll be a cold day on Tyrone before Patrick O'Rourke will follow you.''

"I never said I'd be leader." Munroe was as nervous as he was angry. "Robbie, you can vouch for that. All I said was we needed a change. And that was before we heard all this from the chief." He turned to Shaker. "You can see it from our point of view, can't you? We didn't have all the facts you had, all we knew was, we seemed to be going nowhere. Now we've heard the plan, everything's different.''

"Not different from where I'm sitting." Shaker had his back to the other three. "I've heard my competence questioned—aye, and had a gun raised against me, when everyone here knows I'm a man who never carries a weapon.''

"Joe didn't mean it, Chief." Pat O'Rourke moved around the cabin, so he could see Danny Shaker face to face. "He was just being hasty. You've said yourself that's his biggest fault.''

"And one I admit to," said Joe Munroe. "I'd never have fired that gun, Chief, you know that. If you could find a way to forget it, and all we said about needing a change—''

"I can't. I told you, go find somebody else to do the worrying.''

"There's nobody else," Robert Doonan wheezed. "An' it's worse than that, Chief. If we go back and tell the others on the *Cuchulain* what we did to you, they'll stuff us out the airlock.''

Danny Shaker was leaning back in his chair, arms folded, staring up at Pat O'Rourke. "Tough. You should have thought of all that before you started. But I'm a reasonable man. I can't forget what's happened, but I'm willing to give it one more go. Only I'll tell you something: If I stay on as chief, there'll be no more threats of violence to me. And I'll not stand any talk of cutting Jay's throat, either. He's the one who gives us our best shot at something more than we've ever had, the Godspeed Drive, and he wants to come over to our side. I'm saying I've accepted him as one of ours. You three had better do the same.''

There was a general murmur of agreement and relief. "I'm sorry, Jay Hara," said Joe Munroe—a more insincere apology I never heard. "Sorry about what I said. You're crew now, as good as the rest of us. If I can help you with anything, let me know.''

"For a start, you fellows can show him how to pilot this beetle," Danny Shaker said. "He's been itching to have a go since first he set eyes on one. Pat, why don't you sit here and give him a bit of a runthrough on the controls. And while you're doing that, I'm going to send a message to the *Cuchulain*. We need a meeting with Doctor Xavier, and I'd rather have it up there than down here.''

He grinned at me. "Time you learned to fly, Jay, if you're going to be a spacer. Ready for a lesson?''

I nodded. But it occurred to me that I had just had a lesson, and one more important than flying a cargo beetle.

CHAPTER 22

I had my spaceflight lesson while we were still on the surface of *Paddy's Fortune:* a short one, and more theory than practice, but enough to convince me that Mel and I could have been in space for days before we reached the *Cuchulain*. The cargo beetle in the hands of Danny Shaker or Pat O'Rourke seemed trivially easy to fly. It was anything but. Half the computer and navigational aids shown on the control panel were actually missing or out of action. When it had been a choice of cannibalizing equipment for the *Cuchulain* or for the beetles, the big ship had won every time.

Pat O'Rourke showed me the basics for seat-of-the-pants navigation and flight without instruments. I would like to have continued at the beetle controls, but once Danny Shaker finished his conversation with Eileen Xavier he wanted a rapid passage back to the *Cuchulain*. At the time I thought it was their talk that provided the urge for speed. Later, I decided that a stronger motive was probably Shaker's lack of confidence in Mel. He didn't know her well, but he was certain of one thing: She had to sit in the dark until the beetle was safely docked at the *Cuchulain* and we had a chance to smuggle her aboard.

I wondered what would happen to Danny Shaker if Mel were discovered by one of the crew members. Then it became obvious. Shaker would tell them that *I* had brought her aboard, unknown to him, while he was away from the ship. Whether the crew were angry or not, he would not be blamed.

I was ordered out of the pilot's chair before liftoff and left reluctantly, convinced that now I *really* knew how to fly a cargo beetle. I was desperate to prove as much to Shaker and O'Rourke, but I was not offered the chance.

There was nothing else for me to do until we reached the *Cuchulain,* and I retreated to an out-of-the-way spot near the cabin wall. After a few minutes I reached in my pocket for the book I had taken from Walter Hamilton's body. I had been carrying it around all this time, but without much thought as to what was in it.

I was not much better informed after half an hour of leafing through the electronic pages. I had not realized that the little book had such enormous storage, and without a road map I was pretty much hunting blind. The first two thousand pages were the result of Hamilton's patient screening of every available record, on Erin or off it, for references to the Isolation. A global data search showed me that the Godspeed Drive was mentioned dozens of times, but never in solid detail. No one who made the old records had ever actually *seen* the drive. What did emerge from my rummaging, clearly and directly enough to horrify me, was the devastating effect that the Isolation had produced on Erin. Walter Hamilton in his search had visited hundreds of deserted towns and villages across the planet, looking for old records. Once each had been a thriving settlement. Now most of them were derelict ruins. The population of Erin had once been more than a billion people. Today it was one thirtieth of that, and shrinking.

I wondered about the drive that powered the *Cuchulain.* It was clearly not a Godspeed Drive, although according to

Danny Shaker it dated back to before the Isolation. I did a general search on the word, "drive," and was offered a dozen different varieties. Apparently there were cargo drives, planet-to-orbit drives, ship drives rated for humans, hundred-gee drives for urgent unmanned shipment only, low-gee drives for bulk cargo, and a perplexingly named "Slowdrive." The last one was described as experimental and unique to the Maveen system, but it was hard for me to see why anyone might find a use for something that went especially *slow*. The electronic book also offered three-D images of the Slowdrive. As I rotated them they outlined a round-cornered cube, a little bit flattened, with underneath it a set of rings of different sizes, placed one above the other so that they formed a blunt cone with its thick end attached to the cube. The written description of the drive was beyond me. I tagged the whole "Slowdrive" entry with a high-level pointer, to draw my attention to it again when I had more time, and glanced over to the control panel.

We would dock at the *Cuchulain* in a few more minutes—and I would have a meeting with Doctor Eileen that I would rather not think about.

I skipped to the last part of the record. Walter Hamilton had swallowed his initial disappointment on arriving at *Paddy's Fortune,* although he had rejected it at once as a possible site for Godspeed Base. I could almost hear his disdainful sniff as he plowed through the head-high vegetation. But then the scientist had taken over, and in spite of himself he had become fascinated by the biology of the worldlet. Before he died, it was quite apparent to Dr. Hamilton that not only was the world itself an artifact, but the present ecology must be sustained by something other than a natural biological balance.

In another half day he would have been thinking in terms of access to the interior of *Paddy's Fortune* and the control mechanisms that ran the little world. If Sean Wilgus had not been such a bloodthirsty fool, Walter Hamilton might have led the crew to what they were seeking.

I closed the book. The right person to have this was not me, it was Jim Swift. He was also the logical person for the new navaid, because of the data on the Godspeed Drive that the controller had loaded onto it. The problem was that without help from Mel neither I nor Jim Swift might be able to read those data.

I hoped I wouldn't be there when Jim was told what had happened to Walter Hamilton. He had described Hamilton as pompous and conceited, but all the same the two had been friends for many years. I found myself thinking that it simplified matters that the person who had killed Walter Hamilton was himself dead. Was that how real spacers dismissed a killer's death, as natural vengeance?

We were docking at the *Cuchulain,* and the automatic procedures from the mother ship had already taken over. I felt a series of unsettling changes of direction. Danny Shaker seemed immune to them as he walked across to where I was sitting.

"I told the crew that I'd be showing you how to lock the beetle in hull storage. So we'll be the last ones off. I'll also be giving you bigger than usual quarters, until you get used to living spacer-style."

There was no wink or change of facial expression, but I knew exactly what he was saying. As soon as the others were gone he and I would smuggle Mel Fury aboard. Mel would occupy the same quarters as me, and it would be my job to make sure she was not discovered until we had a plausible reason for a passenger's presence—or until we had found a Godspeed Drive. After that, the crew of the *Cuchulain* would be so exultant they would not care if Danny Shaker had on board a hundred passengers.

Like everything that Danny Shaker did, the docking and crew disembarkation went without a hitch. As soon as Pat O'Rourke, the last to leave, had gone, Shaker glanced across to me. "Time to get Mel out, and safe into quarters. I'll go and bring her. By the way, I hope she has no special food requirements?"

"No, she eats whatever we—"

I stopped in horror. "How did you know?"

Danny Shaker frowned down at the deck. "You should ask, *when* did I know. That's a harder question to answer. The first hint was when you had been outside on the surface, and I kept Mel in the beetle with me. I asked you when you came back what you had learned inside *Paddy's Fortune*. You didn't know what Mel had said, and you were so keen to avoid that question, you pulled out the navigation aid right away and told me all about the Net and the hardware reservoir. That struck me as a desperate act. You had something to hide. Mel had admitted that there were females inside *Paddy's Fortune*. Yet when I told you I was going to discuss later what *Paddy's Fortune* contained, you never once asked me to do it. I could tell from your face that you didn't want to hear about it. I started thinking, female, and after that there were a dozen clues."

"What are you going to do?"

"I'm going to bring Mel Fury out of her hiding place. And then you are going to take her to your new quarters, while I make sure the crew arc busy elsewhere."

"You're not going to tell them?"

"That Mel is a girl? Jay, you have a good brain. Use it. Why do you think I wanted to leave *Paddy's Fortune* so quickly?"

"In case Mel became impatient, and wouldn't stay hidden."

"That could have happened, but it wasn't my big worry. I was afraid something might change, and young women would start popping out onto the surface of *Paddy's Fortune* like summer locusts."

"They wouldn't. Mel's an exception."

"How was I to know that? And what sort of control do you think I'd have had over the crew if girls—even one girl—appeared on that world? They would have torn the place apart. They're good spacers, all of them, but they can't hold the big picture in their heads. Women are important, and rare, and they could bring riches. They know that, I know that. But the Godspeed Drive is the key to the whole *universe.*"

"Then why did you bring Mel with us at all? Why not leave her back there?"

"That's good, Jay. You're asking better questions, and I'll give honest answers. If the crew learns that she's a girl, we both know what will happen. I won't be able to stop it. So bringing Mel is no real risk to me, but it is a risk to you, and most of all to *her*. You realize that as well as anyone—and that's why I wanted her along.

"You see, Jay, the one person on this ship who can really help or hinder me isn't Joe Munroe, or Robbie Doonan, or Pat O'Rourke. No, and it's not Eileen Xavier either. It's Jay Hara. You know how to work that gadget you brought along, and I don't. Nor does anyone else, except Mel. Now, maybe I could squeeze it out of either one of you. But isn't it a whole lot better if a person cooperates because he has a mind to? If you and Mel work with me, you have my solemn word: Not a man on board this ship will learn from me that Mel Fury is a girl. Of course, I can't guarantee that one of *you* won't give the game away—as you did to me just now. And I'm going to rely on you to explain to Mel Fury just why she needs to stay hidden, because I don't know if she would believe me. Maybe she won't even believe you. But you have Dan Shaker's word for my end of it, my mouth stays shut as long as you play straight.

"Is it a deal then, Jay?" He held out his hand. "You help me, best you know how, and Mel stays our little secret."

After a moment I took his hand and shook it. Of course, I had no choice. For what Danny Shaker didn't need to say was the other side of his promise: If I didn't help him, "best I knew how," he would certainly make sure that the crew of the *Cuchulain* learned that a young female was on board. After that, nothing he said or did would be able to protect her.

Danny Shaker probably realized what we were getting into when we decided to keep Mel Fury smuggled away on board the *Cuchulain* until we reached the Net and the hardware reservoir. I know for sure that I didn't, although I suppose I should have, because I already knew that back on *Paddy's Fortune* she had been in the habit of disobeying the controller.

The sort of problems I might face became clear even before we reached my new quarters. I knew the layout of the ship, and I knew just where we were going. Shaker had told us to wait fifteen minutes after he left, and then he promised us another clear quarter hour during which the interior passageways would be deserted.

The trip from the cargo beetle to the living area would take only a few minutes. I knew we had ample time—and made the mistake of telling Mel that. Then every three steps it was "What's this?" and "What does that do?" and "Wait a minute, Jay, this looks really neat."

I drove her along, ready to scream. When we finally reached our destination I closed and locked the cabin door and pulled the navaid from my pocket.

"You're not going to play with that *now*, are you?" asked Mel.

"I am. Or better still, you are. I want to know just how long it will take the *Cuchulain* to get from here to the Net."

"Why?"

"Because I need to know how long I'll have to sit on your head. Mel, you don't seem to understand that you're in *danger* until we get there."

"Phooey. I heard Shaker talking to his crew before we

took off. They came in mad as could be, and in two minutes
he had them wrapped round his finger.''

"Sometimes. But you didn't hear what Shaker said to me
after we took off, did you?''

"I couldn't hear anything. There was too much engine
noise.''

"Then let me tell you. He said—and I believe him—that
if the crew ever learn that you are on board and are a girl, he
won't be able to stop them.''

"What will they do?''

I felt myself going red. Back on Erin I had been told lots
about sex, but never with girls present. And what I had to tell
Mel was pretty extreme.

"They'll *want* you.'' And, when she didn't seem worried
by that. "I mean, they'll fight over you.''

"So?'' She certainly wasn't making this easy for me.

"And they'll rape you. You do know what rape is, don't
you?''

Mel didn't say anything, but her eyes widened and her
pale face went even paler. She reached out without a word
and took the navaid from me. As she started to manipulate
the indents on its surface I realized that what I had learned
about the navaid in my blind experiments with Paddy
Enderton's stolen model was nothing. Displays flickered into
existence around Mel's busy hands, and were gone again
before I had time to take in what they were.

She asked one question: "What's the top acceleration of
this ship?''

"It ought to be seven-tenths of a gee, but the engines are
in terrible shape. No one dares to run the *Cuchulain* at
anything more than a quarter gee. Even then it feels like the
ship is falling apart.''

She touched one more indent, and nodded to the display
that formed in the air. "It's an eight-day trip at a constant
quarter gee, allowing for Maze direction changes. Twelve
days if you use boost-and-coast.''

Danny Shaker would go as fast as the failing *Cuchulain* could manage. At best, I would have the job of controlling Mel's curiosity for at least eight days. But she knew the stakes now: her body, and then probably her life.

"Make yourself comfortable," I said. "Shaker told me to go along to the main control room as soon as I could, otherwise the crew may start to wonder. Before I go, though, show me what you did to get that time-of-travel calculation."

She ran through it again, this time including a display of thrust times and attitudes. It was done almost too fast for me to follow completely, but it would have to be enough for the moment.

I grabbed the navaid from her.

"And whatever you do, don't leave this place."

She nodded. Maybe I wasn't going to have a problem with her after all.

I headed for the main control room—the same place where Danny Shaker had reached into the air duct and lifted me out like a landed fish. That had happened two days ago. It felt like two centuries.

I didn't waste a second going from my new quarters to the control room, but Mel's dawdling and my own use of the navaid had taken longer than I realized. The only people there when I arrived were Tom Toole and Robert Doonan, who gave me a wheeze and a glower and at once hurried out.

Tom Toole was standing near the controls, examining a display of the *Cuchulain*'s interior. He pushed his long jaw out at me and sniffed. "So you're one of us now, are you? Replacing old Sean, as the chief says it."

I couldn't tell from the look on his cleanshaven red face if he approved of that. "Not a replacement. I don't know enough to be a replacement."

"Don't know enough." Tom Toole grinned. "And don't flare up nor cuss enough, neither, to be Sean. You'll manage,

Jay. Anyway, the chief says, soon as you got here, you follow him to Doctor Xavier's quarters. Better get along.''

I think Tom Toole regarded me as being a bit under his wing, because he was the first on the *Cuchulain* that I'd ever done a job for, back before we even left Erin. And I'm sure he was delighted to hear that I wanted to join the crew, and leave Doctor Eileen, because the two of them had been at each other the minute they met. Certainly he didn't need to add, as I was turning to go, "Before you leave, Jay, here's a word to the wise. There's some on board the *Cuchulain* who are no friends of yours. I don't know what you did down there on *Paddy's Fortune*—and don't want to know, neither, not right now—but whatever it was, it got up the nose of a couple of people. That, and the chief saying we have to partition off your living quarters in the *Cuchulain* with heavy duty bulkheads, which is going to be a lot of work and was certainly a surprise to me. Some people will blame you for their share in that work, too. Anyway, don't count on Joe Munroe as a friend, nor Robbie Doonan, neither. And now scat out of here. I've spoke too much already.''

For Tom Toole, he certainly had. He was one of Danny Shaker's right-hand men, but he was more of a doer than a talker. I pondered his warning as I retraced my steps and headed for the part of the ship where Doctor Eileen and the rest of our group were quartered. On the way I passed tubby Donald Rudden and Connor Bryan. They were dangerously close to my quarters, hauling heavy-duty partitions. They pointed to them as I passed.

"To keep you in, or somebody out?" Connor Bryan called to me.

They seemed to think I knew all about the proposed separation of my living quarters from the rest of the ship, but it was as big a surprise to me as it was to them. On the way to my old quarters, though, I had an answer to Connor Bryan's question.

To keep me in, or them out? *Both,* and maybe more than that. Danny Shaker never did anything for just one reason.

The meeting with the Erin group had begun when I arrived. I could tell from Jim Swift's stunned expression that Danny Shaker had already given him the bad news about Walter Hamilton. Jim was sitting well away from the table, with Duncan West and Eileen Xavier closer to it and facing Danny Shaker.

I received one quick glance from everybody as I came in, and that was all. I sensed the strained atmosphere as I tiptoed across to Jim Swift.

"Here," I whispered, and handed him the electronic book. "I don't understand most of this, but he was making notes just before he died."

No need to say who "he" was. Jim nodded absently, and tucked the book away without even looking at it.

"Well, why don't we look at the contract, then?" said Uncle Duncan. He was using his most casual and easygoing voice, and it sounded as though he was trying to lower the tension.

"No need for that," said Doctor Eileen. She was *miffed.* "I know very well what it says."

"One trip," Shaker said. "To a destination to be given to me upon our departure from Erin. And then a return journey. Nothing about a second destination."

"But my God, Captain!" Doctor Eileen glared at him across the table. "I mean, this is ridiculous. Of course the contract was written for one trip—we had no reason to expect more. And you were paid triple rates."

"That's standard for winter work."

"And *you* are the one who's telling me we ought to be looking elsewhere for Godspeed Base."

"No." Danny Shaker pointed to me. *"He's* telling you."

I became the center of attention.

"Tell them, Jay." Shaker's expression was unreadable. I

wasn't sure what I was supposed to say, but I was very aware that my words alone stood between Mel and the crew of the *Cuchulain*.

I took the navaid from my pocket. To Eileen Xavier and the rest of them, it must seem identical to the one I had found on Paddy Enderton's body. "There's more information in here," I said. "It provides the course from *Paddy's Fortune* to a place known as the Net. It looks as though there, if anywhere, we'll find a Godspeed Drive."

"So why don't you want to go there?" Doctor Eileen addressed Shaker in exasperation.

"You misunderstand me." He crossed his arms and began to massage his biceps. "Speaking for myself alone, I would love to go. But there are complications. The first is the ship itself. The engines of the *Cuchulain* were in poor shape when we left Erin, and they are worse now. I can nurse them along, but they need a major overhaul. They can only receive that back at Upside Muldoon, and the crew know it very well. It will require a major effort on my part to talk them into a new journey, to another unknown destination. *Paddy's Fortune* was as big a disappointment to them as it was to you."

"I doubt that." But Doctor Eileen had calmed down. "What's the second reason?"

"He is." Shaker was pointing at me again. I knew something horrible was on the way, and I didn't know why it was necessary. When it came to finding a Godspeed Drive, Danny Shaker was as keen as Eileen Xavier. Why not just agree, and go?

"While we were down on the surface," Shaker said, "Jay came to me and asked if he could join my party. I considered his request, and discussed it with the rest of the crew. They agreed, but that put me in a difficult position. The information that Jay has about the new destination no longer belongs to your group. It belongs at least as much to mine, and I am forced to respect their rights."

"The navigation computer is ours!"

"Are you sure? I'd say from what I've seen that it's *his.* What do you say, Jay."

"The navaid was given to me." I couldn't bear to look at Doctor Eileen.

"Oh!" She gasped in exasperation. "This is quite ridiculous. Let's get the farce over. Captain Shaker, tell me what you are proposing."

"The minimum that I believe my crew—I am including Jay—will accept. I suggest that in addition he is still entitled to whatever he was promised by your group."

That made Doctor Eileen squirm. No one had promised me anything definite, and she knew it.

"Assuming that the engines hold out," Shaker went on, "I and my crew will fly the *Cuchulain* to the destination that Jay provides to us. If we find nothing there, then you will simply pay us triple rate for the additional journey that we make. If we find something valuable, you will cut us in for twenty-five percent of whatever is found there."

I know nothing at all about business, but what Danny Shaker was asking didn't sound like a lot—a quarter share, but to be split among all his crew. I had expected him to ask for a lot more.

So clearly had Doctor Eileen, because she frowned at him and said, "Twenty-five percent of the value of what we find. And nothing more?"

"One thing more."

"Ah!" Doctor Eileen said, meaning, *Here it comes.*

"Only one thing," Shaker said quietly. "If we do discover a Godspeed Drive, I want to be the man who pilots it on its first interstellar trip."

I don't know what she had been expecting, but Shaker's last condition bowled Doctor Eileen over. All the tension vanished from her face. She stared at him, and shook her head.

"Captain Shaker, you never cease to amaze me." She didn't say, *you have a deal.* But that's what her words meant, because she was turning again to me. "Jay, I am in a very awkward position. I promised your mother that I would look after you while we were away. Do you realize I will not be able to do that if you join Captain Shaker's crew?"

"*I* realize it," Danny Shaker said, "even if Jay does not. I intend to take precautions against anything happening to him. His new living quarters will be reinforced. My crew have orders not to enter them without my permission."

Doctor Eileen was beginning to nod, at least partially satisfied, when Shaker added, "And I expect no less from you and your group. Keep your hands off him, too. Jay is smart, he'll learn fast—if he's left free to learn."

"He *is* smart," Doctor Eileen agreed, to my surprise. Then she spoiled it by adding, as though I was not there, "And I'm afraid he knows it."

Danny Shaker grinned at my reaction. "The right combination. As I understand it, Jay has wanted to be a spacer all his life."

He understood it very well, and Eileen Xavier knew it better than anyone aboard. She was in a very awkward position, because Danny Shaker was being unreasonably *reasonable.*

At last she nodded. "It is impossible for me not to go along with this. But I too have a condition: Jay must have a direct line to me."

"I told you I don't want you talking to him."

"I accept that. Give him a communication line that can only be activated from his end. If he needs me, I insist that he be able to reach me."

"No problem. Provided that I can listen in on it, too."

"Agreed."

That was it, and the meeting broke up. As I headed for my living quarters I felt more than ever convinced that the new walls around me were going to serve multiple purposes: to keep the crew out; to keep Doctor Eileen from talking with me in a way that Shaker couldn't monitor; and to keep Mel Fury—and maybe me, too—safe inside.

CHAPTER 23

The new bulkheads around my quarters made the inside pretty well soundproof, and the single entrance, which could be locked from either inside or outside, gave privacy. Mel and I ought to be safe.

Of course, you could view it another way. Unless I wanted to go crawling through the air ducts again, Danny Shaker had created a fairly good prison.

I didn't tell Mel that. More and more, I was realizing what a handful she could be.

I had evidence of that on the first evening, as the *Cuchulain* made ready to leave *Paddy's Fortune*. Mel and I were preparing for our first meal onboard, which I had carried over from the dining area. The automatic ovens produced as much food as anyone asked for, so providing enough for two was no problem.

I started to eat, but Mel wrinkled her nose in disgust at the first mouthful.

"This tastes *lousy*. What's wrong with it?"

I tasted mine. "Nothing. It's perfectly fine."

"*Fine?* No wonder the crew on this ship are always in a foul temper. I wish I'd brought some *decent* food with me."

But she was starving, and after a moment she went on eating.

The curious thing is, I had thought that the food on *Home* had something wrong with it. Reminded of that now, I fished the little silver box of pills out of my pocket and laid it on the table.

"You're supposed to take one with each meal," Mel said.

"I know. How come *you* don't have any?"

"Because I don't need them." She sounded grouchy and bossy. "What's the matter, afraid you'll be poisoned? The controller's health monitors decided you need those, and they're never wrong. Swallow your pill."

"Suppose their programs are designed for females? I don't want to be fed pills for *women*." But after a few more seconds I took a little blue capsule from the box and washed it down with water. It tasted of nothing.

I didn't have time to worry about its possible effects, because within a few seconds a vibration shook the whole room. My weight increased from near nothing to something substantial. Mel, a spoon at her mouth, missed it and hit her chin. She gave me a surprised glance.

"It's all right," I said. "That's the drive heading up to power. We're on our way."

She jumped up. "Wonderful. Come on."

"Come on where?"

"I want to take a last look at *Home*. It could be months before I'm back."

So much for explanations and warnings. "You can't do that! You can't go near a viewing port or a display screen. You can't go *anywhere* until we get to Godspeed Base."

I wasn't sure what would happen after that. Danny Shaker had said things would change, but he hadn't told me how.

"It's going to be at least an eight-day trip," she said. "Eight whole days! I'll go out late at night, when no one is around."

"Mel, this isn't Erin, or *Paddy's Fortune,* with a night and a day. It's a *ship*. Things happen around the clock."

"Well, I can't stay stuck in this little hole forever. It's worse than being back at *Home*. You have to do something. You're the one who got me into this."

That was so outrageous I couldn't do more than glare at her.

"You *did*," she said. "You told me that I'd have more space to wander around in than I could ever imagine."

"I meant *on Erin*, when we get there—not on this ship."

"Well, you should have been *clear*. You should have—"

How long we might have gone on with that, I don't know, because Mel's next objection was interrupted by a rattling sound from the outer door of the living quarters. It was locked, and in principle only Shaker had a key. But Mel made a dive for the inside room, while I stared at the table and realized that if anyone did manage to get in I would have a hard time explaining why there were places set for two.

It was Danny Shaker. He looked grim. He came right to the table, settled down in Mel's chair, and glanced around him. "Where is Mel Fury?"

"Inside. We heard you coming."

"Get her. I have to talk to both of you."

Mel had recognized his voice, and was already on her way back into the room.

"Two problems." Shaker wasn't one to mess about, and he came to the point at once. "Nothing you can do about either of them, but you need to know what they are. First, the ship. When we came up to full drive, the engines of the *Cuchulain* showed an imbalance. We'll keep going for five or six days, but when we turn and prepare for deceleration we'll have to switch off and do another overhaul. That means a period of free-fall, and since we'll be under reduced power it adds a few days to the trip time."

I could imagine Mel's reaction to that, but Danny Shaker didn't wait to hear it.

"That's the practical problem. The other one is more worrying. It's the crew." He stared at Mel. "When we left, did you bring anything with you? Trinkets, or gadgets, or anything else?"

Mel shook her head. "I didn't bring anything. Just what I'm wearing."

She saw me glance across at the counter. "Well, that as well. But it's just my backpack. I carry it all the time, it's like part of my clothes."

"What's in it?" Shaker asked.

"Oh, bits and pieces, all sorts of things."

"Did you lose anything from it?"

"No, I'm sure I didn't."

I wasn't sure. Nor was Danny Shaker.

"You *think* you didn't," he said. "But Joe Munroe and Robbie Doonan did the final inspection of the cargo beetle before it went into mothballs for the trip, and I think one of them got a sniff of something that shouldn't have been there. Not a word was said to me, but I sense trouble. Too many little private meetings, too much silence when I'm around."

Danny Shaker wasn't a man to rant and rave about anything, and Mel didn't know what a band of cutthroats the rest of the crew were. So it's not surprising that she didn't realize the significance of what he was saying.

I did, though. "What should we do?"

"Not one thing. Lie low, stay quiet, don't move unless I tell you otherwise. I'll have to bring you out for part of the time, Jay, you're crew now and you have to work. But don't give a hint, ever, that there's anything aboard this ship from *Paddy's Fortune*. And especially don't let anyone suspect there might be more than one person in here."

It was exactly what I wanted Mel to hear, but it might have had little effect on her if Shaker hadn't backed words with action. "I'll do my best to stay on top of things," he said, "but don't be misled by that session back on the cargo beetle. I handled the problem, but there's still a lot of anger and hot blood in the crew. I don't know how well I can control it. In case I can't"—he reached into his own pocket—"I think you ought to have this."

He pulled out Walter Hamilton's white-handled pistol and handed it to me. I took it—nervously. "Is it loaded?"

"Full magazine. No point in handing somebody an empty gun." He studied my face. "I'm giving it to you, Jay, and you ought to carry it with you all the time. But I'll be honest: I don't know if you've got the guts to shoot, no matter how you're threatened. Just remember this: Don't ever point a weapon you're not willing to use."

He was finally getting through to Mel. She had seen this gun before. It was the one Dan Shaker had used when he killed Sean Wilgus, and Mel could not take her eyes off it.

Shaker had been watching her closely. He nodded. "All right, then." He was standing up when he saw the little silver box, sitting on the table. "What's that?"

"Pills," I said. "I got them on *Paddy's Fortune,* they're supposed to make me healthier. Do you think I shouldn't take them?"

"That's up to you. But it's exactly the sort of thing I was warning about. Take the pills out and put them in your pocket, and give me the box."

I did as he ordered, and he tucked it away in his jacket.

"One look at that," he went on, "and any smart crew member would start wondering where it came from. It's workmanship like nothing on board the *Cuchulain.*"

He left, closing and locking the door behind him. I tucked the little white-handled gun away in my other pocket, where it made an awkward bulge. Mel sat down again at the table. Her expression was somewhere between guilty and defiant.

"You think I did it, don't you? You think I left something on the cargo beetle."

"It doesn't matter what I think. Shaker thinks so, and there's trouble with the crew. That's good enough for me."

She stood up, reached across for her backpack, and

headed for the inner room where she would be sleeping. "Well, I didn't," she said over her shoulder. "No matter what you and your great Captain Shaker believe."

She closed the door behind her. I picked up a glass, walked quietly across to the door, and set one end gently against the crack where it opened. Then I put my ear on the other.

It was a trick that Duncan West had taught me, so long ago I don't know when I learned it. The glass amplified all sounds coming to its open end, so I could hear very well what was happening in the next room.

I heard a strange rattling noise, hard and soft objects hitting the floor all at once.

I knew what it was. Mel was emptying out her backpack.

She didn't say what was in it. I didn't ask. But for the next few days she was on her best behavior, and she didn't cause me one moment of extra worry.

She didn't need to, because I did plenty of worrying without Mel adding more.

If it was important that Mel stay hidden away in my living quarters, it was just as vital that I appear every day to work with the rest of the crew. There was lots to do, too, because the *Cuchulain* was in awful shape and the senior men, Shaker and Toole and O'Rourke, spent most of their time monitoring the ailing drive. That, plus the absence of Sean Wilgus, meant extra work for everybody. There were more than enough unpleasant chores to pass on to me.

I didn't mind. Checking the work of the cleaning robots, or rebalancing the mass around the cargo spindle, was not fascinating work, but it helped to keep my mind off Mel—and whatever she might be doing, cooped up by herself.

For the first three days I couldn't complain. She mooched around the restricted space of my quarters, and if she seemed bored when I returned late in the day it was no more than natural. And on the fourth day I had an idea of my own.

"Here," I said. Then I had to pause to clear my throat. I must have picked up a minor bug, here or in the damp jungle of *Paddy's Fortune,* and my voice sounded rough and scratchy. "Here, why don't you take a look at this when I'm away."

I handed her the navaid. "We used it to get the coordinates for the Net and the hardware reservoir, but the controller said it put all sorts of other information in about the Godspeed Base and the Godspeed Drive. I have no idea how to get those data out. Maybe you can do it."

Mel took the navaid. "Humph," she said. It wasn't exactly a sign of enthusiasm, and I wondered how long it would keep her quiet. Not long enough, I felt sure. I hadn't told Mel, but we were making slower progress than expected. The engines had to be constantly nursed.

The problem came to a head early on the fifth day. We were still far from the turnover point when Shaker called the crew together. The engines were still deteriorating. We had to switch off the drive later in the day and service it.

That would not please Mel when she heard about it, but for the moment it pleased me.

To explain why, I have to describe something in a bit more detail. Seen from a distance, the *Cuchulain* looked like a long, knobbly stick, with a round ball on the "top" end and a flared cone—rather like a bathroom plunger—at the other, "bottom," end. The knobbly stick was the cargo area, capable of changing shape, when the ship was fully loaded, to a bloated oval bag; the round ball contained all the crew living quarters. And the words "top" and "bottom" make sense, because the cone was the drive unit, and when it was turned on, anything a person dropped would "fall," accelerating from the round ball of the living quarters toward the drive unit.

The place where we all had our living quarters looked like a smooth ball from outside, but of course it had lots of internal structure. Thinking of the whole ship as standing upright on its flared conical end, there were five main layers to the ball. At the very top were the living quarters used now by Doctor Eileen, Jim Swift, and Duncan West. Below that was a general area of crew quarters, some for sleeping but mainly for exercise and recreation. In the next layer came the central control region for the whole ship, buried deep in toward the center where it was well-protected from hull leaks or outside impact. The place where Mel and I lived now was off to the side of that same layer, near the outside hull.

The fourth layer contained kitchens, food machines, and storage areas for food, raw materials, and water. And finally, the bottom layer provided additional crew sleeping accommodation, plus access to the cargo region and, beyond that, to the drive.

It wasn't hard to get between the different levels when the drive was on. There were spiral staircases between them. But when the drive was off, those staircases actually became harder to negotiate.

I had learned long ago that most crew members were lazy, and wouldn't take on any effort that wasn't needed. When the drive was off, and they were going back and forth to work on it, it was easier to stay down on the fourth and fifth levels. They would not come up to the third level, where Mel was hidden, unless they had a good reason to do so.

I didn't tell Mel—I didn't want her deciding it was safe to roam around—but I felt a good deal of relief when the drive went off an hour or two later, and Mel and I were suddenly in free fall.

"Let me find out how long this will take," I said, and left her fiddling moodily with the navaid.

I didn't expect to meet anyone, because the crew ought to be already down near the drive. It was a surprise, and a real opportunity, when I came to the stairway leading down from our level and saw Duncan West right in front of me.

"Uncle Duncan!"

He was floating easily along, no more hurried or worried now in free fall than if he were lounging in an easy chair at our house by Lake Sheelin. He turned and gave me his slow, easy smile.

"Going along to give a hand, Jay? Me too. I got the word from Captain Shaker, he thinks I can be useful."

"Maybe later. Uncle Duncan, stop a minute. I need to talk to you."

He halted, and inspected me carefully from head to foot. "You've changed, Jay. You look different, and you sound different."

"Never mind that. I haven't had any chance at all to talk privately to Doctor Eileen, and I've got a lot of things I must pass on to her. Will you do it for me?"

"Sure. When I get back up there—as soon as we finish playing around with the drive. What's going on, Jay? Keep it short, I'm expected down below in a few minutes."

Keep it short! I had so much to tell, I hardly knew where to begin. I gabbled at him. Everything. What I had overheard on the *Cuchulain* about the crew's plans, Walter Hamilton's murder on *Paddy's Fortune,* my flight from Sean Wilgus, finding Mel Fury—or being found by her—the interior of *Paddy's Fortune* and the new navigation aid, Mel's arrival on board the *Cuchulain*—

He stopped me at that point. "You mean she's *here*. On board the ship right now?"

"Yes. Nobody knows. I mean, Captain Shaker knows, but no one else. But listen, that's not the main thing. You have to tell Doctor Eileen what Shaker's like—what the whole crew's like. They can't be trusted."

"But you're one of them yourself. You *joined* the crew. Why do that, if they're as bad as you say?"

"I didn't have any choice."

Duncan nodded. "I see."

But he didn't. I could see the doubt on his face. How could anyone be *forced* to work with someone they said was a murderer, and worse? He hadn't heard the crew talking about women, didn't know the threat to Mel.

"I'll tell Doctor Eileen," he said, "everything you've told me. I promise. But I have to be honest with you, Jay. If she were to ask me what she ought to do about it, I wouldn't know what to suggest." In other words, he didn't believe me. He started to move along the stairwell in the direction of the cargo hold. "Now I have to hurry," he said over his shoulder, "before Pat O'Rourke does too much of his 'repair work' without me. The only tool he understands is a hammer. See you down there in a little bit."

He disappeared around the curve of the staircase, with the odd irregular clattering of feet against floor and walls that signalled movement in free-fall.

I stayed where I was, crushed and despondent. The opportunity that I had sought for days had come. And gone. If Duncan West reacted like that to what had happened to me, was Doctor Eileen likely to be any different? It was all very well for Duncan to say that I had changed, but he didn't really think so. He still treated me like a child.

After half a minute I heard the clatter of his footsteps again, and was filled with a new hope. He must have been thinking over what I told him, and decided it was important enough for him to come back and get the details.

The person producing the footsteps came into view, and I had another disappointment. It was not Duncan at all. It was Joe Munroe.

He came steadily up the staircase, and I moved to one side to let him pass. I was too full of my own thoughts to do much more than notice his presence, and I certainly felt no alarm—until he came level with me, grabbed my neck and shoulder, and swung me around hard so that the side of my head smashed against the solid steps.

I was dazed, but I didn't lose consciousness. I heard every word when he said, "Couldn't be better. The perfect time, and the perfect place. Now we can have that bit of a talk I've been wanting."

He was twice my mass, and hardly seemed to notice my struggle to get free. But I must have given him at least a bit of trouble, because he went on, "Not feeling cooperative, eh? Well we can't have that, can we. See if this helps."

I felt myself being swung around in the air again, faster than ever. This time I don't know what piece of the *Cuchulain* tested its strength on my skull, and if Joe Munroe said anything to me, I can't report it.

I vanished into space. I didn't see even a single star.

It was a point of pride with me that I had never thrown up in free-fall. But I came close to it when I swam back to consciousness.

It was my head that *hurt,* dull throbbing pressure all around my skull. Yet it was rolling nausea in my stomach that caused me the most distress. I knew that any movement at all would finish me off and I hung motionless with my eyes closed, feeling thoroughly sorry for myself.

Joe Munroe didn't offer a scrap of sympathy. I can't have been unconscious for more than a few seconds, and he still had me by the neck. He gave a vicious squeeze, and I gasped.

"That's better," he said. "Don't pretend you're not awake. Now, if you know what's good for you, you're going to answer a few questions. Don't move, either, or I'll whack you a good one next time." He shook me, as though I was a child's doll. "Let's talk about *Paddy's Fortune.* You found things there, didn't you, and never told us?"

It's easy to talk about being brave, and a lot harder to do it. "Yes," I whispered. I didn't want him to hit me again.

"And this is one of the things you found, right? Come on, open your eyes and look. *Right now.* Unless you want me to pop your eyeballs out of your skull and make you swallow them.''

I blinked my eyes open. My dizziness increased. The stairway swam around me, and I had trouble focusing. Joe Munroe held me easily in one huge hand. In the other he had something, a hazy pink outline. It gradually became clearer.

''Yes.'' The grip on my neck was so tight I could hardly work my vocal cords. ''That's—that's it.''

Joe Munroe was holding Mel's strange flashlight, the one that produced a beam from its empty middle.

''I knew it!'' he snorted. '' 'Crew member' be damned. You might have Shaker taken in, he's going soft. But you don't fool Joe Munroe. It's the way I said it would be. Treasure finds, and you tried to keep them for yourself.'' He shook me again, and new pain jolted through my head. ''Well, you're going to lose the lot. Come on. Before you're done you're going to show me where you've hid every blessed one of 'em.''

He didn't ask me to walk, but towed me along behind him. My elbows and knees banged painfully against the sides of the stairway and the corridor. In my general misery it was a while before I realized where he was taking me.

To my own quarters. To where Mel was hidden. He was going—with my forced assistance—to search the whole place for objects taken from *Paddy's Fortune*.

I couldn't let that happen. I clenched my teeth, closed my eyes, and thrust my hand into my right-hand pocket. Walter Hamilton's gun was there, as it should be. Loaded.

I knew what had to be done. I had to bring the pistol out, thumb away the safety guard, and shoot.

I couldn't miss. The gun was fully charged, it could rapid-fire over a hundred super-dense pellets, each smaller than a pea. They would expand and explode on impact, any one of them enough to kill.

I tried to bring my hand out of my pocket. And couldn't

do it. I had never fired a gun in my life, but that wasn't the problem. I was too afraid of Joe Munroe, too afraid of what he would do to me if I tried to hurt him—and failed.

And then my best chance was gone. We had reached the door of my quarters. Munroe changed his grip, twisting my arm so it came out of my pocket and went up behind my back. He forced it higher, until I thought my shoulder would rip out of its socket.

"Unlock it." His breath was wheezing at the back of my neck. "Quick."

"My arm . . ."

"You've got two." He gave another jerk and twist. "Use the other one. Do it!"

I pawed at the combination left-handed, the ciphers blurring in front of my eyes. As I was working, Munroe every second or two lifted my pinned arm an agonizing fraction of an inch higher. When the door finally opened, I felt more relief than worry. Mel might be waiting inside, but at least he was easing his grip.

She wasn't there. The living-room was empty. I had a sudden wild hope that she had done what she wasn't supposed to do—gone roaming.

Joe Munroe didn't waste time. He slammed the door shut, took one quick look at the room's simple layout, and swung me around to face him. "All right. Where's the stuff?"

"There isn't any." My voice cracked in mid-phrase when I saw his glaring eyes. But before that I must have glanced over to the door of the bedroom, because he grunted and gave me a backhand swat across the side of the head. It was hard enough to send me face-first into the metal frame of a swivel chair.

"There better had be. Or you'll breathe vacuum." He went to the inner door and yanked it open.

I could hardly bear to watch. Even if Mel crouched down by the bunks there was no way to hide from a searcher for more than a few seconds.

She didn't even try. Whatever Joe Munroe was expecting, it wasn't what he got. Mel must have realized there was big trouble on the way when she heard his voice. She came diving out of the door as it opened, and her head rammed Munroe square in the belly. He gave a *whoosh* and doubled over. Mel followed it up with both fists swung hard into his face.

She was doing a hell of a lot better than I had, but it wasn't enough. Munroe was three times her mass, as tough as all the spacers seemed to be, and used to both free-fall and rough-housing.

As her fists came away from his face he grabbed her wrists, crushing both of them in his left hand. She gasped in pain, raised her legs, and bent her back. Then she used the extra leverage of his grip to straighten and kick him in the belly. He didn't make a sound—maybe he had no air left in him—but he let go of her wrists. As she tried to pull away his right hand snapped forward to fix on her shoulder, turning her so she could not kick again.

Mel twisted. Cloth ripped. She broke free, leaving part of her shirt in Joe Munroe's paw. The force of her movement carried her back against the wall.

There was a long, still moment. Mel was panting. Munroe was doubled over in the middle of the room, hands across his belly. I crouched useless by the door, just as I had been since they began to fight. After a moment Munroe grunted, straightened, and glared across at Mel.

He seemed ready to come at her again when his face changed. I could see why. With a shirt on and her cropped hair, Mel might pass for a boy. But with arms, shoulder, and one budding breast laid bare, deception was impossible.

"Well, now," Joe Munroe said in a stupefied voice. He was staring at Mel's pink nipple, oblivious to everything else. "Well, now. Here's a surprise. Black Paddy was right after all."

He was easing forward toward Mel, wary of any sign of

attack from her. Mel didn't try to fight. I couldn't see his expression, but she crouched with her back to the wall and crossed her arms over her body. Munroe reached out, snagged the top of her pants with two thick fingers, and ripped them down. He reached out to grab Mel.

And I, finally, was able to move. I reached into my pocket and dragged out Walter Hamilton's gun. My fingers trembled as I brought my other hand across and thumbed away the safety guard.

I could not shoot—not with Joe Munroe and Mel right in line with each other. I pushed myself off to one side and braced against the door. She was out of the line of fire and I had a clear view of his left side and chest.

And then, I guess—though I don't remember doing it—I fired.

I had the gun on single clip. A stream of eight pellets released one after another but so closely spaced that they sounded like one shot, hit Munroe. They expanded on impact and left coin-sized round holes in his shoulder, arm, and back.

The momentum pushed him back. He turned around and stared at me, a strange expression of surprise in his eyes. I thought for a moment that he was going to come at me, because he didn't crumple or drop. Then I realized that he wouldn't, not in free-fall. And a moment later I knew that Joe Munroe was dead or dying. He was drifting gaping-mouthed off the floor while drops of his blood floated around the cabin, marking whatever they touched.

That was when I ruined the free-fall record of which I had been so proud. With Mel looking on wide-eyed and panting, and Joe Munroe's body no more than a few feet away, I curled up in midair. I closed my eyes. And I vomited every scrap of food that lay within my uneasy stomach.

CHAPTER 24

Call me in an emergency," Doctor Eileen had said.

This was an emergency if anything ever could be. I sent a *Priority Service* message to the cleaning system and hit the line to Level One. She was, thank Heaven, in her quarters.

"It's me," I blurted out when she answered. "I've killed Joseph Munroe." Compared with that, nothing else was important.

"Jay?" Eileen Xavier's voice was sharp. "No good going into hysterics. Calm down."

"I can't. Can you come?"

"I'm on my way. Right now."

The line went dead. I wondered if Danny Shaker, busy with the drive unit at the other end of the ship, was monitoring calls from me to Doctor Eileen. It didn't much matter, because there was no way to keep from him what had happened. I might claim self-defense, but Joe Munroe hadn't been attacking me when I shot him. And I couldn't say I had been defending Mel, because if I did the crew would learn that I had been hiding her.

Considering her narrow escape, the latest arrival on the *Cuchulain* was far calmer than me. Mel had put her torn clothing back into place as best she could, and now she was studying the little cleaning machines as they flew about the cabin, pursuing and absorbing horrible globs of blood and vomit.

"How do they know?" she said. "I mean, how do they know to clean up the mess, but they don't clean up *him?*"She pointed to Joe Munroe's body.

I stared at her in disbelief. Mel must have understood what Joe Munroe planned to do to her, and my performance before I shot him can't have given her much confidence that I'd have been any help at all. But she showed no signs of fear—and not even of disgust.

"Same way they don't try to clean *us* up," I said. It was good to think about something abstract. "Template matching. Shape recognition programs. Thermal signatures. They have programs for those."

"But how about when the body cools off? How long before they'd know he was really just dead meat?"

I was rescued from Mel's morbid line of thought by the arrival of Doctor Eileen. She glanced at me, gave Mel one startled stare, and hurried over to Joseph Munroe. Her examination of him didn't take more than five seconds.

She swore, and said, "Long gone," and then to me, "You did this?"

I nodded.

"Well, you'd better have an explanation, or you'll face murder charges. Most of these shots are in his back."

I gestured to Mel. "He was going to—to—" My voice cracked. "He was going to rape her."

Eileen Xavier turned her attention to Mel. "That's the next item on the agenda. Where the devil did you spring from, girl?"

Mel had her clothes back to normal, but there was no scrap of doubt in Doctor Eileen's voice. The odd thing was, I couldn't see how I had *ever* mistaken Mel for a boy. It wasn't just her growing hair. She was as clearly a girl as Duncan West or Pat O'Rourke were men.

Mel said nothing, and she looked at me for guidance. She had heard a lot about Eileen Xavier, in long evening talks about the very different lives that the two of us had led on Erin and on *Paddy's Fortune.* But it's not the same, hearing about someone and meeting them in person.

"This is Mel Fury," I said. "She lived on *Paddy's Fortune*—not *on* it, but inside it."

I assumed that Doctor Eileen would want to hear more about how anyone could live *inside* a worldlet, and I was ready to explain; but her worries were elsewhere.

"You brought her here to the *Cuchulain,* knowing what the crew is like? You're crazy. This long out of port, they're sex-starved to the last man. If somebody else on this ship ever finds out—"

"Somebody else already found out." The matter-of-fact voice from the doorway jerked us around to face that way. It was Danny Shaker. He came inside, closed the door, and carefully locked it. "Fortunately, that somebody is me—no thanks to you, Jay, leaving an unlocked door."

"The crew—"

"I know. You think they're all working below on the drive. And you happen to be right. But thinking and knowing are two different things."

He moved across to Joe Munroe and gave the body a brief inspection. "Your work?" he said to me.

I nodded. "I had to—"

"Save the explanation," Shaker turned to Doctor Eileen. "And you know about *her,* too. Well, this changes everything." He wandered over to one of the swivel chairs, sat down in it, and drummed the fingers of his right hand on the solid arm.

"This girl is in danger," Doctor Eileen said flatly. "Great danger."

"More than you realize." Shaker was staring absently at

the control board, where lights winked their warnings about
deteriorating drive condition. "And so are you, Doctor. My
ability to control the crew grows less every time the engines
lose another percent of power. My men regard this trip more
and more as a disaster, and what happened here won't help
at all." Shaker sighed. "All right, it's time for a change of
plans. Joe's death will cause all sorts of uproar. These
quarters will be at the center of it. She"—he jerked a thumb
at Mel, without ever looking at her—"can't stay here any
longer."

"Could she go back where she came from?" asked Doctor
Eileen. "To *Paddy's Fortune?*"

"How?"

"The cargo beetles—they're suitable for free-space
travel."

"Sure—up to a hundred thousand kilometers, maximum. We've been going slow enough to annoy everybody,
but we're still a thousand times that far from *Paddy's Fortune.*"
Shaker turned at last from his inspection of the control
board. "I see only one way to do this, Doctor. Mel Fury goes
with you, and stays out of sight. That shouldn't be too hard.
You're up on the highest level, and I can keep the men clear
of it. But Jay will have to stay here and face a crew hearing."

I didn't like the sound of that. Nor apparently did Eileen
Xavier, because she and I started to talk at once.

Shaker cut us off with a wave of his hand. "Doctor Xavier,
I can and will discuss the logic of this with you further. But
not here, and not now. If you want your guest to be as safe as
possible"—he nodded at Mel. Your guest! But Doctor Eileen
didn't react—"then you have to get out of here *at once.* The
drive overhaul isn't going to take forever. The crew will be
back." He stood up. "Mel Fury, collect whatever you need. I
want you out of here in one minute."

Mel gave him a startled look, but she didn't haggle and
hassle him endlessly, the way she did me. She flew through to

the inner room and appeared half a minute later carrying her little backpack.

"The navaid, Jay," she said. "I've been finding some interesting things, new areas for analysis and calculation—"

"Keep it." The way I was feeling, I couldn't add two and two. "Better still, you ought to show it to Jim Swift. He'll—"

"No time for talk." Danny Shaker interrupted me. "If she doesn't get out of here at once, she'll be showing it to Robbie Doonan and Connor Bryan—and a lot of other things, too, if they see her."

"Doctor James Swift," I called after them, as Mel and Doctor Eileen made a dash for the door. "He'll be able to tell you everything that we've learned from the old records."

"Which, when you get down to it, are useless." Shaker did not bother to close the door after them. "Theories are fine, but we've learned more on this one trip than the whole of Erin found out in two hundred years. Come on. There's one thing more we have to do before anyone else gets here."

He went over and made another and closer examination of Joe Munroe's body. "Just as I feared. The gun, Jay. Where is it? I assume you're arguing self-defense."

I moved across and handed the weapon to him. "It really wasn't. I was stopping him doing it to Mel. Joe Munroe knew she was a girl. He was going to . . ."

"I'm sure he was. But the crew's not to know about that, and your problem is that these wounds are in his *back*. Oh, well. This can't do Joe any harm. Stand clear."

He thumbed off the gun's safety catch and set it for multiple clips. While I watched, he pumped forty to fifty shots into Joe Munroe's chest and side. The lifeless body shook and twitched as though it was filled with dreadful new life. It slowly turned under the impact.

Shaker paused, waited, and fired one more clip. He examined the result like an artist studying his creation. "That's a lot better," he said. "Know why I did that, Jay? Because of what you'll have to say to the others. You had to defend yourself, see, and you had the gun on full automatic. He started coming straight for you, and he was facing you, but the force of the shots turned him away as you fired. So the last clip went into his side and back. Understand?''

He stared at me. "What's the problem? Squeamish?''

"No.'' *Yes*—but I wouldn't admit it to Danny Shaker. "I'm wondering why you're not furious with me. I mean, you were short-handed already because of Sean Wilgus, and now I've killed another crewman.''

"I hate to lose any member of the crew. But Joe was certainly asking for it. He left the drive area without permission, and came hunting around up here for whatever he could find. You may even have done me a favor. There's a point where any asset can become a liability, and the hardest part, if you're a hold-on-to-things sort of person—and I'm that, if I'm anything, it's either my strength or my weakness—anyway, the hardest part is to know you've got something more trouble than it's worth, and let go. Maybe I was at that point with Joe. I'm not surprised he did something wild—he had been out looking for trouble all this trip.'' Shaker came across, handed me Walter Hamilton's gun, and slapped me on the shoulder. "What I am surprised by, Jay, is you. I told you when I gave you that gun, I wasn't sure you'd find it in you to use it. I was wrong.''

He studied me for a few more seconds, while I stood there uncomfortable. And then, oddly enough, he came out with just about the same words that Duncan West had used in the corridor. "You're changing, Jay, and changing fast. You don't look like the lad who came aboard on Erin—and you don't sound like him, either. You're living like a man now.''

And maybe dying like one, I thought, already imagining the sound of boots outside. I was going to be subjected to a crew hearing for killing Joe Munroe. The more I thought about it, the more a "hearing" sounded like a trial. Knowing what I did about this crew—and what they knew about me—I couldn't imagine any penalty but death for a guilty verdict.

* * *

Danny Shaker made the rules clear to me before he went back to see how work was going on the drive.

"This is a crew matter," he said. "When one crew member offends another—and to a spacer, death is just another offense—the matter is settled by a crew hearing. You are crew now, we took you on."

"What will *you* do?"

"Well, I'll be there, of course, and in principle I can override any decision for the good of the ship. But I'm telling you now, I won't do a thing. You'll have to defend yourself, as much as you did against Joe Munroe."

"You just sit and watch?"

"Unless there's no agreement. Then I become involved." He glanced around the cabin. "I have to go. I'll tell the crew what happened as soon as I get with them. Better make this place look the way you'd like it to look, before they come for you. Hide anything that should be hidden."

As soon as he was gone I went across to Joe Munroe's body. Mel's pink flashlight bulged in his pocket, but I didn't see any way to dispose of it. Even the thought of touching the bloody, battered flesh and clothing made me feel nauseated all over again. I sat in a chair and stared mindlessly at the pale, floating corpse. After a few minutes the ship's drive went on and the body slammed to the floor. I went over to it, thinking to straighten the twisted limbs, and found I still couldn't bring myself to touch him. I was standing by the body when Tom Toole came to take me away. He gave Joe Munroe one curious glance and nodded to me. "Come on."

The hearing began half an hour later in the main control room, with Pat O'Rourke as a kind of prosecutor and no one assigned to help me out. The other crew sat like a jury in a neat row, with arms folded. Connor Bryan, William Synge, Rory O'Donovan, Dougal Linn, Tom Toole, Robert Doonan—everyone was present except fat Donald Rudden.

Danny Shaker sat at the end, a little apart from the others. Surveying the line, it occurred to me that Shaker's biggest critics, Sean Wilgus and Joseph Munroe, were both dead. Shaker's own job might be easier.

But that wasn't likely to help me. Pat O'Rourke got down to business right away, and there was no doubt how he felt.

"Joe Munroe was an old shipmate of mine," he began. "He served with me on the *Cuchulain* for fourteen years, and before that on the *Colleen* and the *Galway*. He was a good crewman, one who knew ships and the Forty Worlds like the back of his hand. Now he's dead and gone, God rest his soul. Jay Hara"—he turned to glower at me—"shot him. Shot him over and over, 'til Joe had more holes in him than Middletown Mere. You all saw his poor body. Do you admit that, Jay Hara? If you do, now's your chance to tell us why you did it."

"I do admit it. I had to do it to defend myself. He'd already beaten me and knocked me out and nearly broken my skull against the stairs. He thought I had valuables with me that I'd found on *Paddy's Fortune,* and he said if I didn't give them to him he'd make me breathe vacuum. When he came at me again, I shot him."

Pat O'Rourke nodded and pointed to Connor Bryan, who stood up and came forward to where I was sitting.

"Don't move," Bryan said. He was the *Cuchulain*'s next best thing to a medic, and according to Doctor Eileen he knew a fair amount in a rough and ready sort of way. Now he felt my head and jaw, then nodded. "A big lump here, right enough, and the skin broken under the hair. He's had a good bash or two, and it's recent."

O'Rourke nodded again. "And Joe thought you had valuable things, from *Paddy's Fortune,*" he said to me. "Did you?"

Mel wasn't a *thing*. "No, I didn't," I said clearly.

"We'll see about that." As O'Rourke was speaking, Donald Rudden came ambling into the room, slow-moving and deliberate as always. He set Mel's pink flashlight down in front of Pat O'Rourke, then went to sit down with the rest of the crew. After a few seconds he lumbered to his feet again. "I looked," he began.

"Not yet, Don." O'Rourke cut him off. "You'll get your turn." He turned to Robert Doonan. "You first, Robbie. Tell us what Joe Munroe told you and showed you."

"Aye. He showed me that light. Said he found it on the cargo beetle, after we left that little world back there. I'd never seen anything like it before, nor had Joe. He said it must have been brought aboard by Jay Hara, and where it came from there had to be more stuff."

"This light here?" O'Rourke held up the pink ring.

"Aye, that's it."

Donald Rudden heaved himself to his feet again. "I've—" he began.

"In a minute, Don. Bide your time. Jay Hara, what do you have to say?"

I suddenly realized what had been going on during the past half hour. All the crew members were supposed to be present at a hearing. But while we had been getting started, Donald Rudden had been absent—and my bet was that he had been in my quarters, searching. Doing what I should have been doing, when I had the chance. Instead I had sat and stared at Joe Munroe's dead body.

The question was, had Mel, in her hurry to get out of there, left something behind that didn't belong on the *Cuchulain*? Had Donald Rudden found something damning?

If he had, that was the end of me. Unfortunately I had no way of knowing.

"I brought that light aboard the cargo beetle, that's quite true," I said carefully. "I found it on *Paddy's Fortune,* and I assumed one of you must have dropped it there. I didn't say anything about it, because I didn't realize it was anything special. I don't see why it *is* special—I mean, it's just a light. And I didn't bring anything else with me from *Paddy's Fortune.* Not a thing."

"What about the gun?"

"That was Walter Hamilton's. I took it after Sean Wilgus killed him." I realized where they could go with that, if they knew what weapon had shot Wilgus. But Danny Shaker didn't seem worried, so chances were no one else had seen the gun after Walter Hamilton had it on his belt.

O'Rourke gave a noncommittal grunt. "Why did you shoot Joe so many times?"

"I didn't mean to." (True enough!) "I'd never fired an automatic before—never fired any gun. Once it started I couldn't stop it, not even after Munroe had a lot of shots in him."

O'Rourke nodded, and Donald Rudden stood up for a third time. I held my breath. This was it.

"Well, Don?" rumbled Pat O'Rourke.

"Nothing."

"Nothing at all?"

"Not one thing that you wouldn't expect to find. And I took my time looking."

I didn't doubt that. Donald Rudden looked too fat to move, but when he started on a job he was a bit like Duncan West taking apart a clock. He was completely methodical, he lost track of time, and he didn't move or stop until the task was done.

There was a sort of collective sigh, and everybody sat a little differently in his seat. It was the turning point, and I realized it when Pat O'Rourke said to me, "Jay Hara, what do you mass?"

It was a weird question. "I'm not sure. Back on Erin, last time I weighed myself, I was fifty-one kilos."

He nodded, and turned to the others. "Joe Munroe, for my guess, was about a hundred and ten. More than twice as much as Jay Hara. Anyone else want to say anything or ask anything?"

Heads shook along the line.

"All right, then." O'Rourke clumped across and sat down with the others, at the opposite end of the line from Danny

Shaker. There was a long, brooding silence, when no one spoke and I was left wondering what came next.

Finally O'Rourke stood up again. "All right, then," he repeated. "That ought to be enough time. Let's get to it. In order, as you're sitting. Connor Bryan?"

"Justified killing, in self-defense," Bryan said. "No punishment. And I have to say, Joe Munroe was a fool. He told me—"

"No speeches," O'Rourke interrupted. "You know the rules. Tom Toole?"

"Justified killing. Self-defense."

"Robert Doonan?"

"Justified killing," Doonan's words sounded dragged out of him, but they came. "In self-defense."

It went along the line. *Justified killing in self-defense.* O'Rourke stopped short of asking Danny Shaker. Instead he shook his own massive head and said, "I don't like it, but evidence is evidence. So I'll make it unanimous. Justified killing, in self-defense. And I have to say, if you can tell me a more stupid, misguided idiot than Joe Munroe, going off half-cocked the way he did, and then being bested one-on-one by a young 'un who's hardly clear of the ground, and letting him—"

"No speeches, Pat," said Tom Toole. "Remember?" He didn't laugh or smile, but with those words the whole atmosphere changed. The crewmen still looked grim, and no one would meet my eye, but a lot of tension had vanished from the room.

"That's it, then," O'Rourke said. "You, Jay Hara, you're free and clear. And I'm going to say it one more time, no matter what the rules are: Joe was a damned fool." He walked across to me, and after what looked like a big internal struggle reached out and shook my hand. "But that's no fault of yours. This hearing's officially over. It'll be back to work as normal for you, next shift."

He nodded, and headed for the cabin exit. I half expected that the others would come over and say something, too, but they didn't. Without looking at me they filed out one by one, until I was alone in the room with Danny Shaker.

"It's not really over," I said, "no matter what Patrick O'Rourke says. They're all still angry as can be."

"Quite true. But it's over, all the same." Shaker hadn't said one word during the whole proceeding. Now he was lolling back comfortably in his chair. "You don't understand spacers, Jay. They're upset, and they're angry. But they're not mad at you. They're mad at *Joe Munroe*. He embarrassed them all. Even his best friend, Pat O'Rourke, is angry with him. From their point of view, what he did was stupid in more ways than you can count. First, he didn't think to frisk you. A gun won't beat a working brain, but it will beat a fist any time. Second, he lost out to a Downside kid, half his mass and less than half his age. Think what *that* does to the spacer image." Shaker stood up. "You've been lucky today, Jay, in three different ways. With Munroe, with me, and with the hearing. Luck's important. Just don't start to count on it. Because if you do, that's the time it won't work."

He headed for the door, too. "Busy day, eh?" he said over his shoulder. "But you've not helped the *Cuchulain* any. Extra work hours for you next shift, to make up. If you wanted to report sick because of that bash on the head, you should have done it sooner."

He was gone, before I could frame the reply I wanted.

Busy day? It seemed years since I had run into Uncle Duncan on the stairway. It had been—I struggled to work it out— no more than three hours. A couple more days like this, and I'd feel as old as Doctor Eileen.

CHAPTER **25**

Life in space,'' Tom Toole said cheerfully, ''is like life in war. You go muddling along for ages with nothing much happening, and you're bored as all get out; then something happens, and all of a sudden you're so busy you don't know which way to turn.''

I was scraping a grease-coated wall of the cargo hold, in a place where cleaning machines, despite Duncan West's best fix-it efforts, refused to go. I grunted, and went on scraping. It was a rare philosophical statement from Tom, made as he watched me labor. I knew nothing about war, and hoped I never would, but the two weeks that followed Joe Munroe's death had taught me that Tom was wrong about space. I wasn't bored, even though we were crawling slower than ever toward our new destination. I didn't have time to be. I was kept busy from the moment I got up to the time I collapsed into my bunk. Between them, Tom Toole and Pat O'Rourke never gave me a moment's peace—particularly since every job took me three times as long as they said it ought to. It had to be intentional on their part. Thinks he's a spacer now, does he? Well, we'll show *him*. He still has a lot to learn.

I could have complained to Danny Shaker. I felt like

doing it a dozen times, but I didn't. I just gritted my teeth, swore under my breath, and stuck at it while the rest of the crew took it easy.

There was a bonus side to all my labors. I was learning about the workings of the *Cuchulain* in a way that no talking or lessons could ever have given me. But I didn't realize how fast my hard work was making time fly by, until I heard an odd, fluting whistle over the communications system.

Tom said at once, "All hands call. Drop that. We have to get to the bridge."

He set off at once and without waiting for me. I, full of worries of onboard disaster, hurried after him to the main control room.

"Can't tell what it is." Danny Shaker was at the controls when we entered, juggling displays. "It's strange, I show a target when I use ultralong radio waves, but nothing on visible or infra-red, or on regular radar."

"What are you going to do?" Pat O'Rourke asked. All the crew were crowding around.

"Keep flying and wait for a better signal. We're still at extreme range, but we're closing fast." Shaker saw that I had joined the huddle. "Score one for the navaid, Jay. I don't know if that's the Net and the hardware reservoir we're looking for, but something is just ahead with the orbital elements and motion you specified. Go get Eileen Xavier. We'll be arriving in an hour or two. She'll want to take a peek at this."

Arriving. At Godspeed Base?

I hurried away, wondering again about Danny Shaker. He had been careful to keep me away from Doctor Eileen and the rest of the Erin party, so I had no idea how they were doing. But now, with the crew certain to stay around the control room for a while, he was in effect inviting me to go along and tell Doctor Eileen and the others anything that I liked.

Why? I didn't know. I understood the ship's workings a

lot better after all my work, but I sure didn't understand Dan Shaker. As Tom Toole had said, he was a deep one. I could now dismiss all the "two-half-man" stuff that had given me nightmares before, but I couldn't get rid of the thought that Shaker might be testing me in some way that I couldn't guess.

It was this feeling, more than any shred of fact, that made me cautious. I intended to do just what Shaker had directed: Find Doctor Eileen, and bring her back to the control room. And if we talked on the way? Well, that wasn't ruled out in his instructions.

I *intended* to do that. What I hadn't allowed for was the possibility that I would run into Mel Fury the moment I entered Doctor Eileen's quarters.

She must have been hiding away and somehow watching the corridor, because she popped out in front of me as soon as I came through the door.

"Hi, Jay!"

"Hey!"

We stood staring at each other in pleasure—and something else, too, at least in my case. Concern.

"Mel, for God's sake—you're supposed to try to look like a *boy*."

With her fair hair growing and combed loose in a different style, she was far more female than she had ever been. She would have been accepted as a girl, even by the primped and pampered primadonnas of Erin.

Mel shook her head, and her lengthening hair floated around it. "I can't, Jay. I mean, I can try to look boyish, but I can't succeed. Doctor Eileen says that any man on board would know, even if I cut my hair again. She says the trick is not to let anybody see me."

Which was exactly what *I* had been saying, from the moment she came on board the *Cuchulain*. I could tell from the way Mel said "Doctor Eileen" that she had been added to the list of Eileen Xavier worshippers, and Doctor Eileen's word was sacred. Even so, the way Mel had jumped out at me didn't suggest great caution. Suppose some crewman had come in right after me?

"Mel, I want you to carry Walter Hamilton's gun around with you. Just as a precaution."

She pulled a face. "I hate guns. I'll think about it. Where is it?"

"Back in my quarters. I'll give it to Doctor Eileen, and ask her to pass it on to you. Where is she?"

"Gone to get Jim—you know, Dr. Swift."

I didn't like that, either. Jim Swift used to be *my* buddy, but from the familiar way she dropped his name, he was now hers.

"I have to find the doctor," I said. "At once. She and I are urgently needed in the main control room."

It was designed to impress, but it didn't work.

"Phooey," Mel said. "If they want *you* urgently, it's to make tea. What happened to your voice? You sound husky and creaky, like one of the crewmen."

"My voice is fine. And I *am* a crewman."

"Playing at being one is more like. Listen, Jay. I've been working on the navaid with Jim Swift—he's really sharp—and we're coming up with something that may be terrifically important. Remember the 'Slowdrive' that you tagged in Walter Hamilton's notebook? Well, I cross-referenced it in the navaid—"

"You can tell me about that some other time. At the moment I'm busy. I must find Eileen Xavier, and I must take her with me to the main control room."

And I swept grandly out, before Mel could say another word.

All right, so I was miffed, and what I did was stupid. But I couldn't forgive her that crack about making tea, and not being a real crew member—maybe because I suspected it was true. So although I felt sorry that Mel and I hadn't had a real chance to talk, I didn't go back. Instead I found Doctor Eileen and headed for the ship's bridge.

I really wanted to talk, to tell her what had been happening. The trouble was, she didn't choose to listen. She wanted an audience of her own, so she could ramble on with *her* worries. If I had changed, Doctor Eileen had changed, too, in the few months since we lifted off from Muldoon Port. I had always thought of her as old, but old like something that has always been around and will be around forever. Now Doctor Eileen looked tired, peevish and depressed.

"The Net, eh?" She laughed, but it was a harsh, barking cough without any humor in it. "The great hardware reservoir. Well, maybe. I've talked enough to Mel to know that *Paddy's Fortune* was set up as a self-sustaining biological reservoir. What comes next?"

"The Needle, The Eye, Godspeed Base—and a Godspeed Drive."

"You think so? It's great to be young. You know, Jay, I've thought a lot since we left Erin. About space, sure, but about Erin, too, and what we are. I used to think of the Isolation as some sort of pure accident, something that couldn't have been prevented. Now, I'm not so sure. I don't think that humanity before the Isolation was just one big happy family. Maybe at one time, during the early, sublight colonization. But then I think that the people who developed the Godspeed Drive came to regard themselves as *special,* superior to planetary colonists and settlers. The Godspeed Drive was so powerful, it made them feel like gods themselves and they wanted to keep it that way. They left the colonies ignorant. And we've stayed ignorant. They placed their supply and maintenance facilities deep in space. No one on Erin knew how the drive worked. No one knew that *Paddy's Fortune* even existed. No one would know it today, if Paddy Enderton had gone overboard that night on Lake Sheelin."

"You think the people with the Godspeed Drive stopped coming to the Forty Worlds *on purpose?*"

"Oh, no. That wasn't planned. I'm sure there was a monstrous accident, a catastrophe of some kind. But Erin wouldn't be in the mess it's in today if the group who controlled the Drive hadn't wanted to feel *superior*. It's a story as old as history, from water control to drug prescription to access to space: The people with the treasure want to keep the keys of the treasure-house to themselves. What they never dream is that one day they might not be around to use them. So they don't plan for that."

Talking about the past, Doctor Eileen sounded like a defeated woman. Maybe Duncan West had it right: *Live in the present.* If you started to dwell on history, you would find a thousand ways to make yourself miserable.

We entered the control room, and what was revealed on the displays there was enough to halt Doctor Eileen's brooding.

The big screen showed a shape like a round balloon made from fishing net. The individual loops of the net were triangular, and at many of the nodes I could see a "knot," a little point of light. It was the Net. Was it also the hardware reservoir?

"Take a look, Doctor," said Danny Shaker. He was busy at the console, but apparently had eyes in the back of his head. "No wonder our first look was just with low-frequency radio. All the radiation shorter than a few kilometers went right on through. But the long wavelengths were right to interact with the mesh and give a return signal."

That was the first hint I had of the size of the Net ahead of us. If those tiny individual loops of the balloon were kilometers across, then each point of light at the nodes . . .

Doctor Eileen pointed to a smaller display mounted next to the big one. It showed a single node at high magnification, a silver point of light expanded to a grainy, lumpy half-sphere. That could be an empty cargo container, a manufacturing facility, even a ship. The surrounding gossamer threads that formed loops of the net were cables or tubes, tens of meters across, running from the partial sphere and anchoring it in space.

Soon I could see something else. The object on the screen was not complete. Jagged break lines ran across the blunt end. At the node floated no more than a shattered remnant, a broken fragment of a complete structure.

As I stared, the display flickered. It changed to show a pair of thick partial rings, battered rust-colored doughnuts intertwined and floating in space. Another flicker, and before I could see any detail on the doughnuts they too were gone. The image had changed to a loose cluster of small objects. Most of them had the familiar bowl-backed shape of a cargo beetle. They were loosely connected by cables almost too thin to see, and when I looked closely I could see individual differences. One lacked its lower half, another had been sheared in two across the center, the upper dome of a third had a great hole punched through it.

Another flicker. I was gazing at a rough partial sphere, like the first object we had seen but even more battered. It was less grainy in appearance. The *Cuchulain* was still approaching the space structure, and the high-resolution imagers were steadily improving the quality of the pictures.

"It's a junk yard." I spoke in a whisper to Doctor Eileen. She had lost her dejected look. "This can't be the hardware reservoir."

"We'll see," Danny Shaker said over his shoulder. "We're making an inventory now. So many nodes, the first look has to be automatic."

"So many nodes" was an understatement. I tried a quick count and gave up after half a minute. Hundreds, maybe thousands. This mess *couldn't* be Godspeed Base. It would take a long time just to visit each node on the Net.

I was still staring when I felt a slap on the back—Tom Toole, grinning all over his face.

"Here we are, Jay," he said. "Didn't I tell you? We're all going to be rich—rolling in money."

"Rich? It's all junk." But as I spoke I realized that the atmosphere in the control room was like a celebration. Crew members were laughing, shaking hands, and hammering their fists on the walls.

"The hell it is!" Tom Toole, in his enthusiasm, reached his arm around his enemy Doctor Eileen and gave her a squeeze. "I've been making trips to the Forty Worlds for half my life, and I've never seen the like of this. Many a time, come Winterfall, the lads and me would go home with nothing to show. Not this time, though. Look at that!" He pointed to the display, where a twisted cylindrical hulk hung in its retaining network of tubes. "Even if it don't work—even if it's *empty*—it's valuable materials. Every one of the things out there is money. Give me a scavenger ship, a decent crew, and half a year in this place, I'd go home Lord of Skibbereen."

Doctor Eileen had become caught up in the mood. She was laughing at the antics of tubby Donald Rudden, bouncing up and down in place until his belly and jowls rippled.

Then I saw Danny Shaker. Ignoring the noise around him he sat at the controls, quietly and carefully making some fine adjustment. I followed his glance to another and smaller screen. At first I saw only a reduced version of the whole net. Then as I moved to stand by Shaker's side I realized that he was performing a controlled zoom, arrowing the display toward a central region of the field.

That center was not empty. Delineated in space, unattached to any point of the network, a slender sharp-ended feature was appearing. I cannot say I saw it, because nothing was visible. I deduced its existence because something was occulting the background field of stars.

"The Needle," Shaker said softly. I could not tell if he was talking to me or to himself. "First the Net and hardware reservoir." He glanced across to the screen showing the results of the node scan, and from his expression he didn't share the crew's enthusiasm. Displayed at the moment was an object like a smaller version of the *Cuchulain*, except that something had snapped it across the column of the cargo hold and twisted the two halves until the flared drive unit sat next to the living quarters. "Reservoir, Net, and Needle. So where's the Eye?"

"The Eye of the Needle," I said. "In the center . . ."

Under Danny Shaker's control, the imaging system was already creeping along the invisible line of the Needle, beginning at one imagined end and scanning steadily toward the other.

I strained my eyes, willing photons to appear and signal the existence of a Needle's Eye. The display offered only a line of cold, starfree darkness from one end to the other.

Danny Shaker sighed, lifted his hands from the controls, and turned to me. For one second I saw tension on his face. Then he gave me a smile.

"Not so easy, eh? Needle, but no Eye. Here." He stood up and gestured to the chair. "Try your hand, Jay. I need a bit of young man's luck."

I didn't think I was particularly lucky, but nothing in the Forty Worlds could have kept me out of that control chair. Three minutes of experiment gave me the hang of it, controlling the movement of the display and the degree of magnification of the zoom.

I moved out to one end of the Needle, and worked my way steadily along it. I saw nothing—but at one point I imagined a hint of a bit more nothing than usual.

"Look at the star field." I halted the display. "I think an extra area is being masked out. Can you change the brightness and pick up fainter background stars?"

Shaker said nothing, but he leaned over and pressed one button. The intensity of the display increased. Thousands of added stars and galaxies filled the screen.

It was easy to see it now. The spike of the Needle, delineated against a deep space backdrop, was thicker at one point. There was a bulge, a broadening of the smooth line. I zoomed as far as the system would go, and still saw only blackness.

I was ready to resume the scan along the Needle, disappointed at my failure, when Danny Shaker leaned over my shoulder.

"Not too fast, Jay. I don't see anything either, but let's try another part of the spectrum. Run us through the wavelengths, ultraviolet to deep radio."

Maybe he thought that was a straightforward request, but it was beyond me. I moved out of the way and watched Danny Shaker exercise another brief command sequence.

"Hard U/V," he said. "No return signal. Same for the visible, full absorption there and in the near infra-red." He was explaining aloud for my benefit. "Let's try thermal. Nothing there either—"

"Wait. Stop it there."

I had seen something. Black on black, a deeper shade of shadow. The whole line of the Needle was dark—but I sensed that one part was darker than the rest.

"That's a thermal signature," Shaker said. "Let's take a look at actual temperatures. Show me where." He touched another set of keys, and a cursor appeared on the screen. He moved it a little way off the point I indicated.

"Not there," I said. "A bit more over to the right."

"I know. We need this for comparison." Numbers appeared below the cursor. "I'm querying at different wavelengths. The background shows a maximum at sixty micrometers, fifty-two degrees absolute. That's about right for ambient, the temperature of a radiating black body this far from Maveen. So this part of the Needle is absorbing shorter wavelength solar energy perfectly, and emitting it as long-wave thermal radiation. Now for the real test. We ask for the temperature as we go, and see what happens. Show me where."

Under my direction the cursor began to move, creeping

to the center of the darkest area. The region below the cursor began to fall—and fall again.

"Thirty-seven. Thirty-two." Shaker was repeating the values to himself. "Twenty-four. Fifteen. My God, how much lower? Eleven, seven—can't go much farther. Five. Four. Three."

The cursor was at the exact center of the dark region, and the numerical display below it had steadied to a constant value.

"Two point seven degrees," Shaker said softly. "How about that, Jay."

"What about it?" It meant nothing to me.

"That point, right where the cursor is sitting, is at the temperature of the cosmic background radiation. How can we observe the background, but not see the stars?" Shaker stared around the room, where the crew still showed high excitement. Finally he was showing signs of that excitement himself. "The answer is, you can't see background without stars, not in any normal region of space. So that's no normal region of space."

He leaned back in his seat. "It's the Eye, Jay, right there. That's where we have to go, through the Eye of the Needle. That's where we look for Godspeed Base. That's where we find the Godspeed Drive."

CHAPTER **26**

Hardware reservoir' is too charitable," Doctor Eileen said. She, Jim Swift and I were by the display, watching an endless array of ruined space structures that came and went on the screen. Her first enthusiasm had faded, and now she sounded nervous and gloomy. *"Graveyard* would be a better term. And by the look of it the heap of junk we're traveling on knows just where it belongs. It came to the right place."

The *Cuchulain* was hobbling toward the black unknown of the Eye, slow as a Lake Sheelin thaw. We were not hurrying for two reasons: caution, and because we had no choice. The engines of the *Cuchulain* sounded as though they were on their last legs. For the past half hour a steady vibration had shaken the whole ship, enough to keep your teeth on edge. At any other time, Danny Shaker would have ordered the drive turned off for maintenance. Today he ignored it. All his attention seemed fixed on the circle of darkness.

Except that he must have been aware of what was going on behind him, because he said, "You claim the glass is half-empty, doctor, but I prefer to think it's half-full. The *Cuchulain* isn't in great shape, but it did exactly what it had to do: It brought us here."

"To a junkyard. Are you suggesting that you can make a working vessel out of that sort of thing?" Eileen Xavier pointed to where a dismembered drive unit hung close to a mangled cargo stem.

"If I had to. It wasn't so different from that a few years ago, putting a ship together from bits and pieces so we could limp home. With injuries, too, and crew deaths, to make everything that much harder." Shaker laughed, as though injuries and deaths were the most natural thing in the world. "But we're facing nothing like that this time. We're well off. That's Godspeed Base ahead of us."

"Or something," Doctor Eileen said. "I hope you know what you're doing, flying straight for that thing."

"No more than you do, Doctor. But spacers are paid to take risks. Tell me if you want to stop, or if you want to play it supersafe. If you like you can leave the *Cuchulain*, hang around in a cargo beetle, and watch while we go in."

He had one eye on Eileen Xavier as he spoke. I was sure that he really knew what he was doing, and that he was just testing her feelings. But suppose she reacted wrong? If she didn't want to continue, after coming so far and so long . . . Worst of all, suppose that she made *me* stay behind and out of danger, the way she had when we reached *Paddy's Fortune*.

I decided that it didn't matter what she wanted. I was crew now, and I would go with the ship.

"Physicians aren't trained to take risks," Doctor Eileen said. "Especially with people's lives. I want an expert opinion on this. Dr. Swift?"

Jim Swift hadn't spoken since he came to the bridge, apart from an appreciative "Mmm," when he saw the Eye. But he had been studying the black pupil as we neared it, and making calculations.

Now he said, "I doubt if my thoughts are any different from Captain Shaker's. The Luimneach Anomaly?"

Danny Shaker nodded. "That's how I'm thinking."

"The what?" asked Doctor Eileen.

"Luimneach is one of the frozen planets, ninth one out beyond Tyrone." Jim Swift looked at Shaker. "Not much that's valuable there, as I recall."

"Volatiles. But nothing you can't find a lot closer to Maveen. Nothing worth hauling."

"The Luimneach Anomaly is something—I'm not sure what to call it—in orbit around the planet. It's a black region, just like that one." Swift pointed to the screen. "Same size, too, according to my estimates."

"And—inside the Anomaly?" Doctor Eileen glanced from one man to the other.

Danny Shaker shrugged. "Not a thing. I've never been inside myself, but I know people who have. There's nothing there."

"Which is why it's so frustrating," Jim Swift added. "Some people even claim the Anomaly is a *natural* feature, a quirk in space-time. I never bought that explanation myself, and now we have proof that it's not true. If we don't take anything else back with us, this makes the whole trip worthwhile."

"I had in mind a rather more tangible result," Doctor Eileen said drily. "I take it, Dr. Swift, that you don't think it would be too risky to enter?"

He shrugged. "Hey, life's a risk."

From her expression it was not quite the reassurance she was looking for. Doctor Eileen sighed and said, "I must be getting old. All right, Captain Shaker. I see that I am in a minority of one. Proceed. Let's see what we've got."

She was agreeing! We were going in! I could breathe easy again, as the *Cuchulain* rattled and creaked its way forward. The Eye grew, until it filled the whole display screen with a dense, unrelieved blackness. And then, while I was still waiting for something to happen, Danny Shaker said casually, "The ship is being slowed. We must be passing through the membrane. If this is anything like the

Luimneach Anomaly, we'll be out again in just a few seconds.''

We entered another one of those periods when time stretches forever. It may have been seconds, but it seemed hours before the screen showed a first ghost of an image, a dim outline like a bottom-heavy figure eight with a tiny extra lobe stuck onto its upper end. As Shaker murmured, ''Nearly out,'' the image brightened and solidified. The middle part flickered and changed randomly before my eyes.

The control room remained silent, until Jim Swift said in a husky voice, ''Well, *this* anomaly's not empty.''

''Far from it.'' Danny Shaker turned to Doctor Eileen. ''I can't guarantee that this is Godspeed Base until we take a closer look. But I'll bet my share of this whole venture on it. The big sphere on the bottom end of that structure is just the sort of hangar where you do deep space service on large ships.''

''What about the Drive?'' I asked.

Shaker nodded. ''Where there's a ship, inside a hangar, inside an anomaly, inside a hardware net, then inside that ship you can hope to find . . .''

He didn't finish his sentence. But I finished it for him, inside my head.

. . . a Godspeed Drive.

The exploring party was itching to be on its way even before the *Cuchulain* reached the structure. Only a skeleton crew would remain on our ship, because everyone wanted to go. As Jim Swift said, with a perverse logic that seemed shared by everyone, ''I'm quite sure it *is*. But if it isn't, I want to know *at once.*''

So did I, only I had worries of my own. I didn't like that talk of a skeleton crew that would stay on the *Cuchulain*.

While Jim Swift seemed to be starting an argument with Danny Shaker and Doctor Eileen about the best way to explore the space structure floating ahead of us, I sneaked away to the top level of the living quarters. I was learning. *Out of sight, out of mind.* I didn't want to be around when the skeleton crew was picked.

On the upper level I went to find Mel, but apparently she was learning, too. She stayed hidden until I called softly, "Mel? It's me. It's safe."

Then she popped out and was at me like a hurricane. "What are you doing here? Tell me what's happening. First Eileen Xavier—she vanishes, and she doesn't come back. Then it's Jim Swift. Gone. Then it's Duncan West. Where did they go? What are they doing?"

"If you'll shut up for a minute, I'll tell you." I paused, savoring the moment until I thought she was ready to burst, then I said, "We've found it, Mel!"

"The Reservoir?"

"The Reservoir, the Net, the Needle, the Eye, *everything*. Godspeed Base, and the Godspeed Drive."

"You've been to them?"

"Well, no. But I will have, in an hour or so. We'll be docking any minute. Then a party will go over there."

"But you won't be part of it. You said Doctor Eileen wouldn't let you go to *Paddy's Fortune* because she thought it might be dangerous."

"This will be different. She only did that because I was standing right in front of her."

I was feeling smug at my own cunning, and it must have showed. Because Mel looked furious, and suddenly I didn't feel so full of bounce. She had been standing right by me, but now she plopped down in a chair. "You've been sitting up on the bridge all fat and happy. And you're going off to find the Godspeed Drive. And I'm trapped here with nothing to do but play Jim Swift's stupid games with the navaid. It's not *fair,* and I've had it. I've been doing my best to act responsibly, but you're hiding me away forever. When we started out I had no idea it would take so much time."

back to Mel. At least she would feel better, knowing that the two of us were in the same boat.

Apparently she did feel better. In fact, when I told her what had happened to me she started to laugh like a lunatic, rolling round and round the cabin.

Sometimes you have to think that the rule, *No women in space,* is an excellent idea.

"No one did. The engines are in awful shape, we'v
to travel really slow."

It wasn't much of an answer, and I knew it. Mel was on
boil, and if I stayed around I was going to be the one that
the heat. "I'll go and ask Doctor Eileen," I said hurried
"She might be able to tell us something."

"Never mind *something.*" Mel glowered at me. "Find ou
how long it will be before we get to Erin."

"Right. I'll be back as soon as I can." (*After* we return
from Godspeed Base).

I escaped before Mel could have another go at me. When
I arrived at the bridge there was just one person present.
Donald Rudden was settled in the most comfortable chair,
staring at the displays. A monstrous multilayer sandwich
waited on a tray in front of him.

"Where is everybody?" I said.

"Eh?" He turned to frown at me. "Why, they've gone,
that's where they are. All but me." He pointed a stubby
finger at the screen. The middle part of the space structure
on the display made me squint and blink. Flickering surges of
light ran around it, and I couldn't bring it into focus.

"What's that? I can't see anything."

"Because you're staring at the wrong bit. Don't try to see
the middle lump, you'll go cross-eyed. Look there." He
jabbed his finger onto the screen, and I saw a humpbacked
cargo beetle, heading for the big ovoid that formed the solid
bottom of the figure-eight space structure. "There they go."

"What about *me?!*"

"You're here."

"But I was supposed to go with them!"

He seemed puzzled, and stared at his sandwich for
inspiration. "Well, you weren't here, were you?" he said at
last. "How could they take you, if you weren't here to be
taken?"

It was no good arguing with him, the great pudding. I fled

It's a strange thing, but one person can enjoy an experience, while another sees the same event only as a source of irritation.

But I'm getting ahead of myself.

One of Donald Rudden's defects had become a virtue: Sit him in a comfortable chair with adequate supplies of food and drink, and an earthquake wouldn't budge him. I decided that since he was nicely settled, Mel and I could safely go to the observation bubble on the topmost level of the living quarters. We sneaked up there together and I turned the highest magnification scopes onto the cargo beetle.

Or rather, we turned them onto where the cargo beetle had been. We were just in time to see it nuzzling in to a rendezvous with a port on the side of the structure's big lobe.

Mel, sitting beside me, gasped. So did I. When the *Cuchulain* was far from the space base there had been no way of judging its size. Now we were closer, and the cargo beetle provided a direct standard of scale.

The base was *monstrous*. I estimated that the fat ellipsoid that the beetle was entering had to be at least as big as *Paddy's*

Fortune. It was a world of its own. Even the "tiny" third lobe on the top end of the figure-eight would be big enough to house the *Cuchulain.* As for the middle section, it still defeated my eyes. There was a now-you-see-it, now-you-don't quality that might make you think that our ship's screen wasn't working—except that everything else on the display appeared normal. I decided that the middle part of the base must be transparent, and lit from *within,* like a hollow ball of glass with a continuous lightning storm going on inside.

The beetle vanished quickly into the side of the base. Mel continued to study the display with every sign of interest, enjoying her first look in weeks at open space. But I, as an experienced and blasé space traveller, watched with huge frustration—because I should have been *there,* inside Godspeed Base, not hanging around on the *Cuchulain* while nothing happened.

In the middle of that thought, something very definite did happen. I heard a noise like the clatter of boots on the stairway that led up to the observation bubble.

Mel heard it, too. She turned to me. "You said that the man who was left behind—"

"I know. He *never* moves if he doesn't have to."

Except that the sound was definitely louder. Someone was ascending the staircase. I stared around, and saw what I should have noticed the moment we came in. The observation bubble had only one exit. It also had no place to hide.

"Mel," I whispered. "The gun that I gave Doctor Eileen. Did she pass it on to you?"

"Yes."

"Good. Let me have it." I had fired it once. If I had to I could do it again.

She stared at me in dismay. "I don't have it, Jay. As soon as I had that gun in my hand I knew I could never bear to shoot anyone. I gave it to Duncan West . . ."

. . . and left us totally helpless. The footsteps were right at the top of the staircase. The only thing left was surprise.

I launched myself feet-first toward the doorway. If I were lucky and timed it right, I would hit the intruder at chest level.

"No, Jay!" The shout came from Mel behind me.

I just had time to bend my legs and draw them up toward my body. I still hit the newcomer, right in his midsection, but I had softened the impact. I saw a mop of flaming red hair above Jim Swift's startled face as he staggered, made a wild grab at the doorway, and barely avoided being thrown back down the staircase.

He must have reached out from pure reflex, because my driving feet had knocked all the wind out of him. For the next half minute he grovelled on the floor, struggling for breath, while Mel and I hovered uselessly around him.

At last Jim raised his head and croaked, "What the hell?"

It was all he could say before he ran out of air again. Mel lifted him up, while I gabbled explanations and excuses.

After a while he nodded. "All right, all right. You didn't mean it. But you sure as hell did it." He straightened up, winced, and felt his midriff.

"But why aren't *you* on the cargo beetle?" I said. I couldn't believe he had missed the boat, too.

"Because they're dummies, that's why!" Anger did him more good than apologies. The color came rushing back to his face. "Total idiots. I tried to warn that stupid crew, and all they did was say that I didn't know about space. Me!"

"But you told me that you don't," said Mel. "You insisted that the trip on the *Cuchulain* was your first time in space."

Jim Swift had probably told her exactly that, but he didn't want to know it. His face became redder. "I don't know about *space*. But I know a hell of a lot about *space-time,* more than the rest of them put together will ever know."

Mel put her hand on his arm. "Calm down, Jim."

It was the perfect way to make him do the opposite.

"What's knowing about space-time got to do with you not going with them now?" I asked hurriedly.

He glared at me instead of Mel. "I'll tell you what. I was brought on this trip because I'm Erin's expert on the theory of the Godspeed Drive, right? I've studied every fact and rumor and half-baked idea to do with the Drive for the past ten years, right? I know what a Godspeed Drive ship ought to look like. But people who don't know *anything* about the Drive—like halfwit spacers—have the idea that a ship with a faster-than-light drive must be just like the *Cuchulain,* only bigger. They associate speed with *size.* And that's totally wrong. A ship with a Godspeed Drive won't need those big, clumsy engines. Because it's superfast it won't need living quarters this size." He swung an arm around, to indicate all the space on the *Cuchulain.* "And if it's a backup ship, for use only in emergencies when the usual Godspeed ships have a problem, it doesn't need a great big space for cargo. It can be *small*—maybe no bigger than a cargo beetle."

It sounded logical to me. Surely it would have impressed Doctor Eileen and Danny Shaker the same way.

"Why didn't you tell them?"

"I would have—if I'd had half a chance." His voice was rising in pitch and volume. "I got there early. I started explaining to Tom Toole, and then that dummy O'Rourke came at me with a stupid question, and jackass Rory O'Donovan joined in. Before I knew it, there was no end of yelling and screaming."

I caught Mel's glance. *I bet there was,* it said, *and I bet I know who was doing most of it.*

"Well, I wasn't going to stand for that. Who would?" Jim Swift stared at us, and we nodded sympathetically.

"You got into a fight?" asked Mel.

"No." He gave a self-righteous sniff. "I left. The hell with them. If they fly over there and get themselves killed, it won't be my fault. But I decided to fly a cargo beetle *myself,* once they were out of the way, and show them I was right in a way they could never dispute.''

"But if you follow them—" Mel protested.

"I wouldn't follow them. I'd go to the logical place where you'd look for an emergency ship with a Godspeed Drive." Jim Swift pointed at the display screen, to the tiny third lobe on the space base. *That's* where you'd store a small ship—not in that great stupid balloon at the other end, or in the flickering middle bit.''

"But why didn't you go?" I asked.

He glared at me, frustration all over his face. "I'll tell you why. Because I'm not one of your bone-brained spacers, that's why. I can't fly one of those stupid, beat-up, crap-heap, space-junk cargo beetles. Half the instruments on them don't even work!''

"Can you?" Mel swung to stare at me, her eyes wide. "He can't, but *can you?* Or have you been boasting to me?''

"I can. I'm sure I can. I *know* I can." I felt dizzy and breathless as I turned to head for the staircase. "Come on. Quick.''

Before I change my mind and decide I can't.

One twenty-minute lesson, weeks and weeks ago. It couldn't be enough. But I was not about to admit to Mel that I had been laying it on a bit thick. I squeezed my eyes shut and told myself that I was a natural spacer. Hadn't I heard it from Paddy Enderton, and the same from Danny Shaker?

"Come *on,*" said Mel's voice from beside me. "What are you waiting for? Let's go.''

Death before dishonor. I opened my eyes. I placed my fingers on the control keys. I took a deep breath. And I flew the cargo beetle. Out of the hold, away into open space, our destination the distant blip of the space base's least significant lobe.

As we moved clear of the *Cuchulain*—and I couldn't help

wondering what Donald Rudden would make of our sudden appearance—I noticed something that should have struck me from inside the ship. The stars were visible. From the outside, the anomaly had been opaque.

I asked Jim Swift how that was possible, and he started on an explanation that involved one-way membranes and thermalization. He probably thought he was being crystal clear, but before he was half-done I had given up and put all my mind into flying the beetle.

Space felt unbelievably huge, our target supernaturally small and remote. I don't think our trajectory would have won any prizes for either speed or minimum distance, and it was a few minutes before I was sure that we were going anywhere at all. But we were getting there. The base was growing on the screen. Soon I could see more details in each part, although no matter what I did I couldn't get a clear view of that middle lobe. It was like trying to see through a dense, patchy fog, details coming and going as you watched. I became convinced that the surface must be more translucent than transparent, like the covering on *Paddy's Fortune*.

At last I had to give up staring, because the third lobe was looming ahead. It had its own port, a tiny one in keeping with its overall proportions. But "tiny" was relative. It was quite big enough for the cargo beetle to creep inside. Once we were there we hung stationary, the three of us peering into the lobe's rounded interior.

We couldn't see a thing. It was pitch-black inside the ovoid. If we wanted an interior look I first had to learn how to work the external searchlight on the cargo beetle. Its pointing stability mechanism was—naturally—broken. That meant another five minutes of frustration, while I struggled to control a wildly oscillating beam of blue-green light.

Mel Fury and Jim Swift had an advantage over me. They didn't have the problem of controlling the instrument, so they could spend all their time watching what was in its beam—and giving me confusing and conflicting instructions.

"Stop it right there!" "No, dummy, don't go that way." "Back up, you had it right before." "Swing it farther over!"

I finally got the beam steadied—no thanks to them. What it showed did not look promising. Square in the searchlight floated a fat corkscrew with a distorted bubble attached to its blunt end. Thin wires held the structure in position and threw off metallic reflections.

It was like no ship I had ever seen or imagined. I was beginning to swing the light in search of a more promising target when Jim Swift howled in protest. "Don't move it, you moron. You have it right there."

It's great to be appreciated. I swore I'd get even with him—sometime, but not now. He was already heading for the airlock.

Even for newcomers to suited flight, the trip across to the object gleaming in the searchlight should take no more than a few minutes. We fixed our suit helmets into position, Mel with my assistance. I pumped the interior of the cargo beetle and waited for the pressure to reduce. At the hatch Jim Swift cursed and swore at how long it took. For a change I could sympathize with him. After so many weeks, those last few minutes were the hardest to take.

The object of our attention did not impress me, even when we closed in on it. The corkscrew was just that, a smooth helix with no external features. The deformed oval bubble was hardly bigger than our cargo beetle. A square port occupied almost all one end of it.

No one had spoken a word since we left the beetle. Now, drawing closer to the port, we halted in unison a few yards away. I suspect we were all thinking the same thing. According to everything we knew about the Isolation, this structure had hung in space, unvisited, for hundreds of years. Inside we might find anything—gutted and empty cabins, crumbling equipment, long-dead corpses of a Godspeed crew.

Mel broke the spell. "Well, we won't find out floating around here. Let's do it." And away she went, heading straight for the port.

The Net, the Needle, the Eye, the Godspeed Base: isolated in space, drifting deep within the protective chaos of the Maze. It should have been totally alien. It wasn't. The port, when we came to open it, was no different from those on the *Cuchulain.*

I realized that the *Cuchulain* and every other ship that flew the Forty Worlds drew from the technology that built this space base. But the masters of that technology were long vanished, along with the instruction manuals. No wonder that Danny Shaker and the rest of the spacers had problems maintaining their ships in working order.

Then we were inside, and I had no time for ghosts of the past. We were entering what was clearly a control room. Unlike any control room that I had seen, everything within seemed fresh and unused as a newly minted coin.

Jim Swift didn't waste his energy marveling. He turned to me. "Do you know how to get air pressure in here? It's a pain working inside these suits."

"I'll see." I had become our space travel and spaceship expert. Fortunately, the controls here were as simple as those of the cargo beetle. I keyed in a sequence that should seal the lock and provide air, then stood wondering. The equipment looked new, but it hadn't been used for an age. The seal was complete, and the interior was filling with gas. But suppose that after all this time it had become poisonous or unbreathable?

Mel was beginning to fiddle with her helmet seals. She and Jim Swift had to be the two least patient people in the whole Maveen system.

"Wait a second."

I checked my suit monitors. It was not quite Erin standard

atmosphere, but close to it. If there was trouble it would come from subtle poisonous fractions, beyond the ability of the suit to detect and measure them.

Death before dishonor again. I cracked my helmet open and took a shallow, nervous breath. It didn't smell right, but I didn't collapse or go off in a fit. After a few seconds I nodded. "All right."

Before the words were out of my mouth Jim Swift was wriggling from his suit and heading for the pilot's chair. "Told you," he said. "Look at those."

His voice was triumphant as he pointed to a meaningless array of switches, keys and dials.

"What are they?" Mel was out of her suit, too, hovering right behind him. "I've never seen anything like them."

"Nor have I. But I've read enough descriptions, in the old pre-Isolation literature." He touched one array lovingly. "This is a coordinate selector."

I looked over his shoulder. "Not like the one on the *Cuchulain.*"

"No. Because these are for *stellar* coordinates. You enter other stars as destinations." He leaned back and took a deep breath. "We're sitting in a ship with a Godspeed Drive. I'll only say this one time: Jim Swift, you're a genius."

"Mm." Mel's tone seemed to offer a second opinion. "So you can fly this ship?"

He turned to glare at her. "That's a dumb spacer's job. Jay can do it, or one of Shaker's tame monkeys. Anyway, even if I *could* fly it, I'd want to take a good look at everything before I'd think of turning on full power. The Godspeed Drive can be really dangerous. It works by taking liberties with spacetime structure, and that sort of thing doesn't come free. Remember, *something* stopped the Godspeed ships from flying to the Forty Worlds."

Mel nodded and said, "Well, if we don't fly it, what *do* we do with it?"

"We loose it from its moorings and haul it back to the

Cuchulain. Then we go over the whole ship in detail. *After* that we make the run home to Erin, before we try anything ambitious." He turned to me. "You can handle the towing, can't you, Jay?"

"Well—"

"Good. Let's get on with it." Jim Swift turned away from me, placed his hands behind his head, and leaned back luxuriously in the pilot's chair. "And when Shaker and his crew of incompetents get back from bumbling around in the rest of the space base, I guess we'll let them examine this ship. Under my supervision, of course."

Of course.

I started to worry about how I was going to loose those metallic wires that held the ship in place, and how it could be balanced for hauling. I had never done anything remotely like it, and I wasn't sure where to begin. But at the same time I couldn't help contemplating—and looking forward to—the prospect of snotty Jim Swift "supervising" Danny Shaker.

CHAPTER 28

Our trip out from the *Cuchulain* had been no great triumph of ship manoeuvering. Compared with our return it was a masterpiece. After endless effort I managed to free from its moorings the corkscrew ship—I still found it hard to think of that misshapen object as a home for the Godspeed Drive. More hard labor attached our prize to the cargo beetle. But what I could not do was balance masses, and once we were under way we yawed and rolled this way and that in every direction that I could imagine. Sometimes the hawsers were taut, sometimes they floated slack and then tightened with a great jerk. Sometimes, don't ask how, the Godspeed ship we were towing flew out ahead of us.

I was not pleased with my performance, and Mel was outright rude. But Jim Swift didn't say one bad word. He was so full of the idea that we had *succeeded*. When we got back to the *Cuchulain* we would be hailed by the others as conquering heroes.

I wasn't so sure. If the crew of the *Cuchulain* had found a Godspeed Drive for themselves in their search of the space base, then what we had done was no big deal. If they had found nothing, we had made them look like a bunch of lamebrains. Dr. Jim Swift was a lot older than me, but in my experience you didn't become popular by showing people what fools they were.

Donald Rudden confirmed my opinion when we called him on the beetle's communicator, to say we were going to moor the object we were towing alongside the *Cuchulain*. "Wondered where you'd got to. Found something, have you?" He laughed. "Just as well, because Tom Toole called a while ago. Said they'd come up with nothing. Crew's all as mad as a pack of Limerick pipers. They'll be on their way back any time now."

That gave me one more thing to worry about. I had to get Mel on board the *Cuchulain* and safely into Doctor Eileen's quarters before the other party returned. Jim was too full of himself to worry about that or much else, so as soon as I had fought us to a rough docking I left him to gloat. I steered the beetle to the *Cuchulain*'s cargo region, and Mel and I made a quick run through the interior to Eileen Xavier's empty rooms.

"Sit tight," I said as I left her. "I'll be back as soon as I can."

"How long?"

"Don't know. But hang in. We'll soon be on our way home."

I was at last beginning to believe it myself. It's an odd thing, but when you wait for something long enough you can't believe it has arrived, even when it does. But Jim Swift, in spite of his uncontrollable temper, was Erin's top expert on the Godspeed Drive. If *he* was convinced that the oddity hanging next to the *Cuchulain* had inside it a device able to bring the stars close enough to touch, who was I to question?

As for his worries about disturbing space-time, I dismissed them. He had been dwelling too much on his own specialty subject. Jim with his space-time obsession was like the Lake Sheelin fishermen, who saw all the whole world in terms of hooks, lines, baits, and nets.

By the time that I returned to the *Cuchulain*'s bridge, Donald Rudden was showing signs of stirring. "Chief's on his way over there," he said. He nodded his head to a display screen showing the corkscrew ship, hanging where Mel and I had left it. "And I hafta go over myself, with some tools they want. Rory's supposed to spell me here."

That wasn't good news. Rory O'Donovan was the worst possible choice—not very bright, but full of energy. I couldn't trust him to stay put in the control room.

"What's going on at the other ship?"

"That thing's a ship?" Rudden puffed out his cheeks. "I'll believe it when I see it fly. Anyway, Rory says there's hell to pay over there. That redhead friend of yours, Swift, he's full of it. Been laying down the law about ships and drives. He don't know beans about ships, and anyway the lads won't take that stuff from a Downsider. He's been warned twice by Pat O'Rourke, but he takes no mind."

I wondered if Jim Swift knew how much danger he was in. After seeing Walter Hamilton shot, I wouldn't argue with an angry crewman. The only thing Jim had protecting him was Danny Shaker's control of the crew—a control that Shaker said became less every day.

As soon as Rudden left the bridge I made another quick run for the top level. I had to tell Mel what was happening, and warn her to lie low once O'Donovan was aboard and running loose. She didn't take it well.

"I've had it with skulking away. You say hang in, but when do I get *out*?"

"Soon. But *don't take risks.*"

I headed for the control room, wondering when I was going to take my own advice. Every trip to the upper level was a risk, for me as well as Mel.

When I reached the bridge Rory O'Donovan was not there, but Doctor Eileen was, staring at the displays. Her shoulders were slumped and she seemed half-asleep. She knew I was present, though, because as I moved to her side she said, "Jay," in a far-off voice, as though I was some sort of ghost.

"Are you all right, Doctor Eileen?" As she turned to me I saw that her eyes had dark rings under them.

She gave me a faint trace of a smile. "As good as I'll ever be. I'm tired. And I'm beginning to think I'm mortal."

"What happened?"

"Oh, nothing much. We had an exhausting and aggravating sixteen hours, that's all, and we didn't find anything inside the big lobe except confusion. I gather you did better."

"Jim Swift says we found the Godspeed Drive. He's sure of it."

"And I'm sure he believes he can fly it better than any crewman in the Forty Worlds." Doctor Eileen sighed. "You know, this ought to be the greatest day of my life. Erin will get what I've wanted and worried about for fifty years: a new future. That's what I *ought* to be thinking. But I can't get out of my head the notion that things aren't as they seem to be. That's what being old does to you, Jay. It won't let joy have a clear run in the sunlight, not even for one hour."

"I don't know what you mean."

"At your age, I should hope not." She stared at me, studying my face. "Jay Hara, I hardly know you." Instead of explaining what she meant by that, she nodded at the image of the corkscrew and the twisted bubble on the end of it. "That little mystery will give us the stars, eh? Well, maybe. In my life I've seen stranger things."

She reached out as though she was going to tousle my hair, the way she had ever since I was tiny. But this time she didn't do it. She stroked my cheek instead. "Another month or two and I won't know you at all," she said. "I guess I ought to be pleased. Keep an eye on things here, and let me know if anything happens. I've got to take a little rest."

Doctor Eileen left me on the bridge, wondering what on earth she had been talking about. *She* was the one who had changed, and that upset me. Doctor Eileen had always been as constant as the stars.

I went across to stand in front of the big convex mirror at the exit to the bridge, situated so that people entering and leaving through the angled doorway would not run into each other. Its rounded surface reflected a miniature and distorted image of my face, thin and dark-shadowed.

I stretched my arm out in front of me. My jacket sleeve showed three inches of bare wrist. It was the same coat that mother had made for me the night before I left home. It used to fit perfectly.

How long I stood standing in front of the mirror is anyone's guess. I had intended to take one quick look and get back to the controls, but as I examined the neat stitching on the jacket sleeve my mind went spinning away: to lamplit winter evenings in the comfortable house by Lake Sheelin, to long summer days with old Uncle Toby, and finally to my secret sailing trips across the lake to Muldoon Spaceport. That wasn't just a different *world,* it was a different universe.

When I came back to life and returned to the control room displays, I learned that in *this* universe things had been happening. The ship containing the Godspeed Drive had turned, so that the axis of the corkscrew now pointed away from the *Cuchulain.* Shimmering rings of violet haze were running back and forth along its length before spiraling away off the end. They moved on like ghostly smoke rings through open space for a few seconds, then at last faded.

Was the crew going to use the Godspeed Drive at once, without Doctor Eileen (or me) there to be part of it?

I hated that idea, but my worry vanished when all the shimmering rings suddenly disappeared. The Godspeed ship again hung motionless in vacuum. A minute later, a cluster of suited figures appeared from the distorted bubble at the end. They moved along the line of the corkscrew, apparently inspecting it, then jetted as a group toward the *Cuchulain.*

Doctor Eileen had to be told what was happening. For the

third time in an hour I started at top speed for the upper
level. The door of Doctor Eileen's quarters was open, and I
hurried in without knocking. She was there, sitting at a table
with Mel next to her. I also saw—my heart jumped inside my
chest—a broad male back, in a blue-clothed spacer jacket.

The man turned, and I realized with huge relief that it
was Duncan West.

"Uncle Duncan!"

He nodded at me, and smiled as though my sudden
appearance was the most natural thing in the world. "Just
came to tell Doctor Eileen the good news. The ship that you
and Jim Swift found has a Godspeed Drive, we're all sure of it.
And from the first look it seems in good working order."

If the whole universe was ready to change, Duncan West
didn't show much sign of it.

"Have they tested it?" I asked. "I saw the violet rings."

"Fly it here, inside the Eye? That would really be asking
for trouble. What you saw was just preliminaries." The deck
of the *Cuchulain* groaned, and gave a dreadful quivering
lurch. Duncan put his hand to the table top, feeling the
continuing vibrations. "That's our own drive going
on—what's left of it. We'll be leaving the Eye and towing the
Godspeed ship along with us. I came to tell you and Mel and
Doctor Eileen what's going on, and say it's captain's orders
that you stay in quarters while we're flying out. When we get
clear of the Eye, he'll announce it. You can take it easy until
then."

Duncan ambled out, not back to the bridge but along the
corridor that led to his own berth. Doctor Eileen stared after
him enviously.

"Know where he's going, don't you?"

"No," said Mel.

"To take a nap," I said. "He won't worry about the
vibrations."

Doctor Eileen nodded. "Or the fact that the fabulous

Godspeed Drive is being pulled along behind our ship. You know what your mother says, Jay.''

"That Uncle Duncan is the best eater and sleeper she ever met.''

"We should all be so lucky.'' Doctor Eileen stood up. "I've got to lie down for a few minutes myself, or I'll fall apart. You two can stay if you like, I don't mind.''

She wandered away into one of the rooms equipped with a couple of bunk beds. Mel and I were left to sit and stare at each other. Doctor Eileen must be feeling really out of it, because she knew as well as we did that Mel had to stay here. She couldn't safely go anywhere else in the *Cuchulain*.

We went through the other sleeping area and locked the door. Mel turned off the lights, and each of us climbed onto one of the side-by-side beds. We lay there in shuddering darkness, for so long that I began to think that Mel had fallen asleep despite the vibration from the engines. I envied her. For more than twenty hours the two of us had been busy with hardly a break, and now my brain would not stop running. I kept reliving the discovery of the Godspeed Base, and our decision to fly to it. My hands were again on the cargo beetle's controls, guiding us to our rendezvous in space.

Finally Mel said softly, "Jay?''

I came back from miles away. "What?''

"What's going to happen to me?''

"You'll be fine. Girls and women on Erin do very well. They are treated as something really special and precious, unless they happen to be like my mother and won't put up with it. And when we get there we'll all be rich. You can make trips to *Paddy's Fortune* as often as you want.''

The snort in the darkness could have been disgust or frustration. "I'm not thinking of Erin, you dummy—or of *Paddy's Fortune*. I'm worrying about the next few days. If the *Cuchulain* is in as bad condition as everyone says, it won't be able to fly to Erin. And you've seen the Godspeed ship. The living space on it is tiny. Maybe the ship can reach Erin in record time, but I don't see a hiding place on board for me."

Mel was right, and I was the world's prize idiot. I could blame Doctor Eileen a little for not seeing the problem either, but I was the one who had allowed Mel to guide me to the cargo beetle, back on *Paddy's Fortune,* and let her stay there. Looking back on it I decided that I should have insisted that she leave me, the moment that I caught sight of the beetle.

"Well?" Mel said at last.

"I'll ask Danny Shaker. I'm sure he'll have an answer."

"You mean you're sure you don't."

"Maybe the engines on the *Cuchulain* just need a thorough overhaul to carry us home."

Mel didn't comment on that. A dreadful shudder through the whole ship did it for her. The engines sounded ready to die. But I had no more thoughts to offer.

We lay there without speaking, in an uneasy darkness thick enough to feel. At last I did what I most needed to do. I fell asleep.

CHAPTER 29

Jay?"

I awoke from deep-down slumber. Sensations cut in, one after another. Free-fall. Darkness. Silence. A cold hand touched my face.

"Jay!" It was Doctor Eileen's voice, insistent, whispering close to my ear.

"What's wrong?" The ship's engines been turned off.

"Nothing. Shh! I don't want to wake Mel. Come on." She tugged at my sleeve.

"Wait a second." I had to disentangle myself. Mel was sleeping with one arm across me. As soon as I was free I drifted after Doctor Eileen, out into the general living area.

"What's happening?" I saw that the lighting level had been cut way back, and the little blip of the communicator was like a winking red eye in the darkness.

"You didn't hear it?" Doctor Eileen was no longer whispering. "I wish I could sleep like you and Duncan. I gave him a good shake, but he went right back to sleep. A call came through two minutes ago. We're clear of the Eye. Captain Shaker wants us in the control room."

"But why were you whispering?"

"Do *you* want to explain to Mel why she can't go along with us to the bridge?"

And I thought I was the one who found her hard to handle.

"We may have a real problem coming up." I followed Doctor Eileen outside, and locked the door of the living quarters. "If the drive on the *Cuchulain* isn't able to take us back, we're going to have trouble with Mel."

As we started toward the control room I explained that the Godspeed ship was far too small to conceal a stowaway, even for a minute.

Doctor Eileen listened, but I think that her mind was mostly somewhere else, because when I was done she said, "You're overreacting, Jay. If we fly back to Erin in the ship with the Godspeed Drive we won't need to hide Mel, because we'll get there in no time. And the crew aren't animals, you know. They've had the excitement of finding the Base and the Godspeed Drive, and their mood must be a lot better than it was when they were plowing through the mud on *Paddy's Fortune.* I'm sure they'll treat Mel with respect when they find out she's on board."

There was no point in arguing. Doctor Eileen hadn't seen Joe Munroe's face after he ripped away Mel's shirt. She hadn't heard Rory O'Donovan and Connor Bryan talking about women. If the crew weren't animals, it was because animals were better behaved.

The trouble was, Doctor Eileen took her cues as to what spacer crew members were like from Danny Shaker, and he was simply not typical. When we entered the control room he was standing relaxed by the pilot's chair, his smooth face thoughtful and his long hair neatly pulled back and tied. Tom Toole was at his side. The screens behind them showed open space, with the Godspeed ship hanging close to the *Cuchulain.*

"Just the people I wanted to see," Shaker said affably. "Let me bring you up to date. First, the Godspeed Drive. It's over there in the corkscrew ship. It works, and we know how to use it. That's the good news. Now for some bad news: the *Cuchulain*. The engines still work, after a fashion, but neither I nor anyone else believe the ship is in much shape to fly us back to Erin.''

Doctor Eileen looked puzzled. "That doesn't sound like bad news. Can't the Godspeed ship find room for everyone?''

"It can.'' Danny Shaker was talking to Doctor Eileen, but he was staring at me in an odd, speculative way. I got goosebumps. Something had changed. I could see it in Tom Toole as well as in Danny Shaker. Tom was grinning at some private joke, and eyeing Eileen Xavier.

"It has enough room,'' Danny Shaker said. "And even if it didn't, you could make ten trips to Erin and back in the time we'd take to overhaul the engines once on the *Cuchulain.*''

"So what's the problem?'' Doctor Eileen's voice had changed. She was beginning to sense something offkey.

"It's the crew. You see, they've had a meeting. And they don't like the deal we made. Don't like it at all.''

"Ah.'' Doctor Eileen went forward, and sat down uninvited in the pilot's seat. "So that's it. A little bit of blackmail. I have to agree to better terms for you, right, or you won't agree to fly us back? Well, Captain Shaker, I don't know if you're in on this yourself, or if it's really all the crew's doing, the way that you say. But either way, it's no deal. We needed you to fly us to *Paddy's Fortune,* and to get us here to the Needle and the Eye. But we don't need you now. James Swift assures me that he is perfectly capable of flying the Godspeed ship himself. Do you disagree?''

"I believe that James Swift knows how to fly the Godspeed ship.''

"So we stick with the original terms of the deal. And I'm being generous doing so—because you and the *Cuchulain* are in no position to fly us home, which is what you agreed to do. I suggest that you go and inform the rest of the crew of that, wherever they are.''

Tom Toole laughed, and Danny Shaker frowned at him in disapproval. "I don't think that the original terms are relevant, doctor," he said. "James Swift may know how to fly the Godspeed ship, but he will not be doing so. For several reasons. Here's one of them.''

He turned and gave the fluting whistle that I had first heard at Muldoon Spaceport. Patrick O'Rourke entered the control room. Floating along behind, dragged by his mop of red hair gripped in O'Rourke's huge hand, came the body of Jim Swift. His face was a bloody mess. When O'Rourke released him, he came drifting toward us.

Doctor Eileen gasped. She was already moving forward. On Erin or in space, a patient took priority over everything.

I felt sure that Jim Swift was dead, but Doctor Eileen was feeling for a pulse and lifting an eyelid.

"His own doing entirely," Shaker said. "He became involved in a dispute with Alan Kiernan—and Swift was the one who started it. Isn't that right, Pat?''

O'Rourke nodded. "Bloody fool took a swing at Alan. Lucky he's not a dead man. If I hadn't stepped in . . .'' His voice deepened to a chesty rumble.

Doctor Eileen had finished her first examination. "Doesn't seem too serious," she said. "His nose is broken, and that's where all the blood is coming from. This bruise on his temple is what knocked him out. He'll feel awful when he comes around, but he won't be unconscious for more than a few minutes. It won't stop him from flying us home.''

Danny Shaker was standing with his arms folded. He made a little gesture of his head toward Pat O'Rourke and Tom Toole. They left the control room without a word.

Shaker moved to stand in front of Doctor Eileen. "I mentioned that there are several reasons why Doctor Swift will not be flying you home on the Godspeed ship. The fight was just one of them, and not the most important. As you remarked, doctor, the crew wants to change the deal. But not in the way that you seem to be thinking.''

"In what way, then?" Doctor Eileen was busy wiping the blood from Swift's face with the front of his own shirt. She did not look up.

"My crew believe that they are the legal owners of the Godspeed ship and the Godspeed Drive, and that you have no claim to either. They are spacers, and space salvage rights traditionally go only to spacers. You and your group are Downsiders, and have no such rights. However, the crew does not wish to be unreasonable. They are willing to give you the *Cuchulain.*''

Doctor Eileen froze in place, her fingers at Jim Swift's temple. "That is a totally preposterous suggestion, as you well know. The *Cuchulain* is not fit to fly. You told me yourself that it's in no condition to take us back to Erin."

"I told you that if I had to make this ship fly to Erin, I would find a way to do so." Shaker might have been discussing a minor change in flight plans for all the emotion in his voice. "But I do not have to fly the *Cuchulain*, Doctor. You do. You and Doctor Swift. Just half an hour ago, he was boasting to the crew of his abilities as an engineer and space navigator as well as a scientist. He will have an opportunity to prove himself."

Danny Shaker turned to me, and the coldness left his voice. "But you, Jay, you don't need to prove anything. The crew agrees that you already did that. You made your decision when we left *Paddy's Fortune,* to become a spacer and a crew member. And you've been blooded. When it came to the point you killed your man. The crew's vote was unanimous: Joe Munroe deserved what he got. There's a place for you with us."

"A *vote.*" Doctor Eileen let Jim Swift float free and stood up to glare at Danny Shaker. "There's no voting on any ship of yours, Captain Shaker, and you know it. The crew takes your orders. You don't take theirs. My God, what an idiot I've been, to trust you and believe you for so long. If there's a plot to rob us of our rights—and of our lives, too, from what I can see of it—then it's not a scheme hatched by the crew. They don't have the brains for it. Anything like that starts in your head, and nowhere else.''

"You flatter me, Doctor.'' Shaker uncrossed his arms and stuck his hands into his jacket pockets. "A ship can have only one captain, true, or it will run into chaos. But I'm the servant of my crew more than their master. They, not me, decided that the Godspeed ship was theirs. They, not me, offered a place among us to Jay Hara—although I certainly agree with that decision.'' He turned again to face me. "You've not said one word, Jay, though it's you we're talking about. How about it? I'd love to have you aboard. I wouldn't ever mention this with Tom Toole or Pat O'Rourke present, but you have more potential than any crewman on the *Cuchulain*. Sign on with me, and I'll teach you everything I know.''

Those words were designed to tempt me, and they came close. But suddenly all I could think of was *what* Danny Shaker knew how to teach. How to hunt down Paddy Enderton, and hound him to his death. How to manipulate Doctor Eileen, and me, and Mel, and who knew how many others, so that he would be led to the Godspeed Base and the Godspeed Drive. How to trick his own twin brother, so that the hands of Stan Shaker would become those now reaching deep into Danny Shaker's coat pockets.

I thought all that, but I was not fool enough to say it. Doctor Eileen and Jim Swift and I would never be able to fly the *Cuchulain* home to Erin. I knew that, and so surely did Danny Shaker. He might be able to fix the *Cuchulain,* but we could not. Leaving us behind while they flew off on the Godspeed ship was sentencing us to a slow death, drifting in space as our supplies of food, water, and air slowly dwindled away.

Our only hope was to fight *now,* when Danny Shaker was

alone and unarmed. Then we might be able to get back to the upper level living quarters, and find the weapons that Doctor Eileen had taken to *Paddy's Fortune.*

I thought I could hear faint sounds outside the control room. No one entered, but it reminded me that Tom Toole or Pat O'Rourke might be back at any minute.

I had to make Shaker relax by thinking that I was tilting his way, and I had to do it fast.

"I want to come with you," I said. "But what about Mel Fury? Is there any way that she can—"

I never could carry off a lie. My face must have showed the inside of my head, because Shaker at once pulled his right hand out of his coat pocket. It was holding a pistol.

"Nice try, Jay, but I'm too old for that." He saw me start forward. "Don't even think of it. Normally I don't carry weapons, but there have to be exceptions to every rule. And I'd never carry a gun that wasn't loaded."

He was standing with his back to the entrance of the control room. No more sounds came from that direction, but I thought I saw something: a flicker of movement in the big convex mirror that hung in the doorway.

Someone was in the corridor. It might be Tom Toole or one of the other crew members—or, just possibly, it might be Mel. She'd have to be crazy to come out of hiding.

But Mel *was* crazy, that was part of her charm.

"You didn't answer my question." I tried to speak loudly, but instead my voice cracked and squeaked. "You were the one who wanted Mel to come onto the *Cuchulain.* You encouraged her."

I could see the reflection. It was not Mel. It was too big to be Mel.

I felt a moment of despair. And then I realized that the new arrival was Duncan West. He was at the entrance to the control room, and he was holding a gun—Walter Hamilton's white-handled pistol.

I launched myself through the air straight at Danny

Shaker. "Now!" I shouted, when I was just a few feet away. I had little hope of disarming Shaker or knocking him out, but I hoped that by distracting him I would allow Duncan to gain control.

Danny Shaker hardly seemed to move, yet I missed him completely. I went flailing on until I collided face-first with the side of a big display screen. I clutched my nose, convinced that it was broken like Jim Swift's, and spun around dizzily in mid-air.

I had bought Duncan West the time that he needed. He had stepped into the middle of the room. He stood by Danny Shaker, gun raised. And Shaker was lowering his.

But then Duncan was moving right past Danny Shaker.

"Duncan!" Doctor Eileen shouted, and I croaked the same word through a spray of blood from my nose.

"Save your breath." Shaker nodded to Duncan, who casually stuck Walter Hamilton's gun back into his belt.

"Duncan and I had our little talk a long time ago," Shaker went on. "He made his decision before we ever lifted off from Muldoon Spaceport. He was tired of being treated like a nothing. And he wanted to be on the side of the winners. Right, Crewman West?"

Duncan nodded. He smiled at us, the same amiable, charming, uncommitted smile that I had known all my life.

"It's a pity—I mean from your point of view, Doctor," Danny Shaker continued. "Because if there's any man in the Forty Worlds who could coax another flight out of the poor old *Cuchulain,* I'm convinced that it's Duncan. But he'll be going with us." He turned to me. "What about you, Jay? You don't give up, and that's the first requirement of a good spacer. I'd like you with me. But this will be my last time of asking."

I shook my head, and Danny Shaker sighed.

"That's the end of it, then. I guess there's more of your mother than your father in you after all. Duncan and I have to be off. The rest of the crew are waiting. So I'll say good-bye.

And good luck, too, to all of you. I hope that you make it back to Erin, I truly do."

"Wait." Doctor Eileen had not spoken since her one word cry to Uncle Duncan. Now she moved closer to Danny Shaker. Duncan put his hand on the gun in his belt.

"Stop that, Duncan West," she said reprovingly. "I'm not one for violence, and you know it. I want to say something to Captain Shaker. It won't take long."

Shaker nodded to Duncan. "No gun needed here. Go on ahead, tell Tom Toole that I'm on my way." And, as Duncan left the control room, "All right. Say your piece, doctor."

"You're going to maroon us in the middle of the Maze, on a ship with a dying drive. You can pretend that we have a chance to get home again, but you and I both know better than that. Anyone who stays on the *Cuchulain* is doomed. I can live with that thought for myself. Space is as good a place to die as anywhere else."

"Better than anywhere else. You're a wise woman, Doctor Xavier, and a brave one. Pity you're not a man. You'd have made a great spacer."

"I don't need flattery. I'm too old for it. But Jay Hara and Mel Fury are *children*. Jay will say he wants to stay with me, because I've known him all his life and he feels loyal. But I want you to take him with you, no matter what he wants. And Mel too. Don't kill children, Dan Shaker. It's beneath you."

Shaker sighed, and shook his head. "You are a fine advocate, Doctor. There's just one problem with what you're suggesting: It's wrong. Jay and Mel are not children. Look at them. He's become a tough, self-assured young man in the past couple of months. It would be insulting—and dangerous—to treat him as a child. And from what Duncan tells me, Mel is now very much a young woman. I think he's had his eye on her himself, and compared with most of my crew he's an absolute gentleman.

"So it has to be no. I admit that I control most of what the crewmen do, but I recognize my limits. I'd be insane to take a woman—just *one* woman—onto the Godspeed ship. I owe my crew something, but that's not the way to give it to them. After we've made a trial run of the Drive I propose to take another look at *Paddy's Fortune*. I gather we'll find enough inside to please everyone.

"That's enough of future plans. I have to leave. The Drive is primed."

Shaker nodded to one of the screens. The Godspeed ship hovered in the middle of it. Once more the shimmering smoke rings of violet haze were running back and forth along the axis of the corkscrew and spiraling away into space.

"Goodbye, Doctor. And good luck. I'd like to think we'll meet again. Somewhere, somehow. And good-bye and good luck to you, too, Jay. I only wish you could have seen things differently, and come with me. But remember the Golden Rule: Don't give up—ever."

He turned and left without another word. His departure from the bridge drained the room of every particle of life and hope. Doctor Eileen leaned on the pilot's chair, head bowed in exhaustion or despair. Jim Swift, beginning to twitch and groan and groggily move his head, floated a few feet away from her.

And I, the "tough, self-assured young man" who could no longer be "treated as a child"? I put my swollen cheek and bleeding nose against the cool metal of the cabin wall, and I cried until big globular tears mingled with drops of blood, and floated away across the control room.

CHAPTER **30**

Eileen Xavier didn't waste time on pity, for herself or anyone else.

She made a quick review of Jim Swift's condition, came over to where I was still holding on to the cabin wall, and grunted: "Nothing much wrong with you. Snap out of it. You're in charge. I'm going to find Mel and bring her to the bridge."

I believe she was callous on purpose. Her statement that I was in charge surprised me, but it was her other comment that got me moving. There was no way I would let Mel Fury arrive on the bridge and find me sniveling and weeping.

As soon as Doctor Eileen had gone I released my hold on the cabin wall. I staggered along the corridor to a washroom, soaked two towels in cold water, and carried them back to the control room. As I moped my face with a cool cloth and delicately touched it to my sore nose, I wondered how to handle Jim Swift. He was regaining consciousness, but as he came awake he was beginning to thrash about with his arms and legs. Maybe he thought he was still fighting. Whatever the reason, he wasn't safe to go near. One hit from those flailing fists and I could be in worse shape than he was.

Finally I grabbed one of his arms and at the same time threw a heavy, soaking cloth right into his face. Either the cold or the pain got through to him, because he gasped and reached up to grab the towel.

"Oooh!" He groaned. "Where am I?"

"On the bridge of the *Cuchulain*. You're going to be all right. Don't touch your nose!"

Too late. He had moved the wet cloth to his face. As soon as it reached his nose he gasped and his left eye popped open. He glared sightlessly around him, until his one staring eye focused on me.

"Your nose is broken," I said. "Mop the blood if you want to, but touch it very carefully."

He grunted, and moved the cold towel to set it delicately against his right temple and closed right eye. "Never mind my nose. This is where it hurts *bad*. What hit me?"

"Alan Kiernan. You got into a fight. You lost."

"Tell me something new," Swift muttered. He belched, and I thought for a moment that he was going to throw up. But he just put his hand on his middle and stared at me, wall-eyed. "You, too?"

"I'm not sure mine is broken." I took the cloth away from my face. "Could be it's just bruised."

"Kiernan did it to you?"

"No. I did it to myself."

"It takes all sorts." Jim Swift tried to open his right eye, and failed. The whole area from his nose to his right ear was red and swollen. But his brain was working all right, because he pointed to a wall display showing the Godspeed ship, where the shimmering rings on the corkscrew were brighter than ever. "The Drive has been primed. Who's doing that?"

"The crew of the *Cuchulain*. Or what used to be the crew of the *Cuchulain*. Now I guess we're that."

Jim was going to hear the bad news sometime, it might as well be now. I started to give him a summary of what had been happening, from Danny Shaker's arrival on the bridge with Tom Toole to their final departure. I omitted their claim that Jim had started the fight that broke his nose, and I didn't mention Shaker's attempts to recruit me to his new command.

Before I was finished Jim interrupted. He glared around the control room with his Cyclops's stare. "Fly this heap to Erin? Never. Duncan said the engines are good for one or two more short runs, and that's it. Unless he can do one of his magic fixes."

I hadn't yet got to Duncan's change of allegiance. After I explained that, Jim moved over to stand behind the pilot's chair. This time he held the towel over his whole face. "That's it, then. Marooned in the middle of nowhere. Can you fly the *Cuchulain?*"

"I know how to do it. But I don't know how far we'd get with the engines the way they are."

"Anything's better than nothing." Swift peered out from behind his towel and pointed a finger at the display. "Take us away from that. Do it now."

He was indicating the Godspeed ship. Bright rings of light were flickering faster and faster along the twisted spiral.

"Come on, Jay," he said, when I hesitated. "Get a move on. Can't you see the priming is almost done? The release could come any moment now. Someone on that ship is crazy. I tried to warn them, but they're preparing for a jump at full power."

I didn't understand what he was talking about, but the urgency of his tone got through to me. I moved to the pilot's chair and performed the steps to activate the drive of the *Cuchulain.* We were soon ready to fly. Then I hesitated. Would the engines function as I turned them on, or would they blow apart?

I was still dithering when Eileen Xavier and Mel appeared on the bridge.

"What's—" Doctor Eileen began.

"Not now." Jim Swift interrupted her. "First we move, then we talk. Jay?"

"Ready." Or as ready as I would ever be.

"Then *do it.*"

I performed the final sequence. The *Cuchulain* came alive, with a dreadful groan and rumble of off-balance engines. I urged the ship on, trying to move it through space by sheer willpower.

The vibration grew. The smart sensors showed engine stresses beyond the danger level. I sat with my finger on the cutoff key. "We can't—"

"A few more seconds, Jay." Jim Swift was staring at the display showing the Godspeed ship. It was visibly smaller on the screen. But our whole ship was shaking so violently that everything blurred.

"That's all we can take!" I stabbed at the key, and the vibration ended.

"Let's hope it will do." Jim Swift was muttering to himself, not to me. "It will *have* to do."

"Do what?" Mel asked. But no one answered.

Nothing seemed to have changed on the Godspeed ship. If anything, the dancing rings of light were a little less brilliant.

"Radiated power peak's shifting into the ultraviolet." Jim Swift had forgotten his black eye and broken nose. "Any second now. It's praying time. And I'm an atheist."

As he spoke, all the rings of light along the corkscrew vanished. The Godspeed ship hung dark and motionless in space, not a light showing.

Jim Swift gasped, while Doctor Eileen sighed. "So it doesn't work after all," she said. "All our efforts, and for nothing."

I stared at the ship on the screen and thought about Danny Shaker. He and his crew were marooned now, just like the rest of us. He would find a way to get us all home. In spite of everything, I had strange confidence in him.

"Look at the star field," Mel said suddenly. "Should it be doing that?"

The Godspeed ship was not moving. But around it, like bright points on some great wheel, the whole backdrop of stars was turning. As we watched, the rotating pattern began to shrink in toward the central axis, to where the ship sat like the quiet eye of a giant whirlpool.

"Inertial frame dragging," Jim Swift said. "And *strong* space-time curvature. If that effect keeps increasing—"

It did not. The star field blinked back to normal. And in that instant the Godspeed ship was gone. It did not accelerate away, out of our field of view. It did not move, or flicker, or fade. It vanished.

"The Godspeed Drive," Jim Swift said softly. "I've waited all my adult life to see that. But I was wrong about one thing. I was afraid that tapping the vacuum energy would have a permanent effect on space-time structure. Apparently it does not. There's been enough time since the Isolation for an adjustment to take place. We can have—"

I never did learn what we could have, because at that moment Mel screamed and every display in the control room blazed with light. A multicolor pinwheel flared into existence at the place where the Godspeed ship had stood. It grew, in size and intensity, until it filled the screens. Automatic dimmers came into operation, but the intensity of light grew faster than they could adjust. The screens went into overload and darkened in unison.

A moment later, all the lights on the bridge of the *Cuchulain* went out. I waited in shivering darkness, and felt a wave of nausea sweep over me. Through me. Some force was passing *within* my body, squeezing and wrenching and twisting and pulling. A moment earlier I had been in free-fall. Now I was hanging in a gravity field that changed direction every split second—*up* was over my head, then under my feet, now off to one side or another. All around me, loose furnishings flew away to clatter against the walls of the control room. The struts and hull plates of the *Cuchulain* groaned and whined under intolerable pressures.

If it was terrifying for me, it may have been worse for Jim Swift. I had no idea what was happening, while he knew in detail. And when things finally settled down, my own relief was all personal—it simply meant the end of an awful, head-spinning vertigo.

The control room remained dark, until one by one the overloaded displays crept back into operation. The bridge became lit by faint starlight, enough for me to make out the shapes of the other three people in the room. Mel was clinging white-knuckle tight to Eileen Xavier, while Jim Swift floated upside-down near them.

"What in God's name was *that?*" It was Doctor Eileen, sounding as queasy as I felt. There is no way of describing what it is like to have some unknown force *manipulating* the inside of your body.

"Call it space-time's revenge." Jim Swift reached out and grabbed the cabin wall, slowly turning himself until he was the same way up as the rest of us. "That's what I was afraid of. That's what I tried to warn them about—and no one would listen."

"You mean that every time anyone ever used the Godspeed Drive, a region of space near it was affected like that?" I said.

"No, I don't think so. That's what happens *now*, and has ever since the Isolation. But once it wasn't so. This means that the Godspeed Drive can't be used. Maybe can't be used *ever again.*"

"But *they* just used it." Mel released her hold on Doctor Eileen and seemed unaware of the death grip she had taken. Doctor Eileen began rubbing ruefully at her upper arm as Mel gestured to where the Godspeed ship had been floating a couple of minutes earlier. "We *saw* them use it," she said.

"We sure did." Jim Swift nodded, and winced as he

moved his head. "Do you know where they were planning to go?"

"On a trial run," I said. "Maybe to Erin." For Mel's sake, I didn't add that the second stop would be *Paddy's Fortune.*

"Erin can't be much more than a light-hour away." Jim carefully touched the end of his nose, and winced again. "A one-light-hour trip is nothing for a Godspeed Drive. But I'll bet my life that if they set off for Erin, they haven't arrived there. In fact, I'll bet that they never arrive."

"Then where are they?" asked Doctor Eileen. I saw bewilderment on her face.

"That's the great question of my life." Jim Swift groped his way forward and sat down in the pilot's chair. "I could say, they're in the same place as anyone else who used the Godspeed Drive at the time of the Isolation or since. But that's not much of an answer."

"It's no answer at all," I said. The control room was overheated, but I had the shivers. If Danny Shaker and his killer crew had not flown to Erin . . . "Do you mean the Godspeed ship is still around here somewhere, but we just can't see it?"

"Easy, Jay," said Doctor Eileen. "We're all nervous."

And Jim Swift added, in a curiously satisfied voice, "Easy, all of us. Sit down, and I'll tell you what I think, and what I *know*—less of that than I'd like, I'm afraid."

Eileen Xavier sat down. After a few moments, Mel and I followed her lead.

"I wish Walter Hamilton were here to start this off," Jim went on, "because some of what I have to say comes from him, and I don't know how much of that was guesswork. It starts all the way back. Back before the Isolation, before there was a Godspeed Drive. Humans had been spreading through the galaxy, out across the stars. But they'd been doing it *slowly,* on ships that couldn't even get close to light speed. We don't know much about the first colonists of Maveen and the Forty Worlds, but Walter believed that they came to Erin on a multigeneration, culturally homogeneous starship. He claimed to be able to trace most of our place names and family names to a single small region of the original home of human beings.

"I can't vouch for that, but I do feel sure that the old star travelers did it the hard way, creeping out slowly, star after star, planet after planet. Humanity explored and developed and colonized that way for thousands and thousands of years. Nobody in the Forty Worlds knows how long that went on. Then somewhere, sometime, an unknown young genius discovered the Godspeed Drive."

"Genius, yes." Doctor Eileen frowned. "But *young* genius?"

"Yeah." Jim Swift smiled, a bruised, lopsided grin. Battered or not, it didn't take him long to become cocky again. "A young genius, and one who either died young, or wasn't listened to much after the invention was made. How do I know? Easy. Anyone who makes a huge breakthrough like the Godspeed Drive is going to be young, not old. Great discoveries come from people who aren't stuck in an old mindset. And I don't think the inventor was listened to, because any person bright enough to invent the drive would also be bright enough to understand the possible consequences when it was used.

"The Godspeed Drive seems like a perfect something-for-nothing device, the ultimate free dinner. But that's an illusion. You saw how small the drive unit was in the Godspeed ship that we found. Not a hundredth the size of the *Cuchulain*'s engines, but with enough power to toss a ship from star to star.

"So where does the power come from? There was no energy source on the Godspeed ship.

"Well, I tried to explain it to Alan Kiernan and the rest of those numbskulls. The Godspeed Drive taps the vacuum energy of space-time, to create a bridge from one place to another. There's a huge amount of energy available, but the supply isn't infinite. And it's not like pumping water from a well, where you have some warning before it runs dry because less and less water comes out and it gets harder and harder to pump. This is more like a solid stone bridge. You can run loads over it for years with never a hint that the bridge is under stress. Until one day, without any warning, the whole thing collapses.

"That's what happened with the Godspeed Drive—except that I suspect we're talking not just years of use, but many, many centuries. A period so long that people came to rely on it completely. They forgot that the Godspeed Drive might have its limits. They no longer kept old, slow, multigeneration ships as back-up.

"Then one day the bridge broke. The vacuum energy drawdown passed a critical level. The Godspeed Drive failed, all at once and everywhere. Any ship that tried to cross the bridge fell off into the water."

"Water?" I said. He had lost me.

"Sorry. That was just a figure of speech. The Godspeed Drive formed a bridge through space-time, a short route from one place to another. And when that bridge collapsed, a ship that tried to use it fell out of space-time itself."

Apparently he had lost Mel, too. "Fell out of *space-time*," she said. "How can you fall out of space-time? There's nowhere to fall *to*."

"I know. But I can't give you a better description. Let's just say, the ships left our universe, and went *somewhere*, beyond the universe we can perceive."

"But it still doesn't make sense," I complained. "I mean, suppose that the drive suddenly stopped working, the way that you say. Every ship with a Godspeed Drive wouldn't try to fly on that same day. There would be lots of ships left."

"Of course there would. But you see, this wasn't a bridge you could look at, and say, hey, it's damaged, or hey, it's vanished. No one would *know* that the bridge had gone. If they were too close when a Godspeed ship tried to make an interstellar jump, they could have been destroyed the way we were nearly destroyed a few minutes ago. But if people weren't too close, all they would know was that the Godspeed ship had vanished. And that was normal. The ships *always* vanished when they made a jump. Of course, it would be obvious that there was a problem to the people at the other end, when a Godspeed ship failed to *arrive*. But if that happened in your system it would just encourage you to send out a Godspeed ship of your own, to learn what the problem was at the other end.

"After a while there were no ships left to send. Every stellar system became isolated. Then you had hundreds or thousands of populated stellar systems, all totally cut off from each other. They might all be in trouble, but they wouldn't be able to help each other. They weren't even set up to *talk* among themselves without the use of the Godspeed Drive. It's no accident that the word that has come down to us through history to describe the disaster is *Isolation*. The Maveen system is isolated. But so is everyone else."

Isolation. Jim Swift could talk theory and see that word in the abstract, but as he went babbling on I stared up at the nearest display screen. It showed nothing but barren space in all directions. I had spent sixteen happy years on Erin and I hadn't for one moment suspected that I was isolated from anything or anyone—or even in any kind of trouble, except sometimes for skipped chores or homework. Real isolation was here and now: lost in the Maze, without a working ship or the hope of contact with any other humans.

I turned to scan the other screens. We were still in the middle of the Net. I could pick out dozens of nodes as tiny points of light. Tom Toole had told me that this hardware scrap-heap was hugely valuable, enough to make any scavenge-and-salvage crew rich. If they were alive, and hadn't been thrown into another universe as Jim Swift believed, the crew might return here—eventually. Maybe an experienced spacer like Danny Shaker could even sort through the junk pile of the hardware reservoir, and repair the battered *Cuchulain* enough to fly it home. But that sort of work was far beyond our talents. And no one else was going to do it for us.

The four of us were truly isolated. And eventually, when our supplies ran out, the four of us would be dead.

CHAPTER **31**

All over. No hope. No chance of escape. The person who snapped me out of that hangdog attitude was not, oddly enough, Jim Swift, or Mel Fury, or even Doctor Eileen. It was Danny Shaker and his Golden Rule: *Don't give up.*

Even before I thought of that I had a personal proof that I was far from dead. Doctor Eileen insisted that as a first priority Jim Swift and I must have our wounds attended to. She swabbed his temple and his closed eye, then tackled his bent and broken nose. I heard the bone crack horribly when she straightened it. His forehead went pale beneath his thatch of red hair, but he didn't utter a sound.

So then I couldn't let it show, either, not with Mel looking on. Not even when Doctor Eileen probed far up inside *my* nose, to do what she called "a remedial septum straightening."

The inside of my head, from my nostrils to up behind my eyes, caught fire. I thought to myself, *I'm not dead yet. Dead people don't hurt like this.* I didn't cry out, though, but when she was done and had given me a quick injection I muttered that I had to take a look at the *Cuchulain*'s engines. I fled. When I reached the cargo area I stayed there for a long time. I felt dizzy and sweaty, as though I wanted to throw up but couldn't.

When I got to the drive unit the monitors gave me the same bad news as those on the bridge. Of five clustered main engines, three would never fire again. The other two were in poor shape, but by using them in short bursts and turning the whole ship between thrusts, I might be able to move the *Cuchulain.*

The acceleration would be miserably low. I made an estimate. If we used the remaining engines until they both died completely, then coasted all the way to Erin, we would be on our way for seven or eight years.

Could our supplies last so long? I didn't think so. We had provisioned for a dozen people when we set out, but for a far shorter period. Once we were clear of the Maze, though, we could send a distress signal. With lots of luck we would be heard at Erin's Upside Spaceport, and a ship might come out to meet us. If it didn't, the *Cuchulain* with its dead drive would float by Erin and off to nowhere.

I returned to the control room, to tell the others that we faced the problem of surviving for many years in space.

Doctor Eileen was not there. Instead Mel and Jim Swift were crouched together by the control panel. He had Walter Hamilton's electronic notebook in his hand, while Mel was holding the little navaid that we had been given on *Paddy's Fortune.*

"Just the person." Jim looked awful, but he sounded full of pep. I wondered what kind of shot Doctor Eileen had given *him,* and wished I'd had the same.

"Can you fly the *Cuchulain* again?" Jim asked.

"I think so. But not very well."

I tried to explain my idea of coasting toward Erin, but Jim cut me off before I got halfway. "Wrong direction, boyo. We'd never make it. If we're to have any chance at all, we have to go *there.*"

He was pointing to the dark pupil of the Eye. The last

place, it seemed to me, that we wanted to go. It was a dull, glassy black, and it made me think of a dead fish eye.

"Why there?" I said. "Suppose we get in, and the *Cuchulain*'s engines are too far gone to get us out again? You can't even send a signal from inside the Eye."

"It's the Slowdrive," Jim said, as though that explained everything.

"You won't find a drive much slower than what we've got now," I said. I told him about the three dead engines, and the dying pair that remained. "Seven or eight years from here to Erin. If we could last that long."

"Which we can't. Doctor Xavier and I have already talked about supplies. No more than two years, and that's starving ourselves." Jim Swift had killed my only hope, but he went on cheerfully, "Maybe the Slowdrive, even if we find it, will be no better. But I don't have enough information to prove that. The evidence is inconsistent. This"—he held up Walter Hamilton's electronic notebook, and cackled like a madman—"suggests that 'slow drive' hardware was in an experimental state when the Isolation took place. And *that*"—he pointed to the navaid that Mel was holding—"indicates that what it terms the 'slow option' should be here, somewhere within the Net."

"We'll never find it before the drive dies." I was staring despondently at the huge array of nodes.

"Not if we look there," said Jim. "Danny Shaker said there was nothing but bits and pieces at the Net nodes. I know he was a villain, but he was plenty smart when it came to space. So I believe him, there's nothing useful for us in the Net. That leaves the Godspeed Base itself—inside the Eye."

"We already looked there."

"No. Shaker and the crew explored the big lobe, and the three of us found the Godspeed ship in the smallest one. No one ever explored the middle region."

"The flickery one? You said it would be dangerous."

He gave me a horrible one-eyed leer, peering like a

lunatic owl around the plaster beak that Doctor Eileen had placed on his swollen nose. "You sound like Mel. That was then. This is now. The definition of dangerous has changed. Can you fly us in?"

"Of course I can." I found the question insulting. Wasn't I a "natural," according to no less an authority than Danny Shaker?—wherever he might be.

I had changed, too, and in the last five minutes. It didn't occur to me that my injection was doing as much to me as Jim Swift's was to him. But I was certain that I could fly anything, including the collapsing *Cuchulain*.

How far could I fly it? That was a different question. I didn't even care. It was flying time.

Here's my advice: If you have to pilot a ship that you don't know how to fly, into a situation that you've been told is deadly dangerous, first go and ram your face into a wall and break your nose. Then get yourself shot full of drugs. After that you may be out of danger—or at least dead—before you know you're in it.

When we first went into the Eye I had heard Danny Shaker's quiet comment: The *Cuchulain* was *slowed* in its passage through the membrane. Now, nursing failing engines and surrounded on all sides by dense grey fog, I realized how much Shaker had left unsaid.

The power draw of the drive had doubled, but our rate of progress was slowing—and we were not yet to the Eye's interior.

I had to make a choice. Keep going, and ruin the engines forever? Or try to pull back?

It was really no decision at all. We might not survive within the Eye; we would die for sure if we remained outside.

I ignored the screens and kept my eyes on the status monitors. Both engines were about equally bad. Both of them were red-lining. All I could do was balance them as closely as I could; and when Mel, watching the displays, quietly said, "Coming clear," I knew it before she spoke. The engines were in their death rattle, but in spite of that the *Cuchulain*'s speed was increasing. We were through.

I cut the drive. We drifted on toward the base. If I had stared before at its globular middle section, now I couldn't take my eyes off it.

Or keep them *on* it. Flashes of light ran within the surface, with bright afterimages that fooled me into fancying strange shapes within the globe. I could imagine a giant human ear, a human face, a great fist clutching a twisted caricature of a Godspeed ship.

"Who goes inside Flicker, and who stays?" That was Mel, naming the middle region at the same time as she voiced my own question: Who would go? With the drive dead, the *Cuchulain* was no better than a derelict adrift in space. This time I wouldn't remain behind.

"Can we leave the Eye again?" asked Doctor Eileen.

I shook my head. "Not in this ship."

"Then we may as well stick together. Collect anything that you want to take with you. I'll start loading food and drink. There's nothing to be gained by anyone staying here."

She was right. The *Cuchulain* would be our tomb if we stayed. All the same, I hadn't expected her to give the order to leave *permanently*. I had an odd feeling of security abandoned as we closed down the *Cuchulain* energy and life-support systems and went one by one into the cargo hold, adding our little packages of personal possessions to the pile of provisions in a cargo beetle; and soon I was piloting us clear, convinced that I was doing a better job of flying than I ever had before—with no one able to appreciate it.

"Stay together, or separate?" Doctor Eileen asked Jim Swift the next important question as we approached a dark part of the middle sphere, closing on what I hoped might be entry points.

"Both." Jim Swift had thought it through. "We go into

Flicker together, and divide up the interior search when we get there. We'll check back at the entrance on a regular schedule. Anyone who finds something interesting waits at the beetle for the others.''

"And *nobody*"—Doctor Eileen was staring at me—"plays with something he finds that might be a drive, or anything else, until we've discussed it together.''

If anyone was likely to get in trouble with a new gadget, it wasn't me—it was Mel. But there was no time for argument, because the middle section of the base was looming up in front of us like a great, smooth wall. The internal lightning flickered brighter. It showed three dark openings where we might be able to lodge the beetle. I headed for the biggest.

Our arrival was reassuring. The port contained a lock, little different from the airlocks at the other lobe, or even at Muldoon Upside Port. We had been in suits since we left the *Cuchulain,* so the pressure change didn't affect us when the lock cycled us in.

"Close to Erin surface pressure," said Jim Swift. He was examining a wall monitor. "But we won't be breathing this one. Helium, neon, and xenon. Nice inert atmosphere to preserve things, but no trace of oxygen. Keep your suits tight.''

The inner door of the lock was opening. It revealed a featureless corridor, which thirty yards farther on branched into four.

"North, south, east, west," Doctor Eileen said. "I guess that settles one question. Jay, how long do you have?''

I glanced at my air supply. "Thirteen hours, nearly fourteen.''

"Mel? Jim?''

"Sixteen hours.''

"Twelve.''

"So I'm lowest, I've got a bit more than eleven.''

"Back here in nine or ten, then?'' Jim Swift was itching to get started, his eyes glinting behind his visor.

"No!" Doctor Eileen was in charge again. "What happens if one of us gets into trouble and can't make it back? We have to give ourselves enough time to help."

Gets into trouble, I thought. You mean we're not in trouble already? But I didn't say anything, and Jim Swift came back with, "All right. How about six hours? Don't forget we may have to do a lot of looking before we find anything. And the longer we stay here talking . . ."

"Six it is." Doctor Eileen was moving forward. "Prompt. Anyone who isn't back here by then and hasn't met some sort of problem *will* have one—with me. I'm talking to you, Jay, and you, too, Mel. I'll skin you alive if you're not on time. Let's go."

I hung back, making the final series of suit checks that Danny Shaker had drummed into my head time after time. I was the last to arrive at the corridor branch. The other three had taken the top, left, and right forks.

I was left with the bottom branch. The "south" branch. *"Going south."* It was Uncle Toby's favorite expression to describe dying. "Old Jessie, she just packed her bags and went south." Let's hope it didn't apply to me on Flicker.

My branch of the corridor was plain walls, with no rooms or exits leading off it. It headed downward for no more than twenty or thirty yards before it leveled off to run parallel to the way that we had entered. That was puzzling, because I felt as though I was again moving straight toward the center of Flicker. Had I lost my sense of direction?

Soon I had a bigger problem. My corridor was ending. In nothing. Or rather, in a fish-eye circle of misty dark-grey, like the membrane that surrounded the Eye itself.

The gravity inside Flicker was too small to be useful. I had to use my suit controls to slow my forward progress, until I hung just a couple of feet from the dead circle. Ought I to try to go on through? It wasn't just Doctor Eileen's warning about taking risks with new things that held me in place. The circle itself scared me.

I reached out one suited arm and pushed my hand delicately into the darkness. I felt a slight, sticky resistance, but that was all. Unless it was very deep I should have no trouble passing through. I was not sure I dared to try.

The thing that persuaded me to enter the dark eye of the circle had nothing to do with courage. I realized that I was only a minute or two away from the airlock. I was not willing to go back and sit near the cargo beetle for the next five and half hours, then tell the others that my total achievement had been to "explore" less than a hundred yards of blank corridor. I knew how Jim Swift and Mel would react to that confession.

I moved back a few steps along the corridor. It might be difficult to get any traction from the walls or floor once I was within the circle itself. I turned the suit forward impulse to a medium level, built up speed, and plunged feet first into the dark center.

I didn't close my eyes, but I might as well have. The darkness inside was total. It didn't last long enough for my eyes to adjust, and that was fortunate, because before I knew it I was emerging into a light so intense that the suit's visor lagged for a second before it could make a dimming adjustment.

Five seconds earlier I had been in a narrow corridor. Now I had emerged into a chamber so big that portals like the one from which I had emerged were no more than dark pinpricks on the distant walls. For a moment I thought that the interior itself was empty, except for flickering regions of light and dark. Then I realized that the interior patterns of dark and light formed moving shapes.

Familiar shapes. I recognized one that was far away from me. It was the figure of a man, gigantic and insubstantial. He was hundreds of feet high, but no more solid than a pall of light-grey smoke from a bonfire. Through him I could see the far wall of Flicker.

Given that first reference point I began to make sense of

the nearer objects, and at last of the whole scene. On the right-hand side I was looking at a ship's living quarters, with a crew moving around within. And on the left side, spreading all the way to the edge of the great chamber . . .

I peered, and puzzled. This was hard to make out: the shadow of an immense band of light, curving around on itself again and again. But I could not see any place where it closed. It formed a huge, hazy spiral, twisting away into space.

As I followed the turning band back from right to left, I made the final connection. This was not merely a crew and a ship. It was a crew in a ship with the Godspeed Drive. I had been looking at the corkscrew rear portion, drawn in luminous fog. And this was not just *any* crew.

I stared at the closest of the gigantic, lumbering figures. From my position close to its midriff I could not see the face, surmounting a huge body and diminished by distance. But at the level where I hovered I could see a dark band around the midsection. Stuck into it was a foggy white cylinder, thirty or forty feet long, with a bent handle. Like a pistol. Like Walter Hamilton's pistol. Tucked into a belt. Duncan West's belt.

As I stared another shape drifted past the static figure of Duncan, creeping forward with slow, hundred-yard strides. The hair was a dark cloud tied behind the head. Giant hands, bigger than cargo beetles, crossed a prodigious chest and gripped the biceps of arms each longer than the *Cuchulain*.

It was Danny Shaker. According to Jim Swift, Shaker and his whole crew had vanished forever, thrown into another universe by the power of the Godspeed Drive. Yet they walked in front of me now. I could not make out individual faces, but I thought I recognized Donald Rudden's ponderous bulk, a hundred times as large as life, and the cloudy swirl of Tom Toole's carroty-red hair.

I watched and watched, unable to take my eyes off the silent action before me. The crew of the *Cuchulain* were as slow as they were big. Each giant step took an age, each mouth gaped and closed in what I recognized at last as a pattern of glacial speech. I used my suit controls, and found that I could float toward—and through—anything in the chamber. For a long time I hovered right in front of Danny Shaker's face, trying and failing to observe the glint of life in the fog of his grey eyes. On his scale my suited figure would be no bigger than a large beetle. There was no sign that he had any awareness of my presence.

I moved with him, hypnotized, studying his face as we crept backward and forward across the ship's cabin. The rest of the crew was now sitting at a table talking, ten eternal minutes to each sentence. Shaker stood aloof. I decided from his actions that as usual he was worrying about the ship. He went and had a long conversation with a seated giant whom I took to be Patrick O'Rourke. From my point of view it was a perfectly silent discussion. Even with my suit amplifier as high as it would go, all I heard was a deep bass rumble like distant avalanches in the mountains far west of Lake Sheelin; far above it was the hiss of air within my own suit. At last Shaker headed off toward a different part of the chamber.

The sight of his destination, a shadowy wall filled with spectral dials, at last made me consider my own situation.

I queried my suit for the time, and could not believe what it told me. Close to five hours had passed since I had left the cargo beetle.

I took a last look at the crew. It should be safe to leave. At the rate they were going, they would sit and chat for another couple of days.

I headed back to the beetle and arrived there bursting to tell the others what I had seen. No one was present, not even Doctor Eileen, for all her threats about being late.

I went inside, replenished my suit's air supply, and settled down to wait. Four hours later I was still waiting. In that time I had made half a dozen trips as far as the corridor branch point, but seen and heard nothing. In my sixth hour of waiting, when I was absolutely convinced that there had been a major disaster and I was alone in the space base, Jim Swift arrived at the cargo beetle.

He slowly opened the visor of his suit and nodded a greeting.

"What happened?" I asked. I couldn't believe he was so casual.

"Not one interesting thing. Chamber after chamber of experimental equipment, all the way across to the other side of Flicker. No sign of any ship. I hope somebody else had better luck."

"Where have you *been?* You're six hours late."

"Eh!" He scowled at me. "I'm not late—I'm a few minutes early."

"You've been gone for nearly twelve hours."

"Nonsense." He started to query his suit, then changed his mind and pointed to the control panel of the beetle. "Six hours since I left, within a couple of minutes."

The panel chronometer agreed with him. I queried my suit. It reported a time six hours later than the beetle's clock. I stared at Jim Swift.

"What's wrong, Jay?" he said. "Seeing things?"

"Hearing things. Listen." I played out the time again, at external volume.

"I hear it." He shrugged. "But it's wrong. What have you been doing that might have ruined your suit's clock?"

"I've been—I've seen—"

"Don't babble." He scented something interesting, so he was more sympathetic than annoyed. "Start at the beginning, and take it slow. What happened when you left here?"

I explained everything: the dark membrane, my passage through it, the world-sized spherical cavity beyond, and the Godspeed ship with its gargantuan crew.

"No," he said, when I described the dimensions of the chamber. "I traveled miles in the interior of Flicker, and there's no room for anything like what you're describing.

You say everyone was enormous, and they moved in slow motion?"

"I timed a blink of Danny Shaker's eyes. It took nearly a minute."

"That's what you measured. But when you returned here, you believed that you had been gone for six hours. Isn't it obvious that you were really away only a few minutes?—just the time it took you to travel along the corridor to the membrane, and then after you returned through it, the time to come back here."

"I spent a long time inside—"

"You *thought* you did. And as far as you are concerned, that is valid. You, and your clock, were speeded up, by a big factor—a hundred or more. And I'll bet you were only the same fraction of your real size, too, for a consistent change in space-time scale that preserves light-speed. Jay, you found a Godspeed space. A *Godspace*. A place where people can do *experiments* in an alternate spacetime. It's fascinating, but it won't help us go home."

"What about Shaker and the crew? They didn't vanish into another universe, the way you said. They're still here, inside Flicker. I saw them."

"No, you didn't. What you saw is some kind of fading record in Godspace, a trace of what was happening to Shaker and the crew at the time when the Godspeed drive was turned on. *Nothing* in that chamber takes place in normal space and time. If you'll take me there, I'll prove it."

He headed for the hatch. Before I could close my suit visor and follow him we were interrupted. The lock was operating. As soon as its cycle was complete, Mel popped through. Right behind her was Doctor Eileen, saying before she was fully into the cabin, "I know, I know, don't tell me. Six hours and fifteen minutes. It doesn't matter."

Because *she* was the one who was late. But it certainly didn't matter to Mel. She grabbed my hands. Before I knew what was happening she had spun us up and around the cabin. She didn't have complete free-fall control, and we bounced together off walls and ceiling.

"We found the ship!" she sang out, while I struggled to make her let go. "We found it, we found it. We're going home."

"Doctor Eileen?" Jim Swift didn't say anything else, but he didn't need to. I turned in mid-air, to watch Eileen Xavier's reaction.

She had opened her suit and was standing motionless. Finally she nodded, grudgingly. "We found—something. But I don't want to raise false hopes. Until you've examined it, Jim, I'd better say no more than that."

My discovery of the Godspace was lost in the excitement. We heard from Mel and Doctor Eileen in bits and pieces as they rushed us through a maze of corridors and open work areas.

They had started out along different branches of the main corridor, just like the rest of us. "But then then they merged," Mel said, "and we ran into each other again in a few minutes. So after that we stuck together."

"And found nothing useful." Doctor Eileen was being extra cautious, to balance Mel's euphoria. "There were workshops, hundreds and hundreds of them, just like these." We were passing through a long series of chambers, each filled with mysterious machinery. "But we didn't recognize anything that seemed significant—"

"—until we got to this point, and saw *that.*" Mel indicated a spidery structure, cradling a squashed cube that was vaguely familiar. "This is almost on the opposite side of Flicker from where we came in. It's not that far as a straight-line journey from where we started, but we made lots of detours the first time we came here. When we arrived to this point we had been away over five hours. We were ready to return to the beetle."

"You mean I was," Doctor Eileen said. "But while I was making that decision Mel skipped on ahead of me."

"I thought we might be getting close to exit ports, and I wanted to take a look at just one more chamber. Then I couldn't resist a peek at the one after that."

"*And* the one after that. I was all set to cuss at her, and tell her we were going back. But first I had to catch her. And when I finally did—"

"She was looking at *this.*"

Mel had timed our progress perfectly, because as she spoke those last words we were emerging into a docking facility. Hanging in a harness at the far end was another flattened cube. Attached to it was a nested set of fat rings, placed one beneath the other to form a blunt cone.

"It's just the way it ought to be," Mel went on. "Don't you recognize it, Jay?"

Where had I seen it before?

"Well, *I* certainly do," said Jim Swift. "We're looking at the Slowdrive, the way it was drawn in Walter Hamilton's notebook."

"That's what Mel said to me." Doctor Eileen was controlling any sign of emotion. "The question is, Jim, is that really a working ship? Is it something Jay can use to fly us back to Erin?"

A *real* flight through space. I had shivers at that prospect, but Jim took it calmly enough.

"It's smaller than I expected." He moved slowly forward and began to circle the cradled ship. "But big enough for us. If the drive is complete, the way it appears to be, and if the ship has an energy source, to power the drive; and if we can learn to fly the ship, which will be more Jay's job than mine; and if 'Slowdrive' doesn't turn out to mean so slow that Erin's a lifetime away . . ."

He turned to face the rest of us. "I'd have given big odds against, an hour ago. But if we get the right answers to all those ifs, then I think there's a chance.

"Maybe Mel is right. Maybe we'll be going home after all."

CHAPTER 32

Last night I dreamed about Danny Shaker.

I suppose the location and the circumstances made the dream inevitable: cradled in a launch sector at Muldoon's Upside Port, drifting in free-fall, waiting for the go-ahead to fly.

Waiting impatiently. Once we received Upside approval to leave, we would be off. Off to the Maze again, out to the woman-worldlet of *Paddy's Fortune*.

It was here, less than six months ago, in this very place and awaiting Upside flight approval, that Danny Shaker and his crew gave me the first hint of what life in space might be like.

Jim Swift came by and read what I just wrote. He interrupted me—polite and tactful Jim—to explain to me that I am an idiot. I should not waste one more word on Danny Shaker.

"Forget him," he said. "And forget his bloody rough-house crew. They're gone forever. If you're going to describe anything, pick a useful subject. Talk about our trip home. Talk about the Slowdrive."

"Yes, sir."

I will, too. In my own time, and in my own way. But I have a problem. You see, no matter what the learned James Swift may tell me, I can't absolutely convince myself that Danny Shaker is dead and gone.

I have reasons, even if no one else accepts them—or cares.

The ship that we found with the Slowdrive was simple enough to pilot: far easier than the *Cuchulain*, even before that became a dying hulk. On the other hand, Jim Swift's conviction about what had happened to Shaker and his crew made both him and Doctor Eileen nervous and supercautious. They were not about to climb into an unfamiliar ship and cheerily let me switch on the power. Jim wanted to *understand* the Slowdrive, before we tried to go to Erin or anywhere else.

He started studying, filling pages with diagrams and equations and loading endless files of data in and out of the navaid and the ship's computer. He was having a great time, and the rest of us were going out of our minds, because Jim would offer no opinion as to how long it might be before he was satisfied that the drive was safe.

Mel and I visited the Godspace chamber half a dozen times in the next three days. Twice Doctor Eileen went with us, but she quickly became impatient and left. Even Mel refused to go with me eventually. Everything in the Godspeed was so *slow,* she said, it was like trying to watch the stars move. She couldn't stand it. Worse than that, Godspace stretched time. We would spend hours and hours there, but find when we returned to the ship that only a couple of minutes had gone by. Jim Swift would still be halfway through the same sandwich, or staring vacantly at the same knob as when we left.

As a result I made my final visits to Godspace alone. And it was not until the very end that I observed the change.

Every previous visit had been the same: a giant,

insubstantial crew drifting slowly around the shadowy cabin, or sitting at an oval table talking and gesturing to each other in five-minute arm movements. It was consistent with Jim Swift's assertion, that I was seeing no more than a dying record of the moments before the Godspeed drive was turned on and the ship and crew vanished together into nonexistence.

This last time I entered the great chamber and took the usual few minutes, adjusting to the strange light and the distorted scale of things. The difference now was that *everyone*, including Danny Shaker, was sitting down. It took me a little while to realize what they were doing. Then I dived for the grey membrane, emerged into the corridor, and hurried at top speed back to the Slowdrive ship.

"What's the panic?" Jim Swift had cleared away his mess of drawings and calculations from the control panel, and he seemed in high good humor.

"The Godspace chamber. You have to see it."

"For a last look, you mean, before we leave for Erin?" He laughed at my double take. "You heard me, Jay. We're going home. And more than home, because I finally have the whole picture. The Slowdrive *is* slow—compared with the Godspeed Drive. But it's still superluminal, four or five times lightspeed. We've got a shot at the stars again. The Slowdrive doesn't create vacuum distortion, either. It won't throw us right out of this universe."

"Nor does the Godspeed Drive." I saw his raised eyebrows. "Come and look, Jim, you have to see this for yourself. I don't know what the Godspeed Drive did to space-time when the Isolation happened, but it's different now. Space-time repaired itself. The drive is working again."

I led the way to the Godspace chamber at top speed, and dived through with Jim close behind me.

"There you are," I said. "It takes a minute to get used to things, but see for yourself."

He squinted at the monstrous body shapes, like towering smoke outlines in the great spherical chamber.

"See what?"

"Can't you tell what they're doing?"

There was a long pause, while Jim studied slow-lifting arms and gaping mouths in remote, indistinct faces. "I can't be sure. But it seems to me that they're eating and drinking."

"That's right. They're in the middle of a meal. Don't you see what that means?"

He didn't. "You drag me in here," he said in a rising tone, "when I have us almost ready to go home—just to show me a bunch of people *eating?*"

"You don't understand. You told me that what I've been seeing here is an echo of what happened *before* the Godspeed Drive was turned on. That once the drive operated, they vanished."

"That's right. They disappeared from our universe."

"But they're *eating.*"

"Jay, people still became hungry—even when they were getting ready to use the Godspeed Drive. It was their last meal, but they didn't know it."

Jim had spent as much time in space as I had. And he didn't understand spacers, not one little bit.

"They'd *never* sit down for a meal," I protested. "Not just before a ship's departure. Not even if it were a ship that they'd known for years, like the *Cuchulain.* Certainly not on a new ship. What we're seeing happened *after* the drive had been turned on, when they were sure that everything was going well. The drive didn't cut them off from the universe—the Godspace chamber is still in contact with them."

"That's nonsense. The crew were hungry when they went aboard the Godspeed ship. What makes you think you know what they would do?"

Because I think like a spacer, and you won't ever. It would have caused nothing but trouble to say that. "Even if they wanted to sit down for a meal with the Godspeed Drive all ready to fire, that would never happen with Danny Shaker as the boss. He would never have permitted it."

Jim Swift's face was hard to see behind the visor, but his actions were enough. He turned abruptly away and headed for the grey membrane of the exit. "Danny Shaker, Danny Shaker," he shouted, just before he entered it. "That's all we hear from you. You worship that man, he's addled your brain. Can't you see that he was no more than a ruthless savage? Yes, and an incompetent, too. He led the crew to their doom, and his own. Don't waste any more of my time with him."

Jim was going off into one of his rages. It was pointless to argue. I stayed in the chamber for a long time after he had left, trying the impossible task of reading Danny Shaker's expression. That had been beyond me, even face to face aboard the *Cuchulain*. The satisfaction that I read there now was probably all my imagination.

When I returned to the Slowdrive ship no one was interested to hear a single word about Danny Shaker, the crew of the *Cuchulain,* or the Godspace chamber. All that Mel and Doctor Eileen cared about was the Slowdrive. They had become as much monomaniacs as Jim Swift. It was Erin, Erin, Erin. They wanted to fly to Erin, as soon as possible.

And finally, fly to Erin we did.

After all the dangers and difficulties that we had met on the way out, the journey home was pure anticlimax. The ship's controls had been designed to be operated by an idiot (or, as I told myself, by a Jim Swift-like research scientist). At Doctor Eileen's insistence, I held the Slowdrive to its lowest power level. Even so, we snaked our way from the depths of the Maze to Muldoon Upside Port in little more than two days.

Anyone of us who expected excitement at our return to Erin would have been disappointed. I had forgotten the extent to which the Downsiders were wrapped up in their ground-level affairs. Our arrival was greeted with massive indifference. You found a space base? Then go and bring something useful from it, something we can use on Erin. A new drive, you say? We already have ships that can explore the Forty Worlds. A female visitor from the Maze? Don't try to fool us, you took her with you from Erin.

The most interesting response at the end of our trip came not from Erin, but from Doctor Eileen during final arrival. We were together in the control room, just before she and Jim Swift transferred to a ferry ship for Muldoon Downside. Mel and I would follow them down later.

I complained about my husky voice. It had been hoarse and hard to control since we left *Paddy's Fortune.*

"Can you give me anything for it?" I asked.

Doctor Eileen burst out laughing, something she did about once a year. "Not one thing, Jay. Any more than I can do anything for Mel. Maybe you ought to discuss it with her. She's been complaining, too."

And with that baffling comment she was off to the ferry.

Last night I dreamed about Danny Shaker. The two-half-man, face invisible, arms crossed, massaging the red line of scar across his biceps. In my dream he was talking to my mother, telling her of his hopes and plans for me. She was smiling and nodding, and speaking to him like a close friend in the breathless, throaty voice that I remembered from as long ago as I remembered anything. I could tell that she *really* liked him.

That is where I ought to end my story; because tomorrow we leave for *Paddy's Fortune.* Mel can't wait to lord it over the stay-at-home girls she left behind, Jim Swift wants to meet the controller, and Doctor Eileen is keen to study the local plant and animal life.

We expect to be there for perhaps two weeks. After that we will take the next big step. Not the stars—not yet, although the Slowdrive should certainly be capable of it. We will content ourselves with a trial run, out to the far reaches of the Maveen system. On the way, Jim Swift wants to take another look at the Luimneach Anomaly. After visiting the Eye, he's not convinced that the Luimneach is as empty as it is assumed to be.

But the stars are waiting, and we can't ignore them forever. Someday, before very long, we will try the long journey out. Are there other planets and other people waiting and watching the skies, or searching to find a hidden Godspeed Base, or discovering their own version of the Slowdrive?

I know of only one way to find out. And I can't help wondering. If and when we reach the nearest star, what we will find? Dead worlds, fading empires, great living civilizations. And might we find that Danny Shaker and his crew have been before us?

That thought should blow me away. In most ways it does, but it does not dominate my mind as it would have a week ago, because this morning I finally acted on Doctor Eileen's suggestion. I complained to Mel about my hoarse voice.

"You really don't know what's been happening to you?" she said. She was facing half away, but she kept darting me rapid little glances from the corner of her eye.

"My voice—"

"Your voice, and the hair on your chin, and your chest. And your *moustache*. And you've *grown* about four inches."

"Well, you've grown too. And *you*—"

She had changed, more than I. She had a different shape, and her walk had become a woman's walk. Anyone who mistook her for a boy now would have to be blind.

"You've changed," I said.

"Of course I have." She finally turned to face me. "For exactly the same reason. Doctor Eileen explained it to me. But I don't think it's fair to expect me to explain it to *you.*"

And she wouldn't, not one word. I had to wait until I had another meeting alone with Doctor Eileen.

"Good Lord, of *course* Mel wouldn't talk to you," she said. "I was joking—I didn't expect that you would *ask* her. Sit down, Jay."

I did, wondering what came next. Doctor Eileen stood close, studied my face, and nodded.

"Do you remember that you said the food on *Paddy's Fortune* tasted strange, and Mel said the same thing about the food on the *Cuchulain?* And the controller on *Paddy's Fortune* gave you a box of pills?"

"Sure. But I thought they were diet supplements."

"They were. You see, the food we grow on Erin isn't quite right for humans. It's deficient in certain trace compounds. I've known that for a long time. And funnily enough, the food on *Paddy's Fortune* isn't quite right, either, but in a different way. *Together,* though, they can provide everything you need. Which they did—for you and Mel.

"There's nothing unusual about what's been happening to either of you, except the speed of it. You both had delayed puberty. Now you're rushing through the physical changes in about a tenth of the usual time. It's bound to make you uncomfortable. But it's all normal." She nodded at me and started for the door. "Don't worry about it."

Easy enough for *her* to say—it wasn't happening to Doctor Eileen.

I went through into the bathroom and stared in the mirror at my face. It wasn't just hairy. It was spotty as well, and looked different in other ways. The bones of my cheeks and forehead were more prominent, and my eyes sat deeper in my head. I wondered what my mother would make of the new me. She was heading for Upside, anxious to see me before we left and make sure that I was all right. She was in for a bit of a shock.

I was still gazing at my reflection when Mel came in and stood behind me.

"I just talked to Doctor Eileen," I said. I stared at her, but only in the mirror. I couldn't bring myself to turn around.

"I know." Mel's face was pink. "She told me. And she told me to come and talk to you. I want to say one thing. Just don't you."

"Just don't I *what?*"

"Don't you get any ideas. *Funny* ideas. That's all."

And she was gone, without a word more.

The strange thing is, there had been nothing like that in my head until she spoke.

But there is now, and I wonder if she did it on purpose.

If she did, it worked.

I have no idea what the trip to *Paddy's Fortune* and beyond will be like. I don't know what will happen when we make the long run, and rediscover the stars. I don't know if my wildest fear—and, perhaps, my oddest hope and dream—will come true, and one day, far off in space and time, I will meet again with Danny Shaker.

But I do know that things inside me are changing—fast. And I can't keep my head clear of notions that have nothing to do with the Godspeed Drive or interstellar exploration.